A Knock on the Door

Thomas Richard Brown

1st Edition Published by Second Child Ltd

ISBN: 978-0-9956709-3-8 (Paperback)

Proofread by Julia Gibbs
juliaproofreader@gmail.com

Cover design by Simon Emery
siemery2012@gmail.com

Cover illustration by Brenda McKetty
www.brendamcketty.me.uk

Mary Matthews
www.threeshirespublishing.com

British Library Cataloguing in Publication Data

A CIP catalogue record for this book is available from
the British Library.

Table of Contents

Dedication

To the memory of Mike Hirst

Chapter One
Mischief

"What you got there then?"

The question came from a girl perched on a bench in the bus shelter next to the Marquess of Bute pub. It was an early Sunday evening in April and the late afternoon sun was still shining. The girl was sitting beside two other teenage girls and a boy who were all looking towards the recipients of the question, two older boys who had been sauntering past. The taller of the two was holding something which he was half-heartedly trying to conceal. The girl repeated the question.

"What you got there then, Roger?"

She stood up and faced the two boys confidently. They stopped in their tracks.

"Mind your own business, Fanny Adams," smiled Roger, before looking away.

"Huh," sniffed the girl. "Suit yourself, and my name ain't Fanny Adams, you know it ain't; it's Sandra, so there."

Sandra put her hands defiantly on her hips. She was tall and dark haired with a pretty, round face and she was wearing a fawn, long sleeved sweater and a dark green skirt, with white socks and brown shoes. Around her neck was wrapped a thick scarf.

The other three, who had been watching from the bench, rose and moved to join Sandra.

"Come on, Roger! Show us, why don't you?" said the boy.

1

"Don't show 'em, Roger," piped up Roger's companion, Christian, from his vantage point, slightly behind the taller boy.

Roger stood a good four inches taller than Christian, who was slimly built with red hair and a pale complexion. Roger was wearing a jacket and tie, which gave him an air of someone somewhat older than his seventeen years. Christian did not look so well turned out; his jacket fitted badly and the tie looked tatty, his hair had not been brushed and his trousers and shoes were obviously part of his school uniform. He wore small glasses with thin wire frames and had a habit of blinking more than was necessary.

"Don't show 'em," Christian repeated, his voice rising slightly as he glared angrily at the four in front of them.

"He ain't going to show us," shrugged Sandra. "So what? I'm not interested anyway; are you, Simon?"

She turned nonchalantly to the boy in her group. Simon, like Roger, was tall and had fair, wavy hair and wore a tweed jacket and grey trousers. His black shoes had recently been polished.

Simon shrugged and didn't reply, but one of the other girls stepped forward and addressed Roger directly.

"He will show us, I know he will," she said quickly. "He wants to, I know he does; don't you, Roger? You're just keeping us in suspense."

Roger looked at the girl, whose name was Ann, and shrugged. She was a bit younger than the others, and Sandra's younger sister.

Roger continued to say nothing; Ann waited a few more seconds before sighing and turning to Simon.

2

"Come on then, Simon, let's go for a walk if he won't show us; are you coming, Nimpy?"

She turned to the third girl in the group. Nimpy's real name was Joanna but she had not been called that since she was a child.

"Yes, I'll come," said Nimpy, smiling then following the other three away from the pub.

Sensing that he had lost the advantage, Roger called to their retreating backs.

"All right then. I'll show you, but you ain't got to tell no one, see."

Ann smirked at Nimpy and Sandra, and the group turned and gathered around Roger who placed the object proudly in the palm of his outstretched hand.

"That ain't nothing secret," snorted Nimpy. "It's just a honey jar with some…"

She stopped abruptly as she caught sight of another boy cycling into view. Roger clutched the jar to his chest protectively.

"Who's that then?" asked Christian, blinking myopically towards the approaching figure.

"That's Peter," said Simon. "He lives up the road in Covington. I know him pretty well, he's a good mate."

Simon waved towards the approaching figure, who waved back and stopped his bike, an old ladies' model that he had evidently borrowed. He was tall and wearing a jacket and tie, although he had forgotten to turn his collar down at the back. He swung his leg back over the seat of the bike and bent to pull his trouser legs from his socks, having tucked them in to stop them catching on the chain. He moved towards the group.

"You made it then," Simon said.

"Didn't take too long," Peter replied with a smile.

"On that old thing," said Sandra with a sneer as she nodded contemptuously at the bike.

"He probably can't ride a man's bike," added Christian, with a squeaky snigger.

"You can't talk, Christian! You can't even ride a bike," retorted Ann.

Christian reddened.

"You know you're supposed to wear a skirt when you ride a bicycle like that, don't you?" said Roger.

The rest of the group laughed as Peter leaned the bike against the bus shelter by the pub and ignored the jibes.

"What you doing then?" he asked Simon. The assembled group looked at Roger, whose eyes widened theatrically as he produced the honey jar from behind his back, holding it out in front of him again.

"What do you think that is then?" he asked, looking first at Peter and then at the others.

"It's a honey jar, with a hole in the lid and some liquid in the bottom," said Peter, peering over and sniffing at the pierced hole in the lid. "Smells like petrol," he added, looking up at Roger.

"And why's it got a hole in the lid?" asked Roger dramatically, looking from one to another of the assembled company. Everyone shrugged.

"I know," said Ann. "It's to put flowers in."

Roger tutted and turned to Christian.

"Give me one," he demanded.

Christian rummaged in his trouser pockets, pulled out a small cylindrical object about three inches long with a fuse in one end and handed it over. Roger carefully inserted the cylinder into the hole of the jar, noting that it fitted almost perfectly, then he held the jar up like an icon.

"That, my friends," he announced grandly, "is a Molotov cocktail!"

"A what?" asked Sandra, her brow furrowing.

"A Molotov cocktail, are you deaf?" snapped Roger, angry that his grand unveiling had not created as much enthusiasm as he had anticipated.

"And what's a Molotov cocktail when it's at home, may I ask?" said Sandra.

Roger paused, looked around and lowered his voice. Simon sighed loudly, getting impatient.

"Does anyone know?" Roger asked, determined to build the suspense.

"I do," said Christian, eager to share his knowledge.

"I didn't ask you, stupid," said Roger.

None of the others spoke.

"I'll tell you then," said Roger, with a smirk. "A Molotov cocktail is a petrol bomb."

He paused triumphantly and looked around at the others.

"What do you want a petrol bomb for? Who are you going to blow up?" said Simon.

"I'm not going to blow anyone up, not at the moment anyway. But you never know when it might be needed."

"How did you know how to make it? You can't be sure it will go off, can you?" asked Peter.

5

"The instructions are in a manual that my dad had, it must have been from the war or something like that, it tells you how to do it," said Roger, with confidence.

"But not with a banger like that, I bet they didn't have bangers in the war," persisted Peter.

"Well spotted," said Roger. "The banger is my invention, good, don't you think?"

He almost visibly swelled with pride.

"Have you tried it before then?" asked Nimpy, eyeing the jam jar suspiciously.

"No, I haven't," said Roger, who felt his patience was being tried. "It would be in bits if I had tried it before, wouldn't it!"

"Well are you going to let it off then?"

"I might do. I hadn't really thought about it," said Roger, as if he couldn't care one way or the other.

"Go on," said Simon. "Let's see what it does."

"No you don't, Simon," said Ann, tugging at his sleeve. "It might explode everywhere. It won't be safe."

"Go on, Roger, I've got some matches," said Christian, urging him on.

"Shut up, you, I'll do it when I want, see," said Roger, pushing Christian away.

Bored with the lack of action, Sandra said, "Right, who's coming for a walk then? I'm going round the block."

She started to walk off, stopping when she realised that she wasn't being followed. She turned around.

"Come on then. What are you waiting for?"

Nobody moved.

6

"We're just going to see Roger let the bomb off, or try to," said Peter. "I bet it doesn't work though."

He raised an eyebrow at Roger who snorted contemptuously.

"I bet it does."

"Prove it then," said Peter.

"All right, come on, Christian; where's those matches?"

"You can't do it here," Christian protested.

"I'm not going to do it here, stupid. We'll go down to the cricket field, there's a spinney at the back, we'll do it there," said Roger, turning to the others. "Come on then."

Roger marched towards the cricket field, Christian trailing behind him. The others looked at each other, shrugged and followed the pair at a distance. The group walked on past the chapel and the manse and past the small prep school, where Christian lived and where a board on the gate read:

The Hall Prep School
Boys and Girls aged 5 – 13
Head Mistress: Miss E Shaw

By the time the others had crossed the cricket field to the spinney, Roger and Christian were already getting prepared. Christian was holding the matches in his hand; he beckoned excitedly to the others to hurry up.

"Aren't we going to get hurt, being this close?" asked Ann with a small frown.

"No, I'm going to throw it," said Roger confidently. "That's what it says in the manual, but stand back anyway, I'll throw it into the wood."

The watchers took a few paces back.

"Go on then, stupid, light it!" Roger instructed, proffering the jar towards Christian.

Christian lit a match and held it to the fuse, before turning to run to where the others stood. As soon as the fuse properly took, Roger threw it with all his strength into the trees, running back to join the others. The group waited, Sandra, Ann and Nimpy with their fingers stuffed into their ears. After a few seconds there was a small bang, followed by a huge crack as a flame flashed bright from where the bomb had been thrown. There was silence as smoke oozed from between the trees.

Roger grinned and turned to the others.

"Bugger!" said Christian. "It worked."

"Course it worked, you oaf, I told you it would, didn't I?" said Roger.

"What made the big bang then?" asked Ann.

"The petrol, you dope."

"Don't you call me a dope, Roger, I only asked, didn't I?" said Ann, the corners of her mouth turning down. She flicked her hair and made to walk away.

"Come on then, Simon, let's go for a walk, who else is coming?"

"I'll come," said Sandra.

"So will I," said Nimpy, turning to look at Peter. "What's your name again?"

"Peter."

"Oh yes, I remember now, Peter; well are you coming, Peter?" She eyed him curiously.

"Okay, why not," he said, and headed off with the rest of the group towards the village.

Christian and Roger watched them go.

"What you going to do now then, Roger?"

"We're going to make another one. Come on."

The little group made their way into the village. It was small. There were two pubs, one shop, a primary school and a police house where the local constable lived. A stream ran through the middle of the village and the boys selected small stones to skim across the trickle of water in the ford, before moving to stand with the girls on the small footbridge that bypassed it.

"Who's got a fag then?" asked Sandra.

Peter pulled a packet of Players from his pocket, took one out and offered it to her.

"I ain't smoking them. They ain't got no tips."

Peter offered the packet to Simon, who took one, put it to his lips and lit it.

"Do your mum and dad know you smoke, Simon?" asked Ann in a disapproving tone.

"I've never told them," he shrugged, taking a draw on the cigarette.

"Do any of you want one then?" asked Peter, holding out the packet to them again.

"I don't smoke," said Nimpy, blushing and looking away.

"Okay, I'll have one," said Ann, with a grin.

"You haven't ever smoked before," said Sandra. "You don't know how to smoke one."

"Yes I do. And how do you know that I've never had one before?"

9

"'Cos I do, so there."

"Right, give me one then, Peter and I'll show you," said Ann, furious with her sister.

She took a cigarette from the packet and held it between her lips. Peter lit his and offered the lit match to Ann. She steadied the cigarette between her index finger and thumb and craned her head towards the lit match. All eyes were on her as she gingerly poked the end of the cigarette into the flame.

"Go on then, suck!" said Sandra.

Ann drew back and as the match stuttered out she whirled round towards Sandra.

"You put me off, you did! You shouldn't have said that."

Peter lit another match as Ann turned back to face him.

"Come on, try again," he said, offering up the lit match in his cupped hands.

Ann leaned forwards for a second time, bringing the tip of the cigarette into the flame. She shut her eyes and drew the smoke into her mouth. No sooner had she inhaled than she pulled the cigarette from her lips, erupting into a chorus of coughs. The others laughed.

"There, I told you that you didn't know how to do it," said Sandra, grinning as she mocked her sister.

Ann scowled and held the cigarette to her mouth again. Cautiously, she inhaled, took the cigarette from her mouth and puffed a cloud of smoke out towards Sandra.

"There you are, I can do it after all," she said smugly.

Sandra stuck her tongue out at her sister and scuffed at the ground.

"I know," she said suddenly, "let's go and call on Primrose, see if she wants to come out."

"No," groaned Ann. "We don't want her."

"Who's Primrose?" asked Peter.

"She's a girl who lives at the next house, she's our cousin," explained Sandra.

"So what's wrong with her then?" asked Peter.

"She goes to the grammar school," said Ann.

"What's wrong with that then?" said Peter, puzzled.

"All them that go to the grammar school think they're better than they are," shrugged Ann.

"No, not Primrose, she's not like that," chimed in Nimpy. "I know some of them are, but not all of them."

She turned to Peter.

"I bet you go to school at Kimbolton like Simon, don't you?" she said with a smile.

"Yes," admitted Peter, reddening slightly.

"Come on then, I'm going to see if Primrose is coming out," said Sandra firmly, walking up the path to the house's small back gate.

She approached the back of the house and knocked on the door. There was no answer, and as she turned to the others, Ann smirked. Sandra knocked on the door again; as she did so, it was opened by a thick set man in his late forties. He was wearing a vest, which revealed broad shoulders and strong arms. His braces hung down his sides, his trousers held up with a thick leather belt.

"What do you want then, Sandra?"

"I was just wondering if Primrose was going to come out for a bit?" said Sandra, evidently cowed.

"Come out for what?"

"Just a bit of a walk or something like that."

11

The man glared up the path to where the other four were standing.

"Who you got there then? Who are them boys? Up to no good I bet."

There was a shuffle behind the man then Primrose appeared beside her father.

"Are you coming then?" Sandra asked.

"No she ain't," her father answered for her. "She's got to do her homework, and at any rate we're going to chapel in a little bit so she can't come."

He eyed Sandra crossly.

"I'm going to have a word with your mother, young lady, why she lets you roam the streets with them boys I can't imagine."

He shook his head and moved backwards to close the door, just as Primrose skipped past him to stand on the path next to Sandra.

"Now look here, my girl…" started her father.

"I am," said Primrose nonchalantly.

"You are what?"

"Looking at you."

Sandra sniggered and turned away.

"I'm just going to say hello to my friends, Dad," said Primrose. "There's no harm in that, is there?"

She stared at her father, a small grin on her face. The man's shoulders sagged, and he stepped out onto the doorstep and looked critically at the others standing in the street as he relented.

"I suppose not. But you be back in five minutes, my girl, or there'll be trouble."

He stepped back into the house and slammed the door. Primrose turned happily to Sandra.

"Who's here then?" she asked. "I can see Simon and Ann and Nimpy, who's the other one?"

Before waiting for an answer, she ran towards the gate, which Nimpy opened for her.

"Are you coming then, Primrose?" Nimpy asked.

"Can't. Got to go to chapel." She stole a glance at the house behind her. "Who's got the fags then?"

"I have," said Ann with pride, holding up the partly smoked cigarette.

"Come on then, let's have a drag. Make sure he's gone, won't you?"

The others looked towards the house.

"Yes, you're all right now," said Sandra.

Primrose took a puff and blew the smoke out directly into Simon's face. He wrinkled his nose but said nothing.

"You're a long way from home, Simon," she said with a smile. "What brings you here then, off on a bike ride, I expect?"

Simon coloured a little. "Yes, just on a bike ride, nothing much else to do on a Sunday."

"And who's this then, a friend of yours?" asked Primrose, nodding at Peter.

"Yes, he's a friend from school."

"On a bike ride as well, I expect."

"Yes."

"What's your name then?"

"Peter Dunmore."

"Peter Pink more like," said Primrose laughing sharply as she indicated to Peter's red face. The other girls sniggered. "I've got to go, or he will be out again," she said, and she threw her smoked cigarette over the gate as she passed back through it. "I'll see you on the bus tomorrow morning." She waved, turned and went back into the house.

"What are we going to do now then?" asked Nimpy.

The group looked out towards the village; a circuit would take no longer than fifteen minutes.

"Let's just keep walking," suggested Ann.

The group made their way along the street, throwing the occasional stone into the brook as they wandered up past a row of thatched cottages. An old lady was walking up her garden path from the privy back towards her cottage; none of the group had noticed her and Simon chose this moment to hurl a large stone into the brook.

"Who's that there?" said the woman, turning and rushing down the path towards the road. She peered over her gate. "What are you girls doing round here at this time? You should be at chapel, you know that!" She turned her steady gaze on Nimpy. "And you, Nimpy! Do you not know that it's a Sunday?" The woman wobbled her head furiously opening her mouth a couple of times as if gasping for air and exposing her few remaining brown teeth planted at angles along her gums.

"We're just going for a walk," explained Ann politely.

"Going for a walk! I've never heard of such a thing, you've never been for a walk before, I'll bet. Causing mischief, that's what you lot are up to." She pushed her lips together primly and eyeballed the group in front of her. "Who are them boys then?" she demanded of Sandra.

14

"They're just friends of ours."

The two boys looked down and said nothing.

"Up to no good, I bet. Oh yes, I've heard all about you lot, always up to no good; everyone says that."

"We're not doing any harm," Nimpy protested.

The woman smiled. "Not standin' there you ain't but when our backs are turned, there's no tellin' what you get up to." She shook her head and brushed her hands down the pinny she was wearing. "I'm going to see your mother about you, young Nimpy, you mark my words, I will."

With one last scathing look, she turned and walked back towards her front door. The girls stuck their tongues out as she went, the boys making rude signs behind her back. At the door she turned and scowled back towards the group before finally going into the house, slamming the door behind her.

"Old bag," grumbled Sandra. "It's not fair, we haven't done anything. Not to her anyway."

"Is she always like that?" Peter asked.

"Always, but Mum doesn't take too much notice of her now she complains so much."

"We ought to do something," said Simon. "Play a trick on her or something – it would serve her right." He looked round mischievously at the others. "Come on, think of something!"

The group stood looking from one to the other.

"I know," said Peter at last. "Let's take the bucket out of her lav and hide it."

Simon grinned. "Brilliant, come on. She won't see anything we do on this side of the house, there's no windows."

"You can't do that," protested Ann. "What'll happen when she…well, you know, when she goes?"

15

"What do you think will happen?" said Simon.

Everyone started to giggle.

"Where shall we hide the bucket though?" asked Sandra.

"There's a small orchard back up the road there," said Simon. "We'll hang it on a branch of one of the trees."

"Perfect," said Peter with a smile. "You go and fetch the bucket and I'll climb up the tree and wait for you. You girls go and watch her door and shout if she comes out."

Simon smiled conspiratorially at Peter and turned to make his way up the path through the vegetable patch to the privy door. The latch clicked as he crept in, brushing past a copy of the local newspaper hanging from a nail on the door. He lifted the lid on the privy and reached for the handle of the bucket, lifting it gently out. He replaced the lid of the privy, and, holding his nose, trotted out back through the vegetable patch and towards the road. He crawled through a gap in the hedge through to the orchard where Peter was waiting for him in the lower branches of an apple tree.

"Do you have something to tie it with?" Simon called up.

Peter held up a length of broken washing line with a flourish. Simon grinned and held the bucket up towards Peter, who tied the washing line through the handle and then round the branch.

"That should hold," said Peter, as Simon tentatively stopped supporting the bucket and moved away from the tree.

Peter slipped from the lower branches to stand next to Simon. They looked up into the tree. The bucket hung firmly from the branch. Peter laughed and the two boys crept back through the hole in the hedge to meet the girls.

16

"That'll show her," Simon said, as they all made their way towards the centre of village.

The sound of a motor bike could be heard approaching from behind and they all turned. The motor bike screeched round the bend, coming to a scudding halt inches from Simon, who stood his ground, daring the rider to run him over. The driver raised his goggles and grinned at Simon.

"You sod; I nearly hit you."

"You wouldn't dare," Simon replied.

The driver revved the engine and cocked his head.

"Who does he think he is, Sterling Moss?" said Ann.

"Sterling Moss drives cars, stupid," answered the motor bike rider, doing nothing to endear him to his audience.

"Well let's hope he drives cars better than you drive motor bikes," Ann answered. She turned angrily to Simon. "Who's this joker then?"

"This is Peter Tookey, a friend from home."

"Another Peter," said Sandra. "Well, Peter, do you know *this* Peter?" She pointed at Peter Dunmore.

"Yes," replied Peter Tookey. "I do know *that* Peter."

"Let's have a ride then," said Simon, leaping onto the pillion seat and bouncing the bike up and down on its springs.

Peter Tookey laughed. He was tall with fair short hair, and wore a leather jacket with a fur collar over dark trousers and shiny brown leather shoes.

"Go on then," urged Simon, nudging his friend in the ribs.

"I can't," protested Tookey. "I'm only a learner."

"You don't bother about things like that, do you, Tookey?" challenged Simon.

"Yes I do," said Tookey with a smile. "The policeman up here is red hot on that sort of thing and I bet he's about today."

"Yes he is," said Nimpy. "I saw his bike outside the police house before we came out."

"So he's not *outside*," said Simon. "Come on!"

Tookey sighed and held up his hands. "All right, just up to the end and back, that's all, mind."

He revved the engine, threw the bike in gear and tore up towards the junction where he turned, roared back again and skidded the bike to a halt. He smiled at Nimpy.

"Do you want a go?" he asked with a wink.

"Not bloomin' likely. I'll get my skirt in the wheel."

"I'll have a go," said Ann.

"No you won't!" retorted Tookey. "Not after the way you spoke to me when I got here."

"Go on. I'll say I'm sorry! Please, let's have a go."

She smiled pleadingly at Tookey, who looked at the others and then back at her.

"All right then, get on."

Ann grinned and rushed to the bike. She climbed on be-hind Tookey, carefully tucked her skirt underneath her so it didn't flap and threaded her arms around Tookey's waist.

"Go on then," she urged, shutting her eyes as Tookey sped up towards the junction, turned and raced back again.

As they drew to a halt, Ann hopped off, laughing; she grinned at Tookey.

"Where are you lot going then?" he asked, returning Ann's smile.

"We're just having a walk round the block," said Sandra. "Where are you going?"

18

"I don't suppose I know really. Just riding around. I'll follow you if you don't mind, for the rest of your walk."

"As long as you don't run us over," said Simon with a wink.

They continued their progress on to the end of the street, before turning back and crossing the brook towards the bus shelter, Tookey driving in and out of the group as they walked. As they made their way up the hill away from a small farm on their left they noticed someone walking towards them. He was heavily built, wearing wellingtons and carrying a pitchfork. He had white, short hair and a long red face, accentuated by his hanging jowls. He wore an old tweed jacket, tied closed with a piece of binder twine, which looped his waist; a cigarette dangled from between his lips.

"What are you old girls up to?" he asked gruffly, rolling the cigarette over his lips as he spoke.

"We're just out walking," said Sandra.

"And who are these rum 'uns?" said the man, nodding at the boys suspiciously.

"Friends," said Sandra.

His eyes alighted on Simon. "Don't I know you, boy?" he asked, rubbing his chin. "Yes, I'm sure I do, ain't you Jack's son? I'm sure I'm seen you with him somewhere. Do you go beating?"

Simon shuffled uncomfortably. "Yes," he admitted.

"Well, that's where I'm seen you then, beating. I don't know about them others." He looked carefully at the other two boys. "I ain't seen them before. Anyway just you keep out my farm, see," he said firmly, turning to the group. "I don't want

19

any of my stacks going up in smoke, I know what you lot get up to, don't you think that I don't, so just you behave."

"We weren't going to go into your yard," said Ann, indignant.

"Don't speak to me in that tone, my girl," warned the man. "Or I will march you down to your father. You ought to know better than to speak to your elders like that." Ann scowled at the man and turned on her heel, the others starting off after her. The farmer pointed accusingly at Simon's retreating back. "You mark my words, young man. If there's any trouble around here, I'll know who to blame and I'll give your dad a call."

But his words were drowned by the revving of the motor-bike as Tookey shot off ahead of the group, the others jogging to catch him up.

At the church gate, the group turned in and meandered over to the church porch, where they flung themselves on the cold stone benches. Peter pulled the cigarettes from his pocket and offered them around to the girls, but none of them accepted. Tookey drew up on his motorbike, red in the face, having hared round a complete circuit of the village. He propped the bike up against the church porch as the sound of footsteps up the church path alerted them to the reappearance of Roger and Christian.

"Where have you been then?" Sandra asked.

"Look," said Roger proudly, holding up another jar with a banger already jutting out of the top. There was no petrol in the bottom.

"What you going to do with it this time then?" asked Simon.

"I can't do nothing at the moment; we don't have any petrol, Dad's locked his in the shed." He shrugged and looked round at the others. "Anyone got any?"

Everyone shook their heads.

"I know," said Christian, pointing towards Peter Tookey. "You've got petrol in your motorbike, haven't you?"

"You're not having any of that," said Tookey. "How am I supposed to get home then? Anyway it's two stroke, that wouldn't be any good for a bomb."

"Stupid!" said Roger. "It don't make no difference if it's two stroke, that's what I used before, from Dad's shed."

Tookey bridled and stood firm in front of his bike.

"Look who's coming!" he said, looking towards the figure of Primrose who was hurrying towards the group, followed by a younger dark-haired girl.

"I thought you couldn't come out, Primrose?" said Sandra.

"No, I wasn't supposed to. But it's an hour before we have to go to chapel so I managed to slip out, he doesn't know that I've gone."

"What's she doing here?" said Sandra, looking over at the other girl standing at Primrose's shoulder. "Helen ain't old enough to come around with us."

"Yes I am," protested the girl. "I'm fourteen!"

"No, you're not," said Ann. "I know you're not, your birthday isn't till September."

"Well, I'm nearly fourteen then. You're only just fourteen, I know that."

"Shut up, you lot," cut in Primrose. "Leave her alone, she's all right. Anyway, she looks older than fourteen, so what does it matter."

21

Helen pulled a face at Ann, who frowned and looked away.

"What we going to do then?" said Primrose, looking around at the whole gang, which now numbered ten.

"I'm going to find some petrol," announced Roger. "Don't need much, someone will have some. Are you coming, Christian?"

He looked at his companion.

"Not right now," said Christian with a shake of his head. "I ought to go back before long."

"Don't get into trouble, Roger," warned Primrose. "The policeman's at home, I've just seen his bike against the gate."

"I bet no one dare let his tyres down," said Peter Tookey, as nonchalantly as he could manage.

"Well, I'm not going to," said Roger, turning on his heel and trotting off to find petrol.

"Who dare do it?" challenged Tookey again.

"Why don't you do it yourself then, it's your stupid idea," scoffed Ann. "You won't do it, will you, Simon?"

"We don't know where the policeman is, do we? He may not be in the house, he might out be walking about."

"Peter, will you do it then?" said Sandra, turning to Peter Dunmore.

"Not likely, that would be asking for trouble in broad daylight."

Christian stood up suddenly.

"I'll do it," he said.

All eyes turned towards him.

"You'll do what?" sounded a deep voice from beyond the porch.

They all turned; the parson had come up unnoticed. He was tall with a long face, which had a pallor to it that made him look unwell.

"Now, my dears," he began, looking slowly round at the group who had started to shift uncomfortably on the benches, aware that they were not going to be able to escape a telling off. "You really can't assemble here like this. It is not a playground. It's a place of worship. I had a phone call just a few minutes ago complaining about the noise you are making and the sound of the motorbike." He frowned slightly at the boys. "You know it's Sunday, don't you, a day of rest, God's day."

The group looked at one another or at the ground to avoid the parson's gaze. One of the girls sniggered slightly.

"I mean it," reprimanded the parson with a touch of irritation. "I know you girls are from here and so is that boy," he pointed at Christian. "But where do the other boys come from?" he asked, turning accusingly to Sandra.

"They're just friends from round about."

"Well, you must go and be friends somewhere else; this is not the place." He stood and glared at the company. Nobody spoke. Suddenly Sandra got up and walked away, as one by one they filed out of the porch, around the church and across the graveyard to the small gate in the corner and out into the lane. Peter closed the gate behind him and turned to the company in the road.

"That's that then. What are we going to do now? We might as well go back to the bus shelter."

Hearing neither assent nor dissent from the assembled company, Peter turned and made to walk up towards the high street.

23

"We can't go that way," called Sandra.

"Why not? It's the shortest way."

"Mum might see us and then we would have to go in."

"Right, well we will go the other way then," said Peter with a sigh, leading the way down towards the bridge.

"What about the policeman's bike, then?" piped up Tookey. "Come on, Christian, it's just up there, go on, you said that you would."

Christian shrugged and smiled. The police house was the last but one on the left before the lane met the high street. In the distance, they could make out the bike leaning against the gatepost.

"What about it then, Christian?" asked Peter.

"What about what, then?" repeated Christian, wiping at his runny nose with his fist. "None of you dare do it, do you?" He looked from one boy to the other and then at the girls who all looked at the ground. "All right then, I'll do it, keep a look out." He looked to the left and right and started to make his way slowly towards where the bike was parked.

"I'm going to get my motorbike," said Tookey nonchalantly, walking back towards the church now that the parson had gone.

Christian slowly made his way up the lane; he cut a dishevelled figure in his undersized jacket, his red hair sticking out in all directions. As the others watched he crept nearer and nearer to the cottage; he stopped briefly to turn comically and look back at the gang, putting a finger to his lips and winking. At that moment Simon spotted something. Looking across the churchyard over the low hedge he could see the top of somebody's head standing just to the right of the war memorial. It looked like the parson and he was clearly talking to someone who was mostly obscured by the memorial. Simon crept back into the churchyard to see if he could make out who the other person was. With a better angle of vision, it took no time to ascertain that it was Joe Rawlins, the local policeman, in his uniform and helmet. Simon scuttled back into the lane.

"The copper's up there talking to the parson," he hissed to the others. "Christian," he half whispered, half shouted, cupping his hands about his mouth to make his voice carry.

But Christian was now level with the police house and in front of the bike. From where he was he could see neither the parson nor PC Rawlins. He turned and looked back towards the others, grinning and pointing at the bike. He could make out Simon waving and mouthing at him, but his eyesight was poor, and he could decipher no message from the furiously waving arms. He pulled a face and crouched down next to the bike, ready to unscrew the valve of the tyre.

"What the bloody 'ell do you think you're doing, boy?" boomed PC Rawlins' voice from the memorial as he caught sight of Christian. He started to run towards where Christian crouched frozen next to the bike. The unexpected shout had frightened the boy out of his wits, and he couldn't work out where the yell had come from, peering at the door of the police house then back towards the road. Suddenly he made out the figure of PC Rawlins bearing down on him. In his desperation to escape, he tried to stand, but instead tumbled over backwards, his arms windmilling as he sought purchase on something. He landed heavily on the ground, then scrambled to his feet and plunged towards the gang and freedom.

He was too late. PC Rawlins was already on top of him. He grabbed Christian's jacket and shirt collar, holding them tight. Christian scrabbled at his neck, the force of the policeman's hold constricting his windpipe. PC Rawlins was tall and strong and used little effort hoisting Christian to his feet and onto tiptoes. The jacket tightened around Christian's arms and shoulders and he struggled against the policeman, desperate for breath. PC Rawlins lowered Christian back to the ground and bent his face down towards him.

"What were you doing, you little sod?" He glared into Christian's face and then towards the bike. Christian grimaced. "You were going to let my tyres down, weren't you?" Christian looked up at the policeman in terror.

"No I weren't," he stammered.

PC Rawlins scowled and cracked the back of his hand across Christian's face, sending his glasses flying to the ground.

"Yes, you were!" he yelled, pushing Christian away from him to examine the bike.

"I haven't let them down, see?" whined Christian, crawling over in the direction of his errant glasses, patting the ground in front of him desperately.

"Who are that lot then?" said PC Rawlins accusingly, suddenly realising that he had an audience. He peered towards the assembled group, who were standing open-mouthed, watching the unfolding drama. Realising that PC Rawlins was now staring at them, they all turned and pelted back down the lane as fast as they could. "Eh, what are you lot up to?" Rawlins shouted off after them as the group streamed back across the bridge into the backstreet. Simon, Nimpy, Sandra and Ann split one way and Primrose, Helen and the two Peters the other.

PC Rawlins turned back to Christian, who had just managed to find his glasses and stood quaking in front of him, awaiting sentence. PC Rawlins smiled nastily and pulled out his notebook and pencil. He licked the end of his pencil.

"Now," he murmured, "Christian, ain't it?"

"Yes," mumbled Christian.

"What am I going to write in this 'ere notebook?"

Christian licked his lips nervously and looked at the ground. "Don't know," he said, and sniffed, wiping away a small trickle of blood that was running from his nose.

"Well you ought to know," said Rawlins with menace. "And I ought to write a report and I ought to charge you, oughtn't I?"

"I didn't do anything," protested Christian.

"You don't 'ave to do anything, boy," yelled Rawlins, bringing his face closer and closer to Christian's. "You don't 'ave to *do* anything to get on a charge in my book; you just 'ave to look as though you *might* be doing something!"

He inhaled deeply and walked around Christian, scanning him critically.

"You're lucky, boy," he said quietly, standing in front of Christian with his hands on his hips. "You're very lucky. I ain't going to do anything this time as I've got to be on duty in Bedford at six so I have to be leaving soon." He lowered his face towards Christian again. "So you think yourself lucky, young man. I'll have a word with Miss Shaw though, yes I will and you watch out, boy. You make sure you watch out. I'm after your lot and you can tell them others so. There's

27

been complaints about you lot, don't you think that I don't know what you and your gang are up to because I do." He straightened up to his full height and scowled down at Christian. "Now bugger off," he said, and seized his bike and walked with it up the path to his house.

Christian rushed towards the bridge and the backstreet, blood still trickling from his nose.

The others had stopped running and realising somewhat grudgingly that they should go back and check on Christian, they turned and met him on the rise of the bridge. He was limping; he had lost a shoe in the scuffle and they could see that his nose was still bleeding. His jacket was muddy where he had fallen over and his hands were scratched.

"What a mess," said Nimpy, tutting. "Where's your shoe?"

"Back there somewhere, I suppose," he replied, wiping the blood from his nose before assessing his hand to see how much he was still bleeding.

"I'll go and get it. I don't mind what that copper says, it ain't right to hit a boy like that." She marched back up the lane in pursuit of the missing shoe.

"I've got to go," said Primrose. "I'm going to be in real trouble as it is." Without another word she turned and made her way back home. The sound of Peter Tookey's motorbike reached their ears as he skidded round the corner and came to a halt in front of them.

"Cor, you look a mess, Christian. He must've walloped you one really hard." He laughed at the slightly comical figure in front of him.

"Don't laugh at him," said Ann. "He's been hurt."

28

"Only a little. Did you let the tyres down then?"

"No I didn't have time. And then he hit me, the sod." He paused and ran a hand under his nose again. "And he says to tell you that he knows all about us, that we cause a lot of trouble and he's going to get us!"

"The old sod," said Sandra.

Christian shrugged and leaned against the parapet of the bridge, standing on his shod leg. His sock had holes in the toes and heels, which drew attention to the turn-ups of his frayed trousers. Nimpy appeared moments later.

"Looks a bit the worse for wear, Christian," she said, passing him his shoe; a sizeable hole was visible in the sole and the heel flapped feebly.

"Don't worry about that," said Christian with bravado. "It will do for a bit, I ain't got no money to buy any new ones."

"Doesn't Miss Shaw buy you anything?" asked Nimpy.

"No," said Christian. "She offers but it's not her place to, and it's not like she can afford it. My mother will though, when she comes."

Nimpy nodded and didn't pursue the matter.

"Right," said Simon, "I'm off to the bus shelter, my bike's there still."

"So's mine," said Nimpy.

"And mine," added Peter.

Christian slotted the unhappy shoe onto his foot and they set off back to the bikes.

"Peter, your dad's got a farm, hasn't he?" asked Christian out of the blue.

"Yes. It belongs to my grandfather but Father runs it with my uncle."

29

"Does he have any jobs available? I could really do with some money and nobody here will employ me, I've asked all of them."

"I don't think there's anything at the moment. But I can ask him, I suppose. There will be blackcurrant picking in the summer. You can't drive a tractor, can you?"

"He can't even ride a bike, can you, Christian," Ann mocked. Christian didn't respond.

"When's blackcurrant picking then?" he asked Peter.

"At the end of July, it lasts about two weeks and then there's potato picking, but that's a lot later and I suppose you will be back at school."

"I've only got one more year after this," said Christian, smiling happily. "I can't wait to get away from here, but I suppose I ought to do my A Levels, they say that I should pass."

"What will you do for A Level then?" said Peter, with interest.

"Latin, Greek and Greek history."

"Blimey. I struggle with *English*."

"Do you work on the farm then?"

"Yes, we're potato planting at the moment, I'll have to work all of the holiday."

"You're lucky to have holiday, I work all the time," said Sandra. "You wait till you leave school, it ain't as easy as that, although I suppose you do have some money."

"What do you then?" asked Christian.

"I work in Bedford as a trainee hairdresser. I wasn't getting on well at school anymore so I left at Christmas."

They had now arrived back at the bus shelter; Roger was sitting on the bench, a huge smile on his face. The others related their run-in with PC Rawlins.

"The old sod," said Roger, with a shake of his head. "You're sure he's gone, though?"

"Yes," said Tookey. "I saw him go off on his motorbike."

"He said he had to be on duty in Bedford," added Christian.

"Right then, let's go and let this off," said Roger, pulling the second honey jar from his pocket, a small amount of petrol splashing around in the bottom.

"Where are you going to put it this time?" asked Peter.

"In a dustbin." He looked at the others triumphantly.

"Whose dustbin?" asked Helen. "Don't you dare do it in my mum's, she'll never let me out again."

"Right, let's walk down the road and see what we can see then," said Roger, taking charge. "Who's coming?"

"I'm not," said Helen.

The other girls looked at her, nodded their heads in agreement, and they all left together.

"Are you coming, Simon?" asked Roger.

"No," said Simon. "I better go home or I'll be in trouble."

Roger led the two Peters and Christian back past the chapel towards the Hall. Suddenly Roger caught sight of what he wanted, two metal dustbins standing invitingly by the gate.

"You're not going to put it in them," hissed Christian. "If she finds out I've anything to do with it, she'll throw me out."

"She won't know who it is," said Roger, marching up to the first dustbin and peering in. It was half full. He pulled the lid off the second bin and on finding it empty he turned to Christian. "Come on then, light it!"

"No, I'm not going to. I told you already, you do it, I'm going." He turned on his heel and walked away.

"Scared, are we?" taunted Roger. "I thought you were the hard man."

There was no response and Christian continued to walk away. Roger turned back to the job in hand, put the jar on top of the dustbin and fumbled for a box of matches in his pocket.

"Are we all ready?" he asked dramatically, quickly scanning the road for any unwanted observers.

The Peters nodded eagerly.

Roger lit the banger and placed the honey jar gently into the dustbin, replacing the lid quickly and joining the others in sprinting as far from the bin as they could. There was a violent bang; the boys turned to see the lid of the dustbin shooting into the air, a flash of white shot after it from inside the dustbin. A few seconds later the lid came clattering back down to the ground as smoke poured from the dustbin itself.

"Brilliant," breathed Roger happily.

The sound of a door being pulled open at the Hall reached them.

"What on earth was that?" screeched a voice from the door.

The voice came from a woman in her middle age standing, hands on hips, in the doorway. She looked towards where smoke trickled from the dustbin then drifted lazily across the backyard and she bustled across the yard, picking up the lid of the dustbin, which was lying twenty yards from its original location. She was wearing a calf-length pleated woollen skirt with a thick hand-knitted jumper. Her hair was going grey and tied in a bun and her face, long and dreary, showed little by way of emotion. The boys crouched down behind the hedge and watched as Miss Shaw looked into the bin and replaced the lid. She walked to the gate; the boys held their breath in anticipation, if she looked up the road she would catch sight of them.

"Come on," whispered Roger. "Let's make a run for it."

The Peters nodded and raced after Roger up the path towards the bus shelter. The noise of their pounding feet alerted Miss Shaw, who strode into the road.

"Who's that? *Who is that*?" she shouted. "I can see you, Roger, I recognise that black hair, you come back here right now! If you don't do what I say I will phone the police this minute."

Roger stopped in his tracks, both Peters stopping behind him.

"She will, you know," he muttered.

"She will what?" asked Tookey.

"She will phone the police."

"I'll phone your father, Roger, do you hear?" shrieked Miss Shaw. "Do you want me to do that then?"

The boys dithered in the lane.

"What are we going to do?" asked Peter.

"We'd better go back," said Roger. "It's all right for you, she doesn't know who you are. Come on, let's go and face the music, I don't want her phoning my dad."

The boys walked slowly back towards Miss Shaw, stopping shamefacedly in front of her.

"What was that noise then, Roger? What happened to the dustbin?" Roger shuffled his feet and played for time. "Well then?" persisted Miss Shaw, staring intently at Roger. "I know *you* are the ring leader, you always are, so tell me what you have just done."

"We were wondering the same thing," said Roger, looking up at Miss Shaw innocently. "We heard a bang, the lid blew off the bin and it started to smoke. We thought that there must have been something in it, didn't we, Peter?"

"That's right," agreed Peter.

"And who are these others?" Miss Shaw looked beadily at the Peters. "You're all as bad as each other, who are you?"

She turned aggressively to Peter Dunmore.

"We're just friends come down for a while."

"Come down from where?"

"Covington."

She turned crossly to Tookey.

"Yelden," he mumbled.

"Well *you* can go back to Covington," said Miss Shaw, pointing to Peter Dunmore. "And *you* can go back to Yelden." She rounded on Roger. "As for you, Roger, I've a good mind to phone your father."

"There's no need to do that, Miss Shaw," said Roger in desperation. "We weren't doing anything, honest we weren't, were we?" He looked to the two Peters for confirmation. They shook their heads furiously. "You know what my dad's like, Miss Shaw," said Roger, a note of a plea entering his voice.

"Yes, I know exactly what your father is like, Roger," said Miss Shaw with a nasty smile. "Now be off with the lot of you and don't let me catch you again, not any of you."

With one final furious stare at the three boys she turned on her heel and marched back towards the house.

Chapter Two
Mrs Dene

The next Sunday Peter made his way down to Dean again; he was wearing his fine-checked jacket over a shirt and a tie, and some black drainpipe trousers which were newly purchased from Bedford where he had been with Simon the day before. When he arrived in Dean he hid the bike behind the bus shelter, sat down on the bench and waited. The arrangement had been to meet at six o'clock and he was the first one there.

Ten minutes later, Simon arrived, skidding to a stop in front of the shelter. He was sporting a smart blue racing bike equipped with ten gears and an unnaturally high saddle.

"Where's everyone else?" he demanded, glaring up the street.

"I don't know. You're the only other one to turn up so far."

No sooner had he said this than Nimpy rode into view, gliding up the road and parking her bike round the back of the shelter next to Peter's.

"Where are the rest of them then, Nimpy?" asked Simon.

"They're all in trouble. After last week there were a lot of complaints, the others aren't allowed to come out because apparently we shouldn't be allowed to be together." She snorted and flung herself down on the bench.

"But you're here," pointed out Simon.

"Yes, but I don't live in the village, do I, silly," said Nimpy patiently. "My mum and dad didn't stop me because they didn't hear about what had happened."

"We didn't do much," protested Peter.

"Well that's not what the people in Dean think," said Nimpy with a sharp laugh.

Footsteps alerted the three to another arrival. It was Helen.

"How did you get out?" asked Nimpy.

"Dad's up the allotment until the pub opens and Mum's gone next door," said Helen. "Dad doesn't come back until it closes and Mum is always ages, once she gets talking she can't stop, so I think I'm going to be all right."

She threw herself down next to Nimpy.

In the distance they could hear the sound of a small motorbike. Peter grinned at Simon. The sound of Tookey's BSA Bantam was so distinctive it could be heard for miles, despite its pathetically small engine and lack of power. Tookey tore up the High Street as fast as he could manage, applying the brakes at the last minute and letting the back wheel skid round on the gravel. He grinned rakishly and stepped off the bike, pressing the stand to the ground and lifting his goggles in one smooth motion onto the top of his head.

"Come on then, who's got a fag?" he demanded, looking around the meagre collection. He frowned. "Where have all the others gone? I thought we were meeting at six o'clock?"

"We were," said Peter. "It's ten past now, haven't you got a watch?"

"No, I broke mine yesterday when I fell off the bike. Come on now, have you got a fag?"

Peter stood up and pulled a packet from his jacket pocket before offering it around. Tookey looked at Peter critically before emitting a trumpet of laughter.

"What *have* you got on?" he said, pointing at Peter's trousers and snorting with laughter again. "Look at them, where did you get them from?"

"Bedford," said Peter, a little sheepishly.

"You didn't pay good money for them, did you? How do you get into them for a start? You couldn't get into those with shoes on, I bet." He laughed loudly again.

"They're what's fashionable in 1959," said Nimpy, feeling the need to protect Peter and his trousers.

"And look, you're bow-legged," continued Tookey, ignoring her comment, "your knees have never met, you can see that for sure in those trousers."

He stuffed a cigarette into his mouth, accepting a match from Simon who had just lit his own. The boys leaned back and tried to look comfortable smoking, as Simon smothered a cough, blinking furiously as the smoke stung his eyes.

"Where's the rest of them then?" asked Tookey.

"They ain't allowed out," said Helen. "It were all that trouble last week."

"What trouble?"

"Someone tied Mrs Dixon's lavatory bucket up a tree," said Simon solemnly.

Tookey snorted, before doubling up with laugher. "Who did that then, Simon?"

"I don't know," said Simon innocently, taking a small puff on his cigarette.

Tookey laughed and looked up the road; a family of four were making their way towards them dressed in their Sunday best, evidently on the way to chapel. Between the mother and father, the group could make out Primrose, holding the hand of a younger boy who was still in short trousers and dragging his feet. The father made a bee line for Simon, stopped a yard in front of him and looked him straight in the eye. Simon took two steps back and threw his cigarette to the floor.

"Don't I know you, boy?" growled the man, tilting his head to one side like a bird. "I know your father, don't I? Although I don't know why he lets you out on a Sunday to cause mischief, have you been to church?"

"Yes."

"Well, what are you doing hanging around here causing trouble then?" said the man angrily, his voice rising.

"We're not causing trouble. What have we done?"

"Don't you speak to me like that, boy, you should respect your elders, didn't your father teach you that?"

"I respect some of them," Simon retorted defiantly.

Primrose gasped and looked at the ground, smothering a smile.

"What did you say?" the man barked, taking a step closer to Simon.

"Come on," said the wife, grabbing hold of the man's arm. "Let's go, we're already late."

He glared at Simon for another second or two then allowed himself to be led away. Primrose followed them, turning to grin and make faces at her friends as she left. She stuck her tongue out at the back of her father, turned once more towards the group, waved and then trotted off after her family.

"Old sod," said Simon. "I won't have people talking to me like that."

The others laughed and watched Primrose's family receding towards the chapel. A figure came dashing towards them from the other direction, her pleated tartan skirt dancing around her knees as she ran.

"Sandra, I thought you couldn't come out?" said Nimpy.

"Mum and Dad have gone out and my eldest sister's watching the telly," panted Sandra. "Ann's coming in a bit."

"You haven't got a telly!" exclaimed Nimpy incredulously. "When did you get that then?"

"About a month ago," said Sandra with a superior smile. "Haven't you got one then?"

"No. Have you got one, Peter?"

"No," said Peter, as Ann came sprinting up from the same direction as Sandra.

She pulled up beside her, her face red.

"We can't be long, Sandra. Jean hasn't noticed, but that programme will be over at seven," puffed Ann, waving distractedly at the others.

"Don't fuss so," snapped Sandra, turning to look down at Nimpy who was perched in the middle of the bench. "Move up," she instructed. Nimpy shifted to the left and Sandra sat down beside her.

"What are we going to do today, then?" asked Tookey, crunching the end of his cigarette under his boot. The group looked at one another, the girls shrugged.

"Oh, look who's coming," said Simon, pointing to the figure of Christian who was approaching from the direction of the chapel.

"You've got out of jail then?" called out Simon.

"Absent without leave," said Christian, peering at the group through dirty glasses. "She's gone to chapel so I've got just under an hour and then back to the Latin and Greek. Roger can't come though."

"No," said Sandra, "I saw him on the bus, his dad heard about last week and wouldn't let him out, I wouldn't want to be in his shoes, his dad is really strict, you know."

"Well what shall we do?" Tookey repeated. There was silence.

"You know what she said?" said Christian suddenly.

"Who said?" Peter asked.

"Miss Shaw, of course." The others said nothing, waiting.

"Well go on then, tell us," said Peter impatiently.

"She said she ought to find us somewhere to meet so we don't keep wandering around the streets causing trouble."

"Oh yes," said Simon, "I'll believe that when I see it. Anyway, she would want to organise it, and I know what that would mean." He sat on Tookey's motorbike and pressed the hooter.

"No, she means it, I think," insisted Christian. "There's an old out-house that's standing empty and she says we can go in there."

"What are we going to *do* in there then?" Tookey asked dubiously.

"I don't know, do I? I'm just telling you what she said."

"She's right," said Sandra. "We'd be much better somewhere like that, it's bloomin' cold out here at times." She smiled at Christian.

"You can tell her we can clean it out," said Nimpy.

41

"Okay, that's all very well," said Tookey, waving his hand impatiently, "but what are we going to do *now*?"

"Let's go for a walk down to the church and back," suggested Nimpy.

"Great, yeah, let's go for a walk," groaned Tookey. "How exciting!"

"Well, you think of something better then, big head," Ann snarled.

"Right then," said Peter quickly, "let's go now and we can think of something else to do as we walk."

The group got to their feet and trudged off towards the high street, passing a row of cottages as they did. There was a vigorous tapping on a window as they passed the second last cottage in the row.

"It's Mum," said Helen, mortified. "She's seen me; I didn't even think she was in."

The sound of a window catch being released could be heard, as the bottom sash window was dragged up and a woman leaned out to bellow, "What do you think you're doing, Helen? I told you not to go out, didn't I?"

Helen bowed her head and pursed her lips, but said nothing.

"I told you that you wasn't to go out with them boys, there's nothing but trouble when they're about. Now you get back inside this minute, do you hear me?"

Helen chewed her lip furiously and scowled.

"*Do you hear me*?" yelled her mother, leaning angrily out of the window to glare at her daughter.

"Yes, Mum." She turned to the others. "I better go," she said as the window was slammed down. She turned to the cottage where her mother continued to mouth abuse at her through the window, pointing a bony finger her way, and she sighed and dragged her feet back towards the house.

"We'll have to be more careful going past our place," said Sandra to Ann.

Thirty yards up the road, they could hear a car engine starting. Loud noises reverberated from a small low-slung garage as the car burst into life, coughing plumes of smoke out into the road.

"It's Mrs Dene," said Ann. "You wait, she's a hopeless driver, we'll probably need to stand well back."

The car continued to rev in the garage until the smoke finally cleared. There was an uncomfortable grinding noise as the driver tried to engage a gear. The group were now level with Mrs Dene's drive and could see the car preparing to reverse towards them. The engine revved again as Mrs Dene released the clutch; but instead of leaving the garage, the car jerked forwards. There was a loud crunch and the sound of cans falling as the car stalled.

"She hit the back of the garage," said Simon.

The group crept forwards to get a better look. Mrs Dene pressed the starter again; the engine sprang quickly into life, revved once then fell idle. The hideous grinding noise echoed around the garage again and there was a clunk as another gear was engaged. The car revved once more, jerked backwards and stopped suddenly. The engine revved more aggressively, and the group ducked as they saw Mrs Dene twist in the driver's seat to better navigate her exit from the garage, accidentally pressing her hand to the horn as she did so. She turned forwards again in surprise as the horn blared, and released her foot from the clutch, the car shooting backwards out of the garage and across the road.

Confused, Mrs Dene looked to her left and right, and saw the small group staring at her.

"She's got a flat tyre," said Christian. "Look at the front wheel."

The group looked; sure enough, the tyre was completely flat. Mrs Dene disengaged the gear lever and seemed to be looking for something inside the car, as she mouthed enthusiastically towards the group. Eventually, she found what she had been looking for and wound the window down. She was wearing a black straw hat with a large brim above a thick black coat; a poppy was still threaded into the button hole, despite it being spring. She turned slowly towards the assembled group.

"Sandra my dear, how are you?" she said with a smile. "Don't you grow up quickly, quite a young lady now and very pretty as well." Sandra blushed.

"Thank you, Mrs Dene."

"And is that Ann with you? Doesn't she look like your father, don't you think so?" She smiled indulgently at Ann and looked around the rest of the group. "And isn't that Joanna? My, it's a long time since I've seen you, my dear, you've grown as well. Doesn't time fly?" She shook her head in wonder. "And your father and mother, Joanna, are they well?"

"Very well thank you, Mrs Dene," said Nimpy.

"And these boys, Sandra, who are they?" continued Mrs Dene, peering at the boys. "I know that one, don't I, it's Christian. How are you, Christian? How are your Latin and Greek?"

"I'm well thank you, Mrs Dene. Latin and Greek are fine."

Mrs Dene nodded and turned back to Sandra. "And the others, Sandra?" she demanded, looking at the other boys.

"They're just friends, Mrs Dene, that one's Peter, that's Simon and the other one is Peter as well." Mrs Dene leaned forward a little and beckoned Nimpy towards her. Nimpy bent down to listen.

"They look like nice boys. They come from good homes, I expect?"

"Oh yes, Mrs Dene," said Nimpy solemnly, trying not to laugh. "Very good homes all of them."

Mrs Dene took one last piercing look at the boys and fumbled for the window winder again.

"You've got a flat tyre, Mrs Dene," said Christian urgently, stepping forward to the car's window.

"Thank you so much, my dear. Give my regards to Miss Shaw, won't you?" said Mrs Dene airily.

"Yes, Mrs Dene," replied Christian with a puzzled frown.

Mrs Dene wound up her window and revved the car enthusiastically. With a lot of effort, she started to tug the steering wheel round, the wheels ground to the left. She continued to pull the left-hand side of the steering wheel down until the wheels would turn no further. She gazed distractedly down in the direction of the gear lever, located it and wobbled the stick. She pressed down on the clutch and sought desperately to find first gear. The car protested angrily as Mrs Dene

45

ground the gears, waved at the group and turned towards the road, tightly gripping the steering wheel.

The car lurched forwards but the front wheels were now at such an angle that the flat tyre slid straight off the wheel as the car moved and Mrs Dene continued to make her way along the road on the rim of her wheel. Christian pelted off after the car, running alongside, waving and pointing. Mrs Dene smiled and waved back, oblivious. The loose tyre was now starting to bang on the wheel arch. The sharp right-hand bend was waiting at the end of the high street – and despite Mrs Dene's desperate tugs at the steering wheel the car could not properly navigate the bend. With an inevitable bump, the car trundled onto the verge and stalled.

The group ran up to the prone car. Mrs Dene was already trying to clamber out.

"Are you okay, Mrs Dene?" asked Sandra.

"I'm fine, Sandra," said Mrs Dene with a wave of her hand. "But really, my dear, you shouldn't say okay. It's not good English, you will remember that, won't you?"

"Yes, Mrs Dene," Sandra replied, raising an eyebrow.

"I don't know why it did that," sighed Mrs Dene, hauling a leg out of the car in an ungainly manner. Her skirt rode up slightly, revealing long drawers, elasticated just below the knee. The boys blushed and looked away. "Sandra my dear, give me a hand, will you please," and Mrs Dene proffered a hand towards her. Sandra and Nimpy scurried towards her and helped her out of the car. "You are so kind," said Mrs Dene gratefully. She turned and looked with confusion at the car. "I just don't know why it wouldn't go round the corner," she exclaimed. "It always has done before."

"You have a flat tyre, Mrs Dene," explained Simon loudly. "That's why it won't go round the corner."

"A flat tyre?"

"Yes, Mrs Dene, look."

Mrs Dene squinted towards the front wheel of the car.

"My word, so I do, you are clever," she smiled at Simon, then turned with a frown to Sandra, placing a hand lightly on her arm. "I can't remember his name, Sandra," she murmured. "Just remind me, can you?"

"It's Simon, Mrs Dene."

"Yes, that's it, Simon," she said as she turned back to him, "Simon, how observant of you." Sandra stifled a laugh and looked away.

"Do you want us to change the tyre for you, Mrs Dene? It won't take long."

"Can you, my dear? That would be so kind, I'm not sure I could manage that."

"Come on," said Simon to the other boys, "back it into the road, Peter."

Peter leapt into the driver's seat, started the car and backed it into the middle of the road. Simon and Tookey pulled the spare wheel, jack and spanner from the boot. In no time the car was jacked up and the wheel changed. Within five minutes, the car was ready to go again.

"Well, my dears, how splendid you have all been," exclaimed Mrs Dene. "My saviours! I must give you something." She opened her handbag and looked critically at its contents. She frowned, snapped it shut again, leaned into the car and pulled out another larger bag, from which her knitting poked from the top. She peered into it hopefully.

47

"No, nothing," she sighed. "We will have to go back to the house, I'm sure I will have something there, it won't take long to walk back."

"You can't leave the car here, Mrs Dene," protested Simon, "It's in the middle of the road!" Mrs Dene contemplated her car.

"No, I suppose not."

"Do you want me to drive?" said Peter. "I've got a licence; I've passed my test."

"Would you?" said Mrs Dene gratefully, throwing a smile at Peter before turning back to Sandra again. "What's his name, dear?"

"Peter, Mrs Dene."

"Peter that would be kind; thank you so much, we might as well all have a ride."

Mrs Dene walked around the car as Peter opened the front passenger door for her. The three girls climbed into the back seat and Simon and Christian stood on the back bumper, Tookey following on his motorbike.

"Go forward, Peter, and along the backstreet and then you won't have to turn around," instructed Mrs Dene.

Peter started the car and eased it into first gear. The car surged forward, passing a local farmer, who was walking up the road with a pitchfork thrown over his shoulder. As they passed, Simon threw him a military salute. He scowled. They turned right along the backstreet, passing Primrose as she made her way back from chapel with her family. Mrs Dene waved at the foursome, who stared with bemusement at the battered car. Peter tooted the horn and the girls in the back stuck their tongues out at Primrose who reciprocated in turn.

They turned sharp right towards the ford, Peter didn't slow down. There was a bump as the car hit a stone and Simon and Christian yelped and lost their footing on the bumper, bouncing into the water. Simon landed on his feet, but Christian was less agile and lost his balance. He stumbled forwards, throwing his hands out just in time to prevent himself falling face first into the stream. The water was about six inches deep and the two waded out of the water after the car as Tookey came puttering towards them, water sluicing behind the bike as he drove cautiously through the ford. Simon waved him down and leapt onto the back of the bike. Christian followed slowly behind, water squelching out of his tatty shoes.

The car pulled up outside Mrs Dene's house and the group piled out and followed her up the path to the front door, which she opened with a rusty key. She ushered the group into the hallway and went to rummage in her sitting room. They could hear various exclamations from the room before she moved to the kitchen, returning ten minutes later. She was carrying an old white paper bag, which she handed delightedly to Sandra. Sandra peered into the packet – a dozen or so humbugs clung stickily to one another. With a smile Mrs Dene handed Ann a half-eaten pack of Bournville. Ann looked dubiously at the chocolate before smiling up at Mrs Dene.

"Now, where do you come from, Simon?" asked Mrs Dene.

"Yelden."

"I know your parents, don't I?" she said with a small frown. "I am going to phone them to tell them what a wonderfully helpful boy you are." She smiled and turned to Tookey.

"And, Peter, where do you come from?"

"Yelden too, Mrs Dene, you know my mother from the WI, I think, Nancy Tookey."

"Of course, of course," exclaimed Mrs Dene. "Do send her my regards, won't you, such a clever woman your mother." She mused for a moment on the brightness of Mrs Tookey, before turning to Peter Dunmore.

"And the other Peter, where do you come from?"

"Covington."

"Of course, yes, I know who you are then, or at least I know your grandfather, William Dunmore, if I am not mistaken?"

"Yes, Mrs Dene."

"And your father, which Dunmore is your father?"

"Thomas, Mrs Dene."

"Well, well! What a lovely lady your mother is," marvelled Mrs Dene, smiling at the group around her. "Now I can't thank you all enough, you have been so kind, but I really must go, I am so late already." The group said their goodbyes and thronged out into the street.

"We must go," said Sandra, "Come on, Ann, we'll be in trouble, I'm sure."

She grabbed her sister's hand and rushed the short distance up the street to their house. Tookey and Simon headed off in the opposite direction.

"Did you ask your dad about a job, Peter?" asked Christian, as the rest of the group made their way back to the bus shelter.

"There's not much on," said Peter. "But you can come on the potato planter at breakfast and lunchtime if you want, to take over while the men go for their meal."

"That'll do," said Christian, gratefully.

"I could do that too," said Nimpy.

"Okay, I'll ask. I'm sure they will be starting this week, I'll come down and let you know."

The group separated. Nimpy and Peter collected their bikes from the bus shelter and rode off towards Covington.

"Peter," said Nimpy confidentially, as the two pedalled on, "I like your drainpipe trousers, so don't take any notice of what the others say."

Chapter Three
Cold Work

For mid-April the weather was cold. The wind whistled in from the east and the day was cloudy and grey. Peter, Nimpy and Christian stood on the headland of the field waiting for the potato planter to reach them. They were sheltering behind the trailer loaded with trays of seed potatoes, as the planter, pulled by a small crawler tractor, edged its way across the field at a snail's pace.

Colin drew up in an old Bedford Dormobile, the car the farm used for transporting its workers. It had sliding doors towards the front and double doors at the back, from where everybody could climb in to reach the three rows of seats.

"How did you get here, Peter?"

"I biked."

"And what about you lot?" he continued, eyeing Nimpy and Christian.

"I biked too," answered Nimpy. "But it's not far, I only live round the corner there."

"I walked," said Christian.

Colin looked at him closely.

"Ain't you got anything else to wear, boy? It's bloody cold on that machine."

Christian looked down at his attire: he was wearing a grey pullover under a jacket and worn, thin trousers. He was still wearing the battered shoes he'd had on the week before.

"Haven't you got any boots?" asked Colin. "Or a thick coat?"

"No," said Christian with a small shrug. "But I'll be all right, don't worry."

Colin looked back to Peter and Nimpy, who were both wearing coats and overalls with wellington boots; Peter wore a cap, and Nimpy a woolly hat.

"You know what you've got to do then?" Colin asked Christian.

"I'll show them," said Peter, as the crawler trundled to-wards them.

They could see the driver on the crawler as it clanked nois-ily to the end of the field, pulling out the three ridges under which the potatoes had been planted as it went along. The ridges stretched in a straight line to the other end of the field. As he reached the waiting group, the driver leaned behind him and pulled hard on a rope, initiating a mechanism which pulled the planter out of the ground and stopped the potatoes dropping. He turned back quickly and pulled one of the two levers in front of him, pressing his foot hard down on the right-hand pedal. The crawler jerked itself round until it was facing back down the field again.

The three workers, perched on the back, smiled down at Peter as the planter swung round high above the ground. The driver pulled another lever and the planter lowered again, al-lowing the workers to climb down. He then leapt from the crawler, pausing briefly to warm his hands over the exhaust of the tractor as he did so.

"It's bloody cold," grumbled one of the workers, sniffing and wiping a drip from his nose.

"Who have we here then?" grinned another, eyeing Nimpy carefully. "You must be Ned's daughter?"

"Yes," said Nimpy shyly.

"Come on, you lot, let's get back in the warm," instructed the driver, jumping into the seat of the van and nodding towards Colin who turned to the three youngsters.

"Right, Peter, pass the boxes and we'll fill the old girl up."

Nimpy climbed onto the trailer and passed the trays of potatoes down to Peter, who carried them to the planter, where Colin tipped them in. Christian stacked up the used trays.

"Are we ready then?" hollered Colin, as the three took their seats on the planter, Christian slotting into the middle with Peter and Nimpy either side of him.

"What do I do then?" Christian asked Nimpy.

"See that there," said Nimpy, pointing to a wheel in front of Christian, "it goes round and as it does you put a spud in each of them cups as it spins, all right?"

"I suppose so," said Christian, picking some potatoes from the hopper above the wheel.

Colin jumped onto the crawler as the others pulled out of the field in the old van to return to the workshop to have their breakfast and warm themselves by the fire. He buttoned up his coat, rubbed his hands vigorously and pulled on a pair of gloves before tugging down the beret on his head as far as it would go, his ears still exposed. He revved the tractor and engaged the lowest gear, easing the crawler forwards. The tracks of the crawler clanked as they turned and each cup banged as it dropped the potato towards the earth, returning empty for a new potato moments later.

At the back of the planter, four ridging furrows covered over the freshly dropped potato with soil and formed the elevated ridge over them. Peter and Nimpy had no problem with the work, but Christian was finding it difficult to keep up. The wind cut viciously across the field, drawing any heat out of him, his thin jacket and trousers providing little protection. His hands were so cold that he could never pick up enough potatoes, and those he did pick up often dropped from his icy hands. Nimpy found herself having to fill the cups that Christian had missed, which made her work twice as difficult. After twenty minutes they had completed one bout and were back at the trailer of seed potatoes again, ready to fill up.

"Come on, Peter, move the seed trailer up the field a bit," called Colin.

Peter leapt onto the tractor and moved the trailer level with the planter. Colin turned round to check on Nimpy and Christian on the planter.

"Dear oh dear," said Colin, with a shake of his head, "look at you, boy, you look half starved. Are you sure you haven't got anything else to put on?"

"No," said Christian, his teeth chattering as he struggled to stop his body shaking with cold.

"I know," said Colin, "Peter boy, there's some old railway sacks on that tractor, just fetch us a couple, can you."

Peter did as he was told, bringing back the sacks to Colin, who had pulled out his shut-knife. He took the sacks from Peter, turned the first one inside out and cut a slit in each corner and one across the bottom, about nine inches wide.

"Right, come here, boy, and put this on," he ordered, threading the sack over Christian's head, until it sat on his

55

shoulders, "now put your arms through here."

Christian pushed his arms through the holes in the corners of the sack, dwarfed by the huge bag; his small head poked out above the black letters of the sack which read:

LONDON MIDLAND 1947

"Give me that other one, Peter," ordered Colin, grabbing the sack.

He took one corner and pushed it into the other, forming a sort of cloak with a hat on the top. He pushed the hat onto Christian's head, allowing the cloak to fall down his back.

"Now, boy, find a bit of string and tie that round your waist, then get up there and warm your hands," demanded Colin, pointing to the exhaust of the tractor.

"Come on then, Peter, Nimpy, let's get filled up, you get on the trailer, Nimpy, and you pass them trays, Peter. It's no good you looking for them others coming back, they won't be a while yet."

Christian hobbled towards the crawler, the knee-length sack ensuring he could only take tiny steps at a time.

"Here," said Nimpy, moving to him and rolling the sack up round his legs so that Christian could move more easily.

"Come on, get on then, let's go," shouted Colin as Christian hoisted his sack up an inch more as if it were a skirt and hopped back on the planter.

"I don't know what you look like, Christian," laughed Nimpy, picking up a handful of potatoes.

"I don't care," said Christian. "I'm a lot warmer now, that's all I know."

He smiled at Nimpy and reached for a handful of spuds.

Chapter Four
The Clubhouse

The summer came and Miss Shaw finally got round to clearing her outhouse and had a light installed so that the gang could meet in the room; she used Christian as messenger and he informed everyone else.

The grand opening of the clubhouse took place on a Sunday evening in June. Peter cycled over at seven, Miss Shaw having decided that proceedings could not start until she had been to chapel, and by the time he arrived the sun was getting lower in the sky. Everybody was milling around in the backyard of the Hall, some had cycled but most had walked and in all there were ten people.

Miss Shaw had walked back from chapel in her long coat and felt hat. She nodded at the assembled group and went into the house to retrieve the key. When she came back, she had removed her coat, but not her hat and she held a large iron key in her hand. She went to a door to one side of the main house, unlocked it and went in, treading carefully down the three steps and pressing the light switch as she did so. The light, which hung on a thin flex from the ceiling, flickered on, scattering its bright glow across the room and casting a large shadow of Miss Shaw against the far wall. The room was bare save for the benches which lined the walls and it was completely windowless. The air smelt musty and the atmosphere cool compared with the June evening outside.

Everyone piled down the steps into the room after Miss Shaw, taking up positions on the benches. The assembled crowd looked to her expectantly; there was no emotion written on her long face. Her lank greying hair hung down her long neck and rested on the shoulders of her cardigan, which was buttoned up over another thin jumper. Her big bust drooped, prevented from falling any further by the high waistband of her skirt. This was grey and heavy, falling in a straight line to well below her knees and covering most of her thick wrinkly stockings. She wore worn brown sandals, from which the buckles were threatening to fall.

Miss Shaw looked from one of them to the next, but still said nothing.

"What are we going to do, Miss Shaw?" asked Sandra finally.

Miss Shaw turned to her and stared. Everyone was silent.

"I don't know what you are going to do," she said. "What you do is up to yourselves. I will provide the venue to keep you off the street but I can't be expected to organise you as well, now can I?" She looked at Sandra again. "Can I?" she repeated.

"No, Miss Shaw."

"Now, it's seven o'clock," said Miss Shaw in a loud voice. "I will come and lock up at eight-thirty, you understand?"

"Yes, Miss Shaw," the group replied.

"We will have a prayer before I go," she announced, shutting her eyes and putting her hands together.

There were a few puzzled looks, but the group remained silent. Miss Shaw opened her eyes again and looked around.

"Are we ready then?" she said.

Everyone nodded and clasped their hands together, most of them closing their eyes tightly so as not to catch anybody else's eye.

"Dear Lord our Redeemer," started Miss Shaw.

A distracted eye opened in the group, followed by another and another, until most of the group were pulling faces at one another as Miss Shaw continued her prayer.

"Amen," finished Miss Shaw.

"Amen," chorused the group, opening their eyes.

"Now," said Miss Shaw. "Say after me, John Wesley's Rule. Are you ready?" She looked around suspiciously, her eyes alighting finally on Christian. "Are you ready, Christian?"

"Yes, Miss Shaw."

"Now after me," she continued, clearing her throat loudly.

> "Do all the good you can
> By all the means you can
> In all the ways you can
> In all the places you can
> At all the times you can
> To all the people you can
> As long as ever you can"

As Miss Shaw recited a line, the group droned it back to her, some trying their best not to laugh.

"Very good," said Miss Shaw curtly as silence fell amongst the group again. "I will be back at eight-thirty." And with that, she turned on her heel to leave and then turned back again. "I was thinking we'd better have a list of members, Sandra."

"Yes, Miss Shaw."

"You do that for me please and make sure I can read it."

"Yes, Miss Shaw."

"Christian, go and get some paper and a pencil from my office," she said, and turned to leave again.

Everyone gave a small cheer as she shut the door. Simon stood up and looked around the room, the single light throwing a large shadow against the opposite wall.

"What shall we do?" he said.

There was a small groan as soon as the question was asked.

"We could read the Bible," suggested Ann with a snigger.

There was another groan.

"Well, you all think of something then," she challenged, looking around the room.

There was silence.

"Could we play some records? Someone must have a record player in Dean," said Tookey, looking up for confirmation from his friends.

"No one's got one," said Roger. "And anyway I don't think there's a plug in here."

In hope rather than expectation, everyone stood up and looked under the benches; Roger was right, there was no plug.

"What about Radio Luxembourg?" said Sandra.

"Can't get it here," said Christian, who had just come back in with paper and a pencil. "I've tried for ages. We're too low down. We could get some beer though?"

"No good, the pub won't serve any of us," said Primrose.

Christian gave the paper and pencil to Sandra.

61

"Come on, I'd better make the list like she said." Sandra looked at the others, asking "What can I lean on?" as she peered round the room.

"There ain't nowhere," said Nimpy, "you will have to use the wall." Sandra ran her fingers over the lime wash.

"Err it's filthy but there is nowhere else so here goes," and she held the paper against the wall and looked round. "Peter."

"Which one?" two or three voices shouted.

"Peter Dunmore, right here we go," and she printed the names as she shouted each one.

"Peter Dunmore, Peter Tookey, Roger, Christian, Simon, Sandra, Primrose, Nimpy, what's your name, Nimpy?"

"It's Joanna but just put Nimpy."

"Nimpy, Helen, Ann and that's the lot," and she put the list on the bench and sat down.

"What about ping-pong?" piped up someone. "Or snooker? Or darts?"

"Do you have a snooker table to hand?" said Simon. He sighed angrily. "Come on, someone must be able to think of *something*."

"I know something," said Ann suddenly. "What about Postman's Knock?"

"We can't play that," laughed Helen. "That's for children."

"What's Postman's Knock?" Simon asked.

"Yes, let's play that," said Sandra enthusiastically. "Nobody's got any other ideas."

"What do you do then?" asked Peter. "I've never heard of it."

"Right," said Sandra. "How many girls and how many boys?" She counted. there were five girls and five boys. She turned to the room to explain the rules. "We need some bits of paper with numbers one to five written on them."

Christian was sent off to find some more paper from the Hall.

"We want something to put the numbers in," said Sandra.

"I know, there's a flowerpot against the wall on the other side of the yard, someone go and fetch it," said Ann.

Christian returned with a piece of paper as Tookey was sent off to find the flowerpot. Sandra tore the paper up, numbered the pieces from one to five and put them in the flowerpot which she placed in the middle of the room.

"Now what?" said Simon.

Sandra stood up and stamped on the floor for silence. "Now, here's what we do, one person goes outside, shuts the door and knocks on the door a number of times. Any number between one and five."

"Stop, stop!" interrupted Christian, leaping to his feet and visibly paling. "I don't like the sound of this, you can count me out."

"Right," said Sandra again, waving a hand dismissively towards Christian. "Knock a number of times between one and four, if it's a girl outside, and the boys have to pick a number from the flowerpot and the one who gets the number of knocks goes outside and shuts the door."

There was silence.

"That's all?" said Tookey. "That sounds like a stupid game, what happens then?"

"Then," said Sandra, coyly, "then they kiss and the person who was outside comes in and the one left outside knocks up to five times and so on."

For a moment or two there was silence.

"What if you don't like the person that comes out?" asked Helen.

"Hard luck," said Ann.

"You have to do it anyway, even if you don't like them," said Sandra. "Who's going to play then?" She looked around at everyone sitting against the wall. Nobody said a word; some of the girls grimaced, the boys matching their expressions with sly grins. "Right, let's get started, who's going to go outside first?"

There was silence again.

"Right, well who's the oldest then?" she asked, looking around the room. "It must be you, Primrose, there's nobody older than you."

"No," protested Primrose, horrified. "It can't be me, it's one of the boys; Simon, when's your birthday?"

"I'm not the oldest," said Simon. "He is!" He pointed at Peter. "He's nearly eighteen, nobody else here is that close to eighteen. You aren't, are you, Tookey?"

"No," said Tookey, laughing at Peter's discomfort. "It's him! Go on then, Peter, get out there." Everyone cheered as Peter turned bright red and stood up, looking decidedly uncomfortable.

"What do I do then?" he asked Sandra.

"You can't be that thick, Peter Dunmore," said Sandra. "Go outside, shut the door and knock on it between one and four times and wait." She looked at him scornfully. "Do you get it?"

"I suppose so."

"Right. Go on then," she ordered, getting hold of Peter's shoulders, turning him round and pushing him towards the door. The others all cheered as Peter was pushed out and the door shut behind him. Sandra sat down on one of the benches with the others. Simon, who was holding the flowerpot, placed it in the middle of the room and they all waited for the knock. There was silence as the group looked from one to the other.

"Come on then! Knock!" shouted Simon.

There was a muffled "Are you ready?" through the thick door.

"Yes!" everybody shouted back again.

There was another pause and then four deliberate knocks on the door. The girls looked at each other and started to chatter excitedly.

"What do we do now then?" Roger asked Sandra, who was standing up to organise the group.

"We each take a piece of paper from the flowerpot and see what the number is," explained Sandra. Roger got up and reached for a piece of paper. "Not you, stupid! You don't want to kiss him, do you?" The girls shrieked with laughter. "Put the paper back," Sandra instructed, snatching the paper from Roger and throwing it back into the flowerpot. She sat down again. "Right. Just the girls then; someone start."

The girls sat and looked at each other blankly.

"Go on then, Sandra, it's your idea, you take the first one," said Helen.

Sandra frowned slightly, shrugged then gingerly selected a slip of paper, as one by one the other girls followed suit.

"Who's got four then?" asked Sandra, looking down at her piece of paper. "It's not me."

She glanced over at the others who were just starting to unravel their slips of paper. There was silence.

"Come on then," snapped Tookey. "Who is it? Who's got number four?"

"It's not me," said Helen.

"Nor me," said Nimpy.

Ann was silent.

"It's you, Ann!" howled Sandra, pointing at her sister.

Ann smirked, leapt to her feet and with a flourish wiggled her hips, blowing a kiss across the room towards the closed door. She trotted up the steps to the door and sashayed out to catcalls and whistles from the room.

Peter was leaning against the wall of the outhouse in the gathering gloom, smoking a cigarette.

"It's me then," announced Ann, standing and staring at Peter, a small smile on her face, her arms folded across her stomach.

"What do we have to do now?" said Peter, unwilling to get anything wrong at this stage and face the derision of the others.

"You've got to kiss me, that's all," shrugged Ann. "Don't worry; it won't hurt. I bet you've never kissed a girl before though, have you, Peter Dunmore? I can see that you haven't, you're going red."

"I've never kissed anyone as *young* as you," said Peter defensively, trying to deflect Ann's scorn.

66

"I'm nearly fifteen I'll have you know," said Ann. "In just over a year's time I'll be able to get married, if I want to that is," she added, hurriedly. She stood for a while, twisting a curl of hair around her index finger. "Well then."

"Well what?"

"Aren't you going to kiss me then?"

"Suppose so," mumbled Peter, moving closer to Ann and leaning down to peck her on the cheek.

"Can't you do any better than that?" she laughed, as Peter drew away.

Peter shifted uncomfortably. He was a good nine inches taller than Ann when he stood up to the full extent of his height, rather than stooping as he usually did. He took a puff of his cigarette, threw it to the ground decisively and stamped on it. He took another step towards Ann, took hold of her shoulders, leaned down and kissed her hard on the lips, holding on to her for some time before he finally let go. She stood back and looked at him.

"You don't half smell of fags! And you've got lipstick over your face now, come here." She pulled him towards her and wiped it off with a white handkerchief. "Now go on back in there, it's my turn to do the knocking."

Peter nodded and opened the wooden door, almost tripping down the steps as he moved back into the comparative brilliance of the room. Everybody cheered and elbowed him as he sat back down.

"What are you all red for?" said Roger.

"I didn't know you wore lipstick," laughed another.

"Shhhh!" ordered Sandra. "We need to listen for the next knock."

67

The room fell silent as the group waited. Finally, Ann knocked once; eagerly the boys reached for a number from the flowerpot. This time it was Roger who was sent out. As the evening continued, the enthusiasm for the game increased and the amount of time spent outside the door extended longer and longer until Sandra could stand it no longer and imposed a time limit.

Christian, not happy to play, had gone back into the house, returning forty-five minutes later and passing an entangled Nimpy and Peter. The pair, who had been somewhat distracted, sprang apart as Christian brushed past them. He yanked open the door and stomped down the steps into the clubhouse.

"Where's he been?" asked Peter, as the door slammed behind him.

"I don't think he likes this game," said Nimpy, leaning back against the wall. She looked at Peter. "Oh and I nearly forgot. Mum says when are you starting blackcurrants? It must be soon."

"I think it will be another ten days at least, but someone will come round, I'm sure."

"I'll tell her then. She relies on that money, you know."

The door of the barn was suddenly pulled open and Peter was ordered back through into the room to universal reproof that he had overstepped the time limit. Christian sat in the corner, ignoring the banter going on between the rest of the gang. Nimpy knocked twice and it was again the boys' turn to pick.

"Come on, Christian, it's your turn to take a number," Roger shouted over, offering Christian the plant pot. "Come on, take one!"

"No, I ain't playing stupid games like that," said Christian, his voice quiet.

"Yes, you are," insisted Roger. "If you don't take one, I'm taking one for you." Christian looked away, his eyes unfocused behind his thick glasses.

"All right then," he said, taking a piece of paper from the pot and unravelling it on the ground in front of him.

"Look," said Roger, in delight, pointing at the paper. "She knocked twice, that's your number, Christian." Christian frowned.

"Who's outside?" he asked, looking around the room.

"It's Nimpy," said Sandra. "Go on, Christian, she's waiting."

His expression hardened. "I ain't playing."

Roger looked to Simon and Tookey; they all jumped up, pulled Christian to his feet and pushed him out the door, pulling it shut behind him.

"I'm glad that's not me out there," Ann whispered to Helen. "He's got terrible B.O.; he probably doesn't even wash."

"He's not that bad," retorted Helen. "He just ain't got a proper home, has he?" She turned from Ann and moved to sit next to Peter. "Peter, Mum said to ask when are you starting blackcurrants, I nearly forgot, she would kill me if I did."

"At least ten days I think."

The two chattered, waiting for Nimpy to come back into the room.

Outside the door the sun was going. Christian blinked and looked round, trying to get his eyes accustomed to the light. Nimpy was leaning against the wall, running her fingers through her hair. She took a couple of steps to where Christian stood. He looked her in the face, one side of her mouth lifted and she smiled at him, once again running her fingers through her hair. He blinked at her, his eyes meeting hers for a moment before he looked hurriedly away. He bowed his head and looked determinedly at the ground without saying a word. Nimpy crouched slightly to try and attract his gaze but he slung his head even lower. Nimpy reached forward to take his hand but he snatched it away before she could reach him.

"Don't you want a kiss then, Christian?" Nimpy asked kindly.

Christian continued to look at the ground.

"Christian?" she repeated.

This time he looked up and for a moment looked her in the eye, before turning his head away. She could see his lips quiver as he put his fingers under his glasses to wipe away a tear. Nimpy straightened, unsure of what to do. Christian sniffed and looked at her again.

"I'm not into kissing," he said quickly before sniffing again.

"That doesn't matter, Christian," said Nimpy gently. "Not everyone is."

There was silence. Christian looked away again, and another tear brimmed in his eye and rolled down his cheek. Through the door they could hear the others chattering in the barn.

"I'd better go back in again," said Nimpy, turning to open the door.

"Nimpy," Christian said, with sudden urgency, "you won't tell them, will you?"

She looked at him.

"Won't tell them what?"

"Tell them that we didn't kiss?" he said quietly, kicking a stone at his feet, it skittered away across the yard. "You know?" he sniffed.

"Don't worry, I won't tell them," she said with a smile, giving him a little wave as she went back into the room. There was a hushed expectancy as she walked back into the clubhouse and sat down next to Sandra.

"What's he like?" Sandra whispered. "Got B.O., hasn't he?"

"Watch out," said Nimpy, raising an eyebrow, "it could be you next." There was silence as they waited for Christian to knock on the door.

"Come on then, Christian, knock, won't you? We're all waiting," yelled Tookey.

There was no response.

"What's he up to?" asked Simon, turning to Roger. "Go and have a look."

Roger rose and opened the door. There was nobody there. Christian had disappeared.

"He's gone," Roger called back to the others. The boys rushed to the door.

"Where's he gone then?" asked Simon.

"He'll be in *there* somewhere," said Roger, nodding towards the big house that was the prep school.

71

The house was divided into accommodation for Miss Shaw and her assistant Miss Sykes, leaving the rest for classrooms and dormitories for the pupils. To the back was a big hall, which had a glass roof and was two storeys high. Christian knew every nook and cranny of the place.

"Let's go and get him," said Roger.

The boys divided in two, one lot making their way towards the hall and the other moving to the back door of the house to see if they could find Christian's room. The building was a rabbit warren of staircases, halls, landings and corridors. The boarding children would already be in bed so the boys crept quietly from room to room. Passing a downstairs window, Simon caught sight of a figure in the light cast from the room; Christian was crossing the garden. He whistled gently to the others and they rushed back into the garden. Sensing he was being tracked, Christian scooted towards the big hall.

"What are we going to do with him if we catch him?" asked Peter, haring after Christian.

Roger shrugged and sped in through the front door.

The big hall was dark and smelt of polish and damp clothes. Someone found a light and clicked it on; there were groans as the group were momentarily blinded. The room was obviously used as a gym. At each end was a gallery, and standing on the farthest one was Christian looking down towards them, his glasses glinting in the half light.

"Come on then," said Roger, rushing to the door at the other end of the hall. "There must be a stairway somewhere."

With a hunted look on his face, Christian disappeared through a door at the back of the gallery and was gone.

"I'm not going; it's a waste of time," called Tookey. "He knows where to go, we'll never catch him."

Tookey walked back to the clubhouse, Peter following. The girls were still sitting in the room.

"Did you find him?" asked Ann.

"No, not likely to either," said Tookey.

"What did you chase him for then?" asked Nimpy.

The two boys looked at each other and shrugged. A few minutes later the other boys returned and sat down, all out of breath.

"Did you find him?" Helen asked.

"No, but Miss Shaw's coming, we could hear her along a corridor," said Roger. The group sat and waited. The latch of the door clicked as the door creaked open and Miss Shaw trod slowly down the steps into the room. She looked round at them and smiled warmly.

"Now have you had a nice time?" she asked, looking at Sandra.

"Yes, Miss Shaw."

"What have you been doing then?"

"We just played a few games," Sandra said, chewing her lip to stop herself giggling.

"Very good. Now, I think if it has been successful we should carry on when school starts next term, but you can't come in the summer holidays when the school is closed."

There was a groan from the assembled company,

"We wouldn't be any trouble, Miss Shaw, would we," said Nimpy looking at the others.

"No, I have made my mind up, we will start again in September and Christian will tell you the date. We will now have a prayer to close."

The door clicked again and Christian hurried down the steps and took a seat.

"Where have you been, Christian?" demanded Miss Shaw.

"Just to the toilet," he answered, insolently.

"We're going to have a prayer," said Miss Shaw, wafting Christian towards a bench. "Everyone shut your eyes."

She clasped her hands together and said a few words before dismissing the assembled group. One by one the children stood and filed out of the room then Miss Shaw switched off the light and locked the door.

Christian scampered to catch up with Peter.

"Peter, are you blackcurrant picking soon?" he asked. "Is there a job for me?"

"I expect so. But shouldn't you be at school?"

"I don't have to go much, as it's the end of term. Will you be there?"

"Yes, most of the time I will."

Christian nodded, smiled and made his way back towards the school house.

Chapter Five
Blackcurrant Picking

In mid-July, blackcurrant picking started on Peter's father's farm, and everyone from the area who had a need for cash came to help. Anyone from ten-year-old children to old age pensioners turned up to pick, and often there could be up to one hundred and fifty people at any one point in the field.

Some of the pickers were collected in the various farm cars, but most made their own way to the field and started arriving from seven-thirty in the morning, particularly on a hot day. They were issued with a metal bucket and sent to one of the numbered rows where they were allocated a certain number of bushes to pick. The younger boys were all separated off and put in a part of the field on their own, which generally kept the majority of the trouble makers in one area, and made the whole field much easier to run. Once a picker filled their bucket they took it to be weighed and were paid there and then, so much per pound of what they had picked. To do this, vast amounts of small change was needed from the bank, so much so that at least two people had to go to collect it; it being too heavy for one to carry. Simon helped with the weighing of the fruit while another girl was in charge of paying the money out. After the fruit had been weighed, it was poured into wooden trays lined with greaseproof paper and the bucket was handed back to the picker to go and refill.

Peter was one of three who organised the pickers in the field, the younger boys all looked after by one overseer. Of the Dean gang, Nimpy and Helen picked together, while Christian had for some reason been placed with the younger boys.

"What are you doing here, Christian?" Peter asked, having found him on the fringes of the field picking with boys half his age. "Come on, you must come back in the main field; Nimpy and Helen are here, I can put you with them."

"They said I had to come here with the schoolboys," Christian grumbled, as they made their way through the rows of bushes towards the girls. Peter tutted sympathetically. "Peter, how much do you think I can earn in a day at this job? I'm right out of money at the moment. I have been for ages."

"Depends how much you can pick, but you should do five pounds a day if you stay long enough," said Peter, as the pair approached Nimpy and Helen.

Peter showed Christian to a spot further up their row and he started to pick.

Although there were roughly one hundred and fifty pickers in the field, they were difficult to see amongst the obscuring bushes unless they stood up. The main group of pickers were women and girls, most of whom knew each other, but there were also some from Raunds and Rushden, an altogether tougher bunch, which often led to bickering between the groups. The day was hot and sunny and the women took their jackets off, revealing tanned arms. Some had brought another bucket with them which they turned upside down and sat on to pick. Others knelt on the ground, ensuring they could get the currants from the lower branches.

By ten o'clock, both Nimpy and Helen had filled a bucket each and shouted up to Christian.

"Have you got your bucket full then, Christian?" called Nimpy, making her way towards him, Helen close behind.

The pair looked in his bucket, it was less than half full, because he had picked each currant off separately, whereas Nimpy and Helen had picked theirs in clusters, pulling the currants off the bushes on their stalks.

"You don't need to do it like that, Christian," said Helen. "Pull them all off together; it doesn't matter about the stalks, just don't put any leaves in."

Christian stood up, the girls could see that he had worn through one of the knees of his threadbare trousers.

"Look at you, Christian," said Nimpy. "You'll have to make shorts out of them now."

She pointed at the rip in the left leg of his trousers, Christian peered down to where she was pointing, said nothing, but blushed, knelt again and muttered, "I'd better get on then."

The two girls made their way back down the field to get their buckets weighed.

"I've never known anyone so hard on their clothes as Christian," said Nimpy. "He's always a mess."

"I know, it's not like he doesn't have new things either, but they're worn out straight away with him. I'm surprised Miss Shaw doesn't keep a better eye on him."

"I don't think she notices. She's so distracted herself with all those children to look after."

"That's true. Plus, she doesn't look like she cares much about the way she dresses anyway so is unlikely to think about him. Look," said Helen, pointing down one of the rows, and

77

changing off the subject of Christian, "there's Mum." She tugged at Nimpy's arm. "Come on, don't let her see me."

Nimpy looked at Helen, surprised.

"Why don't you want to see your mum then?"

"I didn't tell her I was coming, that's why."

"Why didn't you tell her then?"

"Cos she would make me work with her and I couldn't do that, not with all them other old women."

"They're not old. Not as old as *my* mum anyway."

Nimpy's mother was already grey-haired, but didn't come picking in the mornings as she cleaned at the local pub and served in the bar at lunchtime.

"I know they're not old, but I just don't want to work with her, would you want to work with your mother?"

"No fear," said Nimpy, rolling her eyes.

The two continued on to the pay point stationed in the headland of the field. There was a queue for weighing as there were no empty currant trays; more were being unloaded from the back of the van as they approached.

"Come on, Simon, stop buggering about and get on with it, we ain't got time to stand 'ere doing nothing," came a brazen voice from behind the two girls.

The girls turned to see the owner of the voice, a tall blonde woman with a small scarf keeping her hair in place. She had a pretty face and wore a singlet top, which pulled tightly across her large bust. Her shoulders were broad and her strong arms were bronzed like her face. There were red marks on her top and on the back of her trouser legs where she had wiped off the sticky juice of the blackcurrants.

"Your mum said you weren't coming today, Helen," the woman said loudly, noticing Helen in the queue. "She won't be pleased when I tell her you're here after all."

"Don't tell her, Nell, will you?" begged Helen. "I just don't want to have to work alongside her, I want to work with Nimpy."

"I won't have to tell her," said Nell with a snort. "Look, she's coming with her bucket now."

Nell lifted her chin in the direction they had come from, and sure enough, Helen could make out her mother's pink straw hat bobbing towards her above the rows of currant bushes.

"Here, Nimpy, you take my bucket," said Helen desperately, putting the heavy bucket down. "I'll nip up that row and round the top. I'll see you back in our row." She turned imploringly to Nell and said, "Please don't tell her," before she rushed off without waiting for a reply.

Nimpy sighed and picked up both buckets, staggering forward in the queue, which was now waiting for her, under the weight of blackcurrants. She could only carry them a couple of yards before she had to put them down again. Nell leaned across her and plucked one of the buckets from in front of her, passing it with ease to Simon. Nimpy smiled gratefully as Simon weighed the bucket.

"Eighteen!" Simon shouted to the girl doing the paying, taking the other bucket from Nimpy.

Joyce, Helen's mother, barged her way up the queue towards Nell.

"Who was that run up that row just now?" she asked.

"I don't know," shrugged Nell, smirking at Nimpy, who was concentrating furiously on keeping a blank face.

"On your own?" Joyce asked Nimpy eyeing her with suspicion.

"No, Christian's up there," replied Nimpy.

Joyce grunted in disapproval. "What's that boy doing here, he couldn't knock the skin off a rice pudding, and where are his parents, that's what I want to know?" She eyeballed Nimpy again, setting her bucket down with a clank. "Who was that who just run up that row, Nimpy? It looked just like my Helen, if that girl has come up here, she said she wouldn't come when I asked her." Joyce shook her head. "She's worse than her father to keep in order and that's saying something."

"Nineteen!" shouted Simon, handing the bucket back to Nimpy, who now stood holding two buckets.

"Whose bucket is that?" demanded Joyce, looking severely at Nimpy.

"Christian's," Nimpy said quickly, trotting off before she could be asked any more questions.

"Come on, Simon, buck your ideas up," scolded Nell, as Simon laid greaseproof paper in another tray.

"He's half asleep," said Joyce. "No wonder if you spend all night wandering the streets of Dean." She scowled at Simon. "I seen you," she continued, "don't think I 'aven't, and so's everyone else down our way, and Peter ain't no better and that one on a motor bike." She elbowed Nell. "You can't get no peace down our way you know, Nell. Up to no good, that's what I say, up to no good, like the rest of them."

Simon bit his lip and said nothing.

"It's the girls they're after, Joyce, isn't that right, Simon?" teased Nell, watching Simon turn red, "There I told you, Joyce, look at his face."

"Twenty!" shouted Simon, handing Nell the bucket back, without looking at her.

"I'm sure that was Helen," sighed Joyce, handing her bucket to Simon. "Did you see her, Nell?"

"See who?" asked Nell innocently.

"Are you daydreaming, woman?" Joyce turned angrily to Nell. She was shorter than her friend, with closely permed dark hair, but the same tanned complexion. Like Nell, she was well turned out, even wearing lipstick to picking days. She turned back and glared at Simon.

"I shall see your father, young man," she said, for want of anything better to say.

"Not another one," Simon whispered under his breath, no longer seeking answers as to why his father might be informed of anything he did.

"What did you say, my boy?" demanded Joyce.

But before he could answer, Albert barged past Joyce to the front of the queue.

"Have you seen Master Peter, Simon?" He turned to Joyce, who was shaking with indignation. "You all right then, Joyce?" he said, though he didn't sound interested in whether she was or not, before turning back to Simon.

"No, haven't seen him for half an hour, I suppose," said Simon.

"He was up our row not long back," said Nell. "What's up then?"

Albert looked at her but was distracted. "I'll tell you later," he said, walking off in search of Peter.

Nimpy had returned to her row, where Helen was waiting for her and talking to Christian.

"Your mum's on the warpath, Helen," said Nimpy.

"Did she see me then?"

"She said she thought it were you but I didn't let on and neither did Nell, I bet she finds out before long, mind."

"Come on then. Let's get on with it, we've only got a few more bushes and then we'll need a new place."

The girls took a bucket each and leaned down to start picking. The sun rose higher and higher in the sky, warming the air and the ground. The blackcurrants became more and more sticky; the occasional fruit squashing juicily between their fingers as they tore the bunches from the bushes.

Christian walked down the row from where he was picking towards the girls.

"How you getting on?" asked Nimpy.

"Not bad. Nearly got a full bucket now." He hesitated, before mumbling. "Do you know where the toilet is?"

"The *what* did he say?" said Helen, turning to Nimpy.

"The lav," Nimpy repeated, looking at Christian incredulously.

"Christian," she said slowly, "this, is a field. Fields don't have toilets in them; you have to," she broke off briefly, "You have to *find* somewhere."

Christian blushed and looked down, before turning and marching off. Ten minutes later he returned, walking back past the girls to his bucket without a word.

82

Moments later, there was a cry. The girls looked up to see Christian rushing back towards them.

"Nimpy, have you seen my bucket?" he asked, the note of panic evident in his voice.

"No, where did you leave it?"

"Just up there where I was picking," he said, pointing up the row.

The girls stood and walked up the row, searching the area for the errant bucket.

"It ain't here," shrugged Helen.

"Someone nicked it then," said Nimpy quietly.

"They what?" asked Christian.

"They've taken it and gone and got paid for it," said Nimpy apologetically.

"Are you sure?" said Christian, bringing his hand to his forehead. "After all that work, it's nearly lunchtime."

"Do you know what it looked like?" said Nimpy, with more optimism than she felt.

"Yes, I'm sure I would recognise it, it had a dent in one side. I'm pretty sure that I would know it."

"Well, go down to Simon and ask him," said Nimpy.

Christian nodded and hurried off towards the headland, his sticky hands in his pockets.

"It would happen to him, wouldn't it," said Nimpy, watching Christian's retreating figure. "Some people never have any luck."

Christian arrived at the weigh point, bypassing the queue to make his way to Simon.

"Simon, you haven't seen my bucket, have you? Someone has taken it; it was nearly full."

83

Simon looked at him incredulously. "I've seen no end of buckets today, Christian. How would I know which one is yours?"

"It had a big dent in it, I'd know it anywhere," said Christian with confidence.

"Well there are two or three over there," said Simon, pointing to the other side of the little canvas hut where the girl was paying out money. Christian scurried to the hut to examine the buckets, picking up each in turn and scrutinising it carefully.

"This is the one!" he shouted, picking up the second bucket and rushing towards Simon with it. "But there's no currants in it, someone brought it to you and got paid, who was it?"

"How do I know?" sighed Simon, exasperated. "There's hundreds of people here and hundreds of buckets. I just weigh them and the pickers get paid. Someone has pinched yours and got paid for it, that's about what has happened. But I don't know who it is. Do you?" Christian threw the bucket down angrily.

"Of course I don't! The bugger, I'll kill him if I find out who it is." He snatched up the bucket and walked back to his position in the field.

The two girls had just finished the bushes they had been allocated and were preparing to have their lunch before moving to another spot. They sat on their coats and opened their boxes to examine their sandwiches.

"What have you got?" asked Nimpy.

"Jam," said Helen. "What's yours then?"

"Cheese," said Nimpy, turning up her nose. "I hate cheese."

"Let me have one of yours and you have one of mine," said Helen, handing a jam sandwich to Nimpy.

Nimpy grinned and handed over a cheese sandwich as Christian slumped past.

"You found it then?" said Nimpy, pointing at the bucket.

"Yes, but without the currants. Someone got it weighed and took the money." He squinted into the bright sunlight, his lip quivering slightly. "It's not fair!"

"Don't worry, you'll soon fill it again," said Nimpy. "We'll give you a hand in a minute, just don't let that bucket out of your sight."

Christian sniffed and looked miserably at the girls chewing on their sandwiches.

"Are you going to have your lunch?" asked Helen. "What have you got?"

Christian sniffed and said nothing.

"Have you got anything to eat, Christian?" asked Nimpy quietly, throwing a concerned look towards Helen.

Christian lowered his eyes and scuffed at the ground with his battered shoe.

"I didn't bring anything. I didn't know how long I was going to stay."

"Have one of these," said Nimpy kindly, offering Christian a cheese sandwich.

"And one of mine," Helen added. "Don't look like that, Christian! Come on, cheer up, have a sandwich and we'll help you fill that bucket, we've finished the bushes here, if we help you, then we can all move together."

Christian smiled weakly and accepted the sandwiches, sitting to eat with the girls.

Just as they finished and were getting up to carry on there was a sudden flurry of activity towards the top of the row. The three looked up to see Joyce striding purposefully towards them.

"Don't you run away this time, my girl," she shouted, marching towards Helen and standing in front of her, hands on hips. "What do you think you are doing? You told me you wouldn't come when I asked you and now here you are as bold as brass."

Helen bowed her head and said nothing. Christian and Nimpy edged cautiously away from her.

"Well then, what have you got to say for yourself?"

"I just wanted to come with Nimpy, I didn't want to pick with you and Nell and them."

"I don't mind you picking with *Nimpy*."

"You would have said no, I bet you would, if I had asked you; you would have said we were going with the boys, I know you would have said that."

"Well you *are* with the boys, what's he then?" said Joyce with a laugh, nodding at Christian.

"He doesn't count," said Helen sharply. "He ain't like the rest of them."

In the moment that followed Christian reddened, stood and picked up his bucket, then walked the few yards up the row back to his bushes.

"Well what you going to do then?" Joyce asked.

"I'm staying with Nimpy," said Helen, pursing her lips and glaring at her mother angrily.

86

There was silence. Joyce assessed her daughter wryly.

"All right then, but," and she pointed at Nimpy, "you make sure she behaves, Nimpy, you're older than her and you keep her in order, don't you go chasing those boys, see."

"Yes, Joyce," said Nimpy, as Joyce turned to go. Suddenly she turned back again. "And if you're going to stay you can go and get me some fags from the pub. Senior Service, mind you, I don't want Woodbines, here's the money." She held out half a crown towards Helen.

"I'm not going into the pub, I ain't old enough!" protested Helen.

"I'll come, Helen," said Nimpy. "I know where it is and it won't take long."

Joyce nodded and marched back up to the bushes she was picking.

Nimpy took her friend's arm and led her down along the field.

"Look after our buckets, Christian!" she called back over her shoulder. "We won't be long."

At the weigh station there was a problem. Simon was surrounded by a gang of Gypsies who were demanding a job. There were almost thirty of them and they had been laid off at the next door farm where they had been picking peas.

"Where's Peter?" Simon shouted to Nimpy and Helen who were walking back down the row of bushes, having delivered the cigarettes to Joyce.

"He's up there," said Nimpy, pointing to where Peter was walking between bushes thirty yards away.

"Go and fetch him, we've got a problem here, and tell him to be quick," ordered Simon as several of the Gypsies moved with menace towards the weighing table.

"I'll go," said Helen. "I can run faster." She dashed off, returning a few minutes later with Peter in tow.

The spokesman for the Gypsies was a short, stocky man with dark wavy hair and a swarthy complexion; he wore a ring in one ear, and a smudged tattoo lined the right side of his neck.

"You the boss, then?" he growled at Peter, aggression etched on his face. "You don't look old enough."

He looked Peter up and down. Although young, Peter was still a good five inches taller than the Gypsy was.

"Yes, I'm in charge," said Peter, looking at the man squarely.

"Now, it's like this," said the Gypsy with a frown, "we're been laid off up the road. They don't want no more peas at the market and they said to come down 'ere and you would give us a job."

The group tightened almost imperceptibly around Peter, who looked over to the pile of buckets; there were two or three, but not nearly enough for all of them.

"We can't take you," said Peter, with a shrug. "There's too many of you and we haven't got enough buckets."

The leader took another step towards Peter.

"Now look 'ere, boy," he said quietly. "We want a job and they told us to come down 'ere and you would give us one, see."

"Well, we can't," Peter replied.

"That's no good to us, governor," said the man with a nasty smile. He spread his hands and looked across the field. "Look," he continued, "here *we* are and you're employing all them children. We're grown men and women, look at us."

One of the women pushed forward from the group. A red scarf was tied tightly about her head and she wore a calf-length flowery skirt and a tight top which revealed a lot of cleavage. She pointed angrily at Peter. "Now look here, Mr High and Mighty. It's all right for you in your big 'ouse and flash car, but we poor sods 'ave to work for a living. We've got to put food on the table and shoes on the children's feet. Now you just give us a job like a good chap and we won't say no more about it, that's right, ain't it?" She looked round at the others.

"She's right," said the group leader with a leer. "You give us a job and we'll make sure no harm comes to your place."

Peter bridled at the threat, his face hardening. He'd experienced this situation before and knew to stand his ground. "Sorry. But we can't take all of you; there's no room."

The man's eyes widened; he looked round to the gang behind him and then back at Peter. "Now look here, mister, do I have to teach you a lesson, or what?" and he made to take off his jacket.

"Go on, you show him," encouraged one of the women from the crowd.

The man stood, his bear-like hands holding his jacket open, shifting from foot to foot. But Peter did not move.

Then, as quickly as it had built the atmosphere changed. The man straightened up and let his hands drop to his sides.

"Come on then," he said to the others. "We ain't getting no-where 'ere."

The group turned as one, suddenly docile, and walked away.

Peter watched them go, pleased they'd backed down as quickly as they had.

"That were a close one," said Albert, grinning at him. "You were right though, there were no room for them and any road they would upset all the others and you don't want that."

Nimpy and Helen, having watched the stand-off between Peter and the Gypsies, returned to Christian, whose bucket was now half full.

"Come on, we'll give you a hand for a bit," said Helen, bending to start stripping the fruit off the last two blackcurrant bushes.

Within minutes they were finished. Helen waved to Al-bert, shouting that they wanted a new patch. Albert walked up the headland, followed by a picker they had not seen before. She was in her early twenties, with short mousey coloured hair and a pretty face. She wore a tightly fitting singlet show-ing tanned arms and shoulders. Her shorts were extremely tight.

"Look at 'er," said Helen under her breath. "She don't leave much to the imagination, she ought not to be allowed to walk about like that. Don't look, Christian." She put her hand over Christian's eyes and he laughed.

"Come on, you lot!" shouted Albert. "You bring that num-ber with you, Nimpy, and we'll start another row." Nimpy pulled the numbered metal post out of the ground and fol-lowed Albert. "We'll start two rows," he suggested, setting

Helen and Nimpy in one, with Christian a little further up the row and the new girl at the end of the next. Albert looked up at the sky. Black clouds had started to gather ominously on the horizon. "That looks like a storm to me," he grumbled, pulling down the peak of his cap and walking away. The new woman watched him go, before looking up and smiling at Nimpy and Helen.

"Hello, I'm Ginny," she said. "What are your names?"

Helen and Nimpy were taken aback; they had not expected someone so much older than them to be friendly.

"I'm Nimpy, and this is Helen."

"Have you done this before then?"

"The last two years we have and we've just started this week," said Nimpy. "You?"

"It's my first day, I came this morning. Isn't it wonderful to be out in the fresh air!"

"I suppose it is," said Helen rather dubiously.

"The currants are a bit sticky though, don't you think? I've got them all over my top." She looked down at the red marks on her white singlet, before lowering her voice conspiratorially. "Do you eat them?"

"No fear," snorted Nimpy. "They're ever so bitter, I can't stand them." Ginny smiled and they all turned back to picking.

After a while, Christian passed them with a full bucket to take to the pay station. He looked pleased with himself and beamed at the girls as he passed.

"Is that your boyfriend?" asked Ginny, smiling at Helen.

"Him?" shrieked Helen. "No!"

"He's just a friend," explained Nimpy. "He lives down at Dean, he hasn't got any parents though, or none that we know about."

"Oh, that's sad."

Albert came sauntering back down the row.

"He comes round a lot, doesn't he?" Ginny muttered to the girls.

"I'm not surprised," said Nimpy with a smile. "Peter will come next." She winked at Helen. Sure enough, moments later, Peter came strolling up towards the three girls.

"Everything all right?" he asked, slowly walking up the row.

"Do they come round this often all the time?" asked Ginny.

"They don't come to see *us* that often, no," said Nimpy, looking at Helen slyly. The sun passed behind a cloud, taking with it the heat of the day. Nimpy wiped a hand across her forehead and looked over the row at Ginny.

"They're nice shorts she's got on," Nimpy whispered to Helen, peering through the bush at Ginny. "And that top, that's nice, ain't it, looks a bit small for her though." Helen stood up to look through the bushes. She sniggered as Ginny stood and stretched luxuriously.

"She ain't got a bra on neither, you look, Nimpy, I bet she ain't," Helen whispered as Albert strolled unnecessarily down the row once more, stopping by Ginny to light a cigarette.

"Black cloud up there," he said. "Keep a look out, I would, could be a storm." He absently plucked a handful of currants and dropped them into Ginny's bucket.

"Are you going to be picking some for me then, Albert?"
Nimpy grinned, squinting to look up at Albert.

"Now don't you be cheeky, my girl," said Albert, reddening slightly. He puffed on his cigarette and walked on a little, passing Christian who was walking back towards the girls.

"Did you get paid then, Christian?" asked Helen. Christian grinned and held out his hand, which was brimming with coins. "How much did you get then? Let's have a look."

"Eight and six. I'm a rich man, I'm going to retire now." He put his bucket down and looked at the girls. "Look after my bucket, Nimpy, where's the pub? You went, didn't you?"

"What you going to the pub for, Christian?" said Nimpy, looking at him hard.

"Just to get some fags, that's all. Come on, where is it?"

"Along the top through the churchyard and down the street. But you'll have to knock hard, she won't be open now."

Christian smiled, put the money in his pocket and made to leave.

"You shouldn't be smoking at your age," said Ginny, standing up to look at Christian as the sun emerged from behind its cloud, highlighting her profile against the dark green leaves of the currant bushes. Christian looked at her quickly but didn't reply, simply shrugging before he walked off.

"Funny boy," said Ginny, with a shake of her head, squatting down to carry on picking. Slowly, Ginny's bucket began to fill. Suddenly she stood up and turned to Nimpy. "Nimpy, where's the toilet?" she asked.

"There isn't one."

"What do you mean there isn't one? Where are we supposed to go then?"

"There's one down at the farm, but that's miles, no one goes down there. Go behind the hedge, everyone else does, you could go now if you were quick, although Albert will probably come if you do."

"Speak of the devil," said Helen, as Albert slowly plodded up between the bushes, smiled at Ginny shyly and carried on up the rows.

"Go on then quickly," said Nimpy. "We'll look after your bucket." Ginny looked both ways, and trotted off up the headland. When she returned Nimpy and Helen were eating the last of their sandwiches, sitting in the shade of the bushes out of the sun. Ginny fanned her face with her hands.

"It's hot, isn't it? Really muggy."

"I suppose it is," said Nimpy. "We've taken off our jumpers, but you've got nothing left to take off, have you, Ginny?" She sniggered and looked away. Ginny put her hands on her chest, lightly running them down to her waist.

"No, I suppose I haven't," she said, bringing her hand to her mouth and sniggering too. Nimpy smiled.

"Don't you ever wear a bra, Ginny?" she asked.

"Not often. You want to try it."

"Not on your nelly," snorted Nimpy. "Anyway my mum wouldn't let me out the house without one on, that's right ain't it, Helen?"

"Don't tell me," said Helen, taking a last bite from her sandwich and throwing the crust into the bushes. She rose and helped pull Nimpy to her feet and the three started to pick

94

again, just as Christian returned, a packet of cigarettes clutched in his hand.

Moments later the stillness of the afternoon was broken by a loud clap of thunder. Heads appeared over the tops of the bushes as the pickers looked from row to row to establish what effect the weather would have on their work. The storm was still some way off and the clouds did not look thick, so it wasn't long before everyone went back to picking again.

At the weigh point, Simon could see the clouds building behind the rows of pickers.

"It's going to rain and they'll all come wanting to weigh in at once," Simon called over to Peter who was walking towards him.

"Just wait a bit," advised Peter. "If it does come we'll shut up shop and we can weigh them when it stops, it won't last long."

There was another rumble of thunder, much louder this time, and once again heads appeared above the bushes, looking skyward. The sky was getting blacker, the clouds building in great black-purple banks behind one another. The heat had disappeared to be replaced by a cool breeze and the leaves on the bushes started to rustle slightly.

"That's rain," said Nimpy; "it's coming, I can feel it." She stood up and raised a hand above her head.

"Are you sure?" said Helen, looking to the sky. "It's only thunder, I can't feel rain."

There was a violent crack and a bolt of lightning lit up a large oak tree in the hedgerow. The tree shuddered as a branch slowly peeled off from halfway up the trunk and fell to the ground with a crash. The thunder rolled loudly overhead and continued in a low continuous grumble.

"Bloody hell!" said Nimpy. "We'd better find some shelter." Then looking over at Ginny, who was rooted to the spot with tears pouring down her face, she said, "What's up with her?" But Helen, busy gathering her things, didn't answer. There was another clap of thunder, a couple of people yelped. "What's wrong?" Nimpy shouted over at Ginny. "Come on, we must find some shelter."

Ginny's face was drained of all colour, the tears continuing to roll down her cheeks and her frame trembled. "I'm frightened. I can't help it, I'm just so scared; I can't stand thunder."

"Come on then, come with us," instructed Nimpy calmly. "Get your bag and your bucket." She turned to Helen. "Get them bags, Helen, and don't leave your bucket, someone will pinch it." She looked out across the field, seeing that people had just started to move down the rows towards the weigh station. The first drop of rain splashed onto Nimpy's arm, followed by another and another, the drops heavy and wet, scarring the ground with great angry marks that threw up soil as they splashed down. "Come on!" insisted Nimpy. "Get your bag and bucket, Ginny."

Ginny swung into action, throwing her bag into her half-full bucket before being suddenly overcome with indecision again. She froze, the look of terror creeping back across her face. Nimpy hoisted her bucket, grabbed Ginny's hand and started to run down the row to the headland. Once there, she could see that everyone was doing the same thing, running their currants to the weigh station to be paid.

At the weigh point, Simon had taken the scales down and carried them into the little tent, where he was taking shelter with Albert and the girl in charge of the money. Peter stood in front of the tent, directing people to the farm where they could find shelter. The ground was now wet and as people ran, clay soil started to stick to their feet. Some fell over, some dropped their buckets and within minutes everyone was completely soaked as the rain continued to fall in torrents, whipping round the running figures, and driven by the strong wind. Nimpy and many of the others were at the top of the field, well above the station and a long way from the farm.

"We're not going down there, it's too far. Come on under that apple tree in the hedge, it'll give us a little bit of shelter."

"You're not supposed to shelter under trees," Ginny screeched hysterically.

"Not under big ones," agreed Nimpy patiently, "that's a little one, come on." They ran up the headland to the tree where three others were already sheltering.

"Shit!" cursed Helen. "I'm soaked." She shook her head to get the excess water out of her hair. The three people already under the tree looked at one another and dashed for the next tree down the hedgerow, leaving Ginny, Helen and Nimpy alone. "This ain't keeping much rain off," complained Helen, as the thunder crashed spectacularly once again.

Ginny shuddered and continued to shake with fear. Helen put an arm around her as the rain intensified, the noise of the big raindrops battering down on the foliage and ground, drowning out the rumblings of the thunder. The water started to run down the field in between the currant bush rows and the rain pelted down into the freshly made rivers, adding to

97

the flow down the field. Sheets of rain obscured anything further than ten feet away and the girls could no longer make out the farm or even the pay station. The thunder overhead had now stopped and could be heard moving into the distance. The rain, however, seemed to be getting heavier and both Nimpy and Helen started to shiver as their clothes soaked through. Their hair hung limply around their pale faces, Helen's curls straightening out into lank tresses.

Then, as suddenly as it had started, it was over. The beating of raindrops ceased and the faint roll of thunder was barely audible in the distance. There was silence except for the trickle of water as it ran down the field, creating miniature waterfalls as it went.

Ginny looked up towards the sky warily. "Is it over?"

"It's all gone," reassured Nimpy. "Nothing to be frightened of now."

Ginny shuddered again. "I'm so sorry to be such a fool, but I'm terrified of it," she said, wiping her eyes with her fist. "I thought I would shit my pants."

Nimpy's eyes widened, and she looked towards Helen and raised her eyebrows, before turning back to Ginny. "You haven't, have you?"

"No," laughed Ginny. "Don't worry."

"Where did Christian get to?" asked Helen.

"Don't know," said Nimpy.

They all looked round towards the row that they had left. Christian's head was just visible above the bushes as he stood and started to walk down towards the headland. As he waddled into view, the girls could see that he was completely soaked; great lumps of mud had attached themselves to his

98

poorly shod feet. The girls waved him over, giggling as he came into view, completely bedraggled.

"Look at you," said Nimpy, pointing at Christian's sodden clothes. The two younger girls turned to Ginny. Helen gasped.

"Bloody hell," she said. "You can see right through it!"

"Right through what?" said Ginny, following Nimpy's gaze down her front.

"Your top, silly," giggled Nimpy. "Come on, you must have something to go over it." Ginny pulled open her bag, pulled out a shirt and quickly covered herself up. "Come on, we're not going to pick any more, let's see if we can get paid," said Nimpy, leading the way down to the weigh station.

The sun had come back out, warming the ground, which steamed happily, the myriad mini rivers already starting to dam up. At the weigh station there was chaos, with many people waiting to be paid, mostly women and children. All of them were soaked to the skin with great lumps of mud clinging to their shoes and the bottom of their buckets. The youngest children had been brought in pushchairs which were standing abandoned, the wheels clogged with mud. The women with smart hairdos and make-up looked the same as everyone else now, all perms straightened by the rain.

Peter decided that it was impossible to do the weighing in the field and shouted for everyone to go back to the farm and weigh the currants there. Picking would have to be abandoned for the day as the fruit was too wet. Simon carried the scales, Peter the money, with the money woman following. Albert took the big bundle of greaseproof paper and went to set up where the boxes were stored in one of the barns.

Back at the farm an orderly queue formed as people brought their buckets forward to be weighed. Many of them had a lot of water in them, which had to be drained before the currants could be weighed. Nimpy, Helen and Christian stood in the queue as Joyce approached.

"How are you getting home then?" she asked Helen. "I'm going in the van with Nell, are you coming?"

"No. I've got my bike."

"Well you make sure you do come home. Don't you dare go off with any of those boys, you hear," growled Joyce, pointing at her. Helen said nothing. "Did you hear what I said?"

"Yes, Mum," said Helen grudgingly. "But I'm calling in at Nimpy's on the way home so I will be a little while, isn't that right, Nimpy?" Helen looked pointedly at her friend.

"Yes, of course you are, Helen."

Joyce sighed and walked out of the barn. Nimpy turned to Christian.

"Do you want to go in the van, Christian?"

"Not likely. Not with all those old women." He started to tip his bucket gently to remove excess water.

"One of those old women is my mother," said Helen sharply.

"Sorry," said Christian, without any real hint of apology. "Keep your hair on, you didn't seem very pleased with her a moment ago."

"Come on, stop arguing," said Nimpy, moving to the front of the queue and handing her bucket to Simon. "Are you coming home with us, Simon? We're cycling home the same way as you."

100

"I can't. I've got to stop and help load the lorry, but I'm coming down on Friday, we can meet at the bus shelter, six o'clock, you coming?"

"It's a pity Miss Shaw won't open the club on Sunday, but I'll come on Friday," said Nimpy.

"What about you, Helen?" asked Simon.

"I think she'll let me come if you're there, Nimpy," said Helen. "So yes, hopefully."

"And you, Christian?"

"I'll be there. Now I've got some money, there'll be no stopping me."

"All fixed then," said Simon, weighing the last bucket.

The girls wandered off to find their bikes. Ginny was standing where they had all been stacked up, cleaning the mud from her shoes before she cycled home. The sun was still shining and everyone's hair and clothes were starting to dry off.

"I feel such an idiot," Ginny said to the two girls. "Making such a fuss about a little bit of thunder; you must think I'm a fool, but I've always been the same." She shrugged and laughed. "Me a grown woman too and you just children."

"We're not children!" protested Nimpy.

"Yes, I know you're not children," said Ginny quickly, turning to look more carefully at the girls. "I didn't mean to cause offence." She smiled at the pair. "How old are you?"

"I'm fifteen and she's thirteen," said Nimpy.

"No, I ain't. I'm fourteen."

"Not yet you aren't."

Helen crossed her arms and glared at Ginny. "How old are you then?"

"I'm twenty-seven."

"Are you married then?" asked Helen.

"Yes and no," said Ginny, rather evasively.

"Well either you are or you aren't; you can't be either or," said Nimpy.

Ginny blushed and looked down. "Well I got married. But he left me two years ago."

"Oh," said Nimpy, wishing she hadn't pursued the subject.

She looked absently around for something with which to diffuse the situation. She spotted a stick, seized it and started to clean her shoes with it.

"He ran off with another woman," continued Ginny.

"Oh," Nimpy said again, feeling rather out of her depth with this topic of conversation and, having no idea what to say in response she threw away the stick and turned to Helen. "You ready, Helen? Ginny?" Both girls nodded and leapt onto their bikes, pedalling their way back onto the road. Christian, walking, already had a head start, and was some way ahead of them. Suddenly Helen brought her bike to a stop.

"Look!" she exclaimed. "There's a half crown in the road." She turned her bike skilfully in the road and cycled back a couple of yards. She leaned down and picked it up.

"Here's another!" shouted Ginny.

"It must be Christian who's dropping them," tutted Nimpy. "I'll go and tell him." She sped off, hollering at Christian as she went. "Christian, stop!" she yelled. "You're dropping your money, it's all down the road."

Christian stopped and looked vacantly at Nimpy. He frowned and dug his hand into his trouser pocket, pulling the pocket out to reveal a hole. "Bugger," he cursed. "It's all gone, there was nearly ten shillings there." He shook his head angrily and scuffed his foot on the ground.

"Don't worry, I think they've managed to pick it all up," said Nimpy as Helen and Ginny cycled up with handfuls of coins.

Christian held out his hands for the change but Helen hesitated.

"Maybe we should hold on to it until we get to the Hall."

"That would probably be for the best," agreed Christian with a smile.

Chapter Six
The Fete

The next Friday, the group all assembled at the bus shelter at six o'clock as arranged. The girls sat chatting while the boys circled round on their bikes, skidding back wheels and showing off the best they could. Tookey, with Simon sitting pillion, drove tight figures of eight in the road on his motorbike.

"What we going to do then?" said Sandra. "We've got to be home by seven, haven't we, Ann?"

"So have I," said Primrose.

"And me," said Helen. "Mum says that you boys are causing all the trouble and we are encouraging you. She won't let me stay out long."

Peter Dunmore cycled up to the group, his antiquated bike clanking under him. Normally he would still be on duty in the fields, but they had finished picking one variety of currants and the next wouldn't be ready for a few days.

"Well then, what are we going to do?" said Sandra, more loudly. "We can't just sit here and do nothing.

"Look at this," said Christian, pointing at a poster pinned to the side of the bus shelter, "*Grand Fete: Melchbourne Park – Saturday 18th July 1959*. Why don't we go there? It's not far."

"The eighteenth is tomorrow, stupid," said Sandra.

"I know that," snapped back Christian. "But we could go tomorrow, couldn't we?"

"Go to a fete?" said Sandra scathingly. "You're not catching me at a village fete like that, it's not exactly exciting, you know."

"I'm going," said Primrose.

"You're going?" said Sandra, turning in surprise to Primrose. "Whatever for?"

"I've got to go with Mum and Dad, that's all I know," sighed Primrose.

"Why don't we all go?" repeated Christian, looking round at the others.

"Why don't we what?" said Simon, stepping off Tookey's now stationary motorbike and walking towards the shelter to join in the conversation.

"Go to the fete," said Sandra dubiously, pointing at the poster.

"Yes, let's go," said Simon eagerly. "We could liven it up a bit, I'm sure." He looked round at the doubtful faces. "Come on, it's not far and it won't cost much. And it's something to do." There was another silence as everyone looked at one another.

"Well, there's nothing else to do so I say that we go," said Helen decisively. "Two o'clock it says it opens. We can get there then, can't we?" There was a chorus of nods, some more reluctant than others.

"Good, two o'clock then, everyone agreed?" said Simon. Everyone nodded again.

"What are we going to do now though?" asked Tookey.

"*We* don't have time to do anything now, we've got to go home," said Sandra.

"So have I," said Primrose and Helen in unison. The four girls said their goodbyes and made off in the direction of their respective homes. The four boys and Nimpy looked at one another.

"Well that's them gone," said Peter. "Let's go to the pub."

"They won't serve us, I know they won't," said Christian. "Roger tried the other day, and anyway I don't like beer, do you like it, Peter?"

"Not really. But I'll give it a go."

"Then let's try," said Simon, heading towards the pub. As the pub stood twenty yards from the bus shelter, they didn't have far to go.

"You go, Peter, you're the oldest, you must be eighteen by now," encouraged Tookey.

"Not for another two days," said Peter slowly.

"Go on then, that's good enough," insisted Tookey. "Get us all a half of beer and bring it out, go on!" Peter hesitated, digging his hands into his pocket to search for change.

"Come on then," said Simon impatiently. "If you won't go in I will, I don't care what they say. Come on, Peter, follow me." He turned suddenly to Nimpy. "What do you want, Nimpy?"

"I don't want any beer, I hate the stuff, get me some Golden Lemonade," said Nimpy, "and a bag of crisps, if they're not too old."

Simon nodded to Peter and they marched towards the door, they were followed by Christian and Tookey. At the door, realising they were being followed, Simon sent Christian and Tookey back to the bus shelter to wait. The two older boys approached the front door of the pub, took a deep breath

106

and entered. The outside door led into a small hallway with a door one side that read **PUBLIC BAR** and one on the other labelled **SALOON**. The walls were dingy, painted brown and combed to make them look like the grain of wood. The worn brass handle to the bar was grimy with the sweat of hundreds of filthy hands. A light bulb hung limp from the ceiling, the last inch of flex bare wire from where the insulation had peeled away. The two boys looked at each other, trying to decide which door to enter by, Simon dithered momentarily before turning the handle to the saloon. He pushed at the door but it wouldn't budge, shrugged and turned back to the other door.

The room was dark, lit by one small window and another naked bulb which dangled disconsolately from the middle of the room. The floor was red quarry tile and the walls had once been off-white but were now stained yellow with tobacco smoke. The paintwork on the bar and doors was of the same brown combed style as in the hallway. To one side of the fire-place stood a skittle table, the leather surface and surrounds well-polished from many years of use. To the other, a dart-board, the path to the board well-trodden and cleaner than the rest of the floor.

The publican, a fat bald man in his mid-forties, leaned on the bar talking to the four men who were drinking at it. Behind him, perched on a stool and leaning back against a sideboard housing a few bottles of spirits and a large square tin of crisps, was an equally large lady. She had blonde curly hair and a round face. Rouge was smeared on her cheeks and she wore bright red lipstick, which she had used to exaggerate her pout by painting a good quarter of an inch outside her top and lower lips. Her low cut dress showed a deep cleavage and one arm was folded tightly under her bust, the other moving intermittently to her lips as she took deep draws on a cigarette; the butt of which was stained from the lipstick.

For a moment the two boys stood by the door, looking round the bar, not quite knowing what to do. The inhabitants of the room turned slowly to look at the two boys, then there was complete silence.

The publican pushed himself up straight, holding on to the bar with both hands as the two boys walked across to him. The four men, who were spread evenly along the bar, eyeballed the boys before turning back to their drinks, not moving to let Simon in at the bar. Undeterred, Simon moved to the side to talk around the last man. The publican took a step towards them.

"What do you want then?" he said gruffly.

He had a small moustache and a cigarette dangled from one side of his mouth. He wore a striped shirt, the collar of which had been detached, which emphasised the thickness of his neck. The sleeves of his shirt were rolled up to reveal thick hairy arms and his woollen vest could be seen between the buttons of his shirt which stretched tightly across his ample stomach. One of the men turned to look at the two boys, tapping his pipe into the ashtray on the bar and surveying the boys through the thin haze of smoke.

Simon turned to Peter and in a low voice that didn't quite qualify as a whisper said, "What do we want then?" Peter stepped forward, leaning towards the bar.

"Four bottles of light ale, a bottle of Golden Lemonade and a bag of crisps."

The barman frowned.

"Please," added Peter, quickly.

The publican took his hands from the bar and thrust them into his pockets, making no attempt to serve them. "How old are you lot then?" he asked from one corner of his mouth, the cigarette in the other corner wagging up and down as he spoke.

"Eighteen," said Simon. "Or he is." Simon nodded at Peter, the group at the bar looked at him too.

"He ain't eighteen," said the woman, easing her bottom off the stool and tugging her dress down as she stood, evening out the ripples across her tummy. She took another look at Peter and tottered to the bar. "He ain't long out of short trousers," she snorted. Peter blushed.

"That's 'ow you like them, Frances, ain't it?" smirked one of the men. "Young and out of their trousers." The men guffawed and looked back at Peter, who flushed a deeper red.

"I know that old boy," said one of the men. "He plays cricket, quite a good batsman, if I remember."

"It ain't the bat I'm worried about, it's the balls," said Frances slyly. The men hooted with laughter again.

"Are you eighteen then, boy?" the publican asked Peter directly.

"In two days I am," said Peter, looking from the four men back to the publican and then to Frances.

"Go on then, serve the old boy, Russell," said Frances. "He ain't doing no 'arm and he's about the age." Russell looked at Frances, who shrugged. He pulled a face and bent down to grab the bottles of light ale. The latch on the outside door clicked loudly. Russell stopped and looked over the bar to see the brass handle of the door to the bar turning. In stepped PC Rawlins, wearing his helmet and cape. The steel heels of his boots tapped on the floor as he came into the room. The four men parted like the Red Sea to allow him through to the bar as Russell stood back to let Frances move forward to greet the policeman.

"Hello, Joe, what can we do for you?" she asked, using the bar to support her bosom, which she brazenly adjusted under Rawlins' eagle-eyed gaze.

"You ain't serving them boys alcohol are you, Frances?" said Rawlins severely, letting his gaze fall upon Peter and Simon. The boys cowered as the policeman turned back to look at Russell and Frances.

"Would we do such a thing, Joe?" said Frances indignantly. "You know us, we've got a licence to protect *and* our reputation. It's not easy to make money runnin' a pub these days." She stood up and pushed herself back from the bar.

"They came in for some Golden Lemonade and crisps, didn't you, boys?" she said levelly.

"Yes," said Simon and Peter in unison.

Frances reached under the bar for a bottle of lemonade and pulled the crisps from the tin, placing them on the bar. "Take their money, Russell," she ordered, turning back to the policeman. "What did you say you come in for again, Joe?" she said with a smile, pushing her bosom forward again. Rawlins looked away.

"I just come to see if Vic were in, but I don't see him. Has he bin in?"

"Not tonight," said Frances. "Do you want me to give 'im a message?"

"I wanted to borrow his ferret, mine died a few weeks back and I haven't got another one yet," explained Rawlins.

"I'll tell him then, if he comes in like, but you be careful of ferrets, Joe; they can give you a nasty bite, you know. Don't put them in your trouser pocket."

She winked lasciviously at him.

Peter and Simon, having paid, made their way out the pub and re-joined the others in the bus shelter. They handed over the lemonade and crisps.

"What? No beer?" moaned Tookey, unaware that PC Rawlins had followed Peter and Simon from the pub and was standing directly behind him. "Did the bobby come in the pub while you were in there then?"

Simon didn't reply, instead he gritted his teeth, inclining his head meaningfully towards Rawlins. Tookey's eyes widened and he whirled round to see the policeman standing behind him.

"That your motorbike?" he demanded of Tookey.

"Yes," replied Tookey weakly.

"Let's see your licence then, boy, come on be quick about it, I ain't got all day."

Tookey rummaged in his jacket pocket, pulling out his wallet and extracting his licence. He handed it to PC Rawlins who snatched it and eyed it critically. After a minute he handed it back.

"Now," he said gruffly, "I've had enough of complaints about you lot to last me a lifetime. You can all clear off to where you came from and annoy the folks around there, see. Now move!"

He stood and waited as the group scurried to collect their bikes and cycled off towards their various homes.

The next day, as agreed, all the group made their way to the fete, some walked and others cycled. Primrose went with her parents, sticking her tongue out as, in her father's car, she passed various members of the group. The gang all arrived at the fete in dribs and drabs. Peter and Nimpy cycled together, passing Christian on the way, who was as usual walking. Sandra and Ann had been dropped off by their elder sister. Simon and Tookey came from the other direction, Simon on his bicycle and Tookey on his motorbike.

When they arrived, Tookey was dispatched to pick up Christian, who Peter and Nimpy had passed early on in their journey. The last one to arrive was Helen who came on the back of her brother's motorbike, struggling all the while to stop her skirt blowing up in the wind. All the girls wore dresses or skirts and blouses, their arms, legs and faces now tanned a deep brown, and all were wearing makeup except Helen, who rummaged for some lipstick in her bag as soon as she saw the others.

"Come here, Ann, just hold this mirror for a sec while I do this," she instructed, holding up the lipstick. "Mum won't have me wearing it, so I can't put it on at home."

The boys arranged the bikes against the wall of the churchyard, leaving the girls preening; pulling up their short socks and pushing their hair this way and that until it fell straight.

Helen finished with the lipstick and turned to Ann for approval.

"How do I look then?" she asked, looking up at Ann whilst brushing her skirt straight, before lifting each leg in turn to pull up her socks.

"All right, I suppose," said Ann grudgingly. "Come on then, you can hold the mirror while I do mine again." She passed Helen the mirror and carefully applied her own lipstick. She turned her head from side to side to check that none of her blond hair was out of place, before pulling her socks up too. "I would have worn my stockings," she said, "but it's a bit hot for them, don't you think?" She tossed her hair and marched off to stand with Sandra and Nimpy. Helen shook her head and put the mirror away before trotting off after her.

"You haven't got stockings, have you, Ann?" asked Helen. "You never told me, when did you get them then?"

"I've had them a long time, I just don't wear them much in the summer when it's hot, like I said," said Ann indifferently. Helen said nothing.

"Where have those boys got to?" asked Sandra, looking around.

"Can't see them," said Nimpy. "They're up to no good, I expect, showing off. They always do when they get together."

Helen looked at Nimpy; she was taller than the rest of them and her short straight hair curled under towards her neck.

"Nimpy, have *you* got any stockings?" Helen asked, a little shyly. Nimpy turned to Helen in surprise.

"No, course I haven't," she exclaimed. "My mum would go mad if I had, anyway you've got to have something to hold them up with if you buy some."

"Well Ann said that she's got some," Helen began.

"She said what?" asked Sandra.

113

"She said she's got some stockings," repeated Helen, a touch quieter.

"No she hasn't!" said Sandra firmly. "She's got a pair of Jean's that don't fit, and she can't wear them because she hasn't got a suspender belt." Ann blushed furiously and looked away. Nimpy giggled. "Do you know, she tried Jean's roll-on on the other night so she could wear the old pair of stockings but it was much too big and it fell down." The others laughed while Ann stamped her foot and looked away.

"What's a roll-on?" Helen whispered to Nimpy.

Nimpy raised an eyebrow and smiled. "I'll tell you later," she said, leading the way into the garden where the stalls stood.

Some way back, the boys followed. Simon and both Peters looked quite smart, each wearing a jacket and tie over smart trousers. Peter still had his left trouser leg tucked into his sock, where he had forgotten to pull it out after his bicycle ride. As they approached the girls, Nimpy took him to one side.

"Peter, you look stupid."

Peter blushed and tried to examine his attire as best he could, not noticing the problem. "Why?" he asked, turning even redder. Christian, who had been listening, pointed down towards Peter's foot and he quickly pulled the trouser leg out of his sock.

Christian, as usual, did not look like the other boys. He wore grey trousers over black school shoes, which were at least a new pair although they were already looking worn and grubby, a white shirt with a dirty collar and no tie. His grimy pullover sported a large hole in the front. He took off his

114

glasses, huffed on the lenses and polished them with the corner of his shirt, which he had untucked from his trousers. He peered through the lenses, threaded the glasses onto his face and retucked his shirt.

"What are we going to do now then?" he asked. The group looked from one to the other indecisively.

"I'm going to find Primrose, who's coming?" announced Sandra.

"Oh yes, I know where she will be," said Nimpy, leading Sandra and Ann towards a marquee on the other side of the field.

"Aren't you going then, Helen?" asked Peter.

"Not just now. What are you boys doing then?"

"Let's go and get some beer," said Simon, encouraged by the fact that they had so nearly been successful yesterday. "It said there was a licensed bar on the poster, it must be here somewhere." The others ambled half-heartedly across the grass behind Simon.

The fete was set on an estate, the garden of which consisted of formal flowerbeds in front of the house and a big area of lawn leading to a grazed pasture cut off by a ha-ha. The pasture ran down to a large lake, which had been created by damming the nearby stream. On the lawn there were stalls, tents and attractions, which were being patronised by the local community. A band sounded out their brass instruments from the patio in front of the house and foreheads beaded with sweat in the hot July sun.

"This must be it," said Simon, rounding the corner of a dilapidated tent, expecting to find the bar.

Over the entrance to the tent were strung five big letters; they had been cut out of cardboard boxes, badly painted and read RSPCA. In the tent sat an old lady talking to two elderly men, one of whom wore a dog collar. In front of the woman stood a table littered with various pamphlets, and a rusty collection tin, also with RSPCA written on it.

Simon, taken aback, had started to retreat when the old lady suddenly noticed him and beckoned him forward. Simon smiled reluctantly, recognising the woman as Mrs Dene.

"My dear," she said, "how nice to see you, and Helen, and Christian, and you other two boys, how splendid." She turned to the two elderly men. "Now I must introduce you to these young gentlemen, they were so kind to me the other day, they changed the wheel on my motor car." She leaned forwards and beckoned to Helen. "Helen dear, tell me their names again."

"This one's Simon," said Helen loudly, pointing towards Simon. "This one's Peter, that's Peter too and this one's Christian, but you know him, Mrs Dene."

"Yes, dear," said Mrs Dene with a smile, "I know him." The two men nodded and smiled at the boys. "Oh and yes, I forget, this is Helen," said Mrs Dene, gripping Helen's hand enthusiastically. "Isn't she a pretty little thing, don't you think?" She looked admiringly at Helen.

"Very pretty," they agreed.

Mrs Dene pulled Helen a little nearer and whispered, "That's not lipstick you've got on, Helen?"

"Oh no, Mrs Dene," replied Helen quickly. "I've just had a lolly." She blushed slightly at her feeble lie.

116

"I know this one," said the vicar suddenly, turning his head towards Simon as if he were a Punch puppet on a stick. "I know your father, don't I, from Yelden aren't you?"

Simon did not answer immediately, appearing to be considering how to do so. The longer he didn't reply, the more insolent he looked, he had been spoken to directly and the vicar was still looking hard at him. "Yes, I suppose I do come from Yelden," he finally answered, as petulantly as he could manage.

"Well I am glad you know, what!" the vicar snorted. "Glad he knows, eh?" He laughed at Simon who looked back at him blankly.

"Very good, very good," murmured Mrs Dene. "Now run along you lot."

Helen turned away and pressed her lips hard together, pushing her hair back with the palm of her hand, first one side and then the other. She ran her thumb round the waistband of her skirt, straightening her white blouse enough to tighten it across her small bust and shook her head, letting the curls of her dark hair find their own home. "Come on, we had better find the others," she said, and once outside the tent, turned to walk down the aisle of stalls.

"There it is!" said Simon suddenly.

"There's what?" said Helen.

"The bar, silly, that's what we've been looking for," said Simon, standing behind Nimpy and adding in a whisper; "they mustn't see us or they'll never serve Tookey."

The bar was being run by the Marquess of Bute from Dean and both Russell and Frances were behind the bar. The gang moved into a gap between two of the stalls to consider their next course of action.

"It's no good us going, they won't serve us," said Simon. "And they won't serve Christian either, they must know him. You'll have to go, Tookey."

"Why me?"

"Come on," wheedled Simon. "You're the only one they don't know now. Look all we need are four bottles of light ale!" At that moment the others emerged from the group of stalls.

"What do you lot want to drink?" said Simon pompously.

"'You lot'? What do 'you lot' want? What do you mean 'you lot', don't we have names then?" snapped Ann. Simon ignored her and asked again.

"What do you want? Beer?"

"No, I can't stand the stuff," said Sandra. "Goes right up your nose, I can't see why you drink it."

"What *do* you want then?" said Simon loudly, growing more and more exasperated by the minute.

"Golden Lemonade then and a bag of crisps," said Sandra shortly. Simon turned expectantly to Tookey.

"What am I going to do for money then?" There was a sudden fumbling as everybody groped for change in their pockets or handbags.

Tookey held out his hand for the coins then approached the bar, standing nervously in the queue. The day was even hotter now and Russell and Frances had little shade, both of them perspiring freely in the heat of the midday sun. Frances accepted a customer's change and fanned herself with her hand, standing back and leaning against the trestle table that held the glasses. She pulled a packet of cigarettes from her bag and lit one before dabbing her forehead and the wide expanse of her bosom with a spotted handkerchief.

With a sigh, she tilted her head back and slipped a hand inside her blouse, easing her bra strap off over her shoulder, before doing the same on the other side. She squinted slightly in an effort to stop the cigarette smoke streaming into her eyes. Having readjusted her top, she pulled the cigarette from her lips and looked towards Tookey, whose turn it was to be served.

"What do you want then?" she demanded.

"Four light ales, four Golden Lemonades and four bags of crisps please," said Tookey confidently. Frances looked at him suspiciously.

"Are you old enough?" she said, eyeing him up and down.

"Am I old enough?" repeated Tookey, with a feeble attempt at a snort of derision. "What do you think?"

Frances raised an eyebrow and continued to stare at him. Tookey stood his ground boldly.

"Well I'll believe you today," she said finally, reaching down to pull the bottles from the crates under the trestle. Tookey shrugged and leaned against the bar.

The gang outside was watching expectantly; and as Frances bent down to pull out the beers, Tookey turned with a grin to the group and raised a thumb surreptitiously. He paid for the bottles, stuffing two in either pocket, and carried the rest outside to the waiting group.

"Come on then, Tookey," said Simon enthusiastically, "let's have one."

Tookey passed round the bottles and gave the girls a packet of crisps each.

"How are we going to open them then?" asked Helen sourly, holding up the bottle with scorn. "You didn't think to get her to open them for us, did you?" Tookey frowned.

"Keep your hair on then, who's got a shut-knife on them?" He looked at the other boys, they all shook their heads. "All you need is a sharp edge and I can get them off," he said, undeterred.

The others followed him towards the ha-ha, which separated the garden from the pasture leading to the lake. On top of the ha-ha four small bronze statues were placed equidistant along the length of the wall. The base of each presented Tookey with what he was looking for; all the statues were on bronze boxes which were square and provided a sharp edge about half an inch above the stone.

"Brilliant," said Tookey, striding up to the statue so that he was obscured from view and standing in the dry moat of the ha-ha. "Let me show you what to do."

He took his bottle of beer, put the edge of the metal cap tightly against the sharp edge of the base of the statue and gave the top of the bottle a bang with his fist. The top popped off, followed by an urgent rush of froth which bubbled out of the bottle enthusiastically. Tookey put his mouth to the bottle to catch as much escaping liquid as he could, leaning forward so as not to dirty his shirt.

"Let me have a go," said Peter, pushing past the girls to open his bottle.

One at a time they popped the tops off and moved to find a space in the pasture, close to the ha-ha wall. The boys took their jackets off and spread them on the grass for the girls to sit on, lying back on the back slope of the ha-ha as the sun beat down on them.

"Look, there's Primrose, give her a shout, Ann."

Ann moved up to the wall, she was just tall enough to look over into the garden. "Primrose!" she shouted, ducking down again quickly so as not to be seen. The other girls giggled as Ann stood up again and shouted. Primrose looked up, glancing from side to side, unsure as to where the voice was coming from. She started to walk slowly towards the ha-ha. When she was five metres from the edge, Ann leapt up. "Boo!" she shouted. Primrose leapt a foot in the air in astonishment.

"You sod, Ann – you gave me such a fright!" she exclaimed. "You shouldn't do things like that." She walked to the edge of the ha-ha, looking down at the others lying on the grass. "What are you doing down there then?" she asked with a smile.

"What's it look like?" said Simon languidly. "We're having a rest from all the excitement."

"That's not beer you're drinking, is it?" said Primrose sharply.

"Course," said Simon. "Do you want some?" He offered his bottle towards her.

"I've never tried it," she said doubtfully.

"Come on then, try it now," encouraged Simon.

"How can I get down there?" she asked, looking this way and that to find an easy way down, as the wall of the ha-ha dropped five feet.

"Go on, jump!" said Sandra.

"I can't," said Primrose, shaking her head.

"Yes, you can," insisted Sandra.

Primrose looked furtively around to see if her parents were in view, before edging her way to the top of the wall like a diver, her toes just over the edge.

"Here goes then," she shouted, swinging her arms back and then forward as she leapt into the air. As she dropped down onto the grass, the skirt of her dress blew up like a parachute, revealing her pale pink thighs, which contrasted with her tanned calves and white knickers. The boys' eyes goggled and all of them sat up, with the exception of Christian who was looking off across the pasture and draining the last of his beer from the bottle. Primrose landed and quickly jumped up, brushing down her flower-printed dress.

"Not very ladylike," Nimpy said wryly.

"At least she had knickers on," Helen added with a giggle.

"How do you know I had knickers on?" said Primrose sharply.

"We could all see, stupid," snorted Helen, as Primrose finished rearranging her dress. Then she shrugged and turned to the boys.

"Where's that beer then?" she demanded of Simon. He handed her the bottle, which she grabbed from him, put to her mouth and tipped up quickly. The beer frothed into her mouth and she quickly pulled the bottle away from her lips, leaning forwards as beer dripped down her chin. "It's all gone up my nose," she spluttered, handing the bottle back to Simon and wiping her mouth and nose with her fist. She laughed loudly. "I quite like that," she said with a giggle. "Are you going to get any more?"

"Yes, we are," said Simon. "Come on, Tookey, you go again. Who's got some money?" He held his hand out expectantly and looked at Peter. "Come on then?" he repeated.

"No. I don't like it very much."

"You wimp," sneered Simon, turning to Christian. "Christian, what about you?"

"Yes, I'll have one. But I've run out of money."

"You want one, Primrose?" said Simon.

"Yes, I'll have one," said Primrose with a superior smile. Simon collected the money, giving extra for Christian, and handed it to Tookey.

"There we go, Tookey, four bottles if you're having one."

"No, I don't want another," said Tookey. "And I don't want to go and get them, you go if you want some more."

Simon sighed with exasperation. "Right, I'll go then, you just wait here, I'll do it." He stomped off in the direction of the tent, while the others sat and finished the crisps.

"What are we going to do now?" said Sandra.

"I don't know," said Helen crossly. "You're *always* asking what we are going to do. Why don't *you* think of something!" The remainder lay back in the sun and waited for Simon. Ten minutes later, he was back with three bottles of beer.

"What did I tell you?" he said triumphantly. "I got them, an absolute synch, piece of cake."

"So they served you then?" said Peter doubtfully.

"It was easy," shrugged Simon, passing round the opened bottles.

"Nimpy," Helen whispered, grabbing hold of Nimpy's hand.

"Yes?"

"I want to go you-know-where, are you coming?"

Nimpy sat up. "Yes, come on, I've been wanting to go for ages." The pair rose and started to walk back towards the fete, Primrose got up and went with them.

"Where are you going?" asked Peter.

"Never you mind," said Nimpy, turning and walking away, fanning herself impatiently with her hand as she went.

"It's bloody hot," grumbled Tookey, turning onto his front and hiding his face under the crook of his arm.

"Who's going to drink this then?" asked Simon, holding up the bottle that Primrose had ordered. "It's thirsty work lying here in the sun."

"I'll have it," said Christian, who had just drained his second bottle.

"No you won't," said Simon firmly. "You've not paid for that one yet."

"Go on then; she's gone and they don't want it," said Christian, nodding towards the two Peters who were almost asleep in the sun.

"No," said Simon again. Christian looked down to the lake and wiped the beads of sweat from his brow with the palm of his hand. He sighed and lay back again.

"Anyone got a fag?" asked Tookey drowsily, raising himself onto his elbows to look at the others.

A chorus of "No" answered him. Tookey shrugged and lay back down again.

The sound of the band suddenly stopped, leaving the faint chatter of the crowd echoing back across the lawns as people moved up and down the rows of stalls. The air was still and the boys could hear Nimpy and Helen chatting as they walked slowly back to where the boys lay, Primrose having been intercepted by her parents. The two girls reached the ha-ha and sat down on the wall, their legs dangling.

"I know," said Christian, sitting bolt upright, "I'll swim the lake." The other boys sat up and looked at him in confusion.

"You what?" said Tookey.

"If I swim the lake, Simon has to give me the other beer. That's fair, isn't it?"

"What do you mean, that's fair?" said Simon.

"It's a bet," said Christian. "I bet you that bottle of beer that I can swim the lake." The others laughed.

"If you can't ride a bike, I bet you can't swim," said Helen.

"Course I can," said Christian. "Come on then, Simon, what do you say?" Simon looked at the others and back at Christian, before bursting out laughing.

"You mean now? In the middle of the fete?"

"Yes," said Christian. "Look, the lake's a long way off, I bet nobody even notices." He looked round at the others.

"All right then," shrugged Simon, standing and looking out across the water. "You have to go across and back though, not just one way."

"Course," said Christian. "It's a deal, you wait here and watch. I'll do it, you'll see."

He stood up and marched towards the lake, a hundred yards from where the group were sitting. All of a sudden he stopped, sank down towards the ground and held his head in his hands.

"Are you all right?" asked Nimpy.

"My head's going round a bit," he admitted, staggering forwards a step or two and then standing up straight again.

"You're drunk with all that beer," said Simon with a snort. Christian stood and took a few deep breaths before straightening up again.

"That's better," he said quietly and set off across the pasture.

At the edge of the lake, there were two yards of rushes to wade through before Christian reached the water. The group could see him starting to peel his clothes off. First his shoes, then his shirt and trousers until he stood naked but for an old pair of aertex pants. He looped his fingers through the elastic of the waistband as if he would take them off too.

"Look!" Helen screeched. "He's going to take his pants off; I'm not going to look." She covered her eyes with her hands as Christian, whether hearing Helen or not, evidently decided against stripping naked. He stepped forward through the rushes until the water covered his knees, took a deep breath and suddenly plunged forward, emerging and starting a classy front crawl across the lake to the other side.

The others looked around to check if anybody else was watching, but nobody seemed to be taking any notice. The band had started again and there were fancy dress competitions going on, which seemed to be occupying the crowd. Christian made it to the rushes on the other side, stood up and waved. As he did so, the weight of the material of his pants dragged them down around his knees. The girls shrieked and covered their eyes. Christian hastily threw himself back down into the water and started to make his way towards them. It wasn't long before he was pushing his way through the reeds and making his way up to where he had left his clothes, clutching the waistband of his pants as he came. His legs and feet were black with mud and his hair hung down around his face, wet and bedraggled.

He picked up his clothes and ran back to where the group were standing. He flung his clothes to the ground as the assembled group clapped. He brought an arm across his body and mock bowed, letting go of his pants as he did so and they started to fall once again.

"Christian, put your clothes on, can't you?" shouted Nimpy sharply as the two girls covered their eyes, leaving big enough gaps between their fingers to see plenty.

Christian blushed and held the waistband of his pants, throwing himself to the ground and lying back on the grass in the sunshine.

"I win then," and he grinned at Simon.

"Guess you do," agreed Simon, handing over the last bottle of beer.

Chapter Seven
Potato Picking

The start of potato harvest, or tattering as everyone called it, was the high point of the year for many at the farm. Potatoes were the most profitable crop and since they had built a new store to house potatoes over the winter, the amount of land allocated had expanded. To harvest the crop, up to thirty pickers were employed. They were mainly married women from the local area and they would work in pairs; over the three weeks of the harvest they could earn a lot of money and over the winter some of them would be employed in the grading of the picked potatoes as they were sold from the store. The whole system was very flexible as there was no official start or stop time for work and some just picked in the evening. The men on the farm enjoyed tattering as they were paid a considerable bonus during the harvest; the tattering work was hard and paying out bonuses avoided complaints about how much the pickers were earning.

As well as the married women there were always one or two lots of Gypsies who turned up every year a day before the tattering began. They found a site for their caravans and stayed until the harvest was complete. They worked in pairs, husband with wife, and they always picked up more than anyone else during the day.

The hoover, the machine that lifted the potatoes, took two rows from the ground at a time, leaving them on top of the earth and each pair of women was allocated two rows to pick up. The men moved along in front of the pickers, dropping a sack at regular intervals along the rows and the women carried wire baskets to pick the potatoes into, which they then emptied into the sacks. The men on the farm then returned; one person counted the sacks and gave the women a receipt for how many there were and others loaded the sacks onto trailers to be taken back to the farm where the sacks were emptied onto an elevator which conveyed the potatoes onto the heap in the barn.

Getting started on the first day was always a bit difficult. All the pickers arrived and expected the bags to have been put out and the rows to be ready to start and this never quite happened; but after an hour or two all had been allocated their place and gradually lines of filled bags appeared across the field. The women were of all ages; some wore dresses with aprons over them, some wore skirts and others had trousers on or overalls. The pickers were well spaced out and Peter's uncle, John, who ran the field and decided who should go where, was able to keep apart those who did not get on with one another. Most of the women with families wanted to be home by the time their children came out of school so they packed up at three-thirty; but the Gypsies, who had their children with them, always continued on later. There was always an amount of prejudice towards the Gypsies; but they were the best pickers and John always looked after them as well as he could.

The gang picking up the bags was made up of five people; one drove the tractor and trailer along the row of bags, and one person, usually Albert, or Peter if he wasn't at school, would do the booking. Another would be on the trailer stacking the bags and the two remaining men, with a stick between them, would lift the bags onto the trailer. The pickers all had different styles of picking. Most of them stood with their legs apart and bent from the waist to pick up the potatoes, some knelt on the ground and one old man always brought a trusty stool.

Joyce, Helen's mother, picked with her friend Nell. Joyce was in her forties but had not lost her looks and always wore lipstick and had her hair permed. She was stoutly built but in no way overweight and well used to field work. Nell, on the other hand, was taller and slimmer with blonde hair.

The couple were picking and chatting when Hugh, the man who drove the hoover, passed them. They waved to him. Hugh pulled up and stopped the machine, waiting for all of the potatoes to run off the web.

"What can I do for you lovely ladies?" he grinned, putting his hands in his pockets and puffing away at his cigarette.

"Hugh, have you got a better basket anywhere?" asked Joyce. "Look at this one, it's all bent. I bet you ran it over, didn't you?" Hugh edged closer to Nell; Joyce glared angrily at him.

"Of course I didn't run it over."

"It must have been one of the others then."

"More likely you sat on it, or Nell here," scoffed Hugh, giving Nell's bottom a squeeze.

Nell turned placidly to Hugh, her face betraying no emotion; she reached over to him and in a swift movement, sharply did exactly the same to his behind. Hugh leapt in the air, his cigarette falling to the ground. Joyce looked from one to the other, perplexed.

"What are you doing, you mucky buggers? What about this here basket?" She shook it at Hugh, who retreated quickly to the tractor.

"I'll see what I can do," he promised, revving the engine and engaging the PTO which drove the hoover.

The machine moved off, continuing to lift two rows at a time, the long, flat blade digging into the soil under the crop, forcing the earth and potatoes up onto a conveyor made of long iron slats an inch apart, which carried everything to the back of the machine. The potatoes shone a translucent white with pink patches as they were plucked out of the ground and as the conveyor moved up, the slats bounced gently up and down separating most of the soil, which fell back to the ground. By a certain point, the only things on the conveyor were potatoes, stones and large clods of mud.

The hoover disappeared into the distance as the gang picking up the bags gradually made its way towards Joyce and Nell who were hoisting filled bags into the trailer. Peter came first, counting the bags before moving to Joyce to agree how many there were.

"Twenty-eight," said Peter, writing the number in a small receipt book below their names and the date. He tore the receipt out of the book and handed it to Joyce. She looked at it and then back at Peter.

"Twenty-eight?" she repeated, standing up straight and looking down at the rows of bags that the men were picking up. "Is that all? Are you sure you've counted them right, Peter

Dunmore?" She eyed him critically. "Are you sure your eyesight's good enough for this job?"

Peter smiled and coloured a little. "Yes, I'm sure, you count them, this trailer has only picked up this row so far, I think you'll find I'm right."

"What do you think, Nell?" said Joyce, turning to her friend. Nell shrugged.

"I don't know, you count them if you want, I'm sure he can't be far out."

The day had started off cloudy and rather dull, but the sun was starting to peer out from between the clouds and by eleven o'clock there wasn't a cloud in the sky. The women took their jumpers off and the men picking up the bags hung their jackets on the corner of the trailers as they walked up and down the fields. Pairs of pickers that had started from either end of the field met their opposite numbers in the middle and turned round into the adjacent rows that lay ready to pick back in the opposite direction, towards the edge of the field where they had started. The Gypsy families, since they picked faster than everyone else, had been given complete rows to pick. The other women eyed them with suspicion.

Towards midday, Nimpy emerged, walking across the field to Peter who was helping lift the sacks. "Where's Mum, Peter? I can't see her anywhere."

"Right over there," said Peter, pointing to the other side of the field where Nimpy's mum was fitting in a few hours between her other jobs. "What do you want her for then?"

"Just got her some more fags. I've been down the pub. She could do without them but I suppose I'll have to take them to her anyway."

"I can take them," said Peter. "We'll have to go that way soon to pick up the sacks. Give them to me." He held out a hand for the cigarettes and eyed her curiously.

"Why aren't you at school?" he asked.

"Well that's another story. But I'm sick all right and don't ask questions. Why aren't *you* at school?"

Peter smiled and shrugged. "I just didn't make it to the bus, and we hardly have any lessons today, not ones worth going to anyway."

"Hey," said Nimpy, pointing across the field, "look who's turned up."

Peter turned to see Christian who was standing by the road, looking this way and that about the field. Catching sight of the pair, he waved and made his way over to where they stood. He was in his school uniform minus a tie and he carried his jacket over his shoulder.

"What are you doing here?" Peter asked. "You should be doing your Latin and Greek."

"I've come for a job, I want to do some picking," said Christian. "You said you needed a lot of people, didn't you? So what about it, Farmer Dunmore?"

Peter looked a little bewildered. "You're not exactly dressed for the job, are you, Christian? And anyway, how did you get off school?"

"Oh, that's easy. I just go and register and then come straight back home, no one checks on you after that and I need the money so…" He stood looking expectantly at Peter. "What do I do and where do I go?"

Peter said nothing, looking with confusion at Christian.

"Well come on then, where do I go?" repeated Christian looking to Peter and then to Nimpy.

"You ain't going picking in your school uniform, are you?" asked Nimpy.

"Why not? Anyway, I haven't got any work clothes."

Peter sighed. "Come on then. I'll see John, you can go on the end of one of the short rows over there, but we will have to find you a basket or something to pick into."

"I'll come and show him what to do, Peter," said Nimpy. "I don't mind doing that."

Peter nodded and led the way across the field to find his uncle.

The sun was now high in the sky, and the day hot for early October. Jackets and jumpers lay strewn around the field and the men lifting the sacks rolled up their sleeves and mopped sweat from their brows. Hugh moved up and down the field, the hoover spinning out potatoes, their white and pink skins shining as they were exposed to the sun, dulling as they dried. The rows of bags increased behind each pair of pickers as they slowly edged towards the opposite pair from the other end of the field.

"Who you got there then?" said John to Peter. "He don't look as though he could knock the skin off a rice pudding, he don't want a job, do 'e?"

"Can't he go in those short rows in the corner? He'll get them done," promised Peter.

"I suppose so. But he ain't got a basket and we've run out for the minute. He will have to pick straight into the bag for a bit. Who's this girl with him, she ain't coming as well!"

"No. That's Nimpy, she's come with fags for her mum, she can show Christian what to do."

John grunted and walked off in the other direction, waving at Hugh to move the hoover over as he went.

"Over there," Peter instructed Christian, pointing across the field.

Christian removed his glasses and breathed on them, before wiping them on the tail of his shirt. He squinted in the direction that Peter was pointing.

"I'll show him," said Nimpy, exasperated. "Come on, Christian, follow me, grab some of them bags." She picked up a bundle herself and strode off across the rows, Christian following. She reached the end of the row nearest the hedge and stood looking up it to where her mother was picking from the other direction.

"Now, you lay the bags out about five yards apart like this," she instructed, walking up the row and throwing a bag down every now and again. "See," she shouted back at him.

"Yes," said Christian, looking a little uncertain and balancing on one foot as he picked up the other and emptied soil from one of his black school regulation shoes.

"Then, just pick up the spuds and put them into the bags, see," Nimpy instructed, looking at Christian. He nodded and shifted his weight from foot to foot. "Come on then – what are you waiting for?" she asked impatiently. Christian looked out across the field and then up and down the hedge.

"Nimpy," he said, in a slightly embarrassed tone.

"What now?"

"Where's the toilet?" mumbled Christian, looking away from her.

"Toilet? There ain't no toilet. You know that already, unless you want to walk back to the farm and that's a mile away. What do you think the hedge is for then?" She pointed towards the hedge with a look of contempt.

"I'll go in a minute," Christian said, reddening. "What do I do then?"

"Put the potatoes in the bag," she said incredulously, her voice rising.

Christian got hold of a bag, shook it out, picked up a potato and dropped it in. He smiled, picked up another and did the same, all the time holding the top of the bag with one hand.

"Not like that, silly. Come here, let me show you."

She grabbed the top of the bag and rolled the sides down so it looked like a doughnut with a bottom to it and laid the bag on the ground in front of them. She then picked up the potatoes using both hands until she had six or seven and threw them forward towards the bag; within twenty seconds she had cleared the ground in front of her of potatoes.

She stood up, her legs still apart and her face a little red, pushing her hair behind her ears with each index finger.

"See?" she asked, looking at him.

"I suppose so," said Christian, looking a little more confident.

Nimpy brushed her hands against each other. "I'm going to see Mum now; you should have filled the bag by the time I get back, all right?"

Christian pursed his lips and nodded as Nimpy walked off up the row to deliver the cigarettes she hadn't managed to hand over to Peter after all.

Across the field, Joyce and Nell had met the pair picking towards them and had between them decided it was time for lunch. They picked up a handful of bags and made their way towards the other side of the field to sit under the hedge to eat their food.

"I must have a wee," announced Nell, rising and pushing her way through the hedge out of view of the rest of the pickers. She looked quickly up and down the hedgerow, lifted her blouse and hurriedly pushed her trousers down, squatting behind the hedge. A branch cracked within yards of her. She looked round startled, pulling her trousers up and standing to find the source of the noise.

Christian was standing ten yards away, doing up the fly buttons of his trousers.

"What do you think you are doing there, boy?" she shouted at him. "What are you doing peeping like that, you mucky bugger?"

Christian stood paralysed to the spot, his face drained of colour. "I weren't peeping, I promise I were just…"

"You bloody were," interrupted Nell. "You bloody were, I know your sort, you're Christian, aren't you? I know who you are, don't think I don't, don't think I don't know all about you."

"What's up, Nell?" came a voice from the other side of the hedge. Joyce pushed her way through the branches to see what was happening. "What's up then?"

"It was him," said Nell, pointing an accusatory finger at Christian. "He were peeping at me 'aving a piss." Joyce looked from Christian to Nell and back to Christian.

"I weren't," stammered Christian. "I were just having one myself and she come through. I couldn't say anything, I didn't want you to see me…" He broke off, distress lining his face. "I weren't peeping. I weren't!" he implored, close to tears.

Joyce looked back at Nell. "You know who he is, don't you?"

"He's Christian from the Hall, ain't he, course I know who 'e is."

Joyce spread her hands and lowered her voice slightly. "He couldn't knock the skin off a rice pudding. They tell me he's not interested in women anyway, ain't that right, Christian?" She looked at him slyly. "Ain't that right, Christian?" She sniggered. "I've heard all about you, Christian, you just ain't interested, are you?"

Christian looked away and did not answer.

"Leave him alone, Nell," advised Joyce. "He won't do you no harm. Now you bugger off, Christian, or I'll let Miss Shaw know about you peepin', go on then."

Christian pushed his way back through the hedge and into the field. Nell scowled furiously after him.

"Mucky old boy. What's he doing snoopin' on me like that?"

"He's harmless," assured Joyce, watching Christian desperately scuttling back to his potato sack. "Harmless."

The next day it rained and potato picking was called off. It continued to rain throughout the week, so none of the gang were able to meet until the Sunday when they returned to the club in Dean after the break for the summer holidays, all eager to play their game of Postman's Knock.

Miss Shaw had agreed to the gatherings starting earlier at six from now on.

One or two more people had joined, friends of the original gang, and it had become quite crowded in the clubhouse. Christian still avoided the kissing, hiding in the corners or leaving to roam the grounds when he was bored, but the girls didn't mind, as his dishevelled look and dirty clothes did not appeal to them. Nimpy tried as best she could to be kind to him, but her friendliness was never reciprocated.

"How many bags of spuds did you end up picking the other day, Christian?" she asked him as they stood outside the door of the club. Christian had picked a number at Roger's urging.

"Thirteen," he answered, looking away from her.

"Thirteen? Is that all? Mum said she did fifty, you should have done more than thirteen, it's hardly worth going if you can't do more than that."

Christian scuffed at the floor with his foot.

"I'd better knock and you'd better go back in, Christian," she then said gently, thinking she'd maybe gone too far.

"I'm not going back in there," he said firmly. "I've had enough of all that mucking about." With a scowl, he turned and marched off across the yard towards the road. Nimpy shrugged and knocked on the door three times.

There was a shout from inside and after a few moments Peter opened the door, sauntering out with a grin on his face, and they locked in a passionate embrace. Moments later Peter broke away. "What happened to Christian?"

"I don't know. He doesn't like it, you know what he's like. He says it's mucking about. He walked off over there some-where." She pointed off across the yard.

"You go back in, Nimpy, I'll go and find him after my turn. He must be somewhere about." Nimpy sighed heavily and went back into the clubhouse.

Peter paused and knocked on the door. After a short wait Helen emerged. This time the embrace was interrupted from the timekeeper inside the barn.

"You knock, Helen. I'm going to try and find where Christian has gone. Apparently he went up the road somewhere. Tell them I will be back in a bit."

Peter went out into the road and looked both ways; there was no sign of Christian. He set off in the direction of the village, thinking he was more likely to find Christian skulking around somewhere there. He passed the chapel on the left, and the council houses on the right and approached the bus shelter. Sitting on one of the benches in the shelter was a middle-aged man leaning back against the wall. He had a long beard which he was winding around his finger. On his head, he wore a checked patterned trilby, the brim of which was pulled down around his ears. Around his neck he had tied a red-spotted handkerchief above his best jacket, which was buttoned up down his front. His woolly trousers had string tied round them just above his boots which were black and highly polished.

Peter could see the rows of nails in the sole of the man's boots, as he reclined on the bench, his legs stretched out in front of him. "Hello, Archie," said Peter. "Have you seen Christian?" Archie was Joyce's husband, and Peter knew him well. He looked up when Peter spoke and tipped his hat onto the back of his head.

"Peter Dunmore. What are you doing 'ere on a Sunday night? After all the old girls I've no doubt, up to no good I'm

140

sure and a bloody nuisance to all us folk." He shook his head bemusedly. "And no I ain't seen Christian, why do you ask?"

"No reason. I was just trying to find him, that's all."

Archie stood up, stroked his beard and pulled the sleeves of his jacket down one at a time, before rearranging his hat levelly on his head again and sitting down.

"What are you sitting there for, Archie? There are no buses on Sunday." Archie said nothing for a moment but fixed Peter with a steady gaze.

"What business is that of yours? I'm doin' no 'arm sitting here, am I?" He tilted his chin aggressively. "Am I?"

"No, I'm sure you're not."

"Not like you young buggers, disturbing the peace and creating havoc. That there Christian's no better than the rest of you, 'cept he don't chase the girls, I don't suppose."

"You haven't seen him then?"

"No, I ain't! I told you that afore." He eyeballed Peter again before asking in a more subdued tone, "You got the time while you're standing there?"

Peter looked at his watch. "It's half six."

"Hmm, another half hour."

"Half hour for what?"

"Half hour before the pub opens, what do you think!"

"So that's why you're waiting, Archie? For the pub to open? But why don't you wait at home, it's only thirty yards to your back door over there. You could wait in the warm!"

Archie stroked his beard thoughtfully. "I don't go 'ome, boy," he said slowly, as if talking to someone who was deaf, "Because I can't get in, the door's locked see."

"Why don't you have a key then?"

141

"Because, you stupid boy, there's only one key and Joyce has it and she's gone to see her mother."

"Oh," said Peter, not really understanding. He opened his mouth to pursue the matter just as Christian appeared.

"Look who's here then," said Archie as Christian ambled up, looking as unkempt as ever, his hair uncombed and his glasses so dirty that he must have had a job to see through them.

"Where have you been?" said Peter crossly.

Christian looked at him silently for a moment. "Just around," he said, turning to Archie. "Are you waiting for the pub to open, Archie?"

Archie rose and put his nose in the air. "What I'm waiting for is none of your business, my boy. And at least if I was waiting for the pub then I'd be able to escape the likes of you nosy buggers, you not being old enough to get in."

"I will be soon, Archie," said Christian, "I'm eighteen the week after next and then you won't be able to stop me." Archie glowered at him.

"Come on, Christian, let's go back to the club," said Peter hastily, unwilling to get into another war of words with the belligerent man. Christian shrugged and followed Peter back down the road. "When are you eighteen then, Christian?"

"A week Thursday. And don't tell me I don't look old enough, I'd punch you and you wouldn't forget it."

Peter didn't rise to the bait; he was considerably bigger than Christian and unlikely to sustain much damage from a punch by the younger boy.

"How are you going to celebrate then? Are you having a party?"

"Don't be stupid. Where would I have a party?" He sniffed angrily. "No. I'm going to a pub and I'm going to have a pint of bitter and nobody will be able to stop me."

"Do you like bitter?" continued Peter, eager to deflect the anger bubbling in Christian's voice.

"Course I do. But I ain't going to Archie's pub. I'm going to the Turk's Head, that's a proper pub."

"Where's that then?"

"In Bedford of course, haven't you heard of it?"

Peter hadn't but he didn't reply. They were back at the club and Helen approached Peter and Christian.

"Where have you two been then?"

Christian looked away, leaving Peter to reply. "We've just seen your dad sitting in the bus shelter," said Peter by way of explanation.

"Waiting for the pub to open, I bet."

"Why doesn't your mum let him have a key, Helen?" asked Peter with a small laugh.

"She never has done. She won't let him in the house unless she's there. She says he makes the floor dirty with his boots, so she locks him out."

"Do you really mean that?" said Christian.

"Yes, he sits in the barn if he can't get in," as if it were the most normal thing in the world, and the three of them turned their attention back to the others in the room.

Chapter Eight
Christian's Birthday

It was Christian's eighteenth birthday. It was a Thursday and he went to school in Bedford as usual, but since the afternoon was taken up with cadets, which he did not do, he decided to celebrate instead so after he attended a morning of lessons he left the school just before lunch. He had found a long gabardine mac that must have belonged to a relation of Miss Shaw's and had taken it to school rolled up in his bag. As he left the grounds of the school, he unrolled it and put it on, heading for the Turk's Head in the middle of the town.

The day was overcast and cold and it drizzled as he walked, the droplets spattering his glasses. The mac was one or two sizes too big for him but it covered up his school uniform, which was his intention.

He made his way to the junction in the main part of the High Street, jiggling his recently earned coins in his pocket as he walked and whistling to try and cultivate a nonchalant air. The door of *Roses*, the department store in the middle of the town, swung open as he walked past and an old lady bustled out. She wore a straw pork-pie hat and a long grey woollen coat with brown lace-up shoes. Her stockings, which were thick, were wrinkled, as though they were falling down. Christian immediately recognised the unmistakeable figure of Mrs Dene, who turned to the girl holding the door open for her.

"Thank you, my dear," she said. "You are so kind."

She took a bag from the girl, smiled and looked up and down the street, trying to decide which way to go. She raised her wrist to look at her watch, but in doing so caught the bag that the girl had given her. The bag clattered to the floor and three oranges that had been sitting in the top tumbled out and rolled towards Christian. He bent down and retrieved the oranges, handing them back to Mrs Dene as she picked up the bag from the pavement, covering his head as best he could so that she would not recognise him.

"Dear boy, you are so kind," she said, as Christian put the oranges back into her bag.

She glanced at him but, being distracted, did not appear to recognise him.

"So kind," she said again, looping the straps of the bag on her arm and fumbling with her handbag.

She opened it and with some difficulty found her purse, stirring the coins about in it until she found a sixpence which she gave to Christian with a smile.

"So kind, my dear," she repeated, before turning and walking away from him.

Christian strode down the street, turned right at the next junction and caught sight of the sign for the Turk's Head twenty yards ahead of him. He went straight in at the main door, making every effort to appear confident. Etched in the large glass panel of the door in front of him were the words **PUBLIC BAR**, to the left of this was another door labelled **SALOON**. Christian stopped and looked in confusion at the two signs; he did not know the difference between the two.

145

He tried to peer through the glass in the door labelled **SA-LOON**, but there was a curtain on the inside and he couldn't see anything.

At that moment two men came from behind him, pushing roughly past. "Out the way, boy," growled one as he pushed open the door of the public bar and went in. Christian followed them.

The room was gloomy, just like the Marquess of Bute, as two small lights lit the long bar and a narrow beam cast from a small, dirty window gave little more by way of illumination. Several people stood at the bar and a few more sat at tables arranged along the wall opposite. The air was thick with cigarette smoke and laced with a sour odour of stale beer. Wooden boards covered the floor and the walls were unadorned and painted with a cream gloss paint that had stained to yellow from the smoke; patches peeled miserably in various places on the wall. At the far end hung a dartboard with a single light bulb illuminating it.

The two men in front of him went to the bar and ordered their drinks. Christian edged past them and moved further down the bar, sitting on a stool to wait. It took five minutes for the barman to approach him.

"What can I get you then, lad?"

"Half of bitter please." The barman stood and looked at him for a moment.

"Are you old enough?" A little of the colour in Christian's face drained away.

"Course I am," said Christian, his voice trembling a little.

"You don't look eighteen."

"Well I am, so can I have a half of bitter," said Christian without much conviction. "Please," he added quickly.

The barman did not move, but continued to stare at him for a few more moments. Eventually he grunted, picked up a half-pint glass from a shelf under the bar and slowly drew the lever of the pump, filling the glass and handing it to Christian.

"That'll be a shilling," he said, puffing on the cigarette that hung from his mouth.

Christian handed over a shilling and sipped the beer. He looked round; should he sit at a table or stay where he was? He decided not to move. He did not like the taste of the beer but that didn't matter. He considered buying some cigarettes but decided against that, he had tried smoking and it had made him feel sick so it was not a good idea. He sipped the beer and watched as another customer came to the bar. The man was well dressed in a dark-blue blazer with an emblem stitched onto the breast pocket and grey flannel trousers above well-polished black shoes. His dark hair was brushed close to his head and shone with Brylcreem. Its parting was straight as an arrow.

The barman approached him.

"Usual, Cyril?" he asked, already reaching for the glass.

"Please," said Cyril, taking a large wallet from the inside pocket of his jacket and opening it.

With long fingers that boasted manicured nails the man took a ten-shilling note from the wallet and laid it on the bar, before folding the wallet and putting it back in his pocket. He reached into another side pocket and pulled out a silver cigarette case, which he flicked open. He took one out, snapped the case shut, put it away and tapped the end of the cigarette on the bar before putting it to his mouth. He looked up the bar to where Christian sat, and their eyes met briefly before Christian looked away and down at the beer-stained bar, aware of the older man's eyes upon him.

"Are you going to have one with me?" asked the man in a highly educated accent.

Christian, having looked down, was unsure of whether the man was talking to him or to somebody else. He decided to ignore him, instead taking another sip from his glass. The barman brought Cyril his order, a pint of bitter in one glass and in another a shot of whisky.

"He didn't hear me, did he?" said Cyril to the barman, nodding in the direction of Christian.

The barman took two paces away from Cyril to stand in front of Christian.

"There's a gentleman up 'ere wants to know if you want a drink," he said loudly, learning forward and peering at Christian.

"'E don't look old enough to me, Cyril, does 'e?" the barman said turning back to Cyril. Christian looked up at the barman and then at Cyril.

"Are you talking to me? You mean do *I* want a drink?" asked Christian, clearly surprised.

"That's what I said, wasn't it?" the barman replied.

"Thank you," said Christian, giving Cyril a brief smile.

"Drink up then," said the barman, nodding at Christian's glass.

Christian drank down the last of his bitter and handed it over the bar to be refilled.

"Cheers," said Christian, accepting the refilled glass from the barman and lifting it to his lips. He looked apprehensively down the bar to where Cyril sat.

"Cheers," said Cyril, pulling a silver lighter from his trouser pocket and lighting his cigarette. "Want one of these?" he asked, opening his cigarette case and holding it in Christian's direction.

"No thanks, I don't," said Christian, looking away. There was silence for a minute or two.

"This your regular?" asked Cyril, in an attempt to rejuvenate the conversation. "I haven't seen you in here before."

"No," said Christian. "I haven't been in before." He fell silent.

"You don't look old enough to be in a pub," Cyril started again, looking more intently down the bar towards Christian.

"I am. I'm eighteen. I'm eighteen today."

"You mean it's your birthday!" exclaimed Cyril, standing up and moving his stool down the bar to within a few feet of Christian. "You've come out to celebrate, I suppose?"

"I suppose so."

Cyril took a large swig at his pint, before picking up his whisky glass and emptying it in one go. He pursed his lips tightly together and burped. "That's better," he murmured. He tapped the bar with the whisky glass and pushed it towards the barman to be refilled. "You're still at school then, whatever-your-name-is?"

"Christian," said Christian, the beer starting to loosen his tongue. "Yes I'm still at school, the grammar school."

"Well there's a coincidence, so was I, a long time ago now, mind. Is old Philpot still teaching Latin?"

149

"Yes," said Christian, sitting up and turning to face Cyril more directly. "He teaches me."

Christian smiled more warmly at Cyril as the alcohol seeped into his bloodstream, happy that he had found something in common with the man. Cyril continued to ask more questions about the school and Christian continued to answer more and more freely; he began to tell Cyril about aspects of his life he had never told anyone. Half an hour or so later, he stood up and asked for the direction of the toilets. Cyril pointed him to the back corner of the room; Christian smiled and moved slightly unsteadily in that direction.

Cyril watched him go. As the door swung shut behind him, Cyril looked surreptitiously down the bar to check he was unobserved and swiftly poured his whisky into Christian's glass. He summoned the barman once more and asked for a refill of whisky. Once the barman's back was turned, he poured the new shot into Christian's half pint as well. Christian returned, still a little unsteady on his feet, his eyes slightly unfocused. He slid onto his stool and continued to chat to Cyril.

Quarter of an hour later, Cyril looked at his watch. "Time to go, Christian, where do you live?" he asked. "Do you want a lift home? My car is just round the corner."

"I live in Dean. It's miles away don't worry, I can catch the bus."

"I won't hear of it," insisted Cyril. "I only live in Pertenhall, that's not far away, I can drop you off, no trouble at all. Now, come on, drink up."

Christian shrugged, finished his drink and followed Cyril out of the pub. Once he was in the fresh air of the street, the effect of the whisky hit Christian like a hammer blow. The pavement swam in front of him and he blinked furiously to try and right it. He raised his arms to try and balance himself, but the world continued to spin. Cyril looked round to see Christian tottering towards the road; he launched towards the boy and grabbed his arm before he fell.

"Oh dear, oh dear," he murmured. "A little the worse for wear, are we? Come on then, Christian, the car's only around the corner. You'll feel better in a while, a tad too much to drink, that's all." He held Christian upright to prevent him falling and guided him towards the car, where he helped him in. Once inside the car, Christian let his head loll back against the seat; he shut his eyes as the horizon in front of him see-sawed violently.

Cyril started the engine and headed his car towards Pertenhall. The house was empty when they arrived; Cyril's mother was away with her sister until the end of the week. Christian opened his eyes as the car pulled into the drive, and he looked blearily out of the car window, failing to recognise any of the surroundings. He fumbled in confusion for the door handle, but could not find it. He knew he had to get out of the car, he was seconds away from being sick.

Cyril made his way round to the passenger side of the car and opened the door just in time. Christian bolted out towards the lawn and was indelicately and violently sick in the flowerbed. Cyril watched calmly as Christian coughed and spluttered. Finally, he stood up straight and put his hand to his head again.

"I feel dreadful. Where am I?"

"Don't worry, my boy. You'll soon feel better. Just come inside for a while and you'll be as right as rain. You can have a glass of water and then I will run you home."

Christian looked uncertainly around him. "Where am I?"

"We won't be a minute, Christian. Then I will take you back."

Christian traipsed after Cyril round the side of the house and to the back door, which Cyril unlocked. He followed Cyril into the small kitchen. A cat skittered out of the door as they entered and somewhere in the depths of the house a clock chimed. Cyril held Christian's shoulders and guided him to a deep armchair in the large sitting room which overlooked the garden.

"Now, let's take that jacket off, shall we, and make you a bit more comfortable." Christian did as he was told and slipped it off, handing it to Cyril who loomed over him. "Can I get you anything? A cup of tea maybe?"

"No. No tea. But perhaps a glass of water?"

Cyril nodded and went out to the kitchen. He took a glass from the cupboard and filled it from the tap, before placing it gently on the sideboard. He moved silently towards the back door, turned the key in the lock and removed it, slipping it quietly behind a copper-bottomed saucepan on a shelf next to the cooker. He took the glass of water back to Christian.

"Here we are, that will put you right," Cyril said cheerily, handing Christian the glass of water. "I'm just going to freshen up a little, you will be all right, won't you, Christian? Do you still feel sick?"

"Not so much now," said Christian, taking a small sip of the water.

Cyril smiled and left the room. Christian could hear him moving up the stairs and along the landing above.

He leaned his head against the back of the armchair. His head was still swimming but since he had been sick he felt a little better. He sipped the water and tried to stand up; but no sooner had he made it to his feet than the room started to spin again, so he sat down hastily and looked around the room.

Two armchairs flanked the fireplace and a delicately made table sat under the window, upright chairs at each end. A sideboard stood behind the sofa, littered with family photographs; one of them showed Cyril in a gown and mortar board, standing with a woman who Christian guessed must have been his mother. Between the two chairs and the sofa, in front of the fireplace, was a low table stacked with old magazines and papers, the pages starting to curl with age. On top of the papers a brass shape about the size of an apple was being used as a weight. Christian picked it up and looked at it. It was heavy and modelled in the shape of a sleeping cow; its head tucked round to meet its back legs. The feel of the weight in the hand was pleasing, the contours of it smooth and cool to the touch.

Christian looked up above the fireplace. An oil painting hung from the wall depicting a sleepy village, the church standing out above a village green, where a game of cricket was in progress. He glanced down; a long mirror flanked the fireplace and his reflection gazed back at him, the doorway to the hall lurking behind him. He peered again into the mirror, seeing that his face was as white as a sheet, his hair unkempt and his tie undone. He looked dreadful. He scowled and looked away, taking another sip of the water and letting his head fall against the back of the chair again. His eyelids began

153

to drop closed. As they did so his head started to swim and he snapped his eyes open so the horizon levelled. He took another sip of water and tentatively tried to shut his eyes again; his head still spun but not as violently as it had before and it wasn't long before he felt himself slipping off to sleep.

Five minutes later, Christian was woken by a draught against his cheeks. His eyes opened slowly. He sat up, trying to refocus and work out where he was, his eyes scanning the room in confusion. As he remembered, he relaxed fractionally and took another sip of water. His eyes flickered back to the mirror. Behind his own reflection he could see Cyril standing in the doorway. He was completely naked.

The shock galvanised him. Christian shot up from his chair, spilling water from the glass down his front. He hurriedly placed the glass on the coffee table and turned to face the man, disbelief etched on his face.

"Christian, dear boy," crooned Cyril, "don't look so frightened, you've been through the hoop before, I'm sure you have."

Christian said nothing, his eyes scanning the room for an escape route. His head had cleared, his dizziness gone and he was steady on his feet again. There were two doors, one into the kitchen and one into the hallway. All the windows were shut. Christian stared incredulously at Cyril, trying to work out what he wanted and why he was naked, because he had a feeling that whatever it was that Cyril wanted, he did not want at all. He had to get out and quickly.

Cyril moved to the sideboard, opened the cupboard and took out a bottle of whisky and a large crystal glass. The stopper squeaked as Cyril twisted it from side to side to remove it

154

and it relented with a small pop. He poured a generous measure into the glass before banging the cork back into the bottle with the flat of his hand and returning it to the cupboard. Christian licked his lips nervously, Cyril was blocking the escape route to the kitchen. Christian's eyes flicked to the door into the hallway; it seemed like the only available option, surely there would be a way out through there.

Cyril took a large swig from the glass of whisky and plonked it down on the sideboard. He looked at Christian.

"Would you like some, Christian? It's nice. You've actually had it before, you know." He smiled at Christian and took a step towards him.

This was his moment. Christian dashed for the door and out into the darkened hallway. Straight ahead of him another door lay open, revealing the dining room, where a long wooden table lurked amidst several mismatched chairs. To the left were the stairs, and to the left of them, in the corner, stood a small table over which hung two old army bayonets arranged in a cross. The front door loomed to his right, a small single-paned window at the top of that; Christian dashed to the door and seized the handle, trying desperately to open it. But it was locked, and there was no key anywhere to be seen.

He turned and sprinted into the dining room, looking desperately for an exit, but there was none. He ran back into the hall, the only escape now up the stairs. He scrambled back towards them, navigating the first three steps, limbs flailing, before an icy grip circled his leg and clung to it tightly.

Cyril was a lot bigger than Christian and he pulled the small boy back down the stairs with ease. Christian lay cowering on the patterned rug at the foot of the stairs. Cyril hoisted him to his feet and grabbing Christian's left arm, twisted it behind his back. Christian squealed and had no choice but to allow himself to be marched back into the living room, where he was forced down into one of the armchairs. He could smell the sweat on Cyril's naked body as the man rounded the chair to face him. He lowered his face until it was level with Christian's, their noses no more than six inches apart.

"We're not going to be difficult about this, are we, Christian?" said Cyril, with a thin smile. Christian shuddered and shook his head fractionally. Cyril nodded curtly, stood up and walked over to the sideboard to take another slurp of whisky. He prowled back towards Christian, his glass still in his hand.

"Now," said Cyril, "there are two ways we can go about this, *with* your cooperation, my dear boy, or without." He took another sip. "I don't mind, you see, Christian, which way you choose." He smiled again. "I will enjoy myself no matter what."

He turned and put his glass down on the mantelpiece over the fire. As he did so Christian made another desperate dash for escape, this time through the door into the kitchen. Again, Cyril was too quick for him; his large hand clapping down on the back of Christian's threadbare shirt and pulling the pale-faced boy back into the living room.

"Not so fast, not so fast," breathed Cyril, slamming Christian back into his chair.

Christian squealed. His head snapped against the back of the chair and sent his glasses tumbling from his face. He fumbled on the floor to pick them up again, keeping his eyes firmly on the blurry silhouette of Cyril, who was leaning on the fireplace sipping at his whisky. After much desperate patting of the floor, Christian retrieved his glasses. He put them on and looked up at Cyril whose cheeks were flushed bright red.

"I think it would be better if you had no clothes on, Christian. We could see what you are made of then, couldn't we?"

"What have I got to do that for?" asked Christian shakily, confusion etched on his face. "I don't..."

"Take them off," snapped Cyril, taking a step away from the mantelpiece and leaning towards Christian. His face contorted with anger. "I said, take them off."

Christian leapt to his feet and backed slowly towards the table, still looking frantically for a means of escape as he did so. There was none. Cyril raised his fist and advanced angrily on him.

"I told you!"

"Yes, yes," Christian stammered, shaking uncontrollably.

He started to undo his tie, scrabbling at his neck to loosen it before Cyril came any closer. He laid it on the table and slowly pulled off his shirt and trousers to reveal his tatty grey aertex underwear hanging limply off him like clothes on a line.

"And the rest."

Christian squeezed his eyes tight shut and did as he was told. He stepped out of his underwear and stood trembling in front of Cyril.

"What are you going to do to me?" stuttered Christian, as tears squeezed out of his eyes and ran down his cheeks.

He sniffed, the pale skin of his chest moving over his ribs.

"Come here, boy," said Cyril softly, a smirk flitting across his face.

Christian took a step forward, still trembling. Cyril downed the rest of the whisky and walked towards him, looking him up and down. Christian shut his eyes as Cyril circled him; he could feel the man's eyes raking his body. Cyril lightly placed the back of his hand on Christian's neck and ran his fingers down his back, caressing Christian's skin. Christian shuddered and moaned quietly as a small trickle of urine ran down his leg. Cyril sneered and moved to stand in front of the boy again. Christian opened his eyes as the odour of whisky stung his nostrils.

"You've wet yourself, Christian," said Cyril with a small tut.

Christian looked down and said nothing.

Cyril smirked again. Suddenly his expression hardened, and he stared at Christian, his face red as he reached out a hand towards Christian's waist. Christian leapt backwards, whirling round to run into the kitchen. He ran to the door to the garden, tugging at it in blind panic, but it would not give. He pulled again, throwing his meagre weight against the frame of the door as Cyril's laughter echoed behind him. Christian looked around desperately; the only other way out was the window, so he rushed to it and tried the catch.

"No you don't, you little bugger," snarled Cyril, making his way round the small table and lunging at Christian who jumped away and sprinted back into the living room, Cyril hot on his heels.

Christian reached the other side of the room and turned to see Cyril advancing on him. As Cyril passed the table he trod on one of Christian's discarded shoes, his ankle turned and he crashed to his knees next to the small table, knocking the brass paperweight off the table as he tumbled over. The paperweight rolled across the floor towards Christian. Cyril snarled and started to pick himself up, pushing himself onto all fours. Christian, seeing this as his only chance, bent down and seized the paperweight. He took three quick steps towards Cyril, raised the weight and brought it down with all his strength on Cyril's head.

Cyril made no sound; his arms gave under him and he sank heavily to the floor. Christian raised the paperweight over his head again, ready for another blow, but Cyril did not move. Christian gasped and let the weight fall from his hand where it landed with a dull thud and rolled under the sofa. He looked more closely at Cyril; there was no sign of life.

Christian stood transfixed, unable to think what he should do. He looked around the room, hands shaking and teeth chattering, as tears rolled down his face. He looked at his clothes lying in a crumpled heap on the floor and made his way tentatively towards them.

There was a groan. He looked sharply towards the prone figure as Cyril's eyes opened. He groaned again. Christian shuddered, wiped the tears from his eyes and pushed his glasses back onto his face. Slowly, Cyril started to move, his arm pushing against the floor as he tried to prop himself up. Christian ran from the room in terror, scampering out into the hallway, and starting to run up the stairs. As he ran, the glint of the bayonets on the far wall caught his eye. He changed course and ran towards the weapons, grabbed one from the hook before creeping back into the living room. Cyril was now on all fours and still groaning, unable to form any words. Christian eyed him carefully; the man in front of him was strong and muscled, and in comparison, Christian was a weakling.

Christian blinked and advanced on the moaning man. He wiped a trembling hand across his nose, shuddered and blinked a couple more times. Hesitantly, he raised the bayonet in both hands above his head. Cyril rocked slightly and groaned again; his face was red, contrasting with the pallor of his body, and his stomach bulged towards the floor. Slowly, he started to turn his face towards Christian.

Christian shut his eyes and brought the bayonet down with all the force he could muster into the middle of Cyril's back. Cyril shrieked as the point of the bayonet pierced his skin and tore itself out of Christian's hands, clattering to the floor. Cyril collapsed and rolled to his side, the bulk of his body falling across the dropped bayonet as he did so. The small wound oozed blood which began to pool in the middle of Cyril's back. Christian's face contorted in agony and tears sprang to his eyes as he watched the blood form a small dark puddle on the carpet. There was no way he was going to be able to move Cyril to reclaim his weapon, so he rushed to the hall and grabbed the other bayonet from the wall. Tears tumbled from his eyes, his face wet as he ran to stand back over the body of his abuser.

Cyril's eyes flickered open; he focused on Christian and glowered, his eyes thick with hatred, and he made a sound halfway between a curse and a growl and tried to move his arm. Christian howled and plunged the bayonet into Cyril's stomach. There was a hissing noise as Christian punctured

160

Cyril's gut; a putrid smell of vomit filled the room. Christian tried to pull the bayonet from the man's stomach, but it would not budge. He yanked it once, then again before the weapon tore from Cyril's middle; the wound opened and blood and the contents of Cyril's guts flowed out onto the carpet. Cyril's eyes widened in rage and shock as Christian took the bayonet in two hands, lifted it above his head and brought it down hard and deep into Cyril's chest. He stood and yanked the bayonet out. Blood heaved from the wound, spurting from Cyril's chest in quick pulses, drenching Christian in hot crimson liquid. He gasped and stepped back; already the blood flow was lessening.

Christian looked at the body below him, his breathing laboured. The blood had stopped pumping from the wound and Cyril's head was tipped to one side. Blood trickled from his mouth. Christian dropped the bayonet and stepped back from the body. He stared at his blood-stained hands and started to shake. He looked up and around room, his eyes scouring the walls as if they might find someone who had witnessed what he had just done. His gaze came to rest on his reflection in the big mirror. His face was ashen and the length of his pale body and face splattered with deep-red blood. He looked at himself in terror and shuddered. Slowly, his eyes sank to the blood-stained floor and to the body of Cyril lying lifeless at his feet.

Chapter Nine
Escape

There was silence. Christian took his glasses off and wiped his eyes, but in doing so only smeared more blood over his face. He picked up the bayonet and laid it on a newspaper on the small table. He looked towards Cyril's lifeless body; he needed to get the other bayonet out from under him. He knelt and tried to push Cyril up the best he could, but that got Cyril's gut hissing again and Christian shuddered as green stinking liquid oozed from the gaping tear in his side. He could feel Cyril's body already going cold as he fumbled under it for the bayonet, and kept his eyes clamped shut. Finally, his hand located the sharp edge of the blade and he started to slide it out from under the lifeless body. He yanked the bloody bayonet free and placed it with the other one on the little table. He stared at the two barbed blades, thick with congealing blood, and shuddered again, turning and making for the kitchen.

He moved to the sink and turned on the tap. He closed the tap again, reasoning that there must be a bathroom somewhere. He went back to the living room, out into the hall and up the stairs. He opened the door at the top of the stairs and found it. All the fittings looked old, and under each tap in the basin rusty stains lay obstinately after years of dripping; it was the same in the bath. The bath taps one end had a hand shower attached by a hose. The sealed metal cover of the hose

162

was broken and the rubber inside could be seen. Christian turned the taps on and after a while the water started to gurgle out, warm and cleansing. Christian pushed the large lever across and the water started to trickle from the shower; he climbed into the bath. He took his glasses off, placed them carefully on the side and showered – Cyril's blood streamed from his body down towards the plug. Christian stood under the steaming water until it ran clear. He stepped from the tub, washed his glasses and put them on again before examining himself in the mirror to see if he could see any more blood. He found a smear on his shoulder, so he clambered back into the bath tub again and repeated the process. He turned off the water, climbed out and cleaned the bath as best he could before drying himself with a blue hand towel that had been hanging on the rail. He scrutinised himself in the mirror again; he appeared clean this time. He looked at his pale, skinny body and shivered. He slunk back downstairs to where his clothes lay on the table and got dressed quickly, trying not to look at Cyril. He tied up his tie and rootled around for his shoes; the one that Cyril had tripped over was by the sofa and he could see the brass paperweight lying next to it. He picked it up and put it in his pocket. He then rolled up the two bloody bayonets in the newspaper they were lying on and looked back to where Cyril's lifeless, bloody body lay. The whiteness of his skin contrasted with the bright red of the blood that was already cloying to a deep purple colour. He felt nothing. The body was not a person anymore.

He sat down in the armchair furthest away from where Cyril's body lay and shut his eyes. His head did not go round this time, the effect of the alcohol having worn off with the adrenaline that had been pumping round his body but he felt completely exhausted and sleep was overcoming him. For some time, his eyes kept shutting, the after-effects of the alcohol still taking its toll as he tried to clear his mind and think what he should do next. He was brought round by the rattle of the letter box as someone pushed something through, and the smell of vomit immediately brought back the enormity of what had happened as he stood up and looked at the lifeless body on the floor.

He went to the front door where a parish magazine lay on the carpet and he could see the road through the little window in the top. Once more he tried the handle but the door still wouldn't budge so he went into the dining room where through the net curtains he could see, in the distance, a woman pushing a pram. The clock he'd heard before struck once and when he looked at it, it was only half past three and yet it seemed an age since he had been in the Turk's Head.

In the kitchen, he couldn't find a key to the door so the window over the sink was the only way out. He undid the catch of the metal-framed window, climbed into the sink and jumped out, clinging tightly onto the bayonets wrapped in newspaper. He went to the car to find his mac and school bag, which were on the back seat, but as he was about to retrieve those he heard voices. Knowing he had to hide, he opened the back door of the car, threw the bayonets and paperweight onto the floor and jumped in crouching down and pulling his mac over his head. He began to shake as he heard footsteps on the gravel and then the driver's door clicked and was pulled open.

"Bit of luck," a voice whispered in a distinct London accent, "the keys are in it, come on, get in quick before the buggers catch up." The passenger door then opened and the car rocked as two people got in, slammed the doors and started the car.

"Which way are we going then? Towards the A1?" the driver asked as he put his foot on the accelerator and revved the car and ran his hand through his fair hair backwards over his head and down his neck. He was dressed in blue dungarees and a striped shirt but the only thing Christian could take in from where he hid was that he smelt of pigs. This smell rose into Christian's nostrils and, combined with the putrid stench from Cyril, one that Christian thought would stay with him forever, caught in his stomach and it was all he could do not to puke again.

"No, the other way. They will think we would go towards London so let's go the other way," said the passenger, who was dressed, and smelled, the same as the driver. "Are you sure you can drive this thing?"

"Course I can. I can drive anything, I've stolen enough in my time," he said, and put the car in reverse and looked over his shoulder.

"Wait a mo," the passenger put his hand on the driver's arm. "Look, that window's open, let's go and see what we can nick while we're here." So they both got out but as they made their way to the open window they heard the sound of the bell of a police car. They ducked down behind two dustbins as a young woman walked past pushing a pram. The police car came along the road accelerating, but then slowed down as it came level with the woman, its bell ringing loudly.

"Hey you!" one of the policemen shouted as he wound his window down.

"What do you mean *hey you*? Do you talk to everyone like that, and turn that bloody bell off! You'll wake the baby." The policeman raised his eyebrows and started again.

"Excuse me, modom," he said in a condescending tone instead. "We are looking for two escaped prisoners from the borstal. Have you seen anyone?"

"No, I ain't."

"Two boys, dressed in dungarees and striped shirts; they were on the farm."

"No, no one like that, and keep your voice down. I told you, you'll wake the baby." She peered into the pram and then pushed it on. "They'll be in London by now. I bet they've pinched a car and are on their way, they always do. You lot ain't quick enough off the mark for them; they always give you the slip," and she walked on.

The policeman wound his window up, put the bell on again and headed off towards the A1.

Christian raised his head and carefully looked through the window screen, then seeing the two get up from behind the dustbins, crouched down again.

"That was close!" said the driver, "Come on, let's 'ave a look in this window before we go, see if we can see anything worth nicking," and they made their way over cautiously to peer in the front sitting room window.

"Bloody hell, look at that! I must be going mad," said the driver who stepped back as his passenger peered in.

"Christ, it's a dead body. Look at all the blood; someone's done him in." They looked at each other in panic.

166

"What we going to do?"

"Get out of 'ere and quick, come on," he said and jumped into the driver's seat, started the car and backed it round as the passenger got in the other side, neither of them noticing Christian crouched in the back. They sped off down the hill and through Kimbolton before heading for Higham Ferrers.

The driver looked at his companion as they tore through Tilbrook. "We're going to have to get rid of this car. It must belong to that dead bloke and we'll get the blame."

"What you mean?"

"They will say we done him in."

"You're right. We will have to dump it and see if we can nick another one." They pulled into the next gateway, parked the car out of sight behind the hedge, got out and continued on foot.

When he heard them leave Christian raised his head and looked round and when he was sure they had gone he got out, went through the gateway and looked up and down the road, seeing the two borstal boys disappearing in the direction of Higham Ferrers. He waited until they were out of sight before putting the bayonets and paperweight into his school bag, his mac over his shoulder as he slowly walked in the same direction.

Two hundred yards further along the road, the tarmac became covered in mud from the tractors and trailers taking the potatoes from the fields, back to the farm. This felt familiar to Christian, and comforting. Seeking normality, he pushed the events of the last four hours into the depths of his mind, feeling that the only way he could cope was by temporarily erasing them, and he went into the gateway of the field to see what was happening. It was now late in the afternoon and most of the pickers had gone home; only the Gypsy family were left. Rows of bags filled with potatoes were strung out across the field and the gang picking them up were slowly making their way towards him. Peter waved to Christian and walked over to the gate to talk to him.

"What are you doing here, Christian? You're back from school early."

"You're not even *at* school."

"Well I was, but I get back at four so come and help. Do you want a job then? There's still plenty to pick up."

"I thought you would have finished the field by now," said Christian, looking out across the furrows. "What happened?"

"It's been raining if you hadn't noticed. This is the first full day we've done for nearly two weeks. Look at the mud." As if to prove his point, Peter started to scrape at the mud on his boots with a penknife. "Do you want a job then? We can do with all the pickers we can get, we're even going to pick on Saturday if it's fine."

"I could come on Saturday, I suppose. I don't want to miss too much school or I'll be in trouble. Miss Shaw won't write a note so I'd have to forge my own."

"Saturday then," said Peter.

"All right," agreed Christian, picking up his bag to leave.

"How did you get here then? You're a bit out of your way, aren't you?"

"I just hitched up to have a look," said Christian smoothly.

"In all your school kit?"

"This is my only kit. You know that, it's all right for you people with lots of money." Christian took off his glasses, put

168

them to his mouth and breathed on them, before cleaning them angrily on his shirt, he put them on again and glared at Peter. "Yeah, it's all right for you, but I don't have a posh sports jacket or another pair of trousers."

Another trailer drew into the field.

"Got to go now, Christian," said Peter hurriedly, pleased to be able to get away from this line of conversation. "See you on Saturday."

Christian nodded, watching as Peter hoisted himself onto the trailer to take him to the next row of sacks.

When Christian got back to the Hall the children were being sent into tea and no one noticed him sneak up to his room. He lived an independent life with Miss Shaw, who concentrated all her efforts on the forty or so five-to-thirteen-year-olds in her care, most of whom boarded at her school. Christian could not remember any other home and had been told that his parents were abroad. Miss Shaw fed him and gave him a room of his own, but he had little else. He gained a scholarship to a grammar school in Bedford and the bus there was free. His uniform came from the second-hand shop at the school and Miss Shaw paid all the bills for that. His room was small, with a single bed but he did have a desk with a lamp and a chest of drawers for his meagre selection of clothes. As he put his bag on the table, it fell from his hands with a bang because of the weight of the two bayonets and the brass paperweight. The loud noise brought everything that had happened flooding back into his consciousness with a flash. He wished it had been a dream but when he opened his eyes and looked in the bag the evidence of what he had done was only too clear to see. He squeezed his eyes shut and clenched his fists to his face. He opened them again, and tentatively peered in the bag once more. The contents finally confirming his worst fear that what had happened was no dream and he knew immediately he would have to get rid of the bayonets.

He sat heavily on the bed, opened his bag and took out the brass paperweight, tracing the contours with his fingers. He polished it on the blanket and looked at it again. It was nearly round, but the features of the sleeping cow had been carved exquisitely, the detail of the legs and hooves delicate and clear even after years of human contact. Christian sighed and took out the two bayonets. Blood had started to seep through the newspaper. He had to find a hiding place for them or dispose of them somehow. He thought of the garden, or the sheds, but someone would see him out there. He knew every inch of the house and decided that the tank attic was the place, nobody went in there. He put them back in his bag and crept out of his room. He could hear the chattering of the children below in the dining room as they had their tea; he had some time before anyone would come upstairs. He tiptoed up to the second floor and up the four stairs to the door of the tank attic, went in, snapped on the light and shut the door behind him. He pulled the newspaper from his bag and rolled it open; the two weapons lay there, thickly coated and sticky to the touch, the blood had dried much darker in colour now and looked sinister. He hunted around him to find a hiding place. All of a sudden there was a noise, and he jumped and swung round, but the sound had just come from the ballcock in the tank dropping as someone ran off some hot water. The two tanks nearly reached to meet the low ceiling of the room and the water hissed and splashed as the tank was filled. Gradually the noise subsided as the ballcock rose and soon all was quiet again. He looked round once more for somewhere to secrete the bayonets. There were footsteps on the landing. Christian listened, cocking his head to one side as a voice shouted down the stairs.

"Another half an hour until bath time, send them out in the garden for a bit."

It was Miss Shaw shouting to Miss Sykes from the top of the stairs of the first floor. He heard her take a step on the stairs towards the second floor. The voice came again.

"Drat. Someone has left a light on in the tank attic."

Christian froze. He could hear her footsteps nearing on the stairs. What was he to do? He grabbed the bayonets and looked desperately around the room again. Making a split decision he reached over the top of the tank and dropped the bayonets, with pieces of bloody newspaper still sticking to them, into the water, grabbed the rest of the newspaper and his bag and hid behind the door as the latch clicked and Miss Shaw opened the door. She peered in but as there was nothing out of place she turned the light out and went back down the stairs. As soon as she had gone, Christian returned to his room; he still had the blood-stained newspaper to dispose of but that would be easier, he could put it in the boiler, he often had to help put the coke in. He made his way downstairs, out of the back door into the yard and into the outhouse where the big coke-fired boiler stood. Carefully he opened the door and thrust the newspaper in, watching the stained pages blacken and catch light; after a few seconds the newspaper had burnt up. He grabbed the shovel from the door and threw some coke

171

into the boiler to cover up any potential remains of newspaper, closed the door and went out into the yard again. Miss Shaw was approaching from the garden.

"Christian, what are you doing in there?"

"I just put some coke on for you, Miss Shaw," said Christian, turning his back on her to walk away.

"With your school bag?"

"I just had it with me that's all,"

"What's that on your hands?"

Christian looked down; his hands were stained with the blood from the newspaper mixed with coke dust.

"It's…" he started, searching for something to say, "…it's just some dirt."

"Well, go and wash it off straight away," instructed Miss Shaw, before returning to the house.

Christian sighed, somewhat shaky after the encounter, and went to the scullery to wash his hands. The blood and dirt ran off his hands diluted to dirty shades of pink and brown in the water and disappeared down the plughole. He returned to his room and threw himself on the bed, once again picking up the brass paperweight and rubbing it on the blanket. He closed his eyes and started to drift off. Twenty minutes later the children were ushered upstairs for their baths. He could hear Miss Shaw chatting away to Miss Sykes on the landing.

"I'll surprise the boys tonight," said Miss Shaw.

"You always do," replied Miss Sykes with a sigh.

Miss Shaw separated the boys into two groups, taking the younger ones first as there were not enough baths for them to have one each.

"Clothes off!" she shouted. "Go and turn the taps on, I will be along directly, get in when you are ready."

She went to fetch a new box of soap from the storeroom. On her return to the bathroom, she found six small boys standing around the bath; they were all naked but were staring into the tub dubiously.

"Come on then," she chivvied. "Why haven't you got in?"

"We can't, Miss Shaw, look!" said one, pointing into the bath. Miss Shaw sighed and looked to where he pointed; the water was discoloured. Against the white of the bath it was clearly tinged the palest pink and on closer inspection tiny flecks of brown floated in the tub.

"What on earth?" she murmured. She stared at the bath water for a moment longer, before going to find Miss Sykes.

"Are your baths the same?" she asked on finding her assistant.

"You mean the dirty water?"

"Yes."

"What can it be?" asked Miss Sykes. "I've tried both taps, it's only coming from the hot ones, go and look downstairs in the kitchen."

Miss Sykes hurried off. A few moments later she came to the bottom of the stairs and shouted up.

"It's just the same here, what can it be?"

"I've no idea," said Miss Shaw. "But they can't bathe in it. I'll send Christian to fetch Jeff; he will sort it out."

She marched to Christian's room, entered without knocking and found him fast asleep.

"Christian," she said sharply, "Christian, wake up, boy, I want you to go and fetch Jeff, tell him there's something

173

wrong with the hot water. It's coming out pink, come on quickly now, or he will have gone to the pub."

Christian rose groggily and plodded downstairs and out into the street to find Jeff. Jeff was a plumber who worked in Raunds but in his spare time, and strictly for cash, he sorted out all the plumbing problems in the village. Christian knocked at the door, which stood slightly open.

"Who is it?" a voice shouted from inside.

"It's Christian."

"It's who?" yelled Jeff, coming to the door. He was short and fat with close cropped hair. He was in his vest and held a towel which he was pushing vigorously into one of his ears with his index finger. He looked at Christian suspiciously. "Wait a mo," he said, moving back and picking up his thick glasses from the draining board and putting them on. "Oh!" he said, "It's you, Christian, why didn't you say? What do you want then?"

"Miss Shaw sent me," explained Christian. "She says can you come and help, the hot water's gone all coloured."

"Well you tell 'er I ain't comin'. I'm going to play skittles," said Jeff firmly, looking at his watch. He paused and considered for a second. "I s'pose I could if she pays on the spot," he relented. "I could do with the money. What do you say's wrong, boy?" He peered at Christian.

"She said the water's coloured, the hot water."

"All right then, tell her I will be up in fifteen minutes, it must be something in the tank."

Jeff moved back into the house and closed the door. Christian stood motionless on the doorstep, his mouth agape, heart pounding in his chest. He turned and sprinted back to the

174

school, crept into the house, dodged past Miss Shaw's sitting room and shot straight up to the tank attic. He flicked on the light and crept up to the tank. He put his hand over the edge of the side of the tank and fumbled in the dark water for the two bayonets; it was no good. He could only fit his arm in up to the shoulder and even then his arm reached only halfway down the tank; it was too close to the ceiling. There was nothing he could do. He put off the light, shut the door and went down the stairs. Miss Shaw shouted to him from her room.

"Yes, Miss Shaw," replied Christian, going towards her.

"Well?"

"Well what?" said Christian with a frown.

"Did you see Jeff?" Christian stared at her for a moment, his mind on the bayonets and how he would ever get them out of the tank. Miss Shaw was still glaring at him.

"Oh yes. He's coming in, but you've got to pay him straight away."

"Drat that man."

She shook her head angrily and went down to the kitchen where Miss Sykes was waiting with the freshly arrived Jeff. Christian scurried in behind her.

"What's up then?" Jeff demanded of Miss Shaw.

"It's the hot water, it's discoloured and dirty."

"Let's have a look then," said Jeff with a shrug. He went to the sink and ran the hot tap; the water gushed out, again tinged pink.

"Looks like blood," said Jeff. "Must be something in the tank, in the attic, ain't it?"

"Yes," said Miss Shaw. "Show him the way, Christian."

175

Christian's eyes widened; he forced a smile to his lips and led the way up the stairs and into the small attic. He flicked the light on.

"Well bugger me," cursed Jeff. "We can't get at that one, it's too close to the ceiling."

He stood back and surveyed the tank.

"Perhaps I can get at the ballcock; we can see if it's comin' in like it."

He threaded both hands awkwardly over the top of the tank; he pushed the ballcock down with one hand and with the other he caught some of the water, then hurriedly pulled his hand back from the tank and examined what little water remained in the palm of his hand.

"That's all right," he said. "Come here, boy, you hold this ballcock up here and I'll go and let the water off; don't let it down till I say."

Christian put his arm over the top of the tank and held up the arm of the ballcock as Jeff went down and turned on all the taps he could find. Christian's arm began to ache because of the awkward angle but within three minutes the tank was empty. Jeff shouted to Christian to release the lever. Christian dropped the arm of the ball cock and listened to the tank fizzing full; he closed his eyes and wished that the problem would have resolved itself. He made his way downstairs to join Jeff who was standing by the sink of one of the bathrooms, the water splattering into it, crystal clear.

Chapter Ten
Investigation

On Saturday morning, Nimpy and Helen decided that they would go potato picking to earn some money. It was unusual to pick on a Saturday but due to the wet weather the harvest was not nearly complete and, as they were nearing the end of October, every fine day had to be taken advantage of. The two girls met at the junction of the road from Dean and the main road to Kimbolton. Helen, who had just passed Christian who was walking, was waiting for Nimpy to arrive. Five minutes later she rode up on her bike.

"Where have you been?" said Helen. "I've been here for ages."

Nimpy pulled on the brakes and skidded the back wheel round in a noisy arc. She got off the bike, slightly out of breath. "We've just had the police round our house," she explained.

"What? What have you been up to then?"

"We haven't been up to anything. But there's a car up in the gateway, look, you can see it from here." She pointed to the abandoned car.

"Who's is that then?"

"I don't know, and they wouldn't tell us. But it's been there two days now, I had a look in when I passed it yesterday, there's nothing in it, but the keys are still in the ignition." She lowered her voice dramatically. "Mum thinks there's something fishy about it."

"Where is your mum then?"

"She's up the tatter field already and they're comin' up to see her."

"Who are?"

"The police, stupid, they want to know if she saw anything."

A scuffling footfall behind the girls announced Christian's arrival, he looked his usual untidy self.

"Are you going tattering, Christian?" asked Nimpy.

"Yes, got to earn a bit of money. Are you going to give me a ride on the back?" He pointed hopefully to the back of Nimpy's bike.

"You'll never guess who's just bin to our house, Christian," said Nimpy, ignoring the question.

"No I won't. How could I guess something stupid like that?"

"The police. And *I* was interviewed about that car." She pointed again to the abandoned vehicle. The colour drained from Christian's face.

"What about it?" he said, as nonchalantly as he could manage. "What did you tell them?"

"I didn't tell them nothing, cos I don't know nothing, do I? But it's been there for two days. Mum said there was something fishy about it and they said they think the borstal boys stole it." Christian shrugged his shoulders as though he was disinterested.

"Are you going to give me a ride then?"

"Go on then, get on," said Nimpy, disappointed not to have ensnared her audience with her tale.

Christian put his bag down, tucked his trousers into his socks so as not to get them caught in the spokes and stood astride the carrier. He waited for Nimpy to start pedalling.

"Here, Christian, you stupid oaf," giggled Helen. "You've left your bag!" She bent down and picked up the bag to hand to him. "Blimey what've you got in here, it weighs a ton!"

"Just my dinner and a drink bottle," said Christian quickly, snatching the bag off Helen.

"You ain't got a lot of beer in there, have you?" asked Helen suspiciously.

"No, I haven't,"

"Hold on," instructed Nimpy, keen to stop the bickering, and she started to pedal.

The front wheel wobbled dangerously from side to side as she tried to get going without losing her balance with the added load on the back; but she was practised at taking passengers and it wasn't long before they arrived at the field where Peter was directing everyone as to where they were to pick.

"Are you all picking together?" he asked.

"I'm picking with Helen," said Nimpy. "Who are you going with, Christian?"

"I'm on my own," said Christian. "I don't want to pick in a three, it won't work."

"Where's Mum, Peter?" asked Helen. "I don't want to be anywhere near her."

"Don't worry," said Peter. "She's right at the other end of the field."

179

"Do you know, Peter," started Nimpy excitedly, "we had the police round this morning about the car over in that gateway, they want to know who left it there, they think the borstal boys had it; they're coming to see Mum in a bit to see if she knows."

"I saw it there on Thursday," said Peter. "Whose is it then? I saw a police car come along this morning, it must be what they were looking for."

Christian scuffed the ground with his shoe and said nothing, feigning indifference, but the knot in his stomach gnawed away at him. He waited until he was allocated a place to pick and hurried along to his row.

It was the first sunny day for two weeks and the soil dried quickly as the temperature rose. The potatoes glowed as they were spun out onto the surface and the rows of bags across the field began to grow. The gang picking up the bags trundled up and down the field, trying to keep up with clearing the rows. It was now nearly lunchtime and the team made their way past Christian but he had only filled six bags so they did not stop to collect them; moving instead to the other end of the row.

Christian collected his lunch bag and went to sit down, leaning back on one of the bags he had filled. He pulled out a hastily thrown together cheese sandwich and took a bite. From where he sat he could just see the blue light on top of a police car glinting in the midday sun; it was parked by Cyril's car in the gateway along the main road. He pulled his lunch bag nearer and thrust his hand into it; glancing around to check that no one was looking. He pulled out the brass paperweight and looked at it; he breathed onto the surface of it, rubbing it on his trousers and turning it round and round in his hand, examining its wonderful carving. He looked around again and quickly put the weight back in his bag; there were too many people around, so he continued to eat his sandwich.

An hour passed, the sun was high in the sky and warm and the two girls took their jumpers off and looked at their trail of filled bags.

"How many have we done now?" Nimpy asked.

Helen stood up and shut one eye, with her index finger she counted the bags, mouthing the numbers as she did so. "Twenty-five," she said, looking down the row to where Christian was picking. She shook her head. "He's only got six. Poor old Christian, he can't do it, can he? Just a born loser."

"He's always been like that. He may be able to do Latin and Greek but he has no practical common sense at all," said Nimpy, bending down again to fill her basket.

"Look," said Helen, pointing out towards the road.

The police car that had been at Cyril's car had turned around and now drove towards them, parking on the road verge near the entrance to the potato field. The two officers got out and strode into the field.

"Peter!" someone shouted, waving his arms to attract his attention.

Peter looked up as they pointed across to where the two policemen stood. He walked across the rows and approached the two men.

"You in charge here?" said the larger of the two men, taking his cap off and wiping his forehead with his handkerchief, before wiping round the inside of the brim of his cap. He

181

jammed his hat back onto his head and eyeballed Peter again. "Well?" he said, his tone surly and laced with aggression.

"No. My uncle John is but he's gone to get some more bags right now."

"What's your name then, boy?" said the policeman, pulling a notebook from his breast pocket.

"Peter." And the policeman licked the end of the pencil and opened the notebook.

"Peter what?"

"Peter Dunmore," said Peter, taken aback by the policeman's tone of voice.

The other policeman guffawed. He was shorter and fatter than his colleague and chewed gum like a cow chewing the cud, his jaw moving up and down and up and down.

"Farmer Dunmore, eh?" said the first officer with a smirk. "Well, Farmer Dunmore; what do you know about that car in the gateway of the road?"

"Nothing."

"Nothing," the policeman repeated. "Nothing? You saying you didn't even notice it?" He looked at Peter incredulously.

"Yes," said Peter slowly, trying to keep his cool. "I did notice it was there, it's been there since Thursday, but I don't know anything about it or who it belongs to."

The first policeman raised an eyebrow and scribbled in his book. "Thursday," he repeated, writing slowly and deliberately, not raising his eyes from his notebook. "Are you sure about that, Farmer Dunmore?"

"Yes," said Peter firmly, waiting patiently for another question.

The policeman stopped writing and scanned the field before glancing over to where Cyril's car stood.

"Now, Farmer Dunmore, wouldn't you say that it's easy to see the car in question from this field?"

"Yes."

"And, *Farmer Dunmore*, wouldn't you say that whoever left the car there could have been seen leaving the car from this field?" Peter looked at the car and back to the policeman.

"Well, yes, but not from everywhere in the field, it's too far from across there." He nodded to the other side of the field.

"Did you see who left that car?" asked the policeman angrily.

"No," said Peter patiently as the policeman scowled, licked his pencil and continued to write in his notebook.

"Now, Farmer Dunmore, were all these pickers in the field on Thursday when you say the car appeared?"

"Yes, most of them. Why?"

"I ask the questions, Farmer Dunmore, thank you." Peter said nothing, and the policeman looked across the field again.

"Is that a Gypsy's van over there?" he said suddenly, pointing to where Jim Barber's van was parked across the field by the hedge.

"Yes," said Peter. "He's a good man, he comes every year."

"Is that so," the policeman said, turning to his colleague with a sneer. "We're going to have to talk to all of them, don't you think, Gerald?"

"I think so, Bob," replied Gerald with a nasty smile.

"Let's have a cup of coffee first then," he said, turning his back on Peter and moving towards the entrance of the field where their car was parked. He turned back to Peter. "Do you have a Mrs Maddox over here, Farmer Dunmore?"

"Yes, she's over there," said Peter, pointing across the field.

All eyes in the field were fixed on the exchange between Peter and the two policemen, whispers as to what the men wanted and who was in trouble being exchanged along the rows.

"Are they the ones that came to your house, Nimpy?" asked Helen.

"Yes, I'm sure it's them."

At the other end of the row Christian watched intently, every muscle in his body attuned to the inevitable moment when the policemen discovered his involvement and came to arrest him. As the policemen turned to walk back to their car he breathed a sigh of relief and continued, somewhat shakily, to pick the potatoes.

Twenty minutes later, the pair returned, walking across the field to find Peter, the mud picking up on their boots as they plodded across the rows.

"Your field is makin' my boots muddy, Farmer Dunmore," said Bob with a frown, looking down at his boots. Peter said nothing. "Now we've been in touch with the inspector and he wants us to talk to everyone, all right? So no one's to leave the field unless we've spoken to them, except the tractor and trailer men, I suppose, they always come back, don't they?" Peter nodded.

"You start this side, Gerald, and I'll do the other side, all right? Then we'll move on to them Gypsies, save the best for last."

Gerald made a mock salute and moved over to Hugh, who was driving the hoover. Methodically, the pair made their way around the workers in the field, asking the same questions about the car. They could find no one who had seen anything. By the middle of the afternoon, they had only the five left to question; the two girls, Christian and Jim Barber and his wife. As Helen, Nimpy and Christian were by now at the far end of the field, Bob made a beeline for Jim.

"Name?" Bob said aggressively, planting himself in front of Jim, who stood up from filling his basket, a small frown across his brow. His black curly hair, tanned face and solitary gold earring clearly marked him out from the rest of the men in the field.

"Jim Barber."

"This your wife then?" asked Bob, pointing at Rosie who was picking next to him.

Rosie glanced up, she also had black hair, half covering a pair of large gold earrings. She wore a flowery dress which fell to half way down her calves, showing her tanned legs. She pulled up her socks as Jim spoke.

"Yes; this is Rosie."

"Address?"

"We ain't got no address. We live in a caravan."

"No fixed abode," sneered Bob, licking his pencil again and writing deliberately. "Where is this *caravan*, Mr Jim Barber?"

"Up the other end of the village behind a spinney."

"Right. Well, Mr Jim Barber, we will want to look you up in your caravan so you make sure you don't move it, see?"

"Why?"

"Don't you ask me why, sonny, I ask the questions. That van of yours, what's the number?" Jim told him. "When is it taxed till then?"

"November."

Bob raised an eyebrow. "We can 'ave a look in a mo, can't we?"

He beckoned over to Gerald who was making his way back from relieving himself behind the hedge.

"Petrol or diesel?" continued Bob, turning to Gerald with a smile. "I bet it's diesel, don't you, Gerald?"

"Diesel," said Jim, gritting his teeth.

"And what's the colour of the diesel in your tank, Mr Barber?" said Bob, with a wolfish grin.

"It's white. I always have white diesel."

"They your kids in the back of that van then?" asked Gerald, looking over to where three children were playing.

"Yes," said Rosie. "They're ours."

"Why ain't they at school then, missus?" snapped Bob.

"It's Saturday, ain't it?" snarled Rosie. "What other bloody stupid questions are you going to ask?" Her face was reddening rapidly and she raised a long finger which she pointed at Bob. "Persecution this is. It's always the same, we can't do nuffing right for you bloody lot. Persecution tha's what it is." She shook her head angrily and Bob was momentarily silenced. "Go on then. Ask us another stupid question." She pursed her lips and stared at Bob furiously. Bob looked at Gerald before turning back to the couple.

"Were you in the field on Thursday?" he asked, getting back to the questioning.

Rosie looked at Jim; they both seemed puzzled.

"I suppose we were, we've been in the field every day. Why?" asked Rosie.

"You see that car over there?" said Bob. The pair looked, but the vehicle was obscured by the hedge from where they stood.

"What car?" said Jim.

"There's a car in a gateway behind that hedge over there, have you seen it?"

"Yes," said Jim.

"Did you see who left it there?"

"No, but someone said the borstal boys stole it."

Bob finished scribbling in his notebook before looking up at the pair. It was a moment before he spoke. "We will be back again," he said quietly. "Make sure you don't move your van, see." The two policemen moved off.

"Who've we got left?" said Bob to Gerald.

"Just them kids over there," said Gerald, nodding at Nimpy, Helen and Christian.

Christian saw them coming. They were moving towards Nimpy and Helen first and he would have to do something with the paperweight before they got to him. He looked around him for a suitable hiding place and surreptitiously removed the object from his bag. The policemen were still some way off and could not see him properly. He put the weight on top of the potatoes in his basket and placed some more potatoes over the top of them. He moved as steadily as possible to a half-full sack and tipped the contents of his basket in. He peered into the sack; he couldn't make out the paperweight, it would be about the same size as the potatoes they were picking and nobody would be able to make it out in the gloom of the bag.

He looked up, watching the two policemen move towards Helen and Nimpy, before realising that he should carry on picking. He bent to refill his basket as the two men approached the girls.

"I'm seen you before, ain't I?" Gerald said to Nimpy.

"You came to our house this morning. Can you not remember?" Gerald looked at her carefully.

"Course," he said. "Your mum's Mrs Maddox, ain't she?"

"Yes."

"We don't need to question her then, do we, Bob?" said Gerald, with a touch of uncertainty. "What about this one?" He turned to Helen.

"Name?" he barked.

Helen proceeded to give Gerald her details.

"Were you here on Thursday?" asked Bob.

"No, I were at school."

"That's that then," said Gerald, satisfied. "We're done, Bob."

"No we ain't, Gerald, there's one old boy over there, look." The pair looked at Christian who was slowly stooping to pick up individual potatoes from the ground.

"I ain't walking all that way," said Gerald, waving his arm and shouting. "Oi, you, boy, come over here!"

Christian looked up as Gerald shouted again; he stood and started to walk towards the group.

"Come on then, boy, hurry up," shouted Gerald impatiently. He turned to Bob and muttered under his breath: "He looks a bit of a rum 'un, don't he?"

Bob shrugged as Christian came to stand in front of the policemen. He looked steadfastly at the ground.

"Don't worry, boy, we ain't gonna bite you," said Bob with a chuckle. "Name?"

Christian told him.

"Were you here last Thursday?"

"No."

"Where were you then?"

"At school."

Bob nodded and looked at Gerald. "That's it then, Bob, we're done?"

"We're done," agreed Bob, closing his notebook and moving in the direction of the car without a glance back at the three.

Christian exhaled slowly, watching the two men go.

"What was that all about?" he said impassively, turning to Helen and Nimpy who had returned to picking the potatoes.

"Mum says that the car is something to do with the murder," said Nimpy dramatically.

"What murder?" said Helen sharply.

"Mum said there was a chap murdered in Pertenhall on Thursday. They think that's his car, didn't you hear about it?"

"No," gasped Helen, unable to keep the excitement from her voice. "We didn't hear about that in Dean, did we, Christian?" She turned to him. Christian took his glasses off and blinked rapidly.

"No, I didn't hear anything," he said, looking down and vigorously cleaning his lenses.

"Are you all right, Christian? You look really pale," said Nimpy, before adding with a laugh, "well, paler than normal." Christian laughed weakly and said nothing.

"Look," said Helen kindly. "They've just picked up your bags, Christian, that's a little more money then, isn't it? Look, Peter's coming with your ticket book." She pointed and Christian swung round.

"They've what?" he asked, putting on his glasses and looking across the field, trying to remember where he had been picking. He saw the last of his bags being lifted onto the trailer, before it drove off across the field towards the farm. "Oh no!" he exclaimed, putting his hand to his forehead, a look of agony contorting his face.

"What's up?" said Nimpy with a frown. She looked at Helen who shrugged her shoulders.

"I've got to go," said Christian, setting off after the trailer that was now speeding away from them.

"Don't you want your ticket?" shouted Helen after him.

Christian did not hear. He quickened to a run, stumbling across the field after the trailer.

"What's up with him?" said Peter, arriving with the tickets.

"I don't know," said Nimpy. "He's been a bit funny this morning, but then he's always a bit funny, don't you think? Give me his ticket, Peter, he's got to come back for his bag and jacket. We're going to do a bit more, ain't we, Helen?" Helen nodded and the pair walked back to where they had left off.

Five minutes later Christian arrived out of breath at the farm. He looked desperately from one building to the other, finally locating the potato store. It was a large concrete-framed building, with high brick walls and an asbestos roof; he could see that it was already half filled with potatoes piled nearly to the eaves of the building. In the middle of the shed was an elevator which carried the potatoes to the top of the heap as they were tipped on at the bottom from the trailer. The trailer was already half empty; another sack was tipped out as the wooden slats of the elevator conveyed the potatoes away from the trailer and up onto the heap. The chap unloading looked quizzically at Christian, recognising him from the field.

"What are you doing here?" he asked curiously, dragging another bag forward.

Christian looked at him a little blankly, blinking up at the huge heap of potatoes. A second chap who looked after the elevator, was wheeling a barrow round from the back of the heap, and he parked it by the bottom of the elevator and glanced at Christian.

"What do you want then?" he demanded.

Christian continued to stare at the heap, saying nothing.

"Who's 'e then?" and the pair laughed. "Where's 'e escaped from?"

"What do you want then?" he tried again.

Christian in a daze looked around at them both, his expression a mixture of fright and concentration.

"I've lost something," he said quickly, looking back at the heap.

"Lost what?"

"A screw." Both men chuckled appreciatively.

"Have you tipped my bags?" Christian asked the man moving the bags.

"I don't know. How do I know which were your bags?"

"You picked them up last."

"They were at the back then, so I tipped them a long time ago," he said, dragging another bag forward. "What you lost?"

Christian scanned the pile of potatoes desperately, and said nothing.

The elevator was switched off as the last potatoes fell off the end onto the top of the heap. There was an eerie silence.

"What have you lost then?"

Christian looked at him. "Nothing much. But I put it in the bag and…" He faded out.

"Well I haven't seen nothing, 'ave you?" The other man shook his head and grinned.

"Not today," he said with a smirk, walking round to the pile of empty bags, which he threw on the trailer before climbing back on the tractor and starting it up to drive back towards the field.

"Can I go up there?" said Christian, pointing up the mountain of potatoes.

"What for? If your bags were on the trailer last whatever you lost is under a ton of spuds."

"But can I go up?" Christian asked again.

"You can. But there ain't no point…"

His words of advice were wasted. Christian had already started to climb up the potatoes, they rolled under his feet and as fast as tried to climb up he slid back down again.

"No, no, you stupid bugger. Go up here." He pointed to the elevator. "Walk up here," he shouted again, gesticulating furiously. "I'll stand on the bottom."

Christian scrambled up the slats to the top of the heap and looked around him. There was no sign of the brass paperweight. He walked with difficulty along the top of the pile, potatoes sliding under his feet, nothing. It had gone. The man was right, digging was going to be futile. He slid down the heap, thanked him and made his way back to the field.

"Ain't you going to do anymore?" Nimpy asked as Christian made his way back towards the girls and picked up his bag and jacket. Christian looked at her, but did not appear to have heard what she said. "Are you then?" she said again.

Christian blinked a couple of times. "Sorry. What did you say?"

"I said are you going to do anymore?"

Christian shook his head. "No. No, I think that I need to go back now."

He turned, slung his jacket and bag over his shoulder and moved slowly back towards the gate.

Chapter Eleven
Life at The Hall

The next day the police returned to Cyril's car and removed it, taking it to Bedford for examination. The police then called at every house on the road through Dean to see if anyone had seen anything untoward. They arrived at the Hall just as lunch was being served. Miss Shaw stood behind the table in the dining room, serving the meal to the children who stood waiting in a long line. PC Rawlins entered with another man who wasn't in uniform and approached Miss Shaw.

"Sorry to bother you, Miss Shaw," said Rawlins. "But this here is Detective Constable Drew and 'e wants to 'ave a word if that's all right." Miss Shaw looked over her glasses at the two men and sighed.

"No, that's not all right, Rawlins," she said sharply, continuing to dish out the food. "Can't you see I'm busy, you stupid man." PC Rawlins puffed his chest out a little and stood to his full height. "And don't you know it's Sunday, Rawlins?" continued Miss Shaw. "Not a day for questions, constable; a day of rest."

"Well I'm, erm, maybe DC Drew…" hesitated Rawlins, turning to the other officer helplessly. The other officer took a step forward.

"Madam," said Detective Constable Drew, lowering his voice, but talking forcefully, "we are investigating a murder and I would be obliged if you would answer some questions

I have immediately." He leaned forward purposely towards Miss Shaw, who shrank back a little but continued to meet his gaze.

"There's no need to take that sort of tone with me, my man. If you want to ask me some questions, the least you can do is be polite." She plonked a spoonful of mash on a plate and ushered the next pupil forward. "Christian!" she called suddenly. Christian had been sitting on a window seat, more or less out of sight. "Christian," repeated Miss Shaw, "come here and serve the food out, can you."

She stuck her large spoon into the pot of mashed potato and waited. Christian rose reluctantly; he was wearing his school uniform as usual. His grey jumper had a hole in the middle and the sleeves were too short, showing the dirty cuffs of his white shirt. The turn ups of his grey trousers were frayed at the back where they dragged along the ground and his black shoes were crusted with mud from the potato field.

"Come on, Christian, hurry up," chided Miss Shaw. She tutted at him. "Look at you, if I've told you to do your laces up once, I've told you a hundred times." She pointed at the potato, before thrusting the pot towards him, displeased with Christian's slowness. "And don't give them too much," she said fiercely. "There's got to be enough for us as well." She turned to the waiting detective. DC Drew looked at her and then over her shoulder to Christian.

"Oi," he said, raising his voice and staring at Christian. "Don't I know you, boy?" He walked round the table to look at Christian properly. "Where have I seen you before, boy?"

Christian did not look at him. "In the potato field."

"In the where? Speak up, boy, don't mumble."

"In the potato field," repeated Christian, louder this time.

"'E ain't a suspect surely, Gerald, it must be them borstal boys," said PC Rawlins. "Look at 'im, 'e couldn't knock the skin off a rice pudding." DC Drew said nothing, but pulled out his notebook.

"Name?" he demanded, flicking through the pages without looking at Christian, who shifted from foot to foot uncomfortably but said nothing. "Name?" he repeated loudly, leaning in towards Christian to hiss. "Are you deaf, boy?" Christian wilted under the DC's gaze, licking his lips nervously. "Well?" said Gerald, staring at Christian.

"Christian."

"Christian what?"

"Thompson."

The pages of the notebook continued to flick over. "Ah," he said, finding his notes from the day before. "You were at school it says 'ere." He looked at Christian. "Well, have you got a tongue in your head, boy? You were at school last Thursday, yes?"

"Yes."

DC Drew nodded and walked back to Miss Shaw.

"Name?" he said, turning to a fresh page in his notebook.

Miss Shaw grudgingly prepared herself to answer Gerald's questions.

That evening the whole gang waited outside the door of what they all now called *The Club*. The murder was the only topic of conversation as they waited for Miss Shaw to come and unlock the door.

"Did they question you then, Simon?" Sandra asked, taking a small puff of his cigarette.

"No," said Simon. "But they came to our house to get the warrants signed. Dad's a JP, you know."

"A what?"

"A JP. Don't you know what a JP is?"

"Course I do," snapped Sandra, saved from having to admit her ignorance by the arrival of Miss Shaw.

"Did you get questioned, Miss Shaw, by the police, I mean?" said Nimpy, excited as Miss Shaw unlocked the door.

"Yes, my dear, as did everyone else as far as I can understand," said Miss Shaw pointedly. "But I had nothing to tell them I'm afraid. Poor man, it all sounds dreadful, stabbed to death. They said they were looking for two borstal boys. We are thinking of him in our prayers. Now come along, get sat down, all of you."

The group sat and gradually the talking subsided for Miss Shaw to say her prayers. When she had finished she rose to leave, suddenly turning back before she left the room. "Ah," she said, "I need a tall boy to give me a hand." She scoured the room, her gaze lighting on Peter. "Peter, you will do. The ballcock in the tank in the roof is stuck and it's dripping. It just needs a wiggle and it will stop." Christian froze and looked up at Miss Shaw.

"But, Miss Shaw," he said, in surprise, "I'll do it, I've done it before; I always do those jobs around here. I'll go." He stood up ready to follow her.

"No, no, Christian," said Miss Shaw with an impatient wave of her hand. "I don't want you, you're not as... practical with your hands as Peter. Follow me, Peter." Peter shrugged and followed Miss Shaw into the big house and up to the first floor, then up the next lot of stairs to the second. He could hear the chattering of the children as they prepared to get ready for bed as Miss Shaw led the way up the last four steps to the attic where the tanks stood. Following her, Peter could see her thick stockings rippling down her legs; bunching up as they reached her shoes. She stopped at the door. Standing behind her, Peter could smell a mixture of moth balls and sweat exuding from her body as she panted, out of breath from climbing the stairs.

In the attic, dust and cobwebs covered every surface. The two tanks stood next to each other, one large one with a smaller one at the end of the cramped room standing on a wooden platform. Miss Shaw dragged a beer crate up to the larger tank.

"Stand on this, Peter. It will make it easier to reach." She pointed to the tank. "You know what to do, do you?"

"Yes, it just wants pressing down and readjusting. That should do it, we've got one like it at home."

The tanks were not that high and Peter could reach the ballcock easily; only the proximity of the ceiling, as Christian had found, made it a little awkward.

"Don't fall, Peter, let me hold you," said Miss Shaw, holding onto Peter's legs just above his knees.

"There's no need, Miss Shaw. I won't fall, I can reach easily from here." He pushed the ball at the end of the lever down. The water rushed in for a moment and he then let it go; the ball rose again and the water stopped coming in. "Just wait and see if it stops completely," he said. "It might need some

198

grease on it. Vaseline is good but we would have to take it all apart."

He stood, waiting to see if the tap stopped dripping. He could smell the moth balls again and the sweat as Miss Shaw stubbornly gripped his legs. His whole body tensed; he looked down at Miss Shaw over his shoulder, but could only see the top of her head as she pulled him closer to her. Peter whipped round violently, the speed of his reaction threw Miss Shaw and she stumbled back, losing her footing as she did so, falling backwards onto the floor. Her skirt lifted, revealing white skin above her stockings as the heels of her shoes hit the floor. She rolled over and picked herself up, brushing the dust from her skirt and jumper as she did so. The tight bun which her hair was rolled into had come loose and hair hung down one side of her head. Her permanent grey face unusually flushed.

"Oh dear, Peter!" she blustered. "I don't know what happened there." She looked up at him innocently. "Has the water stopped?"

Peter eyed her warily before turning quickly to check. "Yes, it's fine now," he said, turning and brushing a cobweb from his hair without looking at her. "I'll go back then," he said, leaping off the beer crate and carefully skirting Miss Shaw to dart out the door and back down to the club. As he left the school and approached the club door he could see a couple clamped together like a limpet to a rock. Peter could see the boy sliding his hand under the girl's jumper. The girl leaned back from him and firmly removed the hand. Out of the shadows ten metres from the door emerged Christian, his hands in his pockets and the collar of his jacket turned up to keep the wind from his neck.

"Peter, psssst," hissed Christian, trying to attract Peter's attention without disturbing the kissing couple.

"What are you doing out here, Christian?" Peter whispered as they both stepped back into the shadows and watched. The boy's hand crept under the jumper again, and this time she did nothing.

"Have you got a fag, Peter?" Peter patted the pockets of his jacket as a loud shout erupted from the club door.

"Time's up!" they heard.

The couple broke off their embrace, as the girl pulled her jumper down and patted her hair into place. She opened the door and stepped down into the club where a cheer erupted from inside.

"Shut the door!" someone shouted and the door closed behind her.

In the disappearing light from the club room Peter and Christian made out Tookey's outline.

"Tookey!" Peter hissed. Tookey turned round, trying to make out where the sound was coming from. "Over here."

"Just a mo, it's my turn!" said Tookey, tapping on the door five times.

Everything was quiet on the other side of the door as numbers were drawn. Tookey walked over to where Peter and Christian were standing.

"What do you want then?" he said. "What are you doing out here?" He grinned. "Oh I know, Peter. I bet you've been doing Postman's Knock with Miss Shaw." He laughed and pointed at Peter, who looked away, embarrassed. "Look, Christian, I'm right, he's going red," Tookey crowed.

"Shut up, you bugger," said Peter.

"Keep your hair on, keep your hair on," soothed Tookey. "What's she like then, did you get your hand up her jumper?" Peter reddened further and looked at the ground.

"Have you got a fag, Tookey? We're out," he asked, desperate to change the subject.

"No. I've only got one left and I'm not giving you it." At that moment there was a cheer from inside as number five was drawn. "I've got to go. And don't you buggers stand there and watch, all right!"

The door latch clicked and Nimpy climbed the last step out into the cold. The door shut and the two of them looked at each other. After a moment, Tookey advanced towards her, but Nimpy pushed him back.

"Tookey, have you got any fags? I'm out," she said coyly.

"Yes, I've got two."

"Can I have one for Ann?"

"That will be my last one."

"Well go to the pub and get some then," said Nimpy with a petulant shrug. She watched him curiously.

"It's closed."

"No, it's not; they just open later on a Sunday."

"We'll go," said Peter, stepping out from the shadows with Christian.

"You've been spying on us, you sods," gasped Nimpy indignantly.

"No, we haven't. Anyway there was nothing to spy on."

"Nimpy, do you know who Peter was playing Postman's Knock with?" interrupted Tookey eagerly. He laughed and winked at Christian, who managed a weak chuckle.

"No, who?"

201

"Miss Shaw! Up in the attic, what's more." Nimpy hooted with laughter, as Peter grimaced and tried to smile.

"Time's up!" came the shout from inside the club.

"I've got to go back in," said Tookey. "Just you get me ten fags and I'll pay you back later." He went back into the room, leaving Nimpy and the boys outside.

"We're going then," Peter said.

"Get me ten as well, can you?" called Nimpy after them as the two walked off. As soon as they were out of earshot Christian turned to Peter.

"Did you get the ballcock fixed? In the attic, I mean?"

"Yes. Just gave it a wiggle and it stopped. I bet it needs a new washer, they do that, it's just the same at home. She'll have to get Jeff to do that though." They walked on up the street as the pub came into view, one small light shining weakly over the sign.

"Peter, did you see anything in the tank? I mean, anything that might have caused all the trouble?" asked Christian, looking at him apprehensively.

"What do you mean? The tank was full of water, that's all. You can't see into that tank, it's too close to the ceiling."

"So you didn't see anything?"

"No I told you, didn't I?" said Peter absently, looking at the coins in his hand. "Who's going in then?"

"You are."

"Why me? I always have to do it!"

"Simple, you look older than me; you *are* older than me. They never believe me when I tell them I'm eighteen." Peter sighed and nipped into the pub, returning a few minutes later with three packets of ten cigarettes.

"There, what did I say? It's easy for you, they wouldn't have given me them, even though I am eighteen." He sniffed. "Can I have one then?"

"Why didn't you get your own?"

"Because I haven't got any money and don't ask me why, I just haven't, so there. It's all right for *you*, your dad's got plenty of it. I ain't got a dad to give me money."

Peter opened his mouth to reply, but decided against it. There was silence as he opened one of the packets and offered one to Christian. "You don't usually smoke."

"I know, but sometimes I like one."

They lit the cigarettes and started to walk back. Christian inhaled and immediately started coughing; Peter looked at him, as Christian blushed and cast his eyes down, before resorting to sucking in the smoke and blowing it straight back out again. They walked on a little further, finally reaching the wooden seat close to the entrance of the Hall, where they sat to finish their cigarettes. Christian turned to Peter.

"Peter, what do homos do?"

"What?"

"Homos? You know what they are, don't you?" Peter frowned and shook his head, nonplussed. "Homosexuals, you know."

Peter looked nervously at the cigarette in his hand and appeared to examine it carefully. "I suppose I do know what they are but… Do *you* know what they do then?"

Christian threw the end of his cigarette on the ground, crushing it under his shoe. "No, I thought you would know, do you?"

Peter looked around him, trying to avoid Christian's gaze at the same time as trying to think of something to say that would not betray his ignorance. He could think of nothing. "No, I don't know, what do they do then?" Christian examined the dog-end on the ground.

"I don't know. That's why I asked you." There was silence.

"Why do you want to know then? Are you going to be one?" Christian frowned.

"I was just thinking about it, that's all," he shrugged, rising and making his way back towards the club room. Peter followed him. When they got back to the club there was nobody outside, so they both went into the room.

"Fags at last," said Nimpy. "Did you get me some then?"

Peter searched the pockets of his jacket for the other cigarettes as Christian slipped past him and sat down on one of the benches. He turned sideways and put his arm round his legs, pulling his knees up and resting his chin on them. He sighed heavily and gazed off into the distance.

"Money?" said Peter, handing the cigarettes to Nimpy.

"I haven't got any, you'll have to come along home and get it on the way back." Peter sat down next to Christian, who fidgeted uncomfortably.

"Peter, you are sure that there was nothing in the tank in the attic, aren't you?"

"You keep on going on, Christian. I told you before, you can't see into the tank, even if you wanted to. There was only enough room to get to the ballcock." Christian frowned as Miss Shaw opened the door.

"Come on then, sit down everyone; we will have a prayer."

Those that had not already left sat down and bowed their heads as Miss Shaw said a short prayer then ushered everyone out the door. Peter and Nimpy cycled together, Nimpy in the lead as she had a light on her bike. Suddenly she stopped her bike and turned to Peter and asked, "Peter, do you know what homos do?"

Chapter Twelve
Prejudice

The next day, Monday, PC Rawlins had been instructed by Headquarters to meet with the CID officers at the site where Cyril's car was found to search for the murder weapon; and at ten o'clock sharp he arrived. He waited for twenty minutes before a car arrived with the two others, headed by Gerald Drew.

"What are we looking for then, Gerald?" PC Rawlins asked cheerily. "And more's the point, where are we going to look? When we find them borstal boys all will be clear."

"Well that's where, PC 49, you may be wrong. If we find the borstal boys the water will only get muddier." Gerald took the cork out of his flask and poured steaming coffee into the cup. "It's like this. Missing from the house are two bayonets, that's according to his mother, the deceased's mother, I mean. She says there's a brass paperweight gone too." He took a packet of cigarettes from his pocket and lit one. "It says in this 'ere report, that 'e were hit on the head with something hard and he died from stab wounds; so I think we can assume that the three missing items were used as the murder weapons. However, it also says 'ere that time of death is between two and two-thirty and the borstal boys escaped at three-thirty, so put that in your pipe and smoke it, PC 49."

"It must be a mistake; they must have done it."

"Well our fingerprint man can find no prints of the borstal boys in the house at all; not one, not one."

"So," said Rawlins, "they could have wiped the place clean."

"But there are plenty of other prints and one in particular in the car and all over the house, including the bathroom."

"So?"

"So, PC 49, there is a third party involved here, in my professional opinion, yes a third party indeed."

"Well, there's no one lurking round here, I've looked. So where do we go next?"

"Well, it's like this. I've been told to search the roadsides all the way to Dean that way and Hargrave that way." He pointed his arms in opposite directions.

"That'll take forever with only three of us," complained Rawlins.

"Well, it's like this. We're not going to do that for the moment; I'm going to use my initiative, they always tell us that, Bob, don't they?"

"They do," agreed Bob.

"What we're going to do is to go back to that potato field we were in on Saturday."

"We're not going to search that, are we?" said Bob.

"No. We're going to do something much more positive." He looked from one to the other.

"We're going to interview that gypo again." He took a long drag on his cigarette, before continuing. "And we are going to search his caravan." He stood to his full height and nodded towards the field.

"Good idea," said Bob. "Gypsies are trouble, well some of them are."

"You can't search his van without a warrant," Rawlins said. "And you've not been told to do it, have you, Gerald?"

"I know I haven't. But do you have a better idea? I suppose you want to spend the whole day going up and down the road when we could solve this case in a much simpler manner."

"But he had nothing to do with the murder, he was here picking tatters, we know that." Rawlins coloured. "No, Dunmore's wouldn't have them in the field if they weren't all right."

"No gypos are all right, PC Rawlins," said Gerald with a sneer. "They're all crooks in my book, don't you agree, Bob?" Bob merely smiled.

"Well, what about a warrant?" Rawlins protested again.

"Don't need one, he don't live in a dwelling, he's of no fixed abode, so we can search it as much as we like."

Rawlins shook his head in despair. "If you say so, Gerald."

"I do say so, Constable Rawlins."

"So do we all have to come?" said Rawlins hopefully.

"Bloody 'ell," exploded Gerald. "You never stop, do you? Well, you go and search the bloody verge then. We'll go and nick the gypos. Will that be all right for you, Constable Rawlins *sir*?" he added with a sneer. He turned his back on Rawlins and beckoned to Bob. "Come on, Bob, I'm looking forward to nicking this one, he ain't gonna stand a chance."

The two policemen climbed into the car and drove off to the potato field to find Jim, leaving Rawlins standing by the side of the road.

At the field, Gerald parked the car on the verge and went in through the gate; the gang had moved quite a way across, having cleared all the potatoes from the area around the gate.

"Where is he then?" Gerald demanded, looking up and down the rows where the pickers were bent over their baskets, the rows of bags extending behind them. In the distance up against the hedge was an old pickup truck with two small children playing in the back.

"There's his van," said Bob, pointing. "Over there, look."

"We ain't goin' to walk all that way," said Gerald. "Go and fetch the car, Bob. If he got round there so can we." He took his cap off and smoothed down his short hair. Bob looked doubtful. "Go on then, get it," insisted Gerald. "We can go round the headland, I can see where he's picking right over there, look." He pointed across the field.

"If you're sure. I'm not sure we're doing the right thing, Gerald, he had nothing to do with the murder, we know that, so what are we arresting him for?"

"Go on, bugger off and get it like I said, for God's sake." Bob went back to the car and drove it along the headland to where Gerald stood.

"There I told you it would be easy," said Gerald. "It's nice and dry along here."

He climbed into the car and drove slowly towards the pickup truck; apart from it being a bit bumpy they easily got to the end of the row that Jim was working with his wife. Walking down the row they passed Joyce and Nell, sitting on some bags, having a sandwich.

"Look, it's the Plod," said Nell with a giggle.

209

Gerald scowled and carried on walking. "That's enough from you, missus."

"No need to be like that."

"You got it wrong, Nell," said Joyce. "It's Dixon of Dock Green, didn't you recognise him?" She laughed. Gerald looked round again.

"Shut it, I said. Just shut up, you old bag." He turned and marched on. Joyce and Nell looked round open-mouthed to the other pickers within their area who had been watching this exchange, many of them laughing.

The two policemen approached Jim just as he was picking up a new bag to fill. As he went to lift the empty sack, Gerald put his foot on it and the bag pulled tight. Jim stood up straight and looked at Gerald.

"Not you again," he muttered. "What 'ave I done this time?"

"You bugger," said Jim's wife quietly. She stood up, her skirt swinging round her calves as she turned and took two steps towards Gerald. "You never stop, do you? You just never stop, you come here and blame every little thing on us, it's unfair." Her eyes fixed him with a penetrating stare, her black curly hair shining in the sunlight.

"Shut up, will you, missus, I ain't said nothing yet, 'ave I?"

"You're going to though, I know your type." She stood back a pace and waited as Gerald pulled out his pocket book and licked the end of the pencil.

"Name?" he demanded, writing the date at the top of the page. Jim said nothing, but looked at his wife. "Name!" bellowed Gerald, eyeballing Jim.

"Jim Barber. But then you know that, don't you?"

"I'll do the talking," barked Gerald, leaning menacingly towards Jim. "That your van over there?" said Gerald, nodding towards the headland where the two children were still playing in the pickup.

"What if it is?"

"Don't you take that tone with me, sonny, or you'll be in real trouble," warned Gerald. He turned to Bob. "Go and 'ave a look in it, Bob, see what's in the back," he ordered, turning back to Jim. "Them your children then?" he said, looking first at Jim then to his wife.

"What if they are?" she snapped.

"Why ain't they at school?" he said with a cold smile. "It's Monday morning if I'm not mistaken. All the other kids around here are at school, ain't they?"

"They're sick," said Rosie curtly, standing up to her full height and pursing her lips. She stared at Gerald.

"They don't look very sick to me. Who says that they are?"

"The bloody doctor does," she said, pointing angrily at Gerald. "You go and ask 'im then, go on, ask him. You ain't got anyfing else to do. They got mumps and the doctor said not to send them to school. I'll go and fetch 'em and you can see." She turned to shout at the two children.

"No, no," said Gerald hastily, but it was too late.

The two children were already climbing down from the truck and they then tore across the field to their mother.

"That's enough then," said Gerald sharply and, keen to keep the kids away, he took two quick steps backwards.

"There's no need to be like that," said Rosie angrily. She ran her hand through the taller one's hair. "They're good kids,

211

ain't they, Jim?" she crooned, smiling down at the shorter one. "'Cept their faces are a bit swollen, ain't they?"

"I can see that," said Gerald, a hint of panic lacing his voice. "Just keep them away." Rosie frowned. Suddenly a small smile spread across her face.

"You ain't had mumps, 'ave you, that's the problem, ain't it, you 'aven't, 'ave you?" Gerald glared at her angrily. "Mumps can be nasty for policemen of a certain age; don't you fink, Jim?"

"You're right, Rosie," said Jim. "Very nasty."

"That's enough of that then," said Gerald, taking another step backwards. "Get these kids out of here."

He raised his arm as though he might strike the children and the pair scuttled back to their mother, hanging onto her skirt.

"Jim Barber," said Gerald aggressively, "I'm now going to search your caravan and if I find anything, and I mean *anything* so much as a hair out of place, you will be in a cell in Bedford within the hour."

"You ain't doin' no such thing," said Rosie before Jim could reply.

"I can and I will," said Gerald.

"You ain't got no warrant."

"I don't need one. You ain't got no address to send it to, you've no fixed abode, don't you remember." He smiled nastily at Rosie.

"Don't you let them, Jim," said Rosie angrily. "Just don't you let them, he'll plant something, I know he will. You go with him, Jim."

"I will have to come with you," shrugged Jim.

"What do you mean?" said Gerald.

"I'm coming in the car with you, if you're goin' to search my van, how else are you goin' to get in?" Gerald looked dubiously at Jim's dirty boots and then at his clean car.

"They ain't *that* dirty," scoffed Jim.

"Go on then, get in," said Gerald grudgingly. The three men climbed into the car and made their way slowly round the headland of the field.

"I wouldn't run over that heap of bags if I were you," said Jim, peering out over Gerald's shoulder as he guided the car around various obstacles.

"What bags?"

"The empty ones there, look."

"That won't hurt," said Gerald, ignoring Jim and driving straight over the bags.

There was a flapping and banging noise, which increased in speed and volume rapidly. The car stalled and came to an abrupt halt, throwing Jim against the back of Gerald's seat. Jim put a hand to his mouth; a small trickle of blood ran from under his fingers, his large front teeth having bitten into the soft flesh of his lip.

"What the bloody hell's that?" asked Gerald, looking at Bob and then back to the car bonnet.

"It's them bags," mumbled Jim, fumbling for a handkerchief to staunch the flow of blood.

"What do you mean, bags?" demanded Gerald, turning to address Jim as the blood dripped from his lip.

"The bags got wrapped round the prop shaft and ceased it," explained Jim. "I told you not to drive over 'em, didn't I?"

213

"Don't you tell me what to do," snarled Gerald. "Get out and do something."

"I ain't doing nothing, *you* do it, you ran over them, I'm a prisoner as far as I can see, I ain't movin'." Gerald slammed a fist into the steering wheel and looked out across the field.

"Bob?"

"Yes, Gerald."

"Who's that just come in the gate in uniform?"

"Looks like the inspector," said Bob.

"What the bloody hell's he doing here?" cursed Gerald, as the inspector made his way the short distance across to where the car was stranded. Gerald cursed again and wound down his window, fixing a smile to his face.

"Well, Drew, what are you doing in here, I thought the order was to search the roadside verge for the murder weapon?" said the inspector calmly.

"Yes, Inspector King, sir, it was," agreed Gerald. "But we have a suspect in the car, sir."

"Who's that then?" said Inspector King, bending down to look over the driver's seat to where Jim was sitting in the back, a red handkerchief clasped to his lip. "Who's this then?"

"He's Jim Barber sir."

Inspector King put his hands on his hips, took a deep breath and looked up at the sky.

"Drew, I don't know how many times you have been told that this intolerance towards the, er, travelling folk," he smiled apologetically at Jim, "is baseless and damaging to the image of our establishment. Your obsession is grating; you have been warned before." He looked back at Jim and frowned. "Why did you hit him?" said King crossly.

214

Gerald spun round to look at Jim, the handkerchief proving an ineffective barrier for the volume of blood.

"I didn't hit him," stammered Gerald.

"Well, why's he bleeding then?"

"He cut his lip when we stopped suddenly."

"Well, can't you drive, man?" Inspector King exclaimed as, his face reddening, he took his cap off and glared at Gerald.

"Well it's like this, sir," said Gerald desperately, "we stalled."

"And why did you stall, man?"

"I think something got wrapped round the prop shaft, a bag, I think, sir." The inspector put his hand to his forehead and turned, then he took a few steps away before returning to stand in front of Gerald. "And why did you arrest this man, Drew?"

"We didn't arrest him, sir," insisted Gerald. "We are taking him to search his caravan."

"And what are you searching his caravan for, Drew?"

"For the murder weapon, them bayonets you said about that we've to find."

"And why should this man have them?" asked the inspector, his expression hardening.

"Well he's a gypo, ain't he? It stands to reason, don't it?" said Gerald, a touch uncertainly. A small crowd had now gathered around the car, all listening eagerly to what was going on.

"He didn't do no murder," said Nell, uninvited. "Or he didn't do it last Thursday; 'e were here all the time, weren't he, Joyce?" She turned to her friend.

215

"Course 'e were," said Joyce. "There ain't no time to go and do a murder if you're tatter picking." She grinned and took a sandwich from a paper bag, taking a large bite out of it before starting to chew noisily.

"So why are you holding this man, Drew?" asked the inspector. "Did you check for an alibi? Presumably you have questioned these ladies already, did they not provide him with an alibi on your first round of interviews?" Gerald reddened and said nothing.

"Did you 'ear that, Nell, he called us ladies?" giggled Joyce through a mouthful of sandwich.

"Quite la-di-da, aren't we, Joyce?" agreed Nell. "Just like Mrs Dene; she likes Gypsies, don't she, Joyce?"

"You mean Mrs Verity Dene?" Inspector King interrupted.

"Yeah, she lives up the road in Dean, not far from Joyce's, she a friend of yours then?"

"Well, not quite, but she's a JP and I know her view of Gypsies," said Inspector King. He turned to Gerald. "Release that man immediately, Drew, and get back to searching the verges as you were told to." Gerald didn't reply, an insolent expression on his face. He looked away from the inspector and then back again.

"You want me to let him go then?"

"Did you not hear what I said, you stupid man?" snarled Inspector King, his face beetroot red. He pointed at Jim. "Let that man go and return to your duties," he bellowed. "Do I make myself clear?"

"Yes, sir. What about the car then?"

"What about it?"

"It won't go."

"Well, I would fix it if I were you and quickly, before I really lose my temper. You will be back on the beat, Drew, if you don't pull yourself together. Do I make myself clear?"

"Yes, sir."

Chapter Thirteen
A Leak

The springs of the bed squeaked as Christian sat down to count his money. It had a black metal frame, larger at the head end, with a hair mattress over the woven spring base. The grey sheets and blankets had been roughly pulled up and the flowery patterned eiderdown had been thrown over the top. Feathers were coming out of it and as Christian sat down he could feel the prickles of the fine quills sticking through the thin fabric that held them in. A single bulb hanging on a wire from the ceiling lit the room. To one side of the bed was a table on which were strewn his school bag, books, comics, pens, pencils and some empty shotgun cartridges. The table held one small drawer in the middle from which he had taken a Player's Gold Leaf tobacco tin which held his money.

He tipped the cash onto the bed and stood and emptied his pockets, separating the money from his penknife, a dirty handkerchief and a small glass bottle with a screw top which he shook before he put it down. The pills inside rattled and he opened the lid and looked in at the contents to assess how many pills lurked inside. He then counted the money left over from what he had earned potato picking; two pounds, three shillings, seven pence and a half-penny. He put the money back in the tin and placed it back in the drawer.

For the last ten days he had been working delivering Christmas post but he would not be paid for this until the week after Christmas, so funds were now light. He picked up the small glass bottle again and opened the top, tipping the contents into his grubby hand. The pills were blue, triangular and a little bigger than aspirin; he counted them, there were nine. He cupped his hand and carefully poured the pills back into the bottle, before screwing the top back on.

The room was freezing and he rubbed his hands together to keep warm. In the opposite corner to the bed was a small chest of drawers which held the few clothes Christian possessed, and on the top stood an old oil lamp with a glass reservoir which held the oil. Christian stood up and fetched the lamp, taking off the glass chimney and adjusting the two wicks. Next to the lamp sat a box of matches; he slid them open and lit the lamp. The flame danced up yellow and bright, and as he put the chimney back, it stopped flickering and burnt with a constant orange glow. He placed the lamp on the desk and held his hands over the top, rubbing them together once more until the numbness left his fingers. Perching next to the lamp, he leafed through the comics to find one that he had not read. The desk was chaotic, comics were mixed with half-written essays, books of log tables, Thucydides *History of the Peloponnesian War* and a large volume of the complete works of Plato. Methodically, he turned over the books and rearranged them neatly. Underneath all this and to one side was a carefully folded edition of the *Beds Times*, the local newspaper. The headline on the front of the paper read:

"*Local Man Murdered in Horrific Attack.*"

Christian lifted it to find any more scraps left on the table, but it was the bottom of the pile. He put it back on the desk and covered it with the tome of Plato. Eventually he found the comic he wanted and flicked it onto the bed. He took his school mackintosh which hung on the back of the door, put it on and threw himself on the bed, arranging himself in a comfortable position as the bedsprings squeaked in protest. He laid his head back on the pillow and stretched his arms out in front of him in an attempt to read the comic, but the little light from the single bulb was directly above his head and shone into his eyes. He sat up and took his shoes off, pulling the eiderdown up over his feet and leaning back against the wall, already stained with a greasy grey patch where his head had rested many times before. The comics, like the blue pills, he had bought from an American serviceman whom he had met in Bedford. Floyd Mullhaus Junior was a little older than Christian and worked as a radio operator at Chicksands, a US listening facility south of Bedford. He could get all the things that Christian couldn't; and the horror comic series were his favourite. Floyd, like Christian, had been raised away from his family and had joined the military as he had no real home.

It was now nearly five o'clock and Christian could hear the children chattering in the dining hall, awaiting their tea. Some of the boarders did not go home for Christmas as their parents were abroad or simply did not want them at home. There was a noise from the attic; the tank was filling as someone ran some hot water off downstairs. Christian jumped, his heart racing, the memories of the murder weeks ago flooding back. He shivered and grabbed the eiderdown closer to him, as the colour drained from his face and he started to sweat. He shut his eyes tight and clenched his fists, imagining the now bloodless bayonets sitting ominously in the tank above his head. His thoughts flickered to the brass paperweight; it was in the heap of potatoes now, there was no hope of finding that. He had been back up to see Peter to ask if there was any chance of finding a keepsake that he had accidentally dropped, but the whole heap was now covered in bales to keep the frost out and he had no idea where in the barn the paper-weight might be. He started to shiver so he pulled the eider-down over his head, willing the images of Cyril's pale naked body to leave his head. He didn't hear Miss Shaw shouting at him from the bottom of the stairs.

The door of his room pushed open. Miss Shaw stood in the corridor, a look of resignation on her long face. "Christian Thompson, are you asleep?" she said quietly. "I've shouted up three times and you did not answer."

"I didn't hear you," said Christian, pulling the eiderdown from his face hurriedly.

"You didn't hear me? You mean you didn't want to hear me, didn't you?" She peered at him. "Are you all right? You look a bit peaky and you're shivering." She crossed the room to Christian's bed, her face softening. "Look at you, have you got a fever?" she asked, a note of concern in her voice, and put her hand on his forehead. "We don't want that at Christ-mas time."

Christian looked at her, his eyes not focusing on the woman standing in front of him; all he could think of was Cyril's blood splashed over his arms.

"Christian," said Miss Shaw, reaching for his shoulder, "Christian, what's wrong with you?" Christian's eyes started to focus.

"What did you say?" he asked vacantly.

"I said are you all right?" asked Miss Shaw, her hand hovering uncertainly over his shoulder in a gesture of concern.

"Yes," said Christian quickly. "I'm just cold, it's freezing up here, that lamp's the only heat in this room." She turned to look at the lamp.

"Where did you get that from?" she said. "You'll set the whole place alight if you're not careful, where did you get paraffin from?"

"I found it in the boiler house and the paraffin was with it."

"Ah yes, the boiler house. That's why I came up. I want you to go and fill the boiler. These children need a bath tonight and the water needs to be hot. You know what to do, don't you?"

"Yes, Miss Shaw."

"And another thing, Christian."

"What now?"

"Don't speak to me in that tone." She looked hurt. Christian scowled and looked away.

"It's the club again on Sunday, isn't it?" said Miss Shaw, ploughing on.

"So what?" Miss Shaw raised an eyebrow but chose to ignore Christian's abruptness.

"I thought we could get all your friends to come in and sing carols around the tree," she said cheerily.

"What tree?"

"The tree you are going to cut down from the top of the garden, there's four or five up there that are all too close together, you can get that Peter Dunmore to help you and you can put it in the dining room. What do you think about that?"

222

Christian flipped the eiderdown from his legs, exposing the holes in his socks as he made to stand up. "Look at those socks! I do wish you would let me buy you some new clothes; we could go to Braggins and I could even get you a jacket like the other boys wear." She put her hand on his arm, and Christian turned his head away.

"I told you my mother will get them when she comes," he sniffed and there was silence.

"Well what about the tree then?" Miss Shaw prompted, knowing from her repeated attempts to buy him clothes he wouldn't hear of it.

"I suppose I could ask Peter to help," he said, looking a bit blankly at Miss Shaw. "But how am I going to let him know? He lives up in Covington, I'm not walking all that way."

"I will phone his mother. I've met her before at Mrs Dene's."

She turned to leave, remembering something at the last minute.

"And, Christian, ask that nice girl to come and decorate the tree, what's her name?"

"Sandra?"

"No, not her."

"Ann?"

"No."

"Nimpy?"

"Yes, that's the one, Joanna. You see her on the bus, don't you? You can ask her then. Tell her three o'clock on Sunday and I will tell Peter's mother too and you can cut the tree down ready. They will all be coming to the club anyway, so it's only a little earlier."

Christian looked at her, a little more enthusiastic now. "I suppose so," he said again with a small smile. Miss Shaw looked at him for a moment.

"Don't forget the boiler, Christian. There's a good boy." She smiled and went out of the room. Christian leapt from the bed and called after her.

"Miss Shaw?" She turned on the landing. "Did you hear anything from Mother? She sometimes writes at Christmas, doesn't she?"

Miss Shaw took a step towards him, a flicker of concern evident in her expression. "No, Christian," she said gently. "It's been a long time since I heard from her." She shook her head, turned and started down the stairs, her shoes clomping on the bare boards. "It's God that provides for you, Christian," she said over her shoulder. "You remember that. He's the best friend that we could have."

That Sunday, Peter arrived early to help Christian cut down the tree, which the pair put in the corner of the dining room. Nimpy arrived at three o'clock to decorate it.

"Aren't there any lights, Christian?" she asked.

"No, there's nothing like that. You're lucky there's a tree, we don't normally even have one of those."

"It's so cold in here," she shivered, putting her coat back on. "She said we had to light the fire." At that moment Miss Shaw entered.

"That's lovely," she said, admiring the tree.

"Ain't there any lights, Miss Shaw?" asked Nimpy.

"No, no, we don't want it to look vulgar, do we? Now, Christian, what about the fire? You go and find some paper.

Peter, you come with me and I will show you where the wood is and where you can chop the kindling."

Peter's face dropped. He attempted a smile and followed Miss Shaw down the long corridor to the back door and out into the yard to where the club room stood. Next to the club was a door into a low block of outbuildings.

"The wood's in there, Peter." He tried the door, but it would not open.

"It's locked."

"Oh, so it is," said Miss Shaw, slapping a hand to her forehead. "I forgot, the petrol for the mower's in there so we keep that safe. Just hang on, I have a key somewhere." She lifted up her baggy jumper to reveal a belt encircling her waist; on the belt was strung a chain with a ring of keys hanging on it. Above her belt Peter could see the tight shimmering pink of an undergarment as Miss Shaw fumbled for the right key. "Ah, got it!" she said finally. "Don't move, Peter." She reached forward to put the key in the lock, pinning Peter against the door. Once again he could smell the mixture of mothballs, sweat and carbolic soap which added to her hot breath as her face came nearer his. Her breasts pushed into him through her thick sweater. "There," she said, "it's open now." She retreated, smiling coyly at Peter to reveal white teeth, and for a moment she fixed Peter with a steady gaze, before stepping back. "It's all in there," she said breathlessly. "Chop some sticks and bring the logs and I'll give Christian some matches."

She turned on her heel and left. Ten minutes later, Peter arrived back in the dining room where Nimpy was watching

225

Christian scrunch up newspaper before throwing it into the grate.

"Where have you been, Peter?" demanded Nimpy. She looked carefully at him and laughed. "It's Miss Shaw again. He can't keep away from her, don't you think, Christian? Don't you think they make a lovely couple?" Peter shook his head in despair.

Christian continued to lay the fire before gingerly lighting a match. He held it in front of him as it flared and began to stutter; but before the flame could get to the paper, it had blown out.

"Come here," said Peter, grabbing the matches from Christian. "Let me have a go." He lit a match and put it to the paper, and the flames leapt onto the paper in the grate. Peter stood back and watched as the paper crackled and hissed; gradually the flames started to shrink, then both boys knelt by the hearth and blew furiously on the fire, but to no avail. Peter took charge and re-laid the fire, putting more paper at the bottom and relighting it; this time the flame from the paper caught the sticks and the fire danced up the chimney. Peter put some coal and logs on top of the kindling.

"That's better," said Nimpy, warming her hands against the flames and taking her coat off again. "Is this place always as cold as this?"

"Pretty much. But she's just given me an electric fire for my room, it's not much but it's better than nothing. We can go up there if you like."

"Let's just finish off the tree then," Nimpy said, as the sash window rattled in the wind.

The fire stopped drawing momentarily, the windows rattled again and a puff of smoke came into the room.

"Bugger," exclaimed Peter.

"Don't swear, Peter Dunmore," chided Nimpy. "Miss Shaw will be in and tell you off. Perhaps you'd like that though, don't you think, Christian?" she added with a wink.

Christian grinned. The fire started to draw again, the smoke making its way up the chimney before changing its mind and billowing into the room as before. After quarter of an hour the room was full of smoke.

"What are we going to do?" Nimpy asked desperately. "I'm not staying in here with all this smoke."

"Don't worry. It always does it, it will be okay when the chimney heats up; you'll see. Let's go up to my room, she's not about now, she's getting the tea ready."

Peter and Nimpy followed Christian up two flights of stairs to Christian's room. Their footsteps echoed on the bare boards as they followed the landing to his room.

"Who else lives up here then?" asked Nimpy. "It's a bit spooky."

"Only me at the moment, some of the older ones do if she gets filled up, but that's not happened for a while." Christian pushed open the door to his room and stood back for the others to enter.

"What a dump," said Nimpy under her breath. "And it's freezing cold." She took a few steps into the room.

"I'll put the fire on, it's much better now she's given me a fire." Christian pulled the bedclothes up on his unmade bed and straightened out the eiderdown.

"The complete works of Plato, who reads that then?" asked Nimpy, fingering the huge copy.

"I do, silly, for A Level, I'm doing Latin and Greek, aren't I?"

"Good luck to you, Christian," said Peter, looking at the tome over Nimpy's shoulder. "I'm not sure I could ever get through that."

The single bar of the electric fire began to glow, it smelt a little as the dust burnt off the element.

"I'll light the lamp, shall I? It warms the place up a bit too."

"If you want to, I suppose," shrugged Nimpy, sitting on the bed and bouncing up and down a little to make the springs squeak. Christian lit the lamp and sat down at the table, while Peter sat beside Nimpy on the bed. He pulled the drawer open and picked out the small bottle, shaking it gently.

"What are those then?" asked Peter. "Are you ill?"

Christian unscrewed the top and shook some of the pills into his hand.

"What are they then?" asked Peter again.

"Purple Hearts."

"They're what?" asked Nimpy, craning her neck to see over Peter's shoulder. "But they are blue not purple. What are they for? You haven't got something nasty, have you, Christian?"

"No, nothing like that. They just give you a buzz when you have one, try and you'll see."

"No, thank you very much. At any rate, they look pretty grubby. Are you going to have one, Peter?"

"No, I'm going to have a fag. I can't do two things at once."

"Chicken," said Christian, "you daren't, is what you mean."

"Do you not want a fag too, Christian?" said Peter, ignoring the jibe.

"Not right now," said Christian.

"There you are, you daren't," laughed Peter. "Nimpy will have one, I bet."

Christian pulled the bottle from his pocket and offered them to her. She shook her head and pushed them away.

"Go on, Christian, you have one," said Peter, shaking the packet of cigarettes in front of his face.

"No," said Christian, tipping the pills out onto his hand. "I'll have one of these." He popped a pill into his mouth. Peter and Nimpy looked at him expectantly, as though the threat of him exploding at any moment was inherently possible.

"Well?" said Nimpy. "What's it like, do you feel any different?"

Christian shut his eyes for a moment and opened them again, wide.

"Look, Nimpy," said Peter, with excitement, "he's having a buzz, don't you think?"

"He must be," said Nimpy confidently. "Christian, are you having a buzz?" She laughed and looked at Christian, who said nothing. Nimpy sighed.

"Come on, Peter, have you got a light?"

"I thought you didn't smoke," said Christian.

"I didn't used to," she replied, as Peter pulled some matches from his jacket and they lit their cigarettes.

229

"Phew, that's gone to my head," said Nimpy, lying back on the bed and looking at the ceiling for a moment. She grabbed the metal end of the bed to pull herself up. "Urgh! What is that?" she exclaimed, sitting up rapidly and examining her palm, which was sticky.

"It's all right," said Christian absently. "It's only chewing gum, give it here." He reached over and pulled the gum away from the bed end, putting it into his mouth.

"You're not really going to eat that, are you?" said Nimpy in disgust. "How long's it been there? It must taste revolting."

"It's fine. Do you want some? There's more there."

"No, I do not," said Nimpy, pulling a face. "What do you think I am?" She took another drag of her cigarette. The wind whistled outside the window, rattling the frame. But when the wind dropped there was silence, punctuated by a soft splashing sound.

"What was that?" said Peter, looking at the other two.

"I don't know," said Christian.

They were silent again, looking at each other. Eventually there was another splash.

"There it is again," said Nimpy. She pointed to a wet patch on the boards in the middle of the room. "Where's that come from?"

The three of them looked up to the ceiling to see the next drip already bulging off the light bulb.

"Where is it coming from?" said Christian, standing up and reaching out a hand to catch the drop.

"I bet I know," said Peter. "It must be the tank in the attic, I went up there with Miss Shaw to do the ballcock. I bet it's right above this room."

Christian froze, looking up at the light bulb in anticipation of the next drop.

"Christian?" came a loud shout from down in the depths of the building. "Christian, are you there?" It was Miss Shaw. "Aren't you going to answer?"

"No," whispered Peter. Nimpy giggled as Christian put his finger to his lips.

"Christian, I know you're up there, and who's there with you?" persisted Miss Shaw. The three could hear the clomp of Miss Shaw's shoes as she started to climb up the stairs. "I'm coming to see what you are up to."

"Say something then," hissed Nimpy.

But Christian wouldn't move. The clomp-clomp of Miss Shaw's shoes got nearer and nearer. She was now on the second flight of stairs.

"What's that smell? Are you smoking, Christian? You know what I think about that." As she reached the top landing and took the few steps to Christian's door, Peter and Nimpy urgently stubbed out their cigarettes and tossed them into the metal wastepaper basket. The door swung open and Miss Shaw was silhouetted against the light from the landing.

"It's dark in here," she said, reaching for the light switch. There was a pop from the bulb, a distant bang and all the lights behind Miss Shaw extinguished. "What was that? The lights have all gone."

"It's water on the light fitting," explained Peter. "It must be coming from the tank and running down the flex. Now you've turned on the light it's fused the switchboard." Miss Shaw looked from one to the other as they stood in the dim light from the paraffin lamp. There was another drip from the

231

ceiling; Nimpy picked up the wastepaper basket and put it over the wet patch on the floor.

"I can mend a fuse," said Christian. "I've done it before."

"Well, don't just stand there then, boy, get on with it. I'll go and get a candle so you can see. You stay here, you two, and turn that switch off." She turned and groped her way along the corridor, Christian clattering down the stairs in front of her.

"What are we going to do?" said Nimpy, as a drip echoed into the metal wastepaper bin.

"We could play Postman's Knock?"

"With just two of us?"

"How many more do we want?"

Nimpy grinned and grabbed Peter's tie, pulling him towards her and throwing her arms around his neck. As she pressed herself up against him, Peter slid his hand under her jumper, pulling her blouse from the waistband of her skirt until his hand found her soft skin.

"Blimey, you're cold!" protested Nimpy, pulling Peter's hand away. "I didn't say you could do that." She pursed her lips and glared at him.

"You didn't say I couldn't," said Peter with a frown, standing up straight. The bulb spat another drip onto his head.

"We ought to see where that leak is, don't you think?" she said suddenly.

"There's no light up there, they've all gone out, or hadn't you noticed?" said Peter sarcastically.

"Don't be like that, Peter, we've got that lamp, haven't we? Come on. Bring it and let's see what's happening." They found their way along the corridor and up the short flight of steps to the attic. The latch clicked as Peter opened the door.

"Can you see anything?" Nimpy asked, as Peter edged forward, holding the lamp to examine the tank.

She tugged at his jacket as she stood behind him. Peter raised the lamp above his head, and there was a spark as a cobweb shrivelled and burnt in the heat from the glass chimney.

"Watch out, Peter, you'll set the place alight." Peter lowered the lamp.

"I can see it. Look, there it is, and water's running down the side." He pointed towards a small pinhole in the tank. "It's only a small hole and near the top as well, what can we mend it with?" He looked at Nimpy.

"Well don't look at me like that. How would I know how to mend a tank, I'm only a girl you know?" She crossed her arms across her chest and scowled.

"There's nothing here," Peter said, scanning the attic. "It needs a plumber, they will have to get Jeff in; he'll fix it."

"On a Sunday night? Don't be stupid, Peter, he won't come now."

"No, I don't suppose he will."

"I know!"

"Know what?"

"How to fix that hole."

"Go on then, clever clogs, how's that?"

"Chewing gum. I bet that will do it easy peasy, don't you think?"

"Good idea, even though I say it myself. Go and get some then and I'll wait here, there's plenty more on the bedstead." He handed her the lamp with a smirk.

"Not on your nelly," she said, pushing the lamp back towards him. "After he's been chewing it? You go and get it if you want to, I'm not going to."

The lights suddenly flooded on and they could hear Christian running back up the stairs.

"There," he crowed. "Who's a clever boy then?"

They heard Christian fling open the door of his bedroom, there was a silence as he realised that they were no longer there. Nimpy giggled.

"Where are you?" he shouted, moving back along the corridor. Peter and Nimpy clattered down the stairs from the attic and met Christian halfway along the corridor.

"We've found the leak and we know how to stop it, don't we, Peter?" said Nimpy, turning to Peter for approval. Peter nodded at Christian, who frowned. "Come and have a look if you don't believe me." Christian shrugged and followed her up the stairs. With the light on, the leak was clear to see.

"All we need is some chewing gum, that will plug it. Christian, you go and get some and we can do it. Peter will be able to reach, he's a lot taller than you."

Christian spat the gum he was chewing into his hand and rolled it between his index finger and thumb. He put it back into his mouth, chewed again and repeated the process.

"Here you are then," he said, offering the gum to Peter.

Peter placed the piece over the hole on the outside of the tank and pressed it into place. He stood back and looked at the leak for a while.

234

"There, it's stopped," he said, rubbing his hands together.

"Let's have a look then," said Christian, peering at the leak through his grimy glasses.

"Looks all right," he grunted, turning from the tank and leading the others back to his room.

"Now, where's this water coming from?" demanded Miss Shaw, stomping back up the stairs into the room. She put her hand out towards the switch in Christian's room.

"No, don't do that!" yelled Peter. "The light will fuse again." Miss Shaw seemed taken aback.

"Well, what about the water?" she blustered. "Where's it coming from?"

"It's the tank in the attic," said Peter. "It's got a leak, or rather it did have, we've just fixed it. Well, at least temporarily."

"You can't just fix leaks," snorted Miss Shaw.

"They did, Miss Shaw," piped up Nimpy. "It was my idea as well, wasn't it, Peter?"

"I suppose so," said Peter, a touch grudgingly.

"We did it with chewing gum," said Nimpy proudly.

"Did it with chewing gum? Who has that revolting stuff? I thought only Americans chewed gum." She looked at them disapprovingly.

"Christian's got it," said Nimpy. "He keeps it on his bedpost."

"I might've guessed," sighed Miss Shaw, looking over at Christian, who once again had paled. "I don't know what I'm going to do with you, Christian Thompson, I really don't." She shook her head and looked him up and down, before turning her attention to Peter and Nimpy.

235

"I suppose *you* mended the leak, Peter," she said with a raised eyebrow.

Peter opened his mouth to protest; he didn't want excess praise, especially as he was unsure how it would manifest itself. Miss Shaw waved a hand at him, dismissing his excuses.

"We will have to get Jeff to have a look when he gets time nevertheless," she persisted, then she turned on her heel and left them in the dim light of the oil lamp.

"Christian," said Nimpy suddenly, "is there a lav somewhere? I'm bursting."

"Down on the next floor is the bathroom, at the end of the corridor." Nimpy rushed from the room.

"Was that was all that was wrong with the tank?" asked Christian curiously. "Could you see anything in…"

"No," interrupted Peter. "I've told you again and again, Christian. What have you got hidden in there, a dead body? You keep going on about that bloody tank!"

"It's nothing, it's just that Jeff thought that there was something in there, I was interested."

Peter frowned. "Well I don't know why you keep asking."

Christian said nothing but pulled another piece of gum from the bed head and put it in his mouth, chewing it thoughtfully.

236

Chapter Fourteen
A Sacred Cow

"Switch it off, Hugh," Joyce shouted, as the last of the potatoes fell from the grader into the bag.

"Are you about right then?" Hugh yelled from the other end of the machine where he had been shovelling the crop into the machine.

"Yes, go on, shut it down. We want to get home, don't we, Nell?" She turned to the tall fair-haired woman beside her who was pulling off her rubber gloves.

"Course we do. It's Christmas Day tomorrow, if you haven't forgotten, Hugh."

Hugh rounded the grader to the switch to turn the machine off. Silence fell and Joyce and Nell took a step back from the machine.

"Who's taking us 'ome then?" asked Joyce, looking round at the men standing about.

"Peter is," someone shouted. "He's coming back in a moment, but we've got some seconds in for Miss Shaw and one for Nimpy's mum, if I remember." The small door into the barn opened and Peter stepped through it.

"Are you ready?" he asked Joyce and Nell.

"We've been waiting for ages, haven't we, Nell? We've got to get back, and quickly, it's Christmas tomorra, or hadn't you noticed either, Peter Dunmore?"

"Yes, I know. But we've got to take some seconds on the way, I'm backed up to the door, give me a hand to put them in, will you? Oh and do you both want a bag each?"

"We do but we ain't havin' *seconds*, are we, Nell? Not on your nelly, come on, bring two of the best and put them in front of Miss Shaw's." Everyone helped pass the bags out until the van was loaded.

"Have you got the ticket book, Peter? She'll want a bill, she won't pay, never does," said Joyce.

"Got all that, yes. Jump in then."

He climbed into the driver's seat as the two women clambered onto the bench seat on the other side. Their heavy coats made it quite a squash, and the two of them wiggled to get comfortable. It was mid-afternoon and the light had started to fade as they drew out of the farmyard, the gears of the van grinding as they accelerated away.

"Are you sure you passed your test, Peter? It doesn't sound much like it," said Nell as she lit a cigarette and blew the smoke across Joyce. "And it's bloody cold in here, aren't you got the heater on?"

"I'm all right, Nell. I'm snuggled up to Peter, he's nice and warm, you know that." The two women cackled, and Peter said nothing.

"What do you get up to down that club then, Peter Dunmore?" asked Nell. "We hear all sorts of stories don't we, Joyce?" She winked at her friend.

"We don't get up to anything. Anyway, Helen goes." He stopped, not wanting to get himself into deeper water.

"I'm surprised you let her go, Joyce," reprimanded Nell. "There will be trouble in the end, you mark my words."

238

"I can't stop her, short of tying her to the table leg. She's got a mind of her own that one, you wait, Nell, when your two get old enough you're going to have the same problem, so you needn't act all hoity toity with me!" There was silence for a few moments as the car slowed up.

"What are we stopping for?" demanded Joyce.

"We've got to drop a bag of seconds off for Nimpy's mum."

"Well bloody well hurry up, Peter, we want to get home, don't we, Nell, and you leave that Nimpy alone, we know she's in there, her mum's down the pub. We know what you get up to down Miss Shaw's."

She dug her elbow playfully into Peter's ribs. Peter said nothing, slung the bag of potatoes onto his shoulder and went round to the back of the house. Nimpy answered the door.

"Who's in the van with you, Peter?"

"Just Joyce and Nell, I'm just taking them home; they're complaining that I'm dropping off spuds to you."

"Wicked old bags, they're always complaining. I bet she's been going on about the club; she always does." Peter shrugged as Nimpy went in to get the money.

"Here we are," she said, handing him some change. She stretched her hand out towards him and pulled him to her, reaching up a little and kissing him hard on the lips. "There we go. Joyce shouldn't talk like that then, Helen's just the same as the rest of us, ain't she?" Peter stood back and looked embarrassed. "Don't look like that, Peter, it didn't hurt, did it?" she laughed, shutting the door and turning back into the house.

239

"Come on, come on, we know what you've been up to," said Joyce as Peter made his way back to the van. "Now you haven't got to stop again, just take us home now and drop Miss Shaw's off on the way back; that will give you time to sort her out, won't it, Nell?" The two women cackled again. "They say she likes boys, don't they, Nell?"

Peter shook his head in exasperation and drove on, dropping the two women off before doubling back to call at the Hall with the ten ordered bags. He knocked at the back door and Miss Shaw came to answer it, clearly flustered.

"Oh, it's you. What do you want?"

"I've brought your potatoes." Miss Shaw looked blankly at him. "Potatoes? Oh, yes, yes of course. I wasn't thinking. We've had another leak; you know, all through the ceiling again, it's an awful mess."

"The chewing gum didn't work then?"

"Only for a little while," admitted Miss Shaw, as Jeff appeared behind her.

"I'm done then, the water's on again, but it won't last, you know, the tank's had it, it's very thin in places, probably installed along with all the plumbing in the house and that could be about eighty years ago." He dropped his bag, took his watch out of his pocket and flicked the case open. "That's an hour and a half then," he said, looking at Miss Shaw.

"It's no good you looking at me like that, Jeff. I can't pay you at the moment, I don't carry that sort of cash, send me your bill and I will write you a cheque when the fees come in for next term." Jeff took his thick glasses off, sniffed and put them back on again.

"You mean you ain't going to pay me then?"

"No."

"Well, I don't know. What am I supposed to use for money then?" He looked at her menacingly, but she ignored him. "You ain't going to pay *him* either, I suppose. I wouldn't let her have them spuds, boy, she won't pay you, see." He picked up his bag and pushed past Miss Shaw, stomping off down the drive.

"Have you got the ticket, Peter?" she asked, as if Jeff had never even been there.

"Yes," said Peter, handing Miss Shaw the small piece of paper, having torn it from his account book.

"Put them in the boiler house, they won't freeze there. You know where it is, Peter, don't you? I think Christian's in there making the boiler up."

She shut the door, making no offer to pay. Peter opened the back door of his van, dragged out a bag of potatoes and walked the few steps to the door of the boiler house. As he pushed open the door he saw Christian, who spun round to see who had entered, a guilty look on his face, then, seeing it was Peter he turned back to the open door of the boiler and continued throwing envelopes into the blazing fire.

"What are you doing?" asked Peter, as Christian threw another handful of envelopes in through the door.

"Nothing," said Christian, turning round to look at Peter. "But come in and shut the door quick, Peter, before she sees."

"Sees what?" asked Peter, as Christian took yet another handful of envelopes from his bag and added them to the fire. "What are they?"

"They're Christmas cards," said Christian, peering into his bag; it was empty.

241

"Well, why are you burning them then, shouldn't they be delivered?"

"They should, I suppose, but I couldn't find the addresses for all of them and anyway they gave me far too many to deliver, it's not fair. They don't give the girls anywhere near so many and we don't get paid till next week and it's the last day so…." Christian stopped, trying to think of other reasons to justify the card burning, then he took the big shovel and threw some coke into the boiler to cover up the envelopes. "There," he said at last, satisfied, "no one would ever know, would they? All the evidence has gone." He giggled, slammed the door shut and turned to Peter. "Do you want a hand then, Peter, have you seen her?"

"Yes, she said to put these potatoes in here so they didn't get frosted, but she didn't pay and she didn't pay Jeff either."

"Has he finished then? We had another leak, you know, in the tank, I mean."

"Yes. I saw Jeff on my way in; he said the tank's no good and it will have to be replaced."

Christian looked away and took his small glass bottle from his pocket. He unscrewed the lid, shook out a couple of pills and threw them into his mouth.

"Come on then, let's get these spuds in," said Peter, with a small frown.

By the end of January, half the store was emptied and they could just see the back wall over the top of the potatoes. The work in the store was hard and boring, but at least it was in the dry and certainly warmer than outside. The men took turns to shovel the crop into the grader, which was the hardest job.

Hugh had just taken over from one of the other men and after a few minutes he was warm enough to take his jacket off. He turned and shovelled another load onto the short metal elevator which lifted the potatoes into the grader. There was a bang. He looked up sharply, but saw nothing; it was common to get stones mixed in with the potatoes. There was a rattling as something skittered across the sieve. Joyce looked up from where she stood sorting the graded potatoes. She would take out the seconds, the green or split spuds, and sort them into a different bag.

"Must be a stone," she said, calling across to her friend. "Can you see it, Nell?"

"Not yet," said Nell who was standing at the other side of the machine, doing the same job as Joyce.

There was another bang and the noise of something rolling onto the last elevator which took the potatoes into the bags.

"What the …" exclaimed Joyce. "Stop it, Nell, stop it!" Nell pressed the stop button.

"What are you stopped for?" demanded Hugh. "You are always pressing that button."

"Well come here and look at this, will you, what on earth is it?" said Joyce, picking up the object that had caused the disruption. She took off her gloves and rubbed the mud from the object, holding it up for all to see.

"Bugger, that's heavy, ain't it?" said Hugh, turning the object over in his hand and examining it. "It's brass, it's a cow, a sleeping cow, look!" He pointed to the elements of the cow. "And look, it's flat on one side." He held the paperweight on the palm of his hand.

"I know what that is," said Joyce.

243

"You know everything, you do," grumbled Hugh.

"Well I do, so there. It's a paperweight, ain't it? Mrs Dene's got one, only hers is made of stone and it's not a cow."

"You sure it ain't gold?" said Nell, squinting to look at the cow more closely.

"Course it ain't gold," scoffed Hugh.

"How do you know then, clever clogs?" snapped Joyce. "It looks like gold; maybe she's right, you don't know."

"Well I do know so there, gold would be much heavier and this is tarnished, look, gold don't go like that." Hugh looked round at the others.

"What you going to do with it then?" asked Nell.

"Well, I'll put it here," said Hugh, placing the cow on the weighing machine. "And we'll show it to Peter when he comes back from school and he can give it to his dad."

"What if it's worth something?" said Nell eagerly. "Who gets the money?"

"I do," said Joyce loudly. "I found it."

"That's not fair," complained Nell. "I saw it as well."

"Now, now," said Hugh, looking at the two women, "we don't know it's worth anything yet. More importantly who does it belong to? Who picked it up in the field and who dropped it in the first place? There's no way of telling. We'll leave it here for the moment and see what happens."

He placed the paperweight on the top of the weighing machine and restarted the elevator.

The moon shone brightly enough for Peter to count the cigarettes in the packet he was holding. There were five. He closed it up and put it back in his jacket pocket.

244

"Come on, knock," a muffled cry came from inside the club. Sandra had just gone back in and it was his turn to knock on the door. He considered for a moment, before tapping five times since he had five cigarettes and waited. There was silence whilst the girls drew the pieces of paper and moments later the latch clicked. Helen peered round the door, acclimatising to the dim glow provided by the moonlight. Peter leaned against the wall as Helen walked towards him, coming to stand in front of him. He took her hand.

"Your hands are cold," she said.

"It's a cold night," he replied nonchalantly. She looked at him expectantly.

"Aren't you going to kiss me then?" she asked, looking him straight in the eye. She let go of his hand and crossed her arms, boosting up her small breasts as best she could.

"Well if you don't want to I'll go back in then, the rest of them ain't chicken like you. 'Cept Christian, I suppose." She turned to go back into the club. Peter grabbed her arm, not quite getting purchase on it, latching onto her sleeve instead, as Helen continued to turn. There was a tearing sound as the top button of Helen's blouse pulled off and dropped to the ground. Peter momentarily glimpsed the white of her breast before Helen clasped a hand to her chest. "Now look what you've done. I can't go in there again like this." She drew her hand back to slap his face, but Peter was too quick. He grabbed her hand and tugged her towards him. The pair struggled briefly, their faces inches apart from each other. Helen reached forward and kissed him gently on the lips, before pulling back sharply. Christian was watching them. "Christian Thompson, you shouldn't be spying on us like that."

"I wasn't spying; I was just late that's all, if you want to stand there kissing then that's your fault; you should go somewhere else."

Helen ran her fingers through her shiny hair and held her blouse together with her other hand. "Christian, you couldn't do something for me, could you?" she said suddenly, with a coy smile.

"Depends what it is. I ain't going to kiss you if that's what you want."

"No, it ain't that. I just want you to get my jumper, it's on the bench next to Simon, the green one. Please, Christian, I'd be really grateful." Christian stuck his bottom lip out and looked at her.

"S'ppose I could," he said after a while, opening the door and going down the steps.

The door closed behind him. Helen turned back to Peter, kissing him hard on the lips before breaking away.

"So am I old enough then?" she said smugly.

"You're old enough, Helen," he smiled, as she organised her hair and waited for Christian. She looked at him quizzically.

"Mum said they found something in the spuds the other day."

"Yeah, it was a brass paperweight," he replied as Christian came out the door again, carrying Helen's jumper.

"Did you hear that, Christian?" she said.

"Hear what?"

"Mum found a brass paperweight in the heap of spuds when they were riddling." Christian stopped and stared at Helen, his hands gripping the jumper, his knuckles white.

"She what?"

"She found a brass paperweight in the spuds."

"What was it like?" His voice trembled.

"It were a cow all curled up and asleep; she said it was lovely, was it, Peter?" She turned to look at him.

"Yes, it was very attractive."

Christian was now visibly shaking; he screwed up his face and a tear sprang to each eye.

"Are you all right, Christian? You're shaking," said Helen, reaching for the jumper that Christian was still gripping. He would not let go. "Christian, can I have my jumper?" she asked, pulling it slightly. Christian's eyes were unfocused; he evidently had not heard. "Christian!" said Helen, raising her voice.

"Yes?"

"My jumper?"

"Oh yes," he said, releasing the jumper and wiping his nose with his fist. He lifted his glasses and wiped his eyes.

"You were in the tatter field too, Christian, it could have been you that picked it up, you never know!" said Helen.

"You were there too," snapped Christian, glaring at Helen angrily.

"I know I were. So was Nimpy and lots of other people, it could have been anyone, I suppose."

She held her jumper up to check it was the right way round and then threaded her arms in one at a time before pulling it over her head, her blouse opening slightly as she did so. Christian looked away sharply and wiped his nose again.

"What happened to it then?" asked Helen.

"Mother took it to the police," shrugged Peter.

"She did what?" gasped Christian.

"She took it to the police."

"Whatever for?"

"I don't know. What do you think she should have done, it's not ours, someone lost it? They are probably looking for it. Anyway the police weren't interested."

"You mean Rawlins didn't want it?" said Christian incredulously.

"No, she didn't take it to him, she took it to Kimbolton. Anyway, they didn't want to keep it but they did in the end. Said if no one claimed it in two months she could have it. Finders keepers sort of thing, I suppose."

"Well, my mum found it," said Helen, tugging her jumper straight. "So she should have it, not your mum, Peter."

"Come on! What are you up to, you lot?" Simon shouted, opening the door violently. Peter returned to the club, leaving Christian and Helen outside.

"Are you sure you're all right, Christian? You look a bit funny, and you're shaking."

"Yeah, I'm fine," mumbled Christian, turning away from her.

He crossed to the boiler room, went in and shut the door as Helen turned and knocked three times on the door of the club.

Chapter Fifteen
A Hockey Match

"Mum, do I have to?" complained Helen.

"Yes, you do, my girl; if you are going to play hockey you are going to look the part!"

"But the dirt won't come off, Mum," wailed Helen.

"Give me strength," muttered Joyce, looking heavenwards and then back to Helen. "Well, go in there and put them under the tap and scrub them. You can bring them out here to dry." She pursed her lips.

Joyce and her husband lived in a semi-detached cottage in the middle of the village. Jeff lived alone next door, his wife having left him some years ago. The cottages were small and a bathroom had been added to the back of each on the ground floor. Outhouses behind the cottages led to a long garden which stretched up to parkland at the back of the village.

"I'm done then, Mum," said Helen, offering the plimsolls for her mother's inspection. Joyce looked at her critically.

"I suppose they will do, now put them down there to dry and go and try that skirt on so I can have a look."

Helen dashed off back into the depths of the cottage. Joyce shook her head in despair and walked out to brush down the path leading to the road. Miss Shaw was walking up from the direction of the Hall. She wore her long brown overcoat, a felt hat and heavy, dirty shoes. Her stockings rippled upwards, disappearing under the thick apparel. Joyce stood up and leaned on her brush.

"Mrs Frost," said Miss Shaw, nodding her head to Joyce imperiously.

"Miss Shaw," said Joyce, with as much disinterest as she could muster.

"I'm looking for Jeff. Do you know if he's in?" asked Miss Shaw, looking absently in the direction of the church, away from Joyce.

"I don't know, do I? But I don't know why he shouldn't be. You'll have to knock on the door like normal people do. Mind, he don't get many visitors, least ways not many women." She gave a sugary smile as Helen appeared behind her.

"Is this all right, Mum?" she asked. Joyce turned round to look.

Helen spun round on the spot, her short sports skirt flying up to reveal her green flannel knickers. Miss Shaw's mouth dropped open and she blinked.

"What do you think you look like, girl?" admonished Joyce. "You've turned that skirt up, I know you have, come here let's have a look." Joyce pulled the skirt towards her and examined the hem; Helen scowled. "I thought so. Now you look here, my girl, you go straight upstairs and take out them stitches and let it down to where it was. And quickly! Do you hear me?" She shook her finger at Helen, who grimaced and turned and stomped off, flicking the back of her skirt up as she went and wiggling her backside as she minced round the corner. Joyce tutted. "I don't know what the world's coming to," she said, turning to Miss Shaw who wore a look of disapproval.

"I must go and find Jeff," said Miss Shaw. She nodded to Joyce and made her way round to Jeff's back door. She knocked and waited. Nothing happened. She knocked again.

"Hang on, hang on," came a voice from the house. "You'll just have to wait, whoever you are, I'm busy."

Miss Shaw peered through the window into the kitchen, where Jeff stood at the table shaving. In front of him was a bowl of steaming water, which he swished his razor through after long sweeping strokes of his stubbly chin. He peered through his thick horn-rimmed glasses into a small cracked mirror that was propped against a pile of books on the table. He wore a sleeveless vest and his braces hung down either side of his sizeable belly. The rest of the table was full of empty milk bottles and dirty plates, which were also piled up in the sink under the window she was looking through. She turned away from the window and looked up the garden while she waited. After three or four minutes, Jeff came to the door. His glasses were on his head and he was wiping his face with a grubby towel. He peered at Miss Shaw as he dragged the towel down his face.

"You're early, ain't you?" he said gruffly. "The pub ain't open yet, is it?" He turned his head and sniffed his armpit, before holding each arm up in turn and wiping at his underarms with the towel. Miss Shaw frowned and looked away. "Are you coming in then or just going to stand there?" he asked, pulling the glasses from his head and rubbing the lenses on the towel. He put them on and looked at Miss Shaw.

"Bugger!" he exclaimed, putting a hand to his mouth. "I didn't see it was you, Miss Shaw. What can I do for you?" He pulled his braces up over his shoulders and adjusted his broad leather belt. "Are you comin' in then?" he asked again, taking a step backwards.

Miss Shaw took a small step forward and sniffed the air delicately; the smell from the house, a mixture of sweat, dirty clothes, fried food and onions, was quite overpowering.

"No," she said bluntly. "I won't be long, I've just come to pay you for last time, the tank, you remember?" Jeff nodded slowly. "We want you to come again, there's another leak and we don't want the water through the ceiling again, do we?" She offered an envelope towards him, which he took and stuffed in his pocket.

"Well, I told you already, there's not a lot I can do. The tank's too old; you need a new one; that one must be eighty years old, it was put in when they plumbed the house."

"Well, I know. But that will cost a lot, won't it?"

"Don't know. I'll come and measure up if you want and see what we've got down the yard, I'll call in on my way to the pub."

Miss Shaw nodded and turned to leave, passing back by Joyce's cottage where Helen had just returned with her skirt adjusted.

"That's better," said Joyce, pulling at the hem. "Now go and get the ruler."

"The what?" said Helen, puzzled.

"You heard what I said." Helen frowned and went to collect the ruler from her pencil case.

"Now kneel down," said Joyce, pointing to the concrete path. Helen protested loudly. "Now!" Helen scowled and knelt on the path as Joyce measured the distance from the skirt to the ground. "Should be four inches, that's what they say and if you want to play in the tournament you're going to be right." Helen lifted her eyes to heaven and said nothing.

Christian, in the meantime, had decided to pay a visit to the police house in Kimbolton to see if he could get the brass paperweight back. If the paperweight was ever linked back to Cyril, then where it was found would narrow the suspects and most of the pickers were able to provide alibis for one another. He had found out from Simon that the station was open in the evenings between six and eight, on the pretext that he had found something that he wanted to hand in. The bus from school continued on to Kimbolton from Dean, so Christian remained on the bus; arriving in the middle of Kimbolton at ten past five. With almost an hour to wait, he wandered to the church and sat in the porch reading until the church clock struck six. He stood, thrust the book back into his school bag and proceeded towards the police house.

He dithered briefly at the door, before taking a deep breath and walking in. The room was small, with two chairs against the near wall which faced a counter, behind which a door led in from the house. To one side of the counter was a bell, which he pressed and waited. Through the closed door he could hear somebody talking, and as Christian could only hear one voice, he assumed that the talker was on the phone and turned to sit on one of the chairs. It was at least another ten minutes before he heard the person hang up the phone and the police constable entered the room. He was about fifty years of age and his hair was cut short. He was overweight; with a large paunch and double chins which made him look like he didn't have a neck. He stood at the counter and opened the book that lay on the surface.

"Well, sonny, what can I do for you then? Lost, are we?"

"No," said Christian, getting up and approaching the counter. He licked his lips nervously, and shifted from one foot to the other. "It's like this. Sometime ago when I was potato picking I lost something in the field and a friend of mine said it had been handed in here, so I've come to collect it."

"And what exactly was it you lost then, laddie?"

"It was a brass paperweight."

"And what did this brass paperweight look like then?"

"Oh, it was about the size of my fist; it was a sleeping cow, all curled up like."

"A sleeping cow, eh? And what is a boy like you doing with a sleeping cow paperweight in a potato field?" He looked at Christian enquiringly.

"I was picking potatoes. They pay so much per bag and me and some friends went to earn some pocket money."

The policeman sighed and looked to the ceiling. "You didn't answer my question, laddie. What. Were. You. Doing. With. The. Paperweight?"

"Oh, I had taken it to school to show some friends and it was still in my pocket." He looked at the constable, who was silent. "My mother gave it to me."

"It's an unusually heavy object to have in one's pocket. I don't know how you could have forgotten about it, you could

254

do someone some damage with a thing like that, you know, laddie?" Christian shrugged and looked away. "Well, we had better have some details, hadn't we?" said the constable, pulling out his notebook and pencil. He wrote the date at the top of the page. "Name?"

"Christian Thompson."

"Address?"

"The Hall, Dean."

"Age?"

"Eighteen."

"You don't look eighteen, boy, are you sure about that?"

"Yes, of course. I was eighteen last year."

"Well, I suppose I believe you. You have any proof of identification?" Christian looked blankly at the constable and patted his pockets, while he thought.

"What kind of identification do you mean?"

"I mean a passport, driving licence, something like that."

"No, I haven't got any of them, I've got my bus pass that's got my name on it." He handed it to the constable.

"Well, I suppose it will do," he said, turning it over and looking at the name and the date. "And how do I know you were in that tatter field then?" said the constable suddenly, with a quick frown. "You might have made the whole story up."

"I've got some of the tickets they give you when they pay you," said Christian, pulling out his wallet and finding four or five headed receipts. He handed them to the constable who turned them over in his hands.

"It don't say they're for potatoes, do it? It just says a number, oh wait a moment, '*Thirteen bags*' it says here." He tutted and raised an eyebrow in Christian's direction. "Unlucky for some." He handed the receipts back to Christian and continued to scribble in the book; Christian watched and waited. After a minute or so, the constable stood up and opened a drawer under the counter, pulling out the brass paperweight. He put it on the counter and looked at it carefully, before picking it up again and holding it in the palm of his hand. He tossed it lightly in the air as if judging the weight.

"It's heavy, ain't it?" he marvelled.

"I suppose it has to be if it's a paperweight." There was silence.

"And is there someone who can corroborate that this is yours? Like your mother?"

"No, she's abroad. I just lodge at the Hall." There was silence.

"Well how long are you lodging there?"

"I expect I won't leave till after A Levels in July." The constable looked at Christian and back down at the paperweight. He picked it up again and rubbed it on the sleeve of his uniform jacket.

"Well, I'm going to say that you can take it. I don't want it cluttering up my drawer forever. But you will have to sign for it, mind, and if anyone else claims it I know where to come, don't I?"

"Yes," said Christian, as the constable wrote out a receipt in the book. Christian signed it and took the paperweight, trying not to make the relief obvious on his face.

"Oh boy!" the constable called after him. "If you live in Dean, do you know my mate Joe Rawlins?" Christian turned.

"Yes. He lives in the police house next to the church."

256

"He says the young buggers there keep trying to let the tyres down on his bike, that ain't you, I hope?"

"Oh no," said Christian sweetly. "That must be someone else."

"Well if you see him just tell him Tom Pentlow sends his regards and I'll see him in the pub before long." He closed the book and returned into the backroom; as Christian left the office, clutching the paperweight to his chest.

There was no way of getting back to Dean now without walking, so Christian dropped the paperweight into his pocket and set off, trying to hitch a lift with various cars as they passed. It was getting colder, the sun had gone down and darkness was approaching. The heavy mass of the paperweight banged against his hip as he walked along; he thrust his hand into his jacket pocket to steady it. A van approached from behind; he turned to face it, walking backwards as he did so. As the van came nearer to him the driver tooted and the van came to a halt on the verge just beyond him, the back tyre lodged in a drainage grip. There was a cheer from inside the vehicle, which now looked like it might be stuck and Simon and Tookey climbed out to check their predicament.

"Christian," Simon declared, "just the man! We need a push! Come on, it's your fault we're stuck so you have to push us out, then we'll give you a lift."

Simon climbed back into the driver's seat and the other two pushed from the back; with little effort the van was out of the grip and back on the road.

"Where are you going?" asked Christian.

"We're going to the pictures but we've been to get petrol and we are now on our way to pick up the girls," explained Simon.

"Whose van is this then?" Christian asked, nodding to the vehicle.

"Dad's. What do you think then? Goes like a rocket, doesn't it, Tookey?" said Simon with a wink.

"Like a rocket all right," agreed Tookey, pulling the back door open for Christian to get in. Christian, who was not paying attention, did not step back in time and Tookey pulled the door straight into Christian's left hip; there was a loud metallic bang.

"What the hell was that?" exclaimed Simon. "What did you do to that door, Tookey? I hope it's not broken or I'll be for the high jump."

"I ain't done nothing with it," protested Tookey. "I just opened it and it hit Christian and made a sound like he's made of steel."

They both looked at Christian standing in front of them in his school uniform. He looked somehow lopsided, one side of his jacket hanging much lower than the other.

"What have you got there, Christian?" said Simon inquisitively. "Another bottle full of pills, I bet?"

"No, I haven't."

"What is it then?" demanded Simon. "I bet it is more pills. Peter told us you offered him some."

"It ain't pills," insisted Christian.

"Let's have a look then," said Tookey slyly.

He grabbed Christian by the arm and quickly dug his hand into his jacket pocket, pulling out the paperweight.

"What the bloody hell's this?" he said, turning it round in his hand, as Christian tried in vain to get it back.

"Give it here," begged Christian.

Tookey threw the weight to Simon who held it up to the failing light and examined it.

"I know what this is, Gran's got one nearly the same."

Christian lunged at Simon to recover his weight, but Simon and Tookey were much bigger and more agile than he was and he had no chance of taking it off them. As the two boys threw the paperweight from one to the other Christian rushed between the two, desperation etched on his face. Tears sprang to his eyes, which he scrubbed away with his fist.

"Here we go then," said Tookey, worried on seeing Christian's distress and throwing him the paperweight.

Christian clumsily tried to catch it but his fingers were chilled and the weight slid through, dropping onto the grass of the verge and rolling into the road. Christian grabbed it and put it in his pocket.

"Where did you get that from, Christian?" demanded Simon.

"It came from my mum," said Christian, wiping his eyes with his fingers under his glasses.

Tookey looked at Simon and then back at Christian.

"Get in," said Simon gently. "Let's be off. We'll miss the first film if we don't watch out."

Chapter Sixteen
A Weapons Find

Miss Shaw sat in her office with the door open so that she could see all the way down the long corridor which led to the dining room one way and two classrooms the other. She had a large cheque book in front of her and a heap of bills, which she took off the top one at a time for payment. A child ran out of the dining room with a large handbell and, holding it with two hands, started to ring it loudly. No sooner had the sound echoed round the building than there was a clattering and shuffling of feet and the banging of closing desks sounded from the rooms. Children rushed across the corridor into the dining room. Miss Shaw sucked air through her teeth and stared at the bill in front of her; she was going to have to go soon to supervise the dishing out of the food to make sure it was shared out evenly. Half way down the corridor was a staircase and she could see Jeff descending the last few treads, holding his bag of tools in one hand and two rusty bayonets in the other. He strode along the corridor to her office and tapped on the door before walking in.

"You'll never guess what?" he said, grinning at her through his thick glasses. Miss Shaw finished writing the cheque, tore it carefully from the book and looked at Jeff. "Look what I've found," he said, dropping his bag of tools and holding up the bayonets. "How do you think they got in there?"

"Got in where?" said Miss Shaw impatiently. "What are they?"

"They're bayonets," said Jeff, "First World War, if you ask me. Look, they've got one serrated edge, a bugger to get out once you'd stuck them in someone." He wiped them on his sleeve one at a time.

"Where did you find them?" she asked.

"In that old tank, it's out of the attic now and they were in the bottom, must have been in there years."

"What are you going to do with them?" she asked.

"Well finders keepers, I'd say, Miss Shaw, don't you think?" said Jeff with a wink.

"Well, I certainly don't want them, I don't approve of the military, you know that. God did not send us into this world to kill each other."

"So you don't want them, Miss Shaw?"

"I most certainly do not."

"So I can have them then?"

"I suppose so. When's the hot water going to be on?"

"Oh, that won't take long now the new tank's in place. Only two fittings to do and I can turn it on again."

"Very good then. And take those things away. I don't want to see them again, and make sure you light the boiler when you're done."

Jeff threw the bayonets into his bag, put his finger to his forehead in mock salute and left.

By the time Christian returned from school, the replacement tank was finished and Jeff was standing outside the boiler house waiting for the fire to catch.

261

"What's up with the boiler then?" he asked, swinging his bag around his shoulders.

"There ain't nothing wrong with it, but I've just lit it." Christian looked at him a little vacantly. "What are you looking at me like that for then, boy? Ain't you got anything better to do?"

"I ain't looking like anything. I'm just wondering why you're lighting the boiler."

Jeff went down the two steps and opened the door of the fire box. After giving the fire a poke he shut it again and returned to where Christian was standing.

"You still here then?" Christian did not reply. Jeff lit a cigarette. "I'm just thought. You can give me a hand lifting, can't you?"

"I suppose so. Lifting what?"

"The old tank." Christian's eyes widened, his lip quivering a little.

"What tank?"

"The one in the attic. I've just changed it. Come on, it's not too heavy; we can get it while that burns up a bit."

Christian followed Jeff along the corridor and up the two flights of stairs to the last little flight to the tank attic. The door stood open and the light was on. Christian could see the new tank in position and the old one standing on the floor. He peered into the tank; it was rusty on the inside with a little bit of water and sludge in the bottom. Christian sniffed and wiped his nose with his hand. His whole body started to shake. Jeff looked up at him curiously; Christian smiled weakly.

"Are you ready then?" said Jeff, bending down to pick up the tank. "Come on." Christian did not move. He stood glued to the spot, trembling. "Are you all right, boy? Come on, grab it under the bottom, don't just stand there!" Christian blinked but still did not move. "Did you hear me, boy, grab it under the bottom," demanded Jeff, bending down again. Christian shook his head and did as he was told, bending down, his gaze fixed on the inside of the tank.

"One, two, three, lift," instructed Jeff. The tank lifted off the ground. "You go backwards. You're younger than me."

Christian started to slowly move backwards, feeling his way down the first flight of stairs. Five minutes later they had the tank in the yard, next to the boiler house door. Once again Christian peered into the tank, seeing nothing.

"What you keep looking in that tank for?"

"Was there anything in the tank, Jeff, I was just wondering? You never know with these old houses."

"You're always going on, boy, you never stop wittering and going on, do you? Don't they teach you any manners at that there school you go to? Where I was at school we were taught…"

He broke off to move back into the boiler house, open the door of the boiler and throw three or four shovelfuls of coke onto the blazing fire. The fire crackled and the flames were temporarily extinguished. Jeff shut the door with a bang.

"That'll do then," he grunted, lumbering up the steps, standing up to his full height and stretching out his back. "What was I saying?" he asked Christian, looking round for his bag of tools which lay open by the door of the boiler house. "Oh I know," he said, bending down to pick up the bag, a mischievous grin on his face. "You'll never guess."

"Never guess what?" said Christian apprehensively.

"What I found in the old tank."

"What did you find, Jeff?"

"Look here," said Jeff, opening his bag, "I found these two old bayonets. They're a bit rusty but I'll be able to shine them up." He pulled both from his bag and wiped each one on his sleeve again; he squinted down at one, seeing some writing etched on the blade. "Royal Enfield," he said slowly. "Look here, boy, your eyes are better than mine, what's that say? Does it say Royal Enfield?" He handed the first bayonet to Christian who took it gingerly, his hands now shaking. He tried to focus on the writing but the bile rose in his throat. He shut his eyes. "What's it say?"

Christian opened his eyes and glanced briefly at the engraved letters.

"Well?" Christian sniffed.

"It does say Royal Enfield."

"I knew it," crowed Jeff. "They're old, you know; must be First World War ones, you can tell, you know, they've got one serrated edge, that's how you can tell. Must be years old." He picked up the second bayonet and peered again at the writing. He frowned. "It's the same, ain't it?" he asked, handing the other bayonet to Christian.

"Yes, it's the same," confirmed Christian, with a quick glance.

"They didn't like 'em, you know, not with the serrated edges. Lots of them said that they wouldn't come out again when you stuck them into old Fritz." He chuckled. "Yep they all said that, wouldn't come out again, did you know that, boy?" He looked at Christian inquisitively. "Are you all right, boy, you look a bit funny and you've got the shakes?"

264

"I'm fine," said Christian quickly, handing the bayonets back to Jeff. "What are you going to do with them, Jeff? Don't they belong to Miss Shaw?"

"No they don't. Or not now they don't, she don't want 'em and she said I could 'ave them. Finders keepers after all." He put the bayonets back into his bag.

"Do you want to sell them, Jeff? I'd buy them, I'll give you a good price."

"You ain't got no money, Christian Thompson. You never did have and you never have now. Anyway what do you want with two old bayonets? You would only go and stick them into someone. I know what you're like, you and your mates." He picked up his bag, ready to go.

"What you going to do with them then, Jeff?" said Christian, a hint of desperation colouring his voice.

"That, my boy, is none of your business so keep your nose out all right," said Jeff, holding a threatening finger up to Christian.

Christian winced, cowering under Jeff's gaze. Then Jeff smiled, turned and walked away down the drive, Christian staring helplessly after him.

Three weeks later Jeff was sitting in the public bar of the Turk's Head in Bedford. It was six-thirty on a Saturday evening and he had just played in a cricket match for Dean against Bedford Grammar School old boys.

"How did you get on Jeff? Did you win then?" Robin the barman enquired, handing Jeff his third pint.

"Did we buggery, stuck up bloody lot. Think just cos they went to the grammar school they know it all, I went to a grammar school as well, you know."

"I know you did, Jeff. You've told me often enough."

"It was their bloody umpire give me out LBW as usual and weren't it cold? Cricket in April ain't no fun, I'll tell you." He took another swig of his beer. "Your fire ain't much 'elp either, Robin, can't you get it to go better than that?" Robin shouted across the bar to the woman who sat at a small table reading a paper.

"Give the fire a poke, Doll!"

The woman looked over the top of the paper. Her hair was jet black and grew in thick wiry curls down to her shoulders. Her bloodshot eyes were rimmed with black eye shadow and her black eyebrows pointed upwards at strange angles.

"What you tellin' me to poke?" she grinned, her large red lips opening to show a uniform set of slightly yellow dentures, the top set of which did not open as wide as her mouth. Her voice was deep and rattled as she spoke. "It's you that should be doin' the pokin', Robin, not me," she said, putting the paper down and standing.

She took hold of the poker that leaned against the fireplace and shoved it once into the coals, before putting the poker down and standing back.

"There," she said. "Ain't I a good poker, Robin?" She grinned again, noticing Jeff for the first time. "Oh and look, there's old Jeff over there, there's a good poker there too, one of the best, ain't you, Jeff?"

She bobbed down to pick up her cigarette from the ashtray and her drink from the table, bending her knees to avoid her short skirt riding up any further. She tottered over in her high-heeled shoes to where Jeff stood at the bar.

"Come 'ere, darlin', let me give you a kiss." She pointed to her cheek, offering it up to him. Jeff wrinkled his nose and lifted his glasses, pushing his face against hers. When he withdrew there was a white spot of powder on his nose. Doll turned back to him. "Don't want to spoil my lipstick, you know how it is, Jeff." She shimmied herself onto a stool at the bar and turned to eye Jeff critically. "Well we don't often see you in here do we, Robin? But I suspect you go to posher places than this, he's a grammar school boy, ain't he, did you know that, Robin?" She winked at the barman.

"It's all right in here," said Jeff.

"Well where's the rest of the team then?" said Doll. "They won't come, will they?"

"They've gone to the County Hotel."

"Told you so, we ain't good enough for 'em, are we, Robin?" laughed Doll. She lowered her voice confidentially. "Mind, Jeff, the brewery have said he's got to smarten the place up, ain't they, Robin? They said, Jeff, that 'e lets 'em down with the way he keeps this place and they will be lookin' for another tenant if 'e don't smarten it up." She winked at Jeff. "It's all the rough people you get in here; that's the trouble, ain't it, Robin?" She nudged Jeff with her elbow.

"They say I'm got to put some décor up, to decorate around a theme," said Robin. "Well I ask you, whoever heard of such a thing. Any road, what is a Turk, do you know, Jeff?" and Robin lit another cigarette, offering his packet on to Jeff and Doll.

267

"A Turk is from Turkey, ain't he," said Jeff knowingly, "'e was a warrior at the time of the Crusades. Saladin was a Turk, or a Saracen, I learnt that at school and they had these mighty swords, a scimitar if you know what I mean?"

"Ain't 'e clever, Robin!" marvelled Doll. "Well maybe that's what you need, a couple of scimitars to hang up about the place."

"And where do you think I'm going to find two scimitars then, clever clogs?" said Robin, moving up the bar to serve two men in suits who had just entered.

"Who are they then?" Jeff asked Doll, nodding to the men. "Look a bit smart."

"Police," said Doll. "They're always in here. CID, I reckon, throwin' their weight about I 'spect." She drained the last of her drink.

"Do you want another one, Doll?" asked Jeff, nodding to her glass.

"Don't mind if I do, just a gin and Babycham will be fine."

"What sort of drink's that then?"

"A bloody strong one," said Doll, laughing as Robin came back to serve Jeff.

"I'm just thought, Robin," mused Jeff. "I'm got just what you want to go over the fireplace to liven it up."

"And what's that?" said Robin sceptically, taking the pint glass that Jeff had pushed across the bar.

"It's a pair of First World War bayonets, they would just look right, they're not scimitars, but they're similar." Robin refilled Jeff's pint glass and passed it back to him. "Oh, and a gin and Babycham for Doll."

268

"So how much do you want for a pair of bayonets, then? I ain't made of money you know."

"I don't know. A fiver?"

"Each! Never."

"No. I mean for the pair." Robin thought for a minute,

"I'll give you two pounds each when I'm seen them."

"Done," said Jeff, shaking Robin's hand across the bar.

Two more men in uniform entered.

"Who are they then?" said Jeff. "This place is swarming."

"Screws, end of a shift, I expect," said Doll, sipping her drink.

She grabbed Jeff's jacket lapel and pulled him towards her, whispering into his ear.

"Are you up for a quick one in a minute, Jeff? Ten shillings for an old friend." Jeff pulled back and grinned, laying his hand on her leg and running it up under her skirt.

"Don't mind if I do. But I'm going to finish this drink first and then I'm goin' to have one of his pickled onions. They're bloody good."

Twenty minutes later, the pair stood outside a terraced house while Doll fumbled with a huge set of keys. Jeff jangled the change in his trouser pockets impatiently while he waited, looking up and down the street. Eventually she found the right key, holding it up triumphantly to Jeff who grunted and followed Doll into the house, then down a corridor towards another door. She returned to the key ring and sought the next key for the small downstairs room.

"Come in. You've been 'ere before, ain't you, Jeff?"

She flicked the lights on. The room contained little furniture; to one side was a bed with a counterpane covering a hair mattress. Next to the bed stood a single chair and a small electric fire which she switched on. There was a fireplace and on the shelf above it stood a solitary birthday card.

"Is it your birthday then, Doll?"

"Yes, fifty-three yesterday. I don't know where the time goes. Bert's sixty next month, you know! Mind he keeps himself well, don't go to pubs and all that, and Judy…" Doll shook her head, "she's twenty-five, poor thing."

Doll stubbed out her cigarette in the ash tray on the mantelpiece, took her coat off and threw it on the bed. With a flourish, she pulled her skirt up and her black knickers down, before sitting on the bed to kick her shoes and pants off. Jeff hurriedly started to tear off his jacket, pulling down his braces and fumbling with the buckle of his belt, a task made difficult by the size of his paunch, which obscured his sightline and meant he had to perform the manoeuvre by feel.

"What's up with Judy then?" asked Jeff, pulling his gut up and peering round it to try and see what he was doing. Doll froze momentarily and shuddered.

"It was that bastard Cyril," she said, standing up abruptly and walking across to the fireplace, the pattern of the counterpane dented into her bare bottom. She put one hand in front of her mouth and with one finger pulled her dentures out, placing them carefully on the mantelpiece. She returned to the bed and sat again.

"He picked her up outside school," Doll shook her head angrily. "She was goin' to do her A Levels, she was nearly eighteen, the rotten bastard." Jeff looked up with a frown; he had managed to get his belt undone. "You don't mind?" asked

270

Doll, pointing to her empty mouth. "They've really been givin' me jip today."

"No, no," insisted Jeff, hanging his trousers over a chair and standing in the middle of the room in his stocking feet.

"What happened then?" he continued, tucking his tie into his shirt.

"The bugger attacked her, that's what happened. And her a good girl. Black and blue she were after that."

She lay back on the bed, spreading her legs and squinting into the light which hung directly above her. The absence of her dentures made her mouth like a cavernous hole and when she closed her lips, the skin around her jaw lost all definition, collapsing inwards all round.

"You about ready?" asked Jeff timidly.

"Yeah, get on with it," sighed Doll, adding sharply. "I said a quick one mind, din't I?" Jeff climbed onto the bed and clambered on top of Doll. "Bugger! You've put on a lot of weight, what have you been eating?" She puffed wheezily as she tried to get herself into a more comfortable position.

"You ain't so small yourself," said Jeff defensively. "I don't know whether I can find it." Jeff started to fumble under himself, taking great gasping breaths as he did so, his face contorted as he wiggled and pushed. "Is it there?"

"How do I know, you silly bugger, if you don't, I don't that's for sure. You're too bloody fat for this game and that's the truth."

"So are you," said Jeff, cross as Doll pushed him to one side.

"Just get off and I'll turn over," huffed Doll, pushing Jeff off the bed.

271

She turned and lay on her tummy, pushing herself down to the end of the bed.

"There you are, just get on with it," she muttered, her hair and lipstick in complete disarray. "And mind you don't put your willy up my arsehole or that'll be more money, understand?" She looked round sharply at Jeff, who looked sheepish.

"Okay, Doll."

After much puffing and grunting, Jeff was done; he stood up, sweat pouring down his forehead, his steamed-up glasses obscuring his eyes. Doll sat up and pulled a soiled towel from under the counterpane. She stood up, letting her skirt fall down over her thighs.

"So what exactly happened to Judy? Why couldn't she do her A Levels?" Jeff asked, pulling his braces over his shoulders.

"It was that Cyril. Did you know him, Jeff? He was as rotten as rotten, I've seen him pick them up in the pub, it didn't matter if it were boys or girls. He'd give 'em a drink or two and then that was that, off they went and we'd never see 'em again."

"Well what did he do to her?"

"It were dreadful," said Doll, on the verge of tears. "Really dreadful, she never did end up doing her A Levels, had to leave school."

Doll stepped into her knickers and pulled them up over her tummy, before smoothing her skirt down. She sniffed angrily and continued, "Bert had to go part time and stay at 'ome. You couldn't leave her, or at least not for long and she's been like it ever since. A little shell of a thing." She sniffed again

272

and stared at the birthday card on the mantelpiece. "We're really strugglin' now. Bert don't bring in much and we have to make do on what I can earn and that gets less when you're my age. Too old for all this, me." She laughed and pulled on her shoes.

"What about Cyril then? Didn't he ever get arrested?"

"No, he got murdered, didn't you hear? Somewhere over your way. About six months ago it was. Well good riddance, that's all I say. I'm glad he were murdered and I hope it 'urt. He'll rot in hell."

She rose, pulled her dentures from the mantelpiece and slipped them into her mouth before returning to the bed and opening her handbag.

"Yes, I remember now. The police came up our way about it, I didn't realise it were that Cyril, but then I din't know him that well. Only seen him occasionally in the pub."

"Well you be glad you didn't know 'im, that's all I can say," said Doll, looking in the mirror to reapply her lipstick and mascara. She stepped back and examined herself critically. "There, good as new," she announced, snapping her bag shut.

"I'll walk you back. My car's in the square and I can take those bayonets in to Robin."

Chapter Seventeen
The Penny Drops

The Picture Drome was the least popular of the cinemas in Bedford but showed more X-certificate films than the others. The lights had just come on following the matinee performance of *No Sun in Venice*. The three boys, Peter, Tookey and Simon, made their way up the side aisle to the exit as the gas lights flickered on the walls above them.

"What are we going to do then?" said Tookey. "It's an hour and a half until the bus goes."

He looked at the other two. There were only two buses on Saturdays from Bedford to Kimbolton; one at four-thirty, which meant that if you wanted to catch it you would miss the end of the film, and one at six forty-five, so you could either watch the film again, or find other entertainment.

"We could see it again?" suggested Peter. "It's better than standing out in the cold."

"No, it's not that cold out," said Simon. "Let's wait a bit and go to a pub, we can go to the Turk's Head, I bet you've not been in there."

The others said nothing, but followed Simon slowly out into the light, traipsing after him towards the embankment of the river adjacent to the cinema. Simon turned to face the other two.

"Come on then," he said. "What about it, you'll come, won't you, Tookey, even if he won't?" He sneered slightly at Peter, who said nothing.

"We can't go, it's not open yet, they don't open till six, do they?" said Tookey, taking out a packet of cigarettes and offering it to the other two.

"We'll just have to wait a bit then, that's all," said Simon, sitting on the stone balustrade which flanked the river.

"I bet they won't serve you," said Peter suddenly.

"They will!" said Simon indignantly. "They have to, we're all eighteen. They let us into the cinema, didn't they? So they'll serve us in the pub."

"It's a rough place," persisted Peter. "They all say that."

"Well so what?" said Simon petulantly, leaping off his perch and walking towards the bridge.

Tookey and Peter looked at one another, shrugged and followed Simon. In the middle of the bridge, they were confronted by three girls, who stood shoulder to shoulder, blocking the pavement.

"Fancy meeting you here," said Sandra with a grin. "You're a long way from home, I'm surprised your mothers let you three out, aren't you, Nimpy?" Nimpy giggled. "What you been doing then? You're all dressed up for something."

"We've been to the pictures and we've got to wait for the bus," said Simon.

"So have we," said Nimpy. "What did you see, then?"

"I know," said Primrose, "I bet they've been to that X certificate. Look, Nimpy, they're going red!" she laughed. "Were they all in the nude? I bet they were."

275

The boys shifted uncomfortably, embarrassment etched on their faces. Simon broke the silence. "Just because you're not old enough. I suppose you went to see *Snow White* or something like that." He stuck his tongue out at the girls and made a face.

"Well at least they didn't take their clothes off, did they, Nimpy?" said Primrose, turning to her friend for support. Nimpy said nothing. "Anyway we saw *Oklahoma* so there." She stuck her tongue out at Simon.

"Well did they, then?" persisted Sandra.

"Did they what?" said Simon.

"Did they take their clothes off in the film? It looks like they did from the advert." She looked at Simon, who refused to be drawn.

"I'm not telling you, when you're old enough you can go and see for yourself. And even if they did, what's wrong with that, everyone's got the same underneath, or didn't you know that?" It was now the girls' turn to look embarrassed. There was an uncomfortable silence.

"Where are you going then?" Peter asked finally, taking a puff of his cigarette.

"We're just going for a walk while we wait for the bus, what are you doing?" Nimpy replied.

"We're going to the pub, ain't we, Tookey?" announced Simon forcefully. Tookey grimaced and looked dubious.

"Which one then?" said Nimpy.

"The Turk's Head."

"You're not going in there, are you?" said Primrose sharply. "It's really rough that pub is, even my dad won't go in there."

276

"Course we are, aren't we, Tookey? Are you coming, Peter?" said Simon, puffing out his chest and holding the lapels of his jacket. A whistle behind the boys alerted them to Helen's arrival.

"You didn't bring her, did you?" said Tookey. "Although, s'pose she gets in for a half at the cinema." Simon laughed.

"No I don't, Peter Tookey. I'm fourteen and I pay full price, don't I, Nimpy?"

"Where have you been then?" Tookey asked, looking her up and down disapprovingly.

"I'm just been to the toilet if you must know. Am I allowed to do that?"

Simon looked at his watch. "Come on, Tookey, it will be six by the time we get there." He turned to Peter. "You're not coming I guess, Peter. You'd better stay with the girls, if you're chicken." Simon turned and marched across the river bridge with Tookey trailing behind him, leaving Peter with the four girls.

The St Cuthbert church clock struck six as Simon and Tookey walked across the market square.

"Are you sure we're all right to go in here, Simon? They say awful things about this pub."

"I know. That's why we're going; it's a challenge, don't you think? Anyway, it can't be *that* bad, and we *are* eighteen, aren't we? It's better than standing about with all those girls."

They arrived at the pub, pushing straight into the public bar. Although it was only just six there were several people already sitting at some of the tables and others standing at the long bar. Simon strode up to the bar, followed by Tookey. He turned to his friend. "What's it going to be then?"

277

Tookey looked confused, unsure of what he was being asked. Simon frowned and turned to the barman.

"Two halves of bitter," he said, pushing his hand into his pocket to find some money. The barman reached for two glasses and put them on the bar. He eyed them suspiciously.

"You old enough?"

"Course we are," said Simon, rather aggressively.

"All right, all right. Don't come with that sort of tone or I won't serve you no matter how old you are." Simon scowled and looked down the bar to the man on a stool closest to them, who had been watching proceedings. "I suppose you do look eighteen," said the barman, picking up the glass and pulling the pump forward to fill it. "It's hard to tell these days."

"Having trouble, Robin?" asked the man on the stool, eyeing the two boys with dislike.

"No, no, these two say they're eighteen," said Robin, looking again at the boys. "What do you think, Tom?"

"Yeah, they look eighteen," said the man, looking hard at Simon. He pointed at him. "I'm seen you, haven't I? Your dad's that solicitor, ain't he?" He clicked his fingers in recognition. "Simon, ain't it? I knew I'd remember." He looked quizzically at the boys. "What you doing in here then? Does your dad know you frequent places like this?" He looked from Simon to Tookey and back again. "I bet he don't, does he?" he chuckled.

"We're having a drink just like you," said Simon defensively. "There's no law against that, is there?" Tom sucked his teeth.

"I suppose not," he said, turning back to his drink as Robin placed the second half in front of Simon, who handed over the money. The two boys grabbed their glasses and moved to sit at a small table, trying to be as unobtrusive as possible.

"Who was that then?" Tookey whispered.

"He's the policeman from Kimbolton, he knows Dad."

"Well we're not doing anything wrong, are we?" said Tookey, sounding apprehensive.

"No. Just drink the beer, we'll have another one in a bit."

Tookey looked round at the other customers in the dimly lit bar. Besides the policeman at the bar, there were two men playing darts, while another man sat at a nearby table scoring; next to him sat a woman who was reading the paper. Occasionally she would reach forward towards the fire and warm her hands as the flames flickered and danced up the chimney. Over the fireplace on the wall hung two bayonets wired together in a cross.

Simon had nearly finished his beer already and he gulped down the last mouthful.

"Did you like it?" asked Tookey, taking a more moderated swig from his glass.

"It's all right. Drink up! We've got time for another one before the bus, get a packet of crisps, that'll take the taste away a bit."

Tookey looked at Simon and then at the men playing darts. The woman was looking over the top of her paper at the two boys.

"Go on then, it's your turn," said Simon, pushing the glasses towards Tookey. Tookey looked at the barman dubiously; he was talking to Tom. He picked up the glasses and went to the bar for service and waited patiently. Robin looked

279

down the bar to Tookey and continued to talk to Tom; finally, he was unable to ignore him any further.

"Do you want a drink then?" said Robin indifferently.

"Yes please, two halves please."

Robin sauntered down and collected the glasses, as the woman who had been reading the paper, tottered up to Tookey. She stood close to him with her back to the policeman at the other end of the bar.

"You're a nice looking boy," crooned Doll, fingering the lapel of his jacket. "What are you doing in a place like this, dressed up in a nice jacket like this? You must be wanting something, I guess?" She smiled at him sweetly. Doll's tired face, accentuated by thick lipstick and dark eye shadow, got closer to his. He took a small step backwards.

"No, I don't want anything. 'Cept the beer, I mean." He looked over Doll's shoulder to avoid her gaze.

"You're a nice boy," she said again, stroking his cheek with the back of her hand. "Lovely skin you've got." Tookey swallowed and looked ahead, silently urging Robin to return.

"One and four," said Robin, sauntering back down the bar.

Tookey handed him half a crown and waited for the change. Doll smiled and lowered her hand to Tookey's thigh; she gripped it tightly and brought her face close to his again.

"Do you want a quick one when you've had your beer, only a pound? I'll do it for fifteen shillings each if your friend wants to come. I couldn't say fairer than that, could I?" She leaned back slightly and grinned wolfishly.

Tookey's body tensed, his hand trembling on the bar as he desperately sought a reply. Suddenly the door flew open and two men entered.

"More bloody police," hissed Doll under her breath. "Well, handsome?" she continued, looking into Tookey's face.

"Not today thank you. I haven't got enough money; I need it for the bus." He snatched the beers from the bar and rushed to the table.

"No luck then, Doll?" came a shout from one of the men who had just entered. "I wouldn't worry, doesn't look as if he'd know what to do, a bit wet behind the ears." His companion laughed.

"Just you keep your opinions to yourself, Gerald Drew," said Doll, returning to her chair by the fire.

"What was that about?" asked Simon, as Tookey made his way back to their table, "What did that old woman want?"

"She wanted to know if I wanted a quick one. For a pound, she said, and if you wanted to come along it would be fifteen shillings each. That was what that was about." He looked at Simon and coloured slightly.

"What did you say then?" said Simon with a grin.

"I said that I didn't have enough money and then all that lot started shouting." They looked over to where the two policemen were talking to Tom. "I know one of them that just came in. He's the policeman from Dean, Rawlins. He wanted to look at my licence the other day. You must remember him."

"Maybe. But who's the other one?"

"Don't know. Come on, we'll drink this and go, I've had enough of this place." The two boys drank down their beers and edged towards the door.

"Look who we've got here then," Rawlins grinned catching sight of the boys before they'd managed to escape. He was leaning back against the bar with a pint in one hand. "Do you know this one, Tom?" he asked loudly, pointing at Tookey. "I think I know both of them, seen you lot in Dean, ain't I? You're the lot that tried to let my tyres down, ain't you?" Simon and Tookey looked at each other and then back at the policemen, saying nothing. "What are you doing in here then? You're a long way from home. Up to no good, I expect." The two boys remained silent, still backing towards the door.

"Oi," shouted Gerald, who had been silently observing this exchange with amusement. "Are you deaf or something? Don't you answer when you're spoken to?" The boys stood frozen to the spot. Tookey assumed an air of innocence.

"Were you speaking to us?" he said, trying to be as offhand as possible.

"Well, who do you think we were speaking to?" said Gerald. "Did you let his tyres down then?"

"No one let his tyres down," said Simon clearly. Gerald scowled and stood up to his full height, pointing at Simon.

"Don't you speak to me in that tone, my boy," he said, wagging his finger warningly at Simon.

"What tone?"

Doll approached the bar behind the boys.

"Come on, Gerald," she said reasonably. "Leave them alone, they've done you no harm, have they? Come on, buy me a drink, won't you?"

"She's right, Gerald," said Rawlins with a shrug. "It wasn't them that let the tyres down, it were that snotty one." The two boys saw their opportunity and darted gratefully for the door.

"Whose idea was it to go in there then?" said Tookey as the pair stood breathlessly outside. "I wish we had come on the bike, we could be on our way home by now."

"Well we didn't. So let's get to the bus station." Tookey frowned and followed Simon back to the square.

Back in the bar, Tom was buying a round for Gerald and Joe Rawlins; they were still discussing the Dean youth.

"I had one of that gang in my station a while back," he said. "He said he knew you, Joe. I can't remember his name. Christian something, I think."

"Thompson," said Joe with a scowl.

"That's him. He came to pick up a paperweight."

"A what?"

"A brass paperweight. Someone had handed it in. They found it in a heap of spuds on the Dunmore farm. Have you ever heard anything so stupid? The lad said he put it in a bag by mistake when he was picking the tatters out the field." Tom took another sip of beer.

"Say that again," said Gerald.

"What?" said Tom.

"What you said about the brass paperweight." Tom repeated the story. Gerald was silent for a moment.

"You remember that murder, that bloke Cyril who was stabbed," he said finally.

"He were no good," piped up Robin from the bar. "He used to come in here."

"What about it?" said Joe, ignoring Robin.

"Well he were hit over the head with something before he were stabbed, weren't he?"

"Yes, so what?"

"Well his mother said there was something missing from the house; his house, I mean." Gerald paused for effect. "A brass paperweight."

"I don't remember that, Gerald. I thought we were looking for bayonets or something like that, like them over the fireplace."

"Well we were. But it's a coincidence, ain't it?"

"Yes, I suppose it is. But Christian Thompson ain't capable of killing a man; he couldn't even let my tyres down properly."

"Where did he say he got it from, Tom?" asked Gerald.

"He said his mother give it him if I remember rightly."

Gerald took a sip of his beer and stared at the bayonets over the fireplace; he couldn't remember having seen them hanging in the pub before. He put his beer down on the bar and walked slowly towards the display.

"What you looking at, Sherlock?" said Doll, looking moodily up from her paper.

"Nothing, nothing," said Gerald, walking back to the bar, his eyes still on the bayonets.

"Well, I'm on duty tomorrow," he said with a sigh. "Sunday of all days, it'll give me something to think about for a change."

"Better than chasing Gypsies," said Joe under his breath.

"Don't talk to me about gypos, Joe," growled Gerald. "You know my views on them."

He pushed his glass over to Robin for another pint.

"Anyone else? Robin, what about you?"

"Don't mind if I do. I'll have an 'arf." Gerald looked back towards the fireplace.

"Where did you get them bayonets any road, Robin?" he asked.

"An old mate sold them to me, Jeff, do you know him? He lives in Dean."

"He lives where?"

"Dean."

Joe and Tom looked up sharply.

"I know 'im," said Joe.

"So do I," said Tom. "He's the plumber."

"He said 'e found them when he were takin' out an old water tank. He said the old lady whose tank it was had given them to him. She runs this little school or something like that in Dean."

The policemen looked at each other, a spark of excitement glimmered in Gerald's eye.

"That's it then, ain't it, that's a bit too much of a coincidence," said Gerald. "Joe, what's the name of the school in Dean and the old lady, we went there, didn't we?"

"The Hall is the school. The old lady's name is Miss Shaw, but she's not really old, just looks it."

"Are you on duty tomorrow, Joe?" asked Gerald. "I might need some help if I come out there."

"No I ain't. But a bit of overtime will come in handy."

"You'll let me know how you get on, Gerald?" said Tom.

"Course I will. And what's the name of that old boy, Joe, the lad who let down your tyres?"

"Christian. That's his name, Christian Thompson."

"Well. I think it's time we went to see young Mr Thompson, I feel he might have a bit more to tell us."

Chapter Eighteen
An Arrest Is Made

The next day brought with it club night, and all the members gathered in the yard at the back of the Hall as usual, waiting for Miss Shaw to open the door. All those from Dean had walked, but most of the others had come on bikes, Simon hitching a lift on the back of Tookey's motorbike.

"How did you get on in the pub, Simon?" asked Nimpy. "We didn't wait as you weren't back at the bus stop by the time our bus left and I had to go home."

"Oh, it was fine. We had a pint and left, didn't we, Tookey?"

"Yeah."

"My dad says there's an old tart in there called Doll," said Helen, enthusiastically. "Did you see her?"

"An old what?" said Primrose.

"Tart," said Helen.

"Do you know what a tart is, Helen?" Primrose asked in a superior tone.

"Well it's…" stammered Helen, "I mean she's a…"

"She's a what?" persisted Primrose.

Helen blushed.

"Well anyway, did you meet her, Simon?" said Helen quickly. "Dad says she's always in there." Simon looked embarrassed and glanced at Tookey.

"I don't know. But how does your dad know about her, your mum wouldn't let him go in there, would she?"

"Where's Miss Shaw then? I'm fed up of standing out here." said Ann loudly, bored with the conversation. "Go and tell her it's time, Christian, will you?"

"She'll come in a minute, you'll see. She's just on her way to chapel and she will be putting her hat on."

He raised his hand to his mouth, popped something between his lips and swallowed it.

It was now late spring; the nights were drawing out and the evening was quite warm. The boys had all taken their jackets off and the girls wore dresses or blouses and skirts in the warm air. Christian had his white school shirt on but it was undone at the collar and his tie hung round his neck half undone. His school jacket was slung over his shoulder with one finger through the peg loop. He moved up to Tookey who was polishing the wheels of his motorbike by running a piece of rag between the spokes and pulling from both sides.

"Tookey, what was that pub like that you went in, was it the Turk's Head?" said Christian.

"Yeah, we went in there. Why? Do you know it, Christian? Have you been in for a pint then?" Christian looked sheepish.

"No. But I was talking to Jeff the other day and he'd sold the landlord a couple of bayonets that I was interested in. I thought I'd like one. He said they came from the First World War. He said the landlord wanted them for decoration. Did you see them?"

Tookey looked up. "See what, did you say?"

"Bayonets hung up as decoration in the pub."

Tookey turned his head and thought for a moment. "Yes, there were some, now you come to mention it. There were two of them hung over the fireplace where she was sitting."

"Where who was sitting?"

"Oh no one," said Tookey hastily. "Just an old woman."

Miss Shaw suddenly appeared from the back door. Everyone cheered. She unlocked the door to the clubhouse, flicked on the lights and led the way into the room. There were twelve of them and they sat themselves down on the benches and waited in silence.

"Eyes shut, hands together," said Miss Shaw, before praying for the starving in Africa.

The "Amens" sounded out enthusiastically as all the club members opened their eyes in anticipation of Miss Shaw leaving, but Miss Shaw stood her ground.

"Now. Before I go I want you all to think hard about what you are doing in this club. It seems to me that in the time you have here, nothing terribly..." she paused tactfully, "...constructive goes on. You must think of some aims and objectives and some projects or events. I have not questioned what you do up to this moment and there certainly have been fewer complaints about your behaviour since you started meeting here; but we must move on. Onwards and upwards. Now who's the eldest?"

"Roger is," said Sandra. "But he's not here tonight, so it must be Peter."

She pointed.

"Very well then, Peter, you will be in charge," said Miss Shaw. "I want you to come up with something more constructive to do or to study." She looked over her glasses at Peter before making a peculiar little tour of the room, looking at each of them in turn. As she passed the girls sniggered and the boys made faces behind her back. "I'm going now," she said, reaching the door again. "I will expect some suggestions by the time I return." Then she turned on her heel and left.

Gerald Drew had been at work all day going over the paperwork on the case of the murder of Cyril Merton. He had found the notes on Christian and had driven to the police station at Kimbolton and checked the details of the paperweight against the report of the loss from Cyril's mother. He had been to interview Jeff in Dean and had then returned to the Turk's Head and collected the bayonets as possible murder weapons. He had spoken at length to the police pathologist and with all the evidence accrued he had decided that he should arrest Christian to pursue the matter further and obtain what he hoped would be corroborating fingerprints. He prepared the paperwork and took it to a JP to sign on his way back to Dean. When he arrived at Dean it had just turned seven, and Gerald dropped by the police house to collect PC Rawlins. He knocked at the door and Joe answered it in his slippers.

"I didn't expect to see you this late, Gerald," grumbled Joe. "I ain't even in my uniform."

"Bit between the teeth Joe, bit between the teeth," murmured Gerald, "I'm got this one cracked now. Come on, get your uniform on and we'll go and get our man."

"Boy, you mean."

"He's a man, Joe, eighteen," said Gerald severely. "Old enough to be hanged."

"If you say so, Gerald. But come in and talk to the wife while I get changed."

It had gone quarter past seven when they arrived at the Hall. Joe knocked at the front door. There was no answer, so he banged again. Eventually steps could be heard approaching along the stone flags of the hallway. There was a squeaking of bolts and a click as the lock was turned and Miss Shaw opened the door.

"Who on earth is calling at this time of night on a Sunday?" muttered Miss Shaw, opening the door slowly to reveal the two men. "Oh it's you, Rawlins. What do you want at this time? I hope it's important. I really have better things to do."

"This is Detective Constable Drew. Do you remember he came a little bit back?" Miss Shaw stared at Rawlins blankly. "He wants to have a word."

"A word about what?" said Miss Shaw impatiently.

Joe went to answer but Gerald butted in. "It's like this, missus…" started Gerald.

"Miss!"

"It's like this…" said Gerald, ignoring her, "we have reason to believe…" He looked around him and stopped. "I'll come in to say this, Miss Shaw, please."

Miss Shaw sighed and opened the door further to let the two men in.

"We have reason to believe that Christian Thompson lives here with you?"

"Yes. He's lived here since he was six, so what?"

"And is he here now, madam?"

"Yes I think so, he's in the club with the other boys and girls at the back. Why do you want him?"

"We've come to arrest him, madam," said Gerald with a distinct air of satisfaction.

"Arrest him!" gasped Miss Shaw, shocked and visibly paling, "What for? He's a bit of a tearaway but he's a good boy really."

"We've come to arrest him for the murder of Cyril Merton."

Miss Shaw's mouth fell open, and she put her hand to her forehead, her legs weakening under her. "It can't be true."

"It is, I'm afraid, miss," said Gerald, taking the arrest warrant from his pocket. "All the paperwork's here." He started to read, "On the 5th October last…" He stopped. "No, I'd better not start before I read it to him and give him his rights."

"Come into the office," said Miss Shaw. "I've got to sit down."

She led the two men down the corridor to her office, collapsing onto the chair behind her desk. She blew her nose loudly on a flowered handkerchief. Her face as white as a sheet and she shivered.

"Now, tell me again. You've come to arrest Christian for murder, is that what you said? I can't believe it." She looked between the two men incredulously.

"That's right," said Gerald. "We've got the murder weapon."

"But that doesn't mean he did it. Just because you've got the murder weapon, and where did you find it? You haven't searched here?"

"Well, it were two weapons really," said Gerald with increasing relish. "And we got them from the public bar of the Turk's Head in Bedford. We believe they originally came from a hiding place in the tank in your attic. Jeff found them. He said you told him he could have them, were that right, Miss Shaw?"

He looked at her. A tear came to her eye which she quickly wiped away.

"Is that all the evidence you've got to go on?"

"No," said Gerald, smugly. "There's the matter of a brass paperweight which went missing from the murder scene. It was found in a heap of potatoes on a farm up the road and was handed in to the station in Kimbolton. Christian went to the station and claimed it; it were handed over to him and we believe the object is still in his possession. According to the pathologist, the victim was originally hit over the head with a heavy metal object. This is before he was stabbed, and we believe the heavy object was a sculpted paperweight which has been declared missing from the house."

Miss Shaw sat back in her chair and blew her nose again.

"He did go potato picking for several days, I know that. He's always short of money, he has no family support. And wouldn't let me help." Her eyes brimmed with tears again.

"Where are his parents, Miss Shaw?" asked Joe gently. Miss Shaw chewed her lip and wiped the tears from her eyes.

"I don't know," said Miss Shaw; she hesitated briefly. "I haven't heard from his mother in years and his father went abroad and stopped sending any money some time ago. We have supported him here unassisted since then."

"Well, can you show us where he is, Miss Shaw, please?" said Joe. Miss Shaw nodded hesitantly and led the way to the back door.

In the club Peter had tried unsuccessfully to get the group to agree to organise an event but they had put any decision off until next Sunday and had quickly resorted to Postman's Knock again. He was outside the clubhouse with Helen, and they stood in the doorway of the boiler house so as not to be seen since it was now light at this time of the evening.

"Peter," said Helen, pulling away from him, "did you know that the police were at Jeff's today, you know he lives next to us? They must have been there an hour. What do you think that was all about then?"

"I've no idea. Why should I know?"

"Well I just thought you might, that's all. One of them was in plain clothes." She wiped her lipstick from Peter's mouth with her index finger.

"No, I don't know. Why don't you ask Jeff?" Peter smiled at her then went through the door of the clubroom, closing it behind him. Inside Sandra held the flowerpot with the pieces of paper in. She offered it to each boy in turn, pausing at Christian.

"Go on," said Tookey. "You have a go, Christian, it's not as bad as all that, you know." They all laughed. Christian looked uneasy and didn't reach out for a number so Sandra thrust her hand into the pot and chose one for him.

"Here we are," she said. "Number three and Helen's outside. You'll win with that, you'll see, Christian."

Christian took the number reluctantly. When all the numbers had been taken, they sat and waited for the knock on the door.

"Come on, Helen," shouted Simon.

There were three loud knocks at the door. The assembled company hollered and whooped.

"Told you," said Sandra, as Christian rose shakily to his feet, clutching his jacket.

The door latch clicked unexpectedly and the group fell quiet, ready to admonish Helen for returning prematurely. The door opened and a man in a suit filled the doorway. He bent down so as not to hit his head on the lintel and swaggered down the three steps, straightening up to his full height. Behind him came PC Rawlins in his uniform and carrying his helmet. There was silence as he looked around the room at everyone sitting on the benches. The only one not sitting was Christian. He still stood in the middle of the room, clutching his jacket. Gerald turned to PC Rawlins and Joe nodded at Christian.

"That's him," he said. Gerald pulled the arrest warrant from his pocket and opened it out.

"Are you Christian Thompson?" he demanded.

There was silence as everybody stared at Christian, mouths agape.

"Yes," said Christian, his voice barely above a whisper.

There was the sound of footsteps as Miss Shaw and Helen came to the doorway. Gerald cleared his throat.

"Christian Thompson," he began, "I am arresting you for the murder of Cyril Merton. You do not have to say anything but anything you do say may be given in evidence."

The group said nothing, all looking from one to the other in disbelief. Primrose put her hand to her mouth and looked ready to cry.

"Do you understand?" said Gerald firmly.

"Yes," said Christian, his voice calm as he looked at the ground.

"Empty your pockets please," said Gerald.

Christian put his hands into his trouser pockets and took out a dirty handkerchief, some chewing gum and a few coins. He held them out in front of him, Gerald looked at the contents of his hands and told him to put them back.

"Jacket pockets now," he ordered.

Christian held the jacket by the collar and put his hand into one pocket, pulling out a small glass bottle. He held it out for inspection with a sigh.

"Hmm," said Gerald, "I think we'll keep that." He handed the bottle to PC Rawlins.

"The other pocket," he instructed.

Christian turned the jacket around, putting his hand into the other pocket and pulling out the brass paperweight. He hung his head and held it out towards Gerald, who took it and turned it round and round in his palm.

"I think we'll keep this as well," he said, raising an eyebrow.

The assembled company continued to look on with dismay. Miss Shaw dabbing constantly at her eyes with a handkerchief as she sobbed, and Christian's shoulders slumped.

"Put your jacket on, boy," said Gerald quietly. "It's time to go."

Christian slid his arms into his jacket and shrugged it on. Then with PC Rawlins holding tightly to his arm, and under the disbelieving eyes of the assembled company, Christian allowed himself to be led from the room.

Chapter Nineteen
Bedford Prison

The group stood and stared in astonishment as Christian climbed into the police car and was driven off. Miss Shaw turned and looked round at them. Nobody said anything. Miss Shaw's face was white. She wrung her hands then looked at the ground.

"We had better close for tonight," she said, but she did not move.

"What did the policeman say he did, Miss Shaw?" said Sandra eventually. Miss Shaw's lip quivered.

"They said he murdered a man called Cyril Merton last October," she said, putting her hand to her mouth.

"But he couldn't have done that," insisted Simon. "Christian could never murder anyone, not like that."

"He's right," said Primrose. "Christian couldn't do that, why would he? How did he know that man anyway?" Miss Shaw sighed.

"They have evidence. The two bayonets, I saw them, and the brass paperweight, you all saw that." She stopped and sighed again. "It all adds up, doesn't it? The paperweight being in the potatoes, where he was working. Who was with him there? I know you were, Peter, what about anyone else?"

"We were there," said Nimpy. "Weren't we, Helen?" Helen nodded in agreement.

"He was a bit funny," said Helen slowly. "And he did go up to the farm to look in the heap for something, didn't he?" Nimpy nodded unhappily. There was silence as the group waited for Miss Shaw to say something else.

"Shall we pray for him?" said Nimpy quietly.

"Yes, let's do that," said Miss Shaw gratefully. "And I'll find out what I can tomorrow and if you all come next week I'll let you know what's happening. After all, you are all his friends, aren't you?" They all nodded in agreement.

Christian meanwhile had been taken to Bedford Police Station where he remained until the next day, when he was taken to the magistrates' court. He spoke only to answer questions and did whatever he was bidden to do without argument. At the court his case was remanded to the assizes which would sit in six weeks' time; he was granted legal aid but was to be held in custody. There was no application for bail and after the hearing he was taken to the prison in Bedford to await his trial. Christian had remained relatively unfazed by all the proceedings, as if he were sleepwalking through someone else's life, and it wasn't until he was sitting in the van transporting him to the prison for his induction process, that the terror of where he was going crowded in on him. Christian stood pale and trembling in a queue with four others from the court, waiting to be called forward.

"Next!" shouted one of the officers sitting at the desk. Christian walked forward shakily and stood in front of the men. "Name!"

Christian Thompson answered quietly.

"Offence?"

"Murder."

The officer looked up sharply at Christian, still in his school uniform, his black shoes sitting grubbily on his feet, his glasses dirty.

"Pockets," continued the officer. Christian looked blank. "Turn your pockets out, boy," he prompted.

Christian obeyed. The officer looked up at him again.

"Are you really eighteen, boy?" he asked. "You don't look it."

"Yes," said Christian, looking down at his feet to avoid making eye contact.

"Where we going to put you then?" he said, running his finger up and down the written list of the cells on the clipboard in front of him.

"He won't survive on the wing," murmured one of the officers standing behind the seated officer "They'll make mincemeat of him in a minute, especially as he's in for murder."

The officer at the desk tutted as he ran his finger down the list again. He turned to another book marked "Segregation Unit", glanced at it briefly and shook his head.

"No, I don't want him in there, he'll have to go on the wing for the moment," said the officer, slamming the book shut and writing Christian's name onto the first list, before shouting, "Next!"

Christian grimaced and allowed himself to be led to the showers, where his clothes were taken from him and he was issued with prison uniform. Once clad in his blue uniform he was taken to his meagre cell, the door slamming shut behind him.

The next day, Miss Shaw was sitting in her office when the front door bell rang.

"Go and see who that is," she shouted to one of the boys who happened to be scurrying past at that moment. Two minutes later he was back at her door, an old lady standing behind him.

"It's Mrs Dene, Miss Shaw," said the boy, standing aside to let Mrs Dene into the room.

"Thank you," said Miss Shaw, as the small boy departed.

"Now, Miss Shaw," started Mrs Dene, "Or can I call you Evelyn?" Miss Shaw smiled slightly.

"Call me Evelyn."

"I came about poor Christian, I just can't believe it, I really can't, how can it be true? They must have made a mistake, mustn't they?" She looked desperately at Miss Shaw. "What can we do? Or what can I do? I mean, I know lots of people, you know, JPs and the like. We must be able to do something." She looked earnestly at Miss Shaw who had remained silent. "Do you think he did it?" Miss Shaw shrugged slightly, removed her glasses and rubbed her eyes with her fists.

"I can't believe he did it. It's so out of character; but there's a lot of evidence, and I saw that for myself. All I can think is that if he did do it he must have had a very good reason." They looked at each other in silence for a moment.

"What about his parents?" Mrs Dene asked. Miss Shaw frowned and looked away.

"I haven't heard from his father in years. And his mother…" She broke off with a sigh.

"So where did he come from, Evelyn? What's his history?" Miss Shaw sat back in her chair and took off her glasses.

"He was born in London in 1942. His father was in the army and when the war ended the father stayed abroad in the Far East, where he served. His mother would leave him with me in the school in Putney when she went out to see her husband with promises she would return, and he has been with me ever since. Christian came up here when we moved in 1949 and has been here ever since." Mrs Dene sighed. "What a sad story. Some people have no luck, do they? And you were in London in the war, Evelyn?"

"Oh yes. I was at Royal Holloway, London University until we were bombed."

"Oh really. I didn't think that you... You don't look... I mean you don't..." She stopped.

"You mean I look too old to have been at university in the war? Don't worry, Mrs Dene, I'm not embarrassed." Mrs Dene blushed.

"Be that as it may, what are we going to do about Christian? What has happened so far, do you know?"

"He's now in Bedford Prison. He's on remand to go to the assizes in six weeks. He's got legal aid and I've heard from the solicitor."

"Now, who do we know who can help?" frowned Mrs Dene, chewing her lip. "I know, Patience Pricklow, she's on the Board of Visitors or whatever they call them. She goes in all the time and I know the chaplain at the jail too, do you?"

"No. I'm afraid I don't."

"Well, never mind. When are you going to see him?" Miss Shaw looked up and then away from Miss Dene. She didn't reply for some moments.

"I don't know whether I can. It's, it's so awful. And what will happen to him if he did it? They hang murderers, don't they? If they are going to hang him in the end, I just don't know whether I can." Her lip trembled slightly.

"Now, now," chided Mrs Dene. "Don't talk like that, Evelyn, I won't have it, you are judging the case before it's even been heard. And even if he did do it or was convicted, they hang very few people these days especially if there's good mitigation and I'm sure there is. *If* he did it, that is."

She put her hand across the desk and patted Miss Shaw's hand. Miss Shaw looked up and across the desk at the woman smiling at her. Mrs Dene was wearing a black straw hat and a badly fitting cardigan over a white blouse and cotton flowery skirt; determination was etched across her face. Miss Shaw smiled.

"You are so kind, Mrs Dene," she said, forcing a smile. "I know Christian is a little odd – but he's been with me so long, I would hate to lose him." Her lip quivered again. "All these years," she murmured.

"Yes, yes, dear," said Mrs Dene, clicking open her handbag which she clutched in her lap.

"I think you should call me Verity, my dear," Mrs Dene said absently, rummaging through the bag. She paused and looked up at Miss Dene, before adding quietly, "I lost a son, you know, he died young. Just a little older than Christian. It was very sad." She pulled out a small crumpled handkerchief and blew her nose. "Now, Evelyn, a plan, don't you think?

301

Firstly, what about the solicitor, he's got legal aid you say, so who is the man representing him?"

Miss Shaw pulled a notebook towards her from across her desk and scrutinised a name scribbled on it. She frowned. "His name's Charles Dickens, that's what I wrote down."

Mrs Dene looked up sharply. "You mean that?" she asked dubiously. "It's not a joke?"

"No, that's what he said his name was. He sounded very nice on the phone."

"Well. I've never heard of him and I know a lot of the solicitors. I'll make enquiries and see what I can find out about him. Meanwhile I think I should visit Christian, don't you, but I don't fancy standing in the queue outside the gate; I will see what I can do."

"Are you sure?"

"Yes. I'm certain, it's the least I can do." She smiled, reached forward, shook Miss Shaw's hand firmly and bustled from the room.

By the time Mrs Dene had organised her visit to the prison, Christian had been moved from his cell on the wing into the segregation unit as he was seen as a vulnerable prisoner after he had been visited by Mrs Dene's friend, Patience Pricklow. He was now in his own cell. His solicitor, Charles Dickens, was young compared to most in his profession in Bedford and took the legal aid cases to ensure he had enough work. He was the junior partner in the firm Lane and Clutterbuck, whose senior partner, Lionel Jacobs, was coming to the end of his career and spent minimal time in the office, leaving Charles very much to his own devices. Charles had taken seven years to pass his articles and by the time he had become a partner he was thirty-three. He was married with two children, and much of his social life revolved round the local Round Table, of which he was a keen member. Charles's first trip to see Christian had been less successful than he had hoped as Christian had remained adamant that he would plead guilty. Deciding that the boy must have been confused and upset, he decided that he must make a second visit to see him and duly made his way to the prison.

At two o'clock that afternoon, Christian was escorted into the interview room where Charles sat waiting; the solicitor rose to shake Christian's hand.

"I like your tie," said Christian absently as they sat down. Charles was wearing a large red-spotted bow tie with a dark blue pinstriped suit.

"Yes, I suppose it's all right," he replied, looking suspiciously at Christian who looked relatively smart in his blue prison uniform. "It impresses the ladies, you know."

"I could do with a tie like that," said Christian, suppressing a smile.

"Well you can't have this one!" said Charles with a grin. "Now, Christian, we have business to do, I have to prepare your defence."

"If you say so," said Christian.

"You don't sound very interested."

"Oh, I am though," said Christian slyly. "For the first time in my life I'm famous and I will be till they hang me and then I'll be even more famous. Don't you think?" Charles looked apprehensively at Christian.

"You are still going to plead guilty, then?"

"Yes."

"To both charges?" Christian frowned.

"I didn't know there were two charges, I thought it was just murder."

"No. Those pills you had in your pocket were Purple Hearts. You've been charged with illegal possession of prescription drugs as well."

"Well I'll plead guilty to that as well then, I did have them, didn't I? Have you ever tried them? They give you a real buzz if you have enough of them." Christian looked at Charles, who blushed deep red and looked away. Christian laughed. "I reckon you have, you should see your face, guilty like me," he giggled, sitting back in his chair as Charles pretended to make notes.

"Well, if you intend to plead guilty what mitigation are you going to offer in the case?"

"What do you mean, what mitigation?"

"Why did you do it? Were you threatened by Cyril? Did he attack you? Was it self-defence? What happened to make you kill him?" Charles tapped the table with his pencil, Christian grimaced and looked away. "Well? Are you going to tell me what happened?"

"No. I've forgotten; it's gone right out my mind."

"Well, let's try again, Christian. Where did you get the Purple Hearts from?"

"I'm not telling you. Where did you get yours from?" Christian smiled at Charles smugly; the solicitor blushed again.

"Now, what about the paperweight and the two bayonets? You took them from the house and hid them; that's stealing, isn't it?"

"Yes, I would definitely call that stealing."

"So there's another charge they could bring. All in all you're in real trouble, Christian. If you want me to help you, *you* are going to have to help me." Christian looked at the ceiling. Charles sighed and stood up from the table.

"Now, Christian, look at the facts. You commit a murder, which you admit to, under the possible influence of drugs, and then you steal from the property. Things don't look too good, do they? Just you think about it for a few minutes." Charles shook his head and walked up and down the room a couple of times, hoping to let the gravity of Christian's predicament sink in but Christian looked moodily at the floor and continued to say nothing.

Just after Charles arrived at the prison Mrs Dene had made her way to the main prison gate. It was a sunny day and there was a queue of twenty people along the pavement waiting to go to visit their friends and relatives. The queue was mainly made up of women, one or two had children with them. Mrs Dene walked breezily past the queue; she was wearing her black straw hat over a long grey thick coat even though the sun was shining, and she carried her handbag and an umbrella. She went to the small door cut into the larger main gate and rapped upon it with the handle of her umbrella.

"What she think she's doin'?" someone called out behind her from halfway down the queue, and they raised their voice: "you ain't jumpin' the queue like that."

305

Mrs Dene took no notice and banged the door again. A small square peep hole opened towards the top of the door; she could see the eyes and nose of the officer inside.

"What do you want?" he asked, his manner abrupt.

"I want you to open this door."

"I can't do that, it ain't time." Mrs Dene stood on tiptoe and shouted into the small peep hole.

"Now look here, my man. When I say open the door, you open the door or I will make sure the right authority knows about it." There was no reply from inside and the face disappeared. There was silence. Mrs Dene shook her head and raised her voice. "Open this door."

There was a click and the small door opened. Mrs Dene stepped over the threshold, as the officer stepped back to avoid being walked into. She went straight into the gate house which was dark compared to the bright sunlight outside and she blinked for a few moments to let her eyes adjust. A large woman with a baby barged in after her.

"No we don't, no we don't!" yelled a voice from the room. "Don't let them buggers in." The woman was pushed back out by the officer who had let Mrs Dene in, and Mrs Dene now looked around her.

"Now who's in charge here?" she demanded, looking from one to the other of the six officers who were sitting around waiting to deal with the visitors.

"I am, madam," said the man whose face she recognised from the peep hole. He swaggered across the room and looked down at her.

"Don't talk to me in that tone," said Mrs Dene indignantly, as she looked around the room. "And do not swear, do you understand? Using dockers' language is most unbecoming."

The officer straightened up, adjusted his cap so that the peak was straight over his nose and fingered the key chain hanging from his belt.

"What can we do for you, madam?" he asked in a more conciliatory voice.

"I've come to see Christian Thompson. I would be grateful if you could take me to him." The officer pursed his lips.

"Can't do that, ma'am."

"Why not?"

"It's not time. And you haven't filled in a VO and he's in the Seg and what's more I think his solicitor is with him."

"You mean you won't let me see him?"

"No, ma'am. Not at the moment."

"Well I want to see the governor."

"You can't, ma'am. He ain't here, he's away on a course."

"Well, who is in charge then? Whoever it is, let me see him." She banged her umbrella on the ground, and as if she had summoned him, a tall, thin man in a pinstriped suit with a red handkerchief neatly folded in his top pocket, appeared at the door and strode up to Mrs Dene.

"Can I be of any assistance, madam?" he said, bowing slightly. "I'm the deputy governor." Mrs Dene looked the man up and down.

"My name is Verity Dene."

"I know, madam." Mrs Dene looked at him in surprise. "We met at the Lord Lieutenant's cocktail party in October. My wife's on the RSPCA committee, I believe you know her?

Audrey Watson?" He put his hand out to shake hers, Mrs Dene hoisted her umbrella under her arm and shook the proffered hand. "Now how can we help?" Mrs Dene looked a little overcome and she took a moment to compose herself.

"I've come to see Christian Thompson; I believe he's in this prison."

"Yes, I'll check for you, what offence was it?"

"Murder."

"Yes, of course, he's in the segregation unit. Now, Mrs Dene, you will need to fill in a visiting order, it's procedure." He leaned in confidentially to Mrs Dene. "You know; pieces of paper keep this place going. The SO will show you how, if you follow him then I can escort you."

Mrs Dene followed the SO into the little office in the gate house where another officer sat. As she climbed the steps, he rose quickly and turned round a calendar that had been hanging on the wall. Mrs Dene caught a glimpse of a half-naked girl rising from the sea as she put her handbag on the counter. The form was placed in front of her. She could hear the church clock in the distance striking two as the front gate opened to let in the queue of visitors. All of them had a visiting order with them and handed the form to one of the officers as they passed, before holding out their bags for inspection and turning out their pockets. The queue moved through the second gate to the visitors' room, all evidently confident of where they were going. Mrs Dene had found her glasses and a pen and came gingerly down the steps a while later after having completed the form.

"If you would like to follow me, Mrs Dene, we can go to the Seg and you can see him there," said the deputy governor.

Mrs Dene nodded graciously and followed the man; at every gate he got out his keys and let her through and every door slammed shut and was locked after them. After many doors they arrived at the segregation unit.

"If you would like to wait here, Mrs Dene, I will see if the solicitor is finished."

Mrs Dene stood at the entrance to a wide gallery and gazed around her. A table tennis table stood in the middle of the gallery and there were eight cell doors down one side and four down the other and an office with a window at the end of the corridor, where a prison officer sat. Another door yawned open to reveal an interview room, which also had a window onto the gallery so the officers could keep an eye on the occupants. The final door stood open to a cupboard stacked with cleaning paraphernalia. At the end of the gallery a prisoner in uniform was mopping the floor. He had an unlit cigarette in his mouth and on his forearm was the tattoo of an anchor with some numbers printed underneath it. The governor knocked at the interview room and when he poked his head round the door Christian was fidgeting and staring at the table while Charles leaned nonchalantly against the wall.

"There's a Mrs Dene here to see him when you've finished," said the Deputy Governor to Charles, who pushed himself away from the wall without taking his hands from his pockets. Christian looked up sharply.

"I'm not seeing her." Charles looked at Christian and then at the Deputy Governor, who raised his eyebrows.

"Who's Mrs Dene, Christian?" said Charles. "Why don't you want to see her?"

"She's an old lady from where I live."

"Well she's gone to a lot of trouble," said the Deputy Governor.

"I'm not seeing her," said Christian, more emphatically than before. Charles sighed and shook his head.

"Have we finished then?" Charles asked. Christian did not answer.

"I just don't want to see her, nor Miss Shaw, nor any of them," he said eventually. A tear sprang to his eye. "I want to see my mother, that's all."

"Fine, fine, I'll see what I can do," said Charles. "Let's leave it a week or so and I will come back, if you want me in the meantime just let the officer know."

Charles put his papers in his bag and stood back as the officer entered and escorted Christian back to his cell, where he locked him in.

"Would you like to say hello to Mrs Dene, Dickens?" asked the Deputy Governor.

"It might be helpful," said Charles with a sigh. Mrs Dene came into the interview room and the two were introduced. Charles handed her his card.

"Oh you work for Lionel, do you?" she asked, looking up from the card.

"Yes, but I do this work on my own."

"I was hoping to see Christian," she added, looking round the room.

"I'm sorry, he won't see you, or Miss Shaw. He's just told me that. I'm afraid I'm getting nowhere with this case. I can't discuss the details but if you can shed any light on events I would be most grateful, Mrs Dene. He asks about his mother and whether she can pay a visit but that is all I can get out of the boy, do you know anything of the mother?"

"No, I'm afraid not. But I can enquire of Miss Shaw, she runs the school where he lives."

"That would be most kind." Mrs Dene turned to leave, but hesitated.

"Mr Dickens, do you think he would see some of his friends? They have a club in the village and there's a small group of them; I'm sure some of them would come if he would see them."

"It's worth a try," said Charles with a shrug. "Perhaps they'll talk some sense into him."

Chapter Twenty
A Visit to Gaol

Helen and Primrose were sitting on a bench by the Hall as Nimpy rode up on her bicycle, the brakes squeaking as she stopped.

"Is it open?" she asked, looking through the hedge to the back of the Hall where the door to the club stood.

"No," said Helen. "Miss Shaw wanted us to leave it until she'd been to chapel and she's not back yet."

Nimpy could see Simon and Roger by the door to the club; they were kicking a football between them watched by Tookey, who was sitting astride his motorbike, smoking.

"Where are the rest then?" asked Nimpy.

"I don't know," shrugged Helen. "I expect they're coming, they usually do. Did you hear anything about Christian?"

"No, except Mum said she heard he was in Bedford prison now."

"I can't believe it, can you? Christian murder someone? It's not true, it can't be." The other girls said nothing. "He weren't no good at kissing, were he?" said Helen matter-of-factly.

"You're the expert then, are you, Helen?" said Primrose. "And you only fourteen!"

"Shut up, you," said Helen. "We all know what you get up to on the back seat of the bus, I've seen, don't forget."

"Just keep quiet, you two," said Nimpy. "He just didn't like it that's all, some people are like that. He had no mother to give him a cuddle, did he?"

"Give him a cuddle!" said Helen scornfully. "I never get a cuddle from my mother, do you, Primrose?"

"Only once, as far as I can remember."

Nimpy opened her mouth to reply but was prevented by the appearance of Peter who was cycling up on his old ladies' bicycle. He waved at the girls before catching sight of the boys at the back of the Hall and he turned into the gateway to see them.

"Like your bike, Peter," said Tookey. "Thought you were getting a new one?" Peter said nothing. "'Spect you'll have a car soon though, won't you? Wealthy farmers do, don't they?" Peter didn't answer, but kicked the ball back to Simon who picked it up and stopped playing. "What about Christian?" asked Tookey as the boys grouped together to discuss their friend.

"Dad says he's in Bedford Prison," said Simon. "He knows the firm of solicitors who are acting for him. He says the trial's in six or eight weeks when the assizes come." He bounced the ball a couple of times. "But he says they won't hang him. He's too young and he should have good mitit.... mitig... well, whatever the word is. Dad says he must have a good excuse for doing what he did to that man."

"You sure he did it then?" said Peter.

"Well it stands to reason, he had that brass thing, we all saw that, didn't we? That came from the house apparently and them bayonets, well we saw them in the pub, didn't we, Tookey?"

313

"Yes," Tookey agreed. "They hung over the mantelpiece; they say he killed him with them."

"Who said he did?" Peter said. "It might have been some-one else." Simon bounced the ball again and threw it to Roger who threw it back.

"Here she comes," said Simon in warning as Miss Shaw walked slowly back from chapel.

She wandered past the three girls sitting on the seat, who all rose and followed her towards the club door. She wore her felt hat and a mackintosh over a plain blue dress and cardigan. She went slowly into the Hall to get the key, returning a few minutes later to let them in. By the time she was back, all the usual members had arrived and they followed her down the steps into the club room.

"Now, we will say a prayer first," said Miss Shaw quietly.

The assembled gang closed their eyes and bowed their heads; there was none of the usual sniggering or whispering as Miss Shaw said her short prayer. She finished and looked at her watch.

"I mustn't be late," she said to nobody in particular, but then she looked up and addressed the room. "I'm going to see Mrs Dene, she's seen Christian. I will tell you all I know when I get back." She left the room.

"What are we going to do then?" asked Simon.

There was silence, then Primrose spoke. "She told us last time that we had to think of some aims and things to do, but nobody had any ideas, did they?"

"Well, we're not playing Postman's Knock," said Nimpy. "Not today anyway, it's not right."

"What about football?" said Tookey. "We could have a team." He looked around at the others but got no response.

"That's no good," said Helen. "Girls don't play football, do they? Why don't we play hockey? Then everyone can play."

"Where do we play then anyway?" said Tookey. "Nobody's got any sticks, only you, you're playing in that school team, aren't you, Helen?" Helen looked pleased with herself.

"We're playing the High School next Saturday," she said smugly. "What do you think of that then?"

"Your team against the High School?" said Peter, "You won't stand a chance."

"Yes, we will. Our team's made up from three secondary mods and we're going to beat them, you'll see."

"I know what we'll do," said Primrose, suddenly. "We will all go and watch the match, how about that? We can go on the bus; it gets there before two. When does the match start, Helen?"

"Two o'clock I think, but they are fetching me." Primrose nodded and started to mete out instructions as to how they were to all get to the hockey.

Meanwhile Miss Shaw had arrived at Mrs Dene's. She knocked at the front door. Within half a minute a lady in her fifties answered.

"Evening, Miss Shaw," she said, "Mrs Dene's expecting you, come this way please."

Miss Shaw followed the housekeeper to the sitting room, where Mrs Dene sat listening to the radio. It was gloomy in the room, even though it was still light outside. The windows were dirty and covered with thick net curtains and the wall-paper was peeling off under the window where the rain had crept in.

"Evelyn!" exclaimed Mrs Dene. "Come in, come in, do take a seat. Excuse me for not getting up, but it takes a little while these days. Now what can we get you? A glass of sherry? Or gin and orange? I believe we have some of that, don't we, Keddy?" She glanced up briefly at her housekeeper.

"I don't usually drink," Miss Shaw replied.

"Nor do I," said Mrs Dene, confidentially. "But I think we need one today, don't we? Keddy?" Mrs Keddy, who had been hovering by the door, turned and looked at Mrs Dene.

"Keddy, two sherries please, is that all right with you, Eve-lyn? Sherry?"

"Thank you, Mrs Dene," said Miss Shaw gratefully.

"Do call me Verity," said Mrs Dene with a wave of her hand towards Mrs Keddy, who bobbed and left the room.

"That woman's a drip, you know? Never knew why I em-ployed her, but there we go." She sighed. "Now, where was I? Yes, Christian!" She moved herself to the edge of her seat, sat up a little and continued in a discreet voice.

"I went to see him, as I said, but I'm afraid with no real success. He refused to see me and sent a message that he would not see you either. I spoke to his solicitor, Mister Charles Dickens, and found out who he works for, a good friend by the way. He's a bit of a 'spiv', Mr Dickens, is that what you call them? But he seems nice enough." She hesitated briefly before continuing. "He said that Christian refuses to cooperate and insists on pleading guilty. He won't give any reason as to why he did it."

Mrs Keddy brought the sherry in on a silver tray, handing a glass to Miss Shaw and another to Mrs Dene; they both took a tentative sip. As soon as Mrs Keddy had left, Mrs Dene continued. "The only thing he did say to the solicitor was that he wanted to see his mother." Miss Shaw took another slow sip from her glass.

"I've had no contact with her," she said quietly. "Why won't he see us; do you think?"

"I don't know. I could hear him in the interview room, he was quite adamant that he didn't want to see us." She sighed. "What about some of those friends of his, I wonder if he would see them?"

"Well, they are all in the club tonight. I can go back and ask them, he ought to agree to see them, don't you think?"

"It's worth a try. Someone has to get something out of him or they will hang him."

"Don't say that, Verity," begged Miss Shaw, taking a handkerchief from the sleeve of her cardigan, her face crumpling with despair.

"I'm sorry, dear. We mustn't think about that, must we? I'm sure we can do something; I will have a word with Rawlins to see if he knows anymore but we mustn't waste time, a week has passed already."

"You're right. I'll go and see them in the club now, do you mind if I don't finish my sherry, it goes to my head; you know?"

Miss Shaw rose unsteadily, said her goodbyes and returned to the Hall via the club. She knocked on the door and descended into the room. There was little noise in the room, everyone was sitting around the wall, some smoking, others talking quietly between themselves, Primrose had a pencil and paper in her hand; they all looked up as Miss Shaw entered.

"We're planning a trip, Miss Shaw, we're going to see Helen play hockey," said Primrose proudly.

"Very good, my dear," said Miss Shaw, with a tired smile. She hesitated, the others waited expectantly. "I just want to talk about Christian. Mrs Dene went to visit him yesterday. But he flatly refused to see her, and he won't see me either, so we think some of you should go and see him. We think that he may not refuse that. I would suggest..." She looked from one to the other of the group before continuing. "I would suggest that Simon goes, your father's a solicitor, Simon, and he will tell you what to do and you should select someone to go with you."

"I'll take Tookey and then we can go on his motorbike. All right, Tookey?"

"I suppose so. But who's going to pay for the petrol? It's a long way to Bedford."

"You could come on the bus with us next Saturday when we go to see Helen?" suggested Primrose. Simon shrugged and nodded.

"Thank you," said Miss Shaw gratefully. "That would be very kind." She smiled and left the room.

Four girls and three boys got off the bus at ten to two that Saturday in Bedford. The girls and Peter went in search of the hockey pitch and Simon and Tookey made their way towards the prison. The queue at the gates of the prison was already long, and they tagged onto the end and waited. Within

318

minutes the clock struck two, the door swung open and the queue started to trickle forwards. Simon and Tookey made their way through the small door into the gloom of the gate house, arriving in front of a tall SO.

"Where's your VO?" he demanded, holding out his hand.

"My what?" said Simon.

"VO! Your visiting order, boy, don't you know what a visiting order is?" said the SO. "Anyway how old are you? You're not eighteen, nor's he." He nodded at Tookey, who opened his mouth to protest. "You know where you can go then, back to where you came from." He pointed to the door dismissing them.

"I am eighteen," said Simon defiantly. "And you have to let me in, I know that." He glared up at the officer, who stared icily back at him.

"We've got a right one here then," he said, turning to the officer next to him and back to Simon. "Now look 'ere, Judge Jeffries," and he brought his face very close to Simon's, "if you're eighteen then why are you still in your school uniform then, eh?" He stood back and smirked.

"I'm in the Upper Sixth," retorted Simon wishing he'd changed more than just his tie after a morning at school. "And I am eighteen and so is he." The prison officer said nothing.

"You still haven't let us in," said Tookey calmly.

"I don't have to do anything," said the officer. "Who said I have to let you in, you ain't got any proof you're eighteen."

"No," said Simon. "But I can get it, and my dad says you have to let us in."

"And who's your dad, Judge?"

"He's a solicitor," said Simon. "He works for the Home Office."

The officer said nothing, but there was indecision now on his face. He turned to his colleague, who frowned and inclined his head to the door; the Deputy Governor was approaching. "Trouble?" he asked.

"These two say they're eighteen, sir," said the officer. "But I don't know, he's in school uniform. He says his dad works for the Home Office."

The Deputy Governor raised an eyebrow and took a cursory glance at Simon. "Let them in."

"You sure, sir?" said the officer, surprised.

"Do as I say," said the Deputy Governor, walking away. Simon filled in the visiting order and handed it to the officer with a grin.

"Who do you want to see then?" said the officer, snatching at the paper and not looking at them.

"Christian Thompson," said Simon.

"Thompson?" the officer shouted towards the officer behind the desk at the other end of the room. "Where's he?"

"In the Seg," replied the officer.

"Bugger. We've got to go all the way over there to fetch him. Come here, you two, follow me, we'll take you to him, it's easier." They followed the man into the building apprehensively.

Many gates later, they arrived in the segregation unit where they were shown to the interview room; a cleaner looked up from sweeping the gallery, glanced at the boys and returned to his brush. Simon and Tookey sat down on two rickety looking chairs at a table, at the other side of which were another two chairs.

"Who've they come to see?" asked an officer who had been sitting in the small office.

"Thompson," replied the SO.

The officer raised an eyebrow, before moving towards a cell door, which he opened.

"Someone to see you," Simon and Tookey heard the officer say.

There was a mumbling from inside the room.

"I don't know, it's two boys," said the officer in reply.

The two boys heard a movement across the hallway and hurried footsteps as Christian followed the officer across the gallery to the interview room. He appeared around the door, a look of gleeful expectancy on his face.

"Simon, Tookey! What are you doing here?"

"We've been arrested," said Simon with a grin. Christian laughed. "We've come to see how you're getting on, of course," he added, turning to Tookey with a smile.

"Yeah, we've come to see how you're getting on," repeated Tookey jovially. Then there was silence. Tookey fidgeted and looked at Simon to continue the conversation.

"I'm getting on all right, have you got a fag?" Simon fumbled for the packet in his pocket and handed everyone one. "They said you wouldn't see Mrs Dene," said Simon, lighting Christian's cigarette for him before lighting his own.

"No," said Christian, looking down at the table. "I'm let them all down, haven't I? I don't want to see her or Miss Shaw." He shook his head. "Miss Shaw's an old bag anyway."

"She's given you a home all these years," said Simon. "And she gave us all a place to meet up, I don't think she's that bad."

"Suppose not," conceded Christian, flicking his ash into a tin lid which was standing in as an ash tray.

"Why can't she come and see you then?" said Tookey.

"Because I let her down, I just told you."

"All right, keep your hair on."

"What about the mitigation?" said Simon. "Dad says if you've got the mitigation right they won't…" He stopped. Christian eyed him with amusement from across the table.

"They won't hang me?" he finished. Simon and Tookey looked at each other. "You didn't want to say that, did you, Simon? You're chicken, I don't mind."

There was silence. Simon fiddled with his cigarette and took another long draw on it, Tookey fidgeted and looked up at Christian.

"I like your suit, Christian," said Tookey, adding with a wink, "much better than what you had on before."

Christian laughed, pushed back his chair and brushed his blue uniform down before standing to attention. He paraded up and down the room twice at a march before sitting down again.

"It's all right, ain't it?" he said, looking down at his clothes. "Just like being in the RAF, the underwear's the trouble, it don't fit and they just give you what someone else wore last week." Simon and Tookey looked at one another and grimaced. "The shirt's good though," he continued happily. "They say people collect them." Tookey frowned. Christian then glanced over at the window that looked onto the gallery before he said, "You haven't got a tie I could borrow, have you? They didn't give me one and I want to look good when I go to court."

"I've only got the one I'm wearing," said Simon, looking at Tookey.

"Don't look at me like that, I don't carry ties about with me."

"I suppose you *could* have mine," said Simon. "I've got my school one in my pocket." He looked at Christian, who was nodding enthusiastically then glanced over at the window again as Simon sighed and pulled off his tie.

"Pass it under the table, they're not keen on visitors passing stuff over here," Christian said, tilting his head towards the window where the other boys could only see one officer in the office, and he wasn't looking their way. Christian accepted the tie gratefully when Simon did just that.

"Don't worry, I'll give you it back," he said, tying the tie around his waist under his tunic.

"What you doing that for?" asked Tookey.

"They might take it off me if I put it in my pocket."

"Do you want us to do anything?" asked Simon, producing his school tie from his pocket and starting to put it on.

"Like what?"

"Anything about your mitigation. Father says you will need a character witness and things like that."

"No. Although there is one thing you can do. Ask Miss Shaw if she has been able to contact my mother, you will see her tomorrow, won't you?"

"Yes, it's club tomorrow, isn't it, Tookey?"

Tookey frowned and nodded, unwilling to talk much about life outside the prison for fear of upsetting Christian. Simon turned to Christian.

"We'd better go now."

"Will you come again?"

"Someone will come. We're going to the hockey match now, aren't we, Tookey? We'll see the others there, so we'll ask. One of us will come see you."

Christian rose from his seat, went to the door and opened it, waiting for the officer to take him back to the cell.

"What hockey match are you going to then, you don't play?"

"No, Helen's playing, we're watching," said Simon.

"Oh."

The officer appeared at the door and turned back towards Christian's cell. Christian followed him, turning his back on Simon and Tookey and walking away in silence.

By the time Simon and Tookey arrived at the match it was nearly half-time and Helen's team were winning five–nil.

"They're thrashing them," said Peter as the boys approached. "Absolute walkover, and Helen's scored two." He looked at his watch as the whistle blew for half-time. The girls clapped and turned to face Tookey and Simon.

"Are we allowed to smoke?" asked Tookey.

"You can do what you like. You're not at school now, they can't touch you. *He's* smoking, isn't he?"

Simon pointed down the touchline to a man in a pinstriped suit and bow tie, a trilby on his head. Tookey pulled out a packet of cigarettes as Helen jogged up to the group. She was out of breath, her face red and her white top damp with sweat.

"What do you think then?" she said, a smug smile on her face.

"All right I suppose," said Peter.

"All right?" exclaimed Nimpy, smacking Peter on the arm. "You're very good, Helen, two goals, that's fantastic."

Helen grinned and knelt to pull her socks up over her pink legs. She stood and dragged her fingers through her hair to keep it back from her eyes.

"When's the bus go?" asked Ann with a frown. "I'm going to walk into town, are you coming, Sandra?" Sandra looked round at the others.

"Are you coming, Tookey?" she asked. Tookey puffed on his cigarette.

"Could do, I suppose, but we haven't seen any of the match yet. Simon, are you going?"

"No, I'll catch you up."

Tookey nodded and followed Ann and Sandra back towards the town.

Helen's breathing had returned to normal, as she looked back across the pitch and tucked her top into her skirt.

"I had better go," she said, running off to where the rest of the team were having drinks.

"Simon, what happened when you saw Christian then?" asked Nimpy. "You haven't said anything about it."

"Not much to say. They didn't want to let us in to start with, but you've got to stand up to them, that's what Dad says."

"Was he all right then?" persisted Nimpy.

"Well, he looked cleaner than usual if that's what you mean."

"Shut up, Simon, just tell us how he was," snapped Primrose.

"He's like he always is. He's always a bit strange. He wanted my tie, he said he wanted it to look smart in court. Other than that he was the same as ever. For someone who might be hanged he didn't seem that bothered though."

"Oh don't say that, Simon, they won't hang him, will they?" said Primrose.

"Dad says not a chance. Any mitigation whatsoever and they won't hang him."

"I don't want to think about it, it gives me the willies," shuddered Nimpy.

The whistle sounded to start the second half and the group turned their attention back to the hockey match. Thirty-five minutes later the match finished and Helen's team had won convincingly.

"Come on," said Helen, who had changed. "They say we can all go for tea."

"What? All of us?" asked Peter.

"Yes, all the supporters, they said, that must mean all of us." Peter looked at Helen dubiously.

"Come on," said Simon. "Why not have tea if they're offering?"

Peter, Nimpy and Primrose agreed and followed Helen towards the school.

In the large hall, each of them collected a plate of sandwiches and cakes and sat down on benches at one of the long tables. The man in the bow tie and pinstriped suit who had been smoking moved towards them before sitting himself next to Primrose and opposite Simon.

"What's that prat doing sitting here?" whispered Simon to Peter. Peter said nothing.

"Charles, come on, move up, make room for me," a woman behind the man shouted. She was wearing a tracksuit and a lot of makeup.

"We're sitting with the enemy, do you know that, darling?" replied the man loudly, smirking towards Helen.

"Don't worry, we have to get beaten once a year," said the woman with a snort as she sat down. She looked over at Helen. "You must be the hero who scored all their goals. Let me introduce myself, I'm Mrs Dickens, head of sport here, and this is my husband Charles."

Helen smiled. "Pleased to meet you. I'm Helen and these are my friends, supporters for today."

Mr Dickens took a flask from his pocket, unscrewed the top and took a swig, then offered it to his wife who shook her head.

"And where are you from, Helen?" she asked.

"We're from Dean. Or at least most of us are." Charles looked up sharply.

"From where?"

"Dean," said Helen, taken aback by Charles's interest.

"*You're* not from Dean though, are you, boy?" he said, looking at Simon. "You must be from Kimbolton, that's the school tie you've got on, isn't it?" He took another swig from his flask and offered it to Simon and Peter in turn, but they both refused. "Oh, you spoilsports," he grumbled, taking another swig before screwing the top on and putting the flask

327

into his pocket. "So you all came just to support what's-her-name here?" Charles asked, putting a hand on his wife's thigh and squeezing. Mrs Dickens jumped and smacked her husband's hand.

"We've been to see a friend too," said Simon.

"In Bedford?" asked Charles, but he was losing interest.

"In the prison."

Charles sat up again and leaned over the table, looking at Simon, then at Helen and back at Simon again. "Your friend wouldn't be Christian Thompson, would he?" he asked, straightening his tie.

Simon looked at the others. "Yes. How did you know that?"

"I know that, young man, because I am his defence solicitor and I hope *you* can get more sense out of him than I can."

"He didn't say much."

"They're not to going to hang him, are they?" asked Nimpy quietly.

"Not a chance, not a chance," Charles said, taking a bite from his sandwich. "Hanging's not the done thing nowadays, it will soon be banned, you'll see. All your friend Christian needs is a little mitigation and he will be fine. That is if we can get him to talk." He leaned forward and looked at the assembled group. "Now, you lot, if you can help with the mitigation you'll let me know, won't you? Charles Dickens, Lane and Clutterbuck, can you remember that?"

He winked at Helen, rose and sauntered off across the dining room, his wife striding behind him.

"I doubt we'll forget that," said Simon.

Chapter Twenty-One
Legal Aid

The key turned in the lock of Christian's cell. Christian stood and picked up the bucket at his feet, waiting until the door had opened. He had been dressed for some time, having been woken by the banging of the doors and rattling of the keys as the officers changed watch. Slopping out was the first of the daily routines which he had now got used to. As he stepped out into the hall with the other men and paraded towards the sluice room to empty his bucket, the acrid smell of human waste seeped into his nostrils. Christian swallowed rapidly and hurried towards the room, emptied his bucket and wandered back to his cell. The twelve men in the segregation unit only showered and changed uniform once a week and an odour of sweat and unwashed men pervaded the whole area.

The cleaner, Cliff, was already at work; he had finished the office and the interview room and was now starting on the landing. He was short with wiry grey hair and a red face that made him look quite comical. He always had a roll-up in his mouth, but rarely lit it. He worked with his blue tunic off and the sleeves of his striped shirt rolled up, displaying a blurred anchor tattoo on his right forearm.

The hot trolley bearing breakfast had just reached the gallery; on hearing the rumble of its arrival Cliff took his mop bucket to the cleaner room and joined the queue for breakfast behind Christian. He leaned forward slightly towards him.

"You've got a visitor today," he murmured, taking a cigarette from his mouth and putting it in an old tobacco tin. Christian turned and looked at him but said nothing. "It's your solicitor," said Cliff, licking round his lips with a yellow furred tongue. He wiped across his mouth with the back of his hand, before rubbing his hand down his trousers.

"How do you know that then?" asked Christian.

"Easy," said Cliff; "I read it in the book on the desk in the office. It says *Solicitor to see Thompson 9:30 am*. I can read, you know?" He sucked air through his teeth and grinned at Christian as they edged forward towards the front of the queue. "Mind you, you'll need your solicitor, you being a murderer, like. You need him so you don't swing." He looked gleefully at Christian.

"Is that so?" said Christian apathetically.

"Yup," said Cliff. "But you ain't goin' to hang, Christian, don't worry. They don't like hangin' people these days, upsets the place it does, I've bin in when they've done it. None of them like it, you know, not now they don't, they say they'll ban it afore long, don't they?" He looked at Christian again.

"Suppose so."

"Mind, they're getting it ready, they tell me."

"Getting what ready?" asked Christian sharply, turning to face Cliff.

"I'll tell you later," said Cliff, indicating that Christian take his breakfast as they had reached the front of the queue.

After breakfast there was an hour of association before the prisoners were locked up for the rest of the morning. During this hour Cliff wandered into Christian's cell and sat on the chair whilst Christian lay on the bed.

"Getting what ready?" said Christian again, as Cliff opened the tobacco tin and took out a flat cigarette. He put it in his mouth.

"The gallows," said Cliff. "It ain't right, but I heard the governor went round there." He paused and shifted the cigarette to the other side of his mouth. "You know where they do it, don't you?"

"No."

"Well did you have your photo took when you came in?"

"Yes."

"Well it's in there, they string the rope over the beam and set it up below that." He raised an eyebrow and shrugged. "I heard the governor went to have a look the other day so they're getting it ready." He took a match from the tin and lit his cigarette; he took one puff and then immediately pinched the end and put it out. "They ain't goin' to need it though, it's obvious, you just get that solicitor to sort you out, he'll do it, I know he will. I know him see, your one I mean, he 'elped me."

"What are you in for then, Cliff?" said Christian.

"Buggery," said Cliff with a harsh laugh. "In the toilet in Silver Street, it were lovely, worth every day served." He chuckled. Christian sat up.

"What did you say?"

"Bug-ger-y," said Cliff slowly. "I'm always done for that, then they put me in 'ere. It don't worry me, I ain't got nuffin' to lose, you know, boy." He pointed a bony finger at Christian. "Not like you, boy, you've got your whole life ahead of you. I'm better in 'ere; it's warm, the food ain't bad, no

331

women shoutin' at you. No, I like it 'ere. I ain't got any further to fall, Christian me boy. Arrested in a public toilet, ain't exactly a good qualification, is it then." He looked at the cell floor. "Mind it weren't always like that, no it weren't always like that." He shook his head and looked at Christian. "You just get that solicitor to sort you out and you won't swing. I'd bet on that." He rose and shuffled out of Christian's room, heading back to get on with his cleaning.

At nine-thirty an officer came for Christian and took him to the interview room, where Charles Dickens was waiting.

"Come on, Christian, sit down then, we've got to sort you out," said Charles impatiently.

He sat up and took his hands from his pockets as Christian sat down, sniffed and took his glasses off, wiping them slowly on his shirt.

"Christian, look at me," instructed Charles. "I want to know what happened when you murdered Cyril. We need to know because you are pleading guilty and we need mitigation so they don't hang you. You understand what I'm saying, don't you?" Christian continued to look at his glasses, which he was still polishing.

"Yes," he said finally.

"What about it then?" said Charles, a touch more optimistically. "Are you going to tell me what happened? Did he attack you? Why did he have no clothes on? Was it a sexual attack, Christian?" Christian said nothing. "You do know what I mean?" prompted Charles. Christian placed the glasses back on his face and looked up.

"Yes."

"So, it was a sexual attack then? That's what I want to know."

"No. I mean yes, I know what you mean by a sexual attack." He looked away again and pulled off his glasses once more. Charles watched and waited.

"We're getting nowhere, are we?" he sighed finally. He looked at Christian again. "Saw some friends of yours the other day. They said they came to see you."

"Where did you see them?"

"At a hockey match, they were supporting some girl."

"Helen. Did they win?"

"They did, and all of them from secondary mods, never seen anything like it."

Christian smiled as Charles stood up, straightened his bow tie and thrust his hands in his pockets before starting to walk up and down.

"Now, Christian. There's some reason you're not telling me what happened and I'm going to get to the bottom of it. I'm not going to be beaten by this one." He stopped and stared at Christian. "With no mitigation they *will* hang you, and nobody wants to see that, least of all your concerned friends. So…" He paused and thought for a moment. "So, I am going to Dean to see that old lady, what's her name?"

"Mrs Dene?"

"Yes. And the other one, the one you lived with."

"Miss Shaw."

"Yes, and those boys and the girls, tell me their names." Christian complied and Charles wrote down the names.

"Ask Miss Shaw if she's heard from my mother."

"Of course. When did you last hear from her?"

333

"I don't remember," said Christian. "It's been so long. I've even forgot what she looked like."

Charles sighed, nodded, and closing his bag, left.

Chapter Twenty-Two
Mitigation

Lionel Jacobs was sitting in the lounge bar of the Embankment Hotel in the bay window overlooking the river. He had his back to the window to give him enough light by which to read *The Times*, which he held up in front of him. He wore a tan-coloured suit with a herringbone pattern, a gold chain slung between the pockets of his waistcoat. A large pipe drooped from the corner of his mouth and a small drop of spittle fell intermittently from the bottom of the bowl into his lap. He sucked hard on the pipe, but it had gone out. He closed the paper, took the pipe from his mouth and picked up a large glass of scotch from the table in front of him, taking a sip as he surveyed the room. Through the double doors at the other end of the room strode Charles Dickens, sporting his usual pinstriped suit and red-spotted bow tie. He removed his trilby and sat down opposite to Lionel.

"What's wrong now?" grumbled Lionel. "Let me guess, you want something, you want money, you want time off, you want a divorce, or all of the above?"

Charles put his elbows on his knees and interlinked his fingers, his two index fingers on his chin.

"No, none of those actually," he said flatly.

"What then?"

"Can I borrow your car?"

"No," said Lionel quickly, eyeing Charles suspiciously. "Where do you want to go? A rugby match or something? Those people at the rugby club lead you astray, you know, they're nearly as bad as the Round Table."

"That's not true. I only go to home matches and the Round Table raises a lot of money, some for *your* church, don't you forget." Lionel scowled.

"Suppose so. Well, why do you want my car, what's wrong with yours?"

"I want to go to Dean, I've got this murder case and I need to see some people. Friend of yours, I think, Mrs Dene, do you know her?"

"Mrs Dene!" exclaimed Lionel with enthusiasm. "Of course I do, who's she murdered then?"

"Nobody," tutted Charles, as Lionel chuckled to himself. "It's this boy Thompson, you must have seen it in the paper."

"Yes, yes, you said he's going to plead guilty. I remember. Well what about it, they won't hang him, will they?" He downed his drink and handed the empty glass to Charles. "Get me another one, can you? And one for yourself, put it on the slate." When Charles returned, Lionel was reading the paper again. "Why do you want to see Mrs Dene then?" asked Lionel as Charles handed him the glass. "And why do you need my car?"

"Lucy's taken some girls to a match and won't be back till late," explained Charles.

Lionel tutted. "Well, I suppose you'd better take mine then. I'll have to walk back to the office when I've had my lunch." He handed the car key to Charles. "It's in the car park," he mumbled, picking up the paper again.

An hour later, Charles rang Mrs Dene's door bell and waited. He was just considering leaving when Mrs Keddy answered the door and no sooner had the door been pulled open than a voice from inside the house shouted.

"Who is it, Keddy?"

Mrs Keddy grimaced and turned to Charles.

"Who shall I say?"

"Charles Dickens, I've come in reference to Thompson."

Mrs Keddy nodded and walked back into the house to relay the message.

"Well fetch him in, don't just stand there, woman," said Mrs Dene, as Mrs Keddy hurried back to usher Charles down the hall and into the sitting room. Mrs Dene was in an armchair, knitting a small square of wool. "Just a moment, my dear. Just let me finish this row." She laboriously put in another row of stitches, before laying the bundle on the small table beside her. "Now, refreshments! A cup of tea?"

"Thank you," said Charles.

"Keddy? Tea!" she bellowed.

There was no reply, but the sound of china rattling could be heard along the hall.

"Now, Christian Thompson, how have things developed since we last met?" asked Mrs Dene. Charles briefly outlined his lack of success with Christian. "Well, my dear, how can I help? I will do anything in my power."

She looked up as Mrs Keddy entered, hovering uncertainly at the door.

"The water's off for a while, Mrs Dene," she said apologetically. "I can't fill the kettle, Jeff said it will be on it a bit."

337

"Hasn't he finished yet?" said Mrs Dene, in exasperation. "Where is he?"

There was a shuffle from the corridor as Jeff appeared behind Mrs Keddy in the doorway.

"Nearly done, Mrs Dene, oh sorry, I didn't know you had a visitor."

"Thank you, Jeff, the sooner the better," said Mrs Dene. "This is Charles Dickens, he's Christian's solicitor."

"Pleased to meet you," said Jeff.

"Did you know Christian, Jeff?" asked Charles, seizing the opportunity.

"Of course he did," said Mrs Dene. "And Jeff found the murder weapons, didn't you, Jeff?"

"Did he tell you anything about the murder then, Jeff?" asked Charles.

"Nope," said Jeff. "He didn't say nothing, he kept on about the tank, but I'm guessing that's because he hid the bayonets in it, but nothing else."

"Nothing about Cyril Merton?"

"No," said Jeff. "Cyril were no good though, everyone knew that."

"What do you mean?" asked Mrs Dene.

"I can't really be saying in front of a lady, Mrs Dene."

"What can't you say?" Mrs Dene looked confused.

"If the gentleman would step in the hall, Mrs Dene, I could tell 'im," said Jeff.

"Well if you must, but I really don't know what's so secret." Charles stood and followed Jeff into the hall.

"Well, it's like this," he said, clearing his throat. He looked down and cleared his throat again.

"Here take a little of this," said Charles, offering Jeff his flask from his inside pocket. Jeff sniffed it and took a large swig.

"Much better," said Jeff appreciatively. "Well it's like this. I've got a friend in Bedford, her name's Doll."

"Doll what?" asked Charles, who had pulled out a note-book.

Jeff opened his mouth to reply; a look of puzzlement crossed his face.

"You know; I can't tell you that. But anyway, Doll's got a daughter and she says that Cyril, you know, interfered with her." He paused, Charles nodded at him to continue. "Doll says he raped her when she were only a schoolgirl and she ain't never been the same since, never finished school, never had a job, just sits at 'ome. Doll's husband 'as had to give up work to see to her. Doll says that Cyril were always doin' it, interfering with folk if you know what I mean. And he didn't mind whether it were boys or girls." Jeff looked at Charles and shrugged. "So there, I've told you."

"Well thank you, Jeff," said Charles. "What does Doll do for a living?"

"A bit of this and that," said Jeff vaguely.

"Do you have an address for her then?" asked Charles. Jeff thought for a moment.

"Well, come to think of it, no I don't, but you can always find her in the Turk's Head, she's in there most days." He looked at Charles with amusement. "I don't expect you go in there."

"I know her. That old tart, sits by the fire mostly; drinks gin and Babycham."

"That's her. She's nice she is, I've known her a long time."

"I bet," leered Charles, taking another swig from the flask and offering it to Jeff once more.

"Don't mind if I do," said Jeff, taking a long glug from the flask.

"And what about Christian?" Charles asked.

"A bit odd, but couldn't hurt a fly, could he? 'Ave you met him?"

"Oh yes, I've met him, but he won't say much, about Cyril I mean." He mused for a moment and accepted his flask back from Jeff. "Well thank you, Jeff; I must go and talk to Mrs Dene."

Jeff touched his forehead and returned to the kitchen.

"Now, Mr Dickens, tell me what he said and don't worry about shocking me," demanded Mrs Dene as soon as Charles walked back into the sitting room.

Charles sat himself down and proceeded to explain what Jeff had told him.

"Well it doesn't surprise me, the man must have attacked Christian, it must have been self-defence, I knew it, I knew it."

"That's all very well, Mrs Dene, but unless Christian tells us that himself, we have little to go on," admitted Charles. "Now I was wondering, I met some of his friends the other day and I understand that some of them have been to see him, but that Christian hadn't been that forthcoming; I wonder if perhaps there were others among the group that he was closer to who might be more successful. What do you think?"

"Well it's worth a try. You must see Miss Shaw, she runs this club that they all go to. She'll tell you all about it; Christian lived in the school, as I'm sure you know."

"Yes, well I'll go and find her and then go back to the Turk's Head to see if Doll will make a statement about Cyril."

He rose, said goodbye to Mrs Dene and made his way to the Hall, driving to the front door and knocking. There was no response. He could hear young voices shouting and the sounds of crockery tinkling so he walked round a path to the side of the building in search of the noise. He came to a window through which he could see the children inside, who were being given sandwiches whilst sitting at a long table. He could see a grey-haired woman supervising and he tapped on the window to attract her attention. She looked up and came to the window; she leaned over and tried to open it but it was stuck. She indicated that he should go back to the front door. She was there before him, a questioning look on her face. Charles introduced himself, sure that Miss Shaw paled at his name. He was escorted to the office where he waited while Miss Shaw found someone else to supervise the children.

"Now, Mr Dickens, how can I help?" she asked, once she was able to join him, but as she said this her face crumpled. "This is all so awful, poor Christian; how did he get into all this mess?" She took a handkerchief from her sleeve and wiped her nose.

"That's what I need to know, Miss Shaw. I need to build up some evidence for Christian in this case or…" He stopped.

"Or they will hang him?"

"No, no, Miss Shaw, I'm sure it won't come to that." He edged to the front of his chair and looked earnestly at her.

"What we need are reasons why Christian killed Cyril. From what I have heard this afternoon, he was an unsavoury character; all we need is for Christian to tell us what happened that day. Now I understand, well, shall I say I met some friends of Christian's at a hockey match and they said some of them had been to see him. I was wondering if any of the others were planning on going, he might open up to others in the group."

"Well, he won't see me, you do know that?"

"Yes, I know that. And if I were you I wouldn't take it personally. But could you find out if any more of his friends will see him? I understand you run a club for them." Miss Shaw opened a drawer in her desk and pulled out a pad, which she flicked open.

"I run a club on a Sunday night. And this is a list of who goes." She pushed the pad towards Charles. "I do know that two of them, Simon and Peter Tookey, went to see him last weekend, but I understand that nothing was said about the murder."

"Well, could you select two more? They will only allow two visitors at a time to go and see him. What about a girl? Women are often better at these sorts of things in my experience." Miss Shaw took the list back, bowing her head and running her finger down the pad.

"Yes, she would go, I think, and so would he. Yes, I will see what I can do." She sighed and sat back in her chair; her face was pale and she looked incredibly sad.

"There's one more thing, Miss Shaw. He always asks about his mother; are you able to contact her?" Miss Shaw initially seemed not to hear. Charles opened his mouth to ask the question again but Miss Shaw was shaking her head.

"His father has stopped corresponding. If it wasn't for a bit of help from our church I don't know how we would support him. I have written to his mother at the last known address but we've heard nothing."

"Very good, I'll tell him when I see him. We've got two weeks until the case comes to court, let's hope she makes contact. I feel that she might be the key to his problem and in the meantime let's hope his friends can get something out of him. Now I must get back to Bedford and the Turk's Head." He rose and Miss Shaw showed him to the door, where Charles returned to his borrowed vehicle and made his way back to Bedford.

He arrived there forty-five minutes later, parking the car at the back of the building and walking into the office where he found Lionel asleep in his chair. His waistcoat was undone and the paper lay over his face, rising and falling as the older man snored gently. His pipe had fallen to the floor and the lit tobacco had dropped out and burnt two small holes in the carpet. Charles looked at the clock on the mantelpiece; it was a quarter to six, by the time he had looked through the afternoon post and walked to the Turk's Head it would be open. He retreated from the sleeping Lionel and carried on to his own office.

At five past six, he approached the door of the pub, which was still closed, but he could hear the bolt being pulled back and Robin opened the door.

"Hello, Mr Dickens, you're early. Desperate for a drink are you? Your wife can't approve, I bet," said Robin with a wink. Charles smiled indulgently.

343

"Now, now, Robin. No more of that, you're lucky to get a customer, you need all you can get as far as I hear."

"What can I get you then?" said Robin, not rising to the bait and slouching towards the bar.

"Information first, Robin, then I'll have a gin and mix. What can you tell me about Cyril Merton?" Robin pursed his lips; the smile dropped from his face.

"That bastard! He's dead, ain't he? Some poor kid murdered him they say." He lit a cigarette and looked at Charles, who continued to stare levelly at the barman. "What about him?"

"He came in here then?"

"On and off he did yeah, but I wasn't sad to see the back of him."

"Why?"

"Why? Because, because he used to pick up kids. Girls mainly, but sometimes boys, he'd lace their drinks, then take them God knows where and have his way if you know what I mean. He did Doll's daughter, you know, and she was a real good girl. Picked her up outside the school, the bastard."

"And the day he got murdered, Robin? Was he in here?"

"How the heck am I supposed to know that?"

"Well, do you remember if a boy came in?" said Charles patiently. "Probably around lunch time. Short, slightly built, glasses, red hair?"

Robin thought for a moment. "Yes, I remember him, he didn't look old enough, I didn't want to serve him but…" He frowned and hesitated. "Yes, it were Cyril who told me to give him one, in fact I think he bought it. The old boy said it were his eighteenth birthday and he was going to have a drink."

"And what happened then?"

"Well it were just like I said, the old boy were worse for wear after a bit, and Cyril took 'im out, that's the last I saw of them." Charles nodded.

"Now I need a drink, Robin, you've told me what I want to know, a pint of bitter will do for me, no gin this time." Robin moved to collect a pint glass, as Charles added, "And you saw this Cyril do this kind of thing before?"

"Yes, many times, that were typical. You ask Doll about him, she'll be in in a bit."

"Which rather begs the question, doesn't it? Why did you never do anything to stop him? Presumably you were the one who sold the drinks to Cyril…"

He broke off, the accusation hanging heavily between them. Robin reddened, his fists clenched. "Don't think I didn't want to," he muttered angrily. "But a living's a living and it's not for me to meddle in other people's business."

Charles accepted his pint and said nothing more, reaching into a side pocket in his coat for payment. Robin waved him away and sloped towards the other end of the bar.

Ten minutes later Doll arrived, the clack of her high heels preceding her. The door swung open, with the light behind her as she entered through the door; her hair looked thinner, her grey roots stark against the dye of her hair. She had a cigarette in her mouth and a fox fur round her neck over a white blouse, short black skirt and black fishnet stockings. She tottered up to the bar, put her bag and jacket on one of the stools

345

and perched on the next one. She took the cigarette from her mouth, the butt of which was thick with her red lipstick.

"Who's going to buy me a drink then?" she asked, looking from Charles to Robin.

"Doll," said Charles, straightening his bow tie and running his fingers through his hair, "nothing could give me greater pleasure after all this time." He winked, then moving over to her slid a hand down her back to her bottom.

"Now, young man," said Doll, with a gravelly laugh, "didn't your mother tell you to look, not touch." She giggled and moved in towards him, her lips not quite touching his cheek. Charles turned and faced her. Doll stared at him levelly.

"Gin and Babycham, Robin, that's right, isn't it, Doll?" She nodded. "I want some information about Cyril Merton. I saw Jeff, he told me about your daughter." Doll blanched, her face tightened and she looked away angrily.

"Don't you talk to me about that bastard. Whoever murdered him did us all a favour. Did Jeff tell you what he did?"

"Yes."

"She weren't the only one either, I've seen him in here, picking up poor girls. He liked them young, and I'm seen him pick up boys as well."

"Would you stand up in court and say that, Doll?"

"If I had to I would. But who would believe *me*?" She looked at Charles squarely. "Anyway why you asking all this?"

Charles explained Christian's situation. Doll listened, her face lined with sympathy for the boy's plight.

346

"You mean the boy ain't sayin' anything?" she marvelled, shaking her head. "You mark my word, Mr Charles Dickens, I bet a pound to a penny he attacked that poor boy and it were self-defence."

"Did you do any business with him, Doll?"

"No. I steered clear of him, always did. But I know someone who did do business with him, a colleague, shall we say. The bugger wouldn't pay her; knocked her about something rotten. She's here next week actually, Kathy, she's a stripper, coming for the rugby club do, I think, I'm sure I've seen it on the poster."

"Yup," agreed Robin. "Friday seven-thirty in the upstairs room; are you coming, Charles? You normally do."

"Not now surely," mocked Doll. "He's *married*, Robin, a reformed character is our Charles. Goes out with the county set now, I imagine."

Charles smiled, sipped at his drink, and said nothing.

Chapter Twenty-Three
What's Done Is Done

Peter knocked at the front door of the pebbledash cottage, four hundred yards from the road junction to Dean. The cottage was one of a pair, all of whose occupants worked on the adjacent farm. The curtain in the next door cottage flicked to the side and a bespectacled grey face peered at him for a moment, before the curtain dropped back. A face appeared in the window of the house he was knocking at; it was Nimpy.

She pointed behind her and mouthed something, from which he gathered he had to go round the back of the house, where the door stood open, Nimpy silhouetted in the doorway.

"What are you doing here, Peter? It's not Sunday."

"No. It's Miss Shaw, she rang my mother to say could we go and see her because she wanted someone to go and see Christian, she especially wanted you to go."

"Well, I'm not going on my own. If she thinks that she's got another think coming."

"No. I'll come too, but she thinks Christian might tell you things that he won't tell anyone else because you're a girl." He shrugged and scuffed his feet on the flagstones. Nimpy frowned.

"Have we got to go and see Miss Shaw, then?"

"That's what she wants."

"My bike's got a puncture. How long are we going to be? Mother's out and the baker's coming."

"We won't be long. You can ride on my crossbar if you like, I've borrowed a bike."

Nimpy smiled coyly and agreed, tripping after Peter to where his bike was standing against the gatepost. The two rode to the Hall where they were met by Miss Shaw, who seemed strangely excited, obviously resting her hopes for Christian's salvation on Peter and Nimpy, who both agreed to travel to Bedford on Saturday to see Christian.

That Saturday, Peter stood at the back door of Nimpy's house again and knocked. Nimpy came to the door, flustered and unkempt.

"Just a mo," she said, rushing to open the door, "I'm coming." She darted back into the house for her jacket.

"Nimpy?" came a voice from upstairs.

"What?" Nimpy shouted back.

"Make sure you take your mac, it's going to rain, it said so on the wireless," instructed the voice.

"I'm not taking that. What do you think I am?" And with that she slung the back door shut.

"Come on, Peter. Let's go before she comes down, my bike's still broken so we've got to go on yours, come on or we'll miss the bus."

She skipped to Peter's bike and hitched herself onto the cross bar, as Peter stood on the pedals to get a quicker start. As soon as they got going, he sat down in the saddle, Nimpy's hair blowing in his face.

"Move your head, I can't see where we are going." Nimpy turned her head and glared at him. "Don't wiggle. You'll have us off."

Nimpy looked to the front again, holding her head awkwardly to one side, Peter's arms encircling her, and she could feel his breath on her neck.

"Peter, do you think he's going to tell us anything?"

"Tell *you* anything, you mean. Miss Shaw thinks he will tell you rather than us boys."

"We'll have to see. He's shy of girls, he doesn't like kissing, but then I don't expect Miss Shaw ever showed him any affection, not like a mother would."

The pair approached the bus shelter just as the bus was drawing up to the stop; Peter rushed to park his bike behind the shed.

They arrived at the prison just before two o'clock, as a big black cloud slid over to darken the sky. The queue at the gates was long and as Peter and Nimpy approached the end of it, the woman at the front hammered on the door. The peep hole opened.

"What do you want?" came a voice.

"Come on, let us in," pleaded the woman. "It's just startin' to rain; we're all going to get soaked out 'ere and look, she's got a little 'un in the pram."

"Can't," said the voice, slamming the peep hole shut.

"Buggers, ain't they," said the woman bitterly, turning to her neighbour. "Not a one bit of humanity and now we're going to get soaked."

Huge drops of rain started to fall, slowly at first, then faster and faster. Peter and Nimpy stood dejectedly as the rain fell, running off their hair and soaking into their jackets.

"I'm getting soaked, Peter. Isn't there anywhere else to wait?" Peter looked up and down the street before looking up to the skies; there was nowhere to take shelter and the rain showed no signs of relenting. "It's gone right through to my skin now and it's cold."

"You should have brought your mac like your mum said."

"My school mac? I'd rather get soaked than wear that old thing."

Within a few minutes, and as quickly as it had started, the rain stopped, but the damage had been done. All those standing in the queue looked as if they had been swimming in their clothes. The church clock struck and the queue shuffled up and through the door. Nimpy and Peter knew from Simon that they had to fill in a visiting order and went straight to the office to ask for one. No one asked their age, and they handed in their form.

"Thompson, where's Thompson?" murmured the officer, running his finger up and down the lists in front of him.

"He's in the Seg," said another.

"Who's going to take them over there then?" said the first officer.

"I'll do it," a voice shouted from the back of a group of officers. The man approached Peter and Nimpy. "Follow me," he said, opening the first gate and ushering the pair through.

Nimpy ran her fingers through her hair and took off her wet jacket. They walked across the yard and towards the main building, where they passed through many doors to the Seg unit.

"Visitors for Thompson," the escort shouted as they arrived, opening the final door for Peter and Nimpy and shutting it behind them.

An officer came onto the landing and looked at the bedraggled pair. "Where have you been swimming?"

"It's raining out there," said Peter with a frown.

"Wouldn't know it," the officer laughed, as he pointed to the interview room. The pair wandered into the room and sat down at the table. "Thompson!" he shouted "Visitor!"

Nobody appeared. Nimpy and Peter sat and waited.

"Peter, go and ask where he is," said Nimpy after a while.

Peter got up and peered out of the door. He looked up and down the corridor, before returning to his seat and sitting down.

"There's no one there except a man cleaning the floor," he said.

"Go and ask him then," insisted Nimpy.

"Give it a few minutes," replied Peter as a bucket clanked down outside the door.

Cliff shuffled in, took the two ashtrays from the table and shuffled out again; he emptied the ashtrays and came back into the room.

"Who you come to see then?"

"Christian," said Nimpy. "Christian Thompson, is he here?"

"Yes, he's here all right," chuckled Cliff. "But I don't know whether he'll see you, he's funny like that." He plonked the two ashtrays back on the table. "You friends of his? You ain't solicitors, are you? No, come to think you don't look like it." Cliff pinched the end of the unlit cigarette in his mouth, pulled a tin out of his pocket and nestled the cigarette back in the tin.

"We're friends of his," said Peter. "How's he getting on?"

"All right. But he won't talk about what happened, he'll have to talk soon though or the judge won't be pleased." Cliff went to the door and looked up and down the corridor. "He will talk eventually, you'll see. They don't want to hang him."

Footsteps could be heard. Cliff shuffled out and an officer came to the door. "Ain't he come?" he asked them.

"No," said Nimpy.

"Cliff, go and fetch Thompson, he's got visitors," instructed the officer.

They watched Cliff move slowly across to a cell door. He tapped on it and pushed it open. Christian was lying on his bed staring at the ceiling.

"Got visitors," said Cliff.

"Who?" demanded Christian, not getting up from his bed.

"I don't know."

"Is it old ladies?"

"No."

"Is it the solicitor?"

"No, it's two kids, a girl and a boy." Christian sat up abruptly.

"What's their names?"

"How do I know? You go and ask them yourself."

Christian rose from his bed, put on his shoes and went to the interview room where the officer stood outside. "All right, Thompson?"

"Yes, Mr Welch."

Welch moved to let Christian into the room and his face lit up when he saw who the two sitting in the interview room were.

"Peter! Nimpy!" he exclaimed, shaking Peter's hand and moving to shake Nimpy's. Nimpy took hold of Christian's shoulders and pecked him on the cheek.

"That's a smart uniform you've got on, Christian," she said, standing back and looking him up and down.

"Better than my school suit, don't you think?" chuckled Christian, sitting down opposite the pair. Nobody said anything for a moment.

"How's the club? Still playing Postman's Knock?"

"No, we've stopped that," said Nimpy with a smile. "We're trying to think of something more constructive to do. That's what Miss Shaw told us we should do now that…" She stopped and looked at the table. "Didn't she, Peter?" she finished feebly.

"Didn't she what?"

"Say that we've got to do something constructive, you dope!"

"Oh yes, she did."

"Mind, I don't think she knew we played Postman's Knock," said Nimpy with a sly smile.

There was silence, Christian polished his glasses. Peter took a packet of cigarettes from his pocket and offered one to Christian.

"Fag, Christian?"

"No, I won't. But can I take one for Cliff?"

Peter nodded and handed him the packet, before offering it to Nimpy, who turned up her nose in disgust.

"I've just thought, Christian," she said, "I've got something for you." She put her hand into her jacket pocket and took out a packet of chewing gum which she handed to him. Christian looked at the packet, turning it over in his fingers, a faint smile on his lips.

"I'll save this for later," he said quietly, putting the packet in the breast pocket of his tunic.

Peter lit his cigarette and the three of them waited for someone to say something. Peter puffed at the cigarette and looked out of the window to where Cliff was shuffling about on the landing. Nimpy coughed pointedly and wafted the cigarette smoke away.

"Do you have to, Peter?"

"I'll go and stand outside then." Peter stood just outside the door, pulling it nearly closed behind him to give Nimpy and Christian the privacy that might make him open up. He noticed the officers watching him and felt awkward and determined not to stray any further.

Nimpy looked hard at Christian.

"We saw Miss Shaw the other day, Christian. She said they want you to explain what happened that day. She said it will make a lot of difference when it comes to court, especially if that man attacked you."

Christian said nothing, but his hands were trembling; he wrung them and tried to get the dirt from under his nails. He would not look at her.

"Did you want to tell me anything, Christian? I'm sure it would help, we are friends, aren't we? You've got a lot of friends, you know that."

She could see his face crumple slightly as he bit his lip, unable to stop the tears springing to his eyes. She put her hand across the table to hold his but he pulled it away. He sniffed and looked away from her as his face became red. Nimpy sat back and waited for him to compose himself.

"You're sure you don't want to tell me, Christian?"

Christian pulled out a hankie from his pocket and blew his nose. He seemed to collect himself, took a deep breath and sat up in his chair.

"Nimpy, I know you're a good friend and so are all the others: Peter, Simon and Tookey and them. But what's done is done and there's no going back on it, there's no mending it. I killed someone and I've got to live with that for ever." He stopped and blew his nose again. "I know you mean well, but I don't want to talk about it, it was so awful, you don't realise how awful it was." He looked at his hands again and said quietly, "I can't describe how awful it was." A shudder passed over Christian's body and his hands started to shake again. Without warning he sobbed. "He had no clothes on, you know, I didn't understand what he wanted. I'm so ashamed, Nimpy, I'm so ashamed." He covered his eyes with his hands and said no more. After a few moments he stopped crying, sniffed, wiped his eyes and took the chewing gum from his pocket. He opened the packet and offered a piece to Nimpy.

"Want a bit then?" he said, as she hesitated.

"No," she shook her head. "I want you to keep it for later."

"Where did you get it? I get mine from this American guy."

"The one you get the pills from?"

"Yes, I suppose it is," said Christian. The conversation dried. Nimpy fidgeted awkwardly. "I've let everyone down, haven't I? Everyone. Miss Shaw, Mrs Dene, she was good to me, she even came to see me here, but I couldn't see her; I wouldn't know what to say. And Miss Shaw, she's a funny old thing, but I would have ended up in some home if it hadn't been for her. My mother never came back for me." He sniffed again. "You know I can't hardly remember her. Sometimes I think I can but then I just don't know. Did Miss Shaw say anything about her, Nimpy? Tell me she did." He reached across the table and took her hand for a moment.

"She didn't say anything, Christian. Except that she had tried to make contact." Christian withdrew his hand.

"I've got no one. Not like you, I know you complain about your mum but at least you've got one."

He stood suddenly and went to the window, looking out to where he could see Peter standing. Cliff was mopping the floor at the far end near where the officers were in their office.

"You see him, Nimpy," said Christian, nodding towards Cliff. "He says he's at the bottom, he's got nothing to lose so it doesn't matter what he does. He says he likes it better in prison than on the outside." Christian came back and sat down again, a smile came over his face. "Nothing to lose, that's what he says, he's got nothing, no one and no possessions except his tobacco tin. All he does is clean the floor over and over again." He smiled sadly.

"Oh, Christian," said Nimpy quietly.

"Now tell me who won the hockey match." Nimpy grinned and started filling Christian in on what had been going on in his absence, the two chatting merrily about the other members of the gang until Peter returned.

"Peter," said Christian, looking up with a smile. "I want to look smart when I go to court and Simon lent me a tie, but it's not the right colour, can I borrow yours please?"

"This is the only tie I've got except my school one."

"That's what Simon said. But he still lent me it, you'll get it back."

"Go on, Peter, it's the least you can do," encouraged Nimpy. "You can go and buy another one, we'll have time before the bus goes."

Peter sighed and removed his tie, passing it under the table as instructed by Christian, who looked anxiously towards the door and at the window before wrapping the tie quickly around his waist, tying it and pulling his shirt back down over it.

"What you do that for?" asked Nimpy.

"Right over left, how does it go?" said Christian to Peter, ignoring her.

"Right over left and under, left over right and under, but you don't need a reef knot for your tie," said Peter with a frown.

"No, I don't suppose so," laughed Christian, turning to Nimpy. "I do this so they won't see, they don't like visitors handing things over." He checked that the tie wasn't showing. "Check, Nimpy, won't you? With Miss Shaw, about my mother."

"Yes, Christian. Anything else you want me to tell her? She would come and see you if you want?"

"No, I don't want to see her. I don't mind you lot. You understand, don't you?"

"I suppose so."

The following Tuesday there was a cricket match at Dean; they were playing Yelden. Both Simon and Tookey were playing for the visiting team so the rest of the gang came to support them. As they stood by the pavilion they could see Mrs Dene's car driving into the main entrance at the Hall. The car stopped, leaping forwards a few feet as Mrs Dene had evidently not disengaged the gear. Once the car had stalled Mrs Dene climbed out. She marched to the front door and pushed it, it opened a little but then stuck fast; Mrs Dene looked around surreptitiously then, sure no one could see her, gave the door a boot. It flew open. She walked down the long hallway to the office where Miss Shaw was sitting in front of her account books.

"Verity, I didn't hear you arrive, I'm sorry, do come in," said Miss Shaw, rising hurriedly.

"No dear, I didn't knock," said Mrs Dene. "I know my way about this place, I was born here if you remember." Miss Shaw smiled and nodded.

"Of course, do sit down."

Mrs Dene pulled up a chair and straightened her hat before she started talking.

"Now, my dear, as you might expect I'm here about Christian." Miss Shaw nodded. "I have seen Nimpy and she has

359

told me about her and Peter's visit and I understand she has been to see you as well, so you know all about it."

"Yes I do," agreed Miss Shaw.

"Well, we are no further ahead. He wouldn't tell her much and said he wouldn't say any more than he did. He did say that the man, that Cyril, whatever his name is, was naked. It doesn't bear thinking about, does it?" Miss Shaw looked up sharply.

"Did Joanna, I mean Nimpy tell you that, that the man was naked?"

Mrs Dene nodded. "Yes, she did." Mrs Dene straightened her hat again, making it more crooked than it had been initially. "I've been thinking, Evelyn," she said finally, "that the key to this problem is his mother. Everyone that goes to see him says he asks about his mother. Nimpy says that he told her he could hardly remember her. How long is it, Evelyn, since you have had contact with her? People don't just desert their children, do they?" She looked hard at Miss Shaw, who averted her gaze. "It strikes me that if he could meet his mother it would give him a reason to live. Then if he could tell us that he was attacked by this monster, and he does sound like a monster, it might substantially alter the case."

Miss Shaw looked firmly at the floor, before pointlessly opening and shutting the book in front of her.

"I'm sure you're right, Verity," she said quietly.

"So when did you last see her?"

"Oh, before we moved up here," said Miss Shaw airily. "She's never been to visit him here. You know we bought the Hall from your family then moved our school up here from

London. That was twelve years ago and it was well before that that we last had contact."

"So would he be able to remember her?"

"Maybe not," said Miss Shaw quietly.

Mrs Dene readjusted her hat again and looked intently at Miss Shaw.

"You said you were in London in the war, didn't you, went to Royal Holloway," said Mrs Dene gently. "I had friends there. You didn't finish, did you?"

"No, we were bombed, you know what it was like, the doodlebugs." She laughed nervously.

"Christian is eighteen, isn't he, Evelyn?"

"Yes. Well, he was born in the war."

There was silence.

"Evelyn, you will forgive me, I hope, but I have to ask. Is Christian your child?"

What little colour there was in Miss Shaw's face drained from it. She stood up, tapped her desk impatiently with the palm of her hand and looked as if she was burning to say something. Then, suddenly she sat again, sinking back into the chair as though defeated, before admitting.

"Yes. Yes, he is."

"Do you want to tell me about it?" asked Mrs Dene kindly. "It's none of my business, I know." She looked at Evelyn, whose smile was shakey as she tapped the desk again.

"I'll have to tell you now, won't I? You don't know how relieved I am now someone else knows. All these years of guilt, of shame. All these years of lies about where his mother was, of lying to him, it wears one down." She smiled apologetically. "How did you guess?"

361

Mrs Dene shrugged gently.

"Well, I don't know really, but it was just now when I came in, something about the set of your face. You suddenly looked like him. If you took his glasses off." Mrs Dene smiled. "And I thought of you as much younger. You must have been very young in the war, Evelyn. Then there was a friend that I knew who was at Royal Holloway in the war; I thought of her, she was left with her son, while her husband went to war. Then I thought of you and, well, it all clicked."

She sat and looked at Evelyn who blushed. Tears sprang to her eyes but she brushed them away and composed herself.

"His father was a lovely man," she said wistfully. "RAF reconnaissance, he didn't return one day and that was that. I was unmarried and alone."

"So what did you do?"

"It was easy, I had the baby and my sister brought him up. She was married and her husband was in the army, but we were bombed out so I said all our documents were lost and we called him Christian, after his father, and Thompson was my sister's married name. It was so easy. But it was all the lying, once I started I couldn't stop for fear of someone finding out." She sighed heavily. "And then my sister's husband was killed on D-Day or just after and we moved again. I went to work as housekeeper for a vicar, he had just lost his wife and they ran a small school. After the war he died and left the school and everything to me, as he had no relatives. The lease came up on the building and that's when we moved here. My sister married again and Christian came here as a boarder to the school, and the rest you know." There was silence.

"Well, well, my dear, what a story. But we must deal with the situation that we find ourselves in in the here and now."

"I know, I know. I've got to go and see him and tell him the truth, but will he see me, do you think? You said that he refused before."

"He must do, my dear. He has been asking for his mother all the time."

"It's really quite frightening," admitted Miss Shaw, brushing her lank hair back from her face with her fingers. "What will he say, how will he react when he knows I am his mother?"

"Well, I have no idea how he will take it but it is the only course of action and we must warn him. I will ring Patience, you remember she's on the board of something or other, she's always going in and she can tell him that his mother is coming and you can go and visit him, how about that?"

"That sounds all right," said Miss Shaw a touch uncertainly, as Mrs Dene started to rummage through her bag for her diary.

"Got it!" said Mrs Dene, brandishing it triumphantly over her head then searching through what appeared to be hundreds of scrawled phone numbers. "Where's the phone, my dear, I will ring her right now."

Miss Shaw guided Mrs Dene to the phone in the hall. After ten minutes and a lot of shouting down the phone Mrs Dene returned.

"That's all done, Patience is going in at nine o'clock in the morning to do what she calls an adjudication and she will go and tell Christian that his mother is coming to see him. Now, my dear, you must go with the solicitor, he will need to know

363

the details if Christian is to talk. He's got to prepare the case, it's only next Tuesday, you know, we haven't got much time."

"Can we phone him? He gave me a number and told me I could contact him on that at any time."

"Very good, my dear, go and do it now."

Miss Shaw went to make the call and was back a couple of minutes later.

"I just got his wife. She said he was at the Turk's Head right now and that he wasn't in the office tomorrow morning. Apparently he always has a haircut and a shave once a month and tomorrow is that day. She said to send a note over and she would give it to him."

"Well, my dear, if that's what we must do, let's get on."

"Who will take a letter?"

"Jeff will, he has a van and he's at the cricket, you go and tell him I said he has to. Run along, dear, and fetch him and I will write the letter. I would go myself, but I really can't see well in this light."

It was just before eight when Miss Shaw got to the cricket field. Simon, Tookey, Peter, Nimpy and Helen stood by the pavilion watching Jeff walk out to the crease.

"Hello, Miss Shaw," said Nimpy. "You don't usually watch the cricket."

"No. I want to find Jeff. If he's here we need him to deliver a letter. It's urgent, it's for Christian's solicitor."

"Well, he's just gone out to bat," said Helen. "He had to go in last because he lost his glasses and had to go home and fetch another pair."

"How long will he be then?"

"Depends," said Peter. "You never know with him. He may score fifty or he could be out first ball."

They all watched as Jeff turned to face the first ball. The bowler came steaming down towards the opposite wicket and released the ball. It hit him squarely on the front pad as Jeff moved forward to swing his bat, completely miscuing the shot and making contact with nothing but fresh air. The bowler wheeled round to the umpire, appealing enthusiastically as the umpire raised his finger into the air.

"Out!" came a bark from the pavilion. The others turned to Peter who smirked.

Jeff looked down at his offending pad, flabbergasted; he shook his head and walked back down to the other wicket to shout at the umpire, who grinned smugly and turned away. Jeff marched back to his wicket, took a swing with his bat and threw it into the stumps before turning on his heel and stomping back towards his van. A roar of laughter erupted from the field.

"That's it! We've won," said Tookey as Jeff marched all the way to his van and climbed in.

He ground the van into reverse and shot backwards, nudging into the scoreboard as he did so; numbers cascaded to the ground as he roared off back down the road.

"Now what am I going to do?" said Miss Shaw desperately, looking at the boys. "I've got to get this letter to Bedford, who's going to do it now?"

"I will," said Tookey, turning to Simon. "Do you want to come, Simon, it needs to be done, it's for Christian."

"Of course," said Simon. "What do we have to deliver?"

"It's just a letter," said Miss Shaw gratefully. "Come round to the Hall. Mrs Dene is writing it at the moment."

Tookey nodded and went to fetch his motorbike, which he drove round to the backdoor of the Hall, Simon riding pillion. They sat and waited for Miss Shaw to bring out the letter. Mrs Dene was sealing the envelope as Miss Shaw arrived back.

"Now, Evelyn, I've told this Dickens everything and I have said he has to cancel his haircut and wait for us at his office after informing the prison that you will be visiting. I will take you to Bedford in the morning and we will be there by eleven. Has Jeff agreed to take the letter?"

"No, I couldn't get hold of Jeff, the two boys said they will take it, they have a motorbike."

"Which boys?"

"Tookey they call him, he has the motorbike, and Simon, you know, the tall good-looking one."

"Very good. Let's go and see them."

Tookey was sitting on his little green motorbike with his leather goggles around his neck waiting and chatting to Simon as the two women emerged from the house. Mrs Dene beckoned Simon towards her.

"Now, Simon, this is very important," said Mrs Dene slowly, as Simon approached. "It's about dear Christian and I want you to take it to Mr Charles Dickens. He's Christian's solicitor, you know."

"Yes, Mrs Dene. I've met him, he was at the hockey match, wears a bow tie."

"Yes, that's the one. Now take this to his home and give it to his wife."

She handed Simon the letter, which he put in his jacket pocket before jumping onto the pillion seat; the boys sped off. At the gate the bike suddenly stopped. Simon leapt off and ran back to where the women were standing.

"Where does he live, Mrs Dene?" asked Simon breathlessly.

"Dear me, give me the letter and I'll write it on the envelope," said Mrs Dene. "Evelyn, let's find the address, do you have a phone book?"

The two women hurried inside, returning minutes later with an addressed envelope. Mrs Dene handed it to Simon.

"Forty-five Pemberly Avenue. Where's that?"

"I have no idea," said Mrs Dene airily, "You will have to ask."

Half an hour later Tookey and Simon were driving around the Market Square; it was dusk and the street lamps were just coming on.

"Where's this road then?" asked Tookey. "Have you seen it?"

"No idea," said Simon as they passed the Turk's Head. They went round the square once again, but there was nobody to ask. "Come on. Let's go in the pub, we can have a beer and ask someone in there."

Tookey parked the motorbike and the boys walked in. This time, they marched straight up to the bar.

"What's it to be?" Simon asked Tookey.

"Mine's a bitter, pint please."

"I'll have the same," said Simon, turning to the barman.

"Look, Simon," whispered Tookey, nodding towards the other side of the room, "there's that old tart. Two of us for fifteen shillings, she said, what about it? She's your type."

They both laughed; Doll, sensing an invitation, approached them. They welcomed her as she tottered up, a little unsteady on her high heels.

"Fifteen shillings for the two of us, eh, Doll?" leered Tookey. "That's what you said last time."

"You naughty boys," giggled Doll, pinching Tookey's bottom. "I could do it for that price but not at this time of the evening. Twenty-five shillings and that's my final offer." She smiled, revealing her teeth, red with lipstick.

"Can't," said Simon. "We've got to deliver a letter, very important." He turned back to her suddenly. "Hey, Doll, you'll know, where's Pemberly Avenue?"

"Sorry, I've no idea. It ain't in my part of town, it's up by the school somewhere, I think, what's the name?"

"Dickens, Charles Dickens," said Simon. "Although I don't know why he calls himself that, can't stand Dickens myself."

"Do you mean Dickens the solicitor? Always wearing a bow tie?"

"That's him."

"We know him don't we, Robin?"

"What you say, Doll?"

"Charles Dickens. We know him, don't we, he's upstairs, ain't he?"

"Yeah, he's up there with them toffs."

"Comes down here for a bit of rough if you know what I mean?" said Doll softly, leaning in towards Simon's shoulder.

"You mean he's here?" said Simon with delight. "That'll save looking for his house. Where?"

"Down the end, out the door and up the stairs there, in the long room. But you won't get in."

"Why not?"

"You ain't got a ticket."

"A ticket for what?" Doll laughed.

"A stripper, Kathy, she's a mate of mine. You can go and look if you like."

The two boys hurriedly finished their beer and made their way through the smoke to the door at the end of the room and up the stairs. As they climbed, they could hear music intermingled with cheers and shouting; they approached a set of double doors. Simon pushed one open, it was dark inside and the boys could just make out a stage with a few spotlights illuminating it at the other end of the room. The air was thick with tobacco smoke and the smell of beer; groups of men sat round tables, cheering and leering towards the stage, while others leaned against the walls, all eyes fixed on the illuminated set.

A man was sitting at a table just inside the door.

"Tickets," he demanded, staring at the boys.

"We haven't got any," said Simon.

"Well, that's three pounds each then," said the man, looking at them without blinking.

Simon patted his pockets and looked at Tookey who shook his head. There was a cheer from the audience and the two boys saw a woman emerge at the front of the stage. She stood up, turning in the direction of the audience. She had blonde hair piled on her head and rolled round at the back. Her eye

369

makeup was jet black, her lips blood red. With one hand, she held her bra to her bosom; she was wearing nothing else but a pair of tiny knickers, frilled along the bottom which hung like short curtains. There was another great cheer as she pulled the bra from her front and handed it to a man on the front row. The man turned to the audience for approval; he was wearing a pinstriped suit with a large red-spotted bow tie.

"Money!" the man at the door repeated.

"We haven't got enough," said Simon.

"Well, that's it then, you can't come in." Simon looked to Tookey, who shrugged.

"Do you know Charles Dickens?" asked Simon.

"That prat down there?" said the man, nodding in Charles's direction as the stripper bent down and swung her breasts towards him. There was another big cheer and Charles turned back to the audience again. "What about him?"

"We've got something for him," said Simon. "It has to be delivered tonight *urgently*."

"Well, he ain't coming over at the moment, is he?"

"No," said Simon. "But please can you tell him we're here and we'll wait in the square for him."

"Suppose so. What's so important?"

"Tell him it's about Christian Thompson," said Tookey.

"What's it worth then?" asked the man, eyeing the two boys mischievously. Simon looked at Tookey, who dug in his pocket and produced half a crown. He handed it to the man. "In the square, you said?"

"Yes," said Simon. "By the statue." The man nodded at the two boys and closed the door. Tookey tugged Simon's sleeve.

"Look," he said. "We can see through the door." He put an eye to the crack between the double doors and whistled gently. Simon ducked beneath him and did the same.

"Where did she get tits that big?" marvelled Simon.

Suddenly their vision was obscured, the man collecting the money appeared to have stood up.

"Well that's that then," said Tookey cheerfully, making his way down the stairs, and back through the bar to the square. They waited on the steps to the statue.

"We could still try and find his house, I suppose," said Tookey after a while.

"Let's wait here for a bit and have a fag," said Simon, pulling a packet from his pocket and handing one to Tookey. He looked up absently at the statue. "What's this statue then?" he said, turning and reading from the inscription. "John Howard, Prison Reformer."

"Who was that then?"

"No idea. I couldn't stand history at school. Christian might appreciate his work though."

Tookey was silent. Fifteen minutes later Charles Dickens tottered out from the pub, clearly the worse for drink. He was still wearing his bow tie and pinstriped suit, but he carried his shirt. He saw the two boys by the statue and zig-zagged his way towards them.

"Now, you buggers," he slurred, "what's all this about? Let's be quick about it or I'll miss the second half. What's this about Christian Thompson?" He burped.

"We've got this letter," said Simon, taking it from his pocket and giving it to Charles. He squinted at the envelope, turning it this way and that and blinking hazily at the writing.

"*Charles Dickens*," he read. "That's me!" He grinned fool-ishly.

"Yes," said Simon, unimpressed. Charles looked at him intently.

"I've met you before, boy, remind me where?" He swayed backwards and put a steadying hand out, propping himself up on the thigh of the statue.

"At the hockey match." Charles looked confused.

"Hockey? *Hockey*. Now bless my soul, I do remember. You buggers won, didn't you, and that girl scored all the goals." He looked fondly off into the distance. "Now, the let-ter," he said, trying to fix his face into a serious shape. "Who's it from then to be so urgent?"

"Mrs Dene," said Simon. "It's about Christian, she said."

"Haha," chuckled Charles. "The magnificent Mrs Dene, well I had better open it, hadn't I?" He sat down on the step. "Got a fag?" he asked Simon.

Simon offered him one, lighting it for him as he opened the envelope. The two boys stood and waited while Charles read the letter once, frowned and then read it again. He puffed on his cigarette and looked up at the boys.

"Do you know what's in here?" he asked, looking from one to the other of the boys.

"No," said Simon, as Charles stood up.

"Well I can't tell you but what a bugger, eh? What a bug-ger." He folded the letter and put it in his pocket before look-ing down in apparent realisation that he wasn't wearing a shirt. "Hold this a minute," he said to Simon, removing and handing over his jacket. He stood up, his top half clad only in braces and bow tie; he undid the latter and gave it to Tookey, before slipping his braces off and picking his shirt from the steps of the statue. He clumsily pulled the shirt on and began to laboriously button it up. As he did so the boys noticed bright red lipstick daubing his chest; they looked at each other, and Tookey suppressed a giggle. Having got the shirt on and tucked it in, Charles took the tie from Tookey and tied it up before turning to Simon. "Is that straight, boy?"

Simon, smothering a laugh, adjusted the mis-tied bowtie and handed Charles his jacket. Charles ran his fingers through his hair and once again turned to Simon.

"How do I look then?"

"Well, you look fine I suppose. But you've got lipstick on your face."

"Bloody hell! Where?" He thrust his handkerchief at Simon and indicated that he should rub it off. Simon moved the hankie towards Charles's face, but he batted it away. "Not like that, boy, lick it!"

Simon grimaced and spat on the handkerchief before wiping tentatively at Charles's face.

"Now, I'm off home," Charles said, with a stab at soberness. "Tell Mrs Dene that I am in receipt of the letter and am aware of its contents and I will alert the prison and wait for her in the office tomorrow."

"But we won't see her," said Tookey.

"Damn," said Charles, thinking hard. "Well I will have to phone her then."

"You're not going back for the second half of the show?" asked Simon, in disbelief.

"No, I'm off home. Got to have all my wits about me to-morrow, so I will say thank you to you two, you've done a good job. And now I'll bid you good night."

"Well, if you're not going back, can we have your ticket?" said Simon hopefully.

"You're not old enough." He squinted at them again and chuckled. "Well I suppose you are, but it won't get you both in."

"Don't worry," said Simon, snatching the ticket from Charles's outstretched hand and making a bee-line for the pub. "We'll think of something."

Chapter Twenty-Four
Christian's Solution

The next morning, Charles phoned Mrs Dene to tell her that he had received her letter and would expect to see her, and Miss Shaw, after eleven o'clock at his office. In the meantime, he said that he would alert the prison to the fact that they would be coming in at midday.

Mrs Dene climbed into her car, tooted her horn, a now standard procedure to alert any passers-by, and backed out into the street without looking, to fetch Miss Shaw from the Hall. As she passed the bus shelter she spotted Nimpy sitting on a bench in the early summer sun, and she tooted the horn again and waved cheerily. She drove up to the front door of the Hall, her hand on the horn again and waited for her passenger. Moments later, Miss Shaw emerged into the sunlight and Mrs Dene gasped. Miss Shaw had transformed herself. Her hair had been washed, combed and neatly brushed and her face bore signs of delicately applied makeup. The hem of her dress was nearer her knees than the ground, she wore nylons in place of her usual crepe stockings and she carried a light-coloured jacket and small handbag. She closed the front door behind her and seemed to float towards the car.

"My goodness, Evelyn," said Mrs Dene, as Miss Shaw opened the car door, "what a transformation, you've made me look decidedly dated." She gave a small laugh. "Although that would not be difficult, would it? Now, my dear, on the way up I saw Nimpy waiting for a bus and I thought we should give her a lift; but that would mean that we couldn't talk, if you know what I mean? What do you think?"

"No, Verity, do pick her up, there's nothing I want to hide now. I don't mind what she hears; she's a sensible girl, she'll understand and they'll all find out sooner or later."

"Very well then," said Verity, steering the car out of the drive and onto the road.

She stopped at the bus stop and wound down her window, turning to Miss Shaw and winking before turning back to Nimpy.

"Why aren't you at school, Nimpy?" she asked in a disapproving voice.

"I've got to go for an X-ray on my arm, I broke it two years ago and they say it's not set right."

"You're a brave girl going on your own, Nimpy. Doesn't your mother come with you?"

Nimpy laughed. "No, I'm fine, if I can go into the prison I can go anywhere."

"Well, come on, hop in and we can give you a lift. Evelyn, I mean Miss Shaw, is going to see Christian today, we will drop you on the way."

"Oh, that's nice, Miss Shaw," said Nimpy uncertainly, climbing into the car. "I know that he only didn't want to see you before because he felt he'd let you down." There was silence. "Any news on his mother?"

Miss Shaw looked at Mrs Dene, who turned to look back at her, turning the steering wheel as she did so. The car bumped the verge briefly, before Mrs Dene corrected her course. Miss Shaw took a deep breath and turned in her seat to talk to Nimpy.

"Oh, I like your hair like that," exclaimed Nimpy. Miss Shaw blushed.

"It's nice of you to say so, Nimpy. I've got something to tell you about Christian's mother." Nimpy sat forward eagerly. "*I* am Christian's mother."

"You're what?" Nimpy's mouth dropped open in surprise.

"I'm Christian's mother. It's a long story, but I'm on my way to tell him." Nimpy sat back in her seat and said nothing.

"You're not saying anything, Nimpy," said Mrs Dene, pointedly. "What do you think Christian will say, eh? Do you think he will be pleased?" Nimpy chewed her lip, thinking furiously.

"I suppose he will be. I mean, I'm *sure* he will be, he's always asking about his mother." There was another pause. "Do you think he will tell you what happened? About the murder, he wouldn't tell me but if that man attacked him, if he said that, it would make a lot of difference, I mean it must do, mustn't it?"

"That's what we hope, Nimpy," said Mrs Dene, grinding the gears of the car as she set off along the A6.

"Simon says that his dad says that they will never hang him, he says that his dad says that he could even get off with a lesser charge, I mean manslaughter, that's what he says."

"Let's hope he's right, Nimpy," said Mrs Dene quietly.

"And when he gets out he can come and live with you, Miss Shaw, like he always did," said Nimpy cheerily.

"It won't be in Dean though," said Miss Shaw thoughtfully.

"Why ever not in Dean?" said Mrs Dene sharply.

"Because I am going to sell the school. I have decided my life has to change. I have worked all these years trying to achieve something that is not achievable. I decided last night and it's final."

There was silence as they drove on into Bedford.

That morning in the segregation unit of Bedford Prison the routine progressed much the same as usual. Slopping out was complete, prisoners' cells had been inspected and breakfast served. The prisoners were all back in their cells and the wardens were in the office drinking coffee. Even Cliff had put his mop and bucket away.

Just before nine o'clock a visitor arrived. She was escorted by a single officer who opened the gate and let her into the unit. She waited while he locked the gate behind them, before following him to the office. The senior officer came to the door.

"Morning, ma'am," he said. "What can we do for you at this early hour?"

The woman, Patience Pricklow, was smartly dressed in a cotton skirt, white blouse and linen jacket. She wore gloves and carried a handbag in one hand and a briefcase in the other. Her hair was completely white but her face was tanned, emphasising her deep blue eyes. For someone in their sixties she had not lost her figure and her pretty face completed an attractive picture.

"Good morning, William," she said. "It is William, isn't it?"

"Yes, ma'am," the officer replied.

"Thompson. I want to see him, but just a little background first, I must make a few notes."

"Yes, ma'am," said the officer, stepping aside to let the woman into the office. Without a word, the other officers rose and left the room as she entered, leaving the two of them alone.

"Now, Thompson is in for murder, is that right?"

William opened a book and flicked through a few pages.

"Yes, ma'am, he's in court next week."

"He won't hang, will he?"

"No, ma'am, he shouldn't; only thing is he refuses to speak about the whole affair. Even so, his solicitor should be able to put together enough mitigation, we don't want a hanging, do we?"

"Who's the solicitor?"

"Charles Dickens, ma'am."

"Bloody hell, that prat," muttered Patience under her breath.

"Yes, ma'am, he's coming in this morning, we just had a call."

"Yes, that's what I'm here about, it's his mother who is visiting apparently, he hasn't seen her in a long time and they want me to let him know."

"Yes, ma'am," said William, looking at his notebook. "A Miss E Shaw."

"That doesn't sound like a mother, does it?" said Patience, raising an eyebrow.

"That's what it says here, ma'am, Mr Dickens and Miss E Shaw, I wrote it down; I'm sure it's right."

"Very well then," said Patience in a business like tone. "I'll go and tell him. How many days are there until the trial?"

William turned to the calendar on the wall and counted, trying unsuccessfully to obscure the calendar's picture at the same time.

"Six, ma'am."

"Very good," said Patience, rising before adding, "I don't like your taste in calendars, William."

"No, ma'am," said William, blushing.

"I'll see him in his cell."

William crossed the landing and tapped on the cell door.

Fifteen minutes later, all the cells were opened for an hour of association. Christian went immediately to seek out Cliff.

"Cliff," he said excitedly, "did you see that woman who came to talk to me? She told me!"

"Told you what?"

"She said my mother is coming to visit!" He hesitated, a frown creasing his brow. "Do you think it's a joke?"

"Why should it be a joke?"

"Well, I've not seen her in years and can hardly remember her. In fact I hardly believe I've even got a mother." Christian sat on the chair whilst Cliff rolled a cigarette. "Have you got family, Cliff?"

"No," said Cliff. "All dead, or if they ain't they don't want to see me. I told you, being arrested in a public toilet ain't exactly the best reference for a chap, is it."

"Do you think it is my mother then, that woman must be right, mustn't she?"

"I can check for you."

"What do you mean?"

"I can check it in 'is book, it's always open on the table in the office, I always have a look, it'll say about your visitors, it always does." Christian fidgeted on the chair.

"Can you then?"

"Course. I'm got to go in a minute to empty the ashtrays. I'll have a look for you then."

Ten minutes later Cliff approached Christian's cell with his mop and bucket. Christian stood on the landing, leaning on the wall next to his door. He chewed gum, intermittently pulling it from his mouth, holding one end with his teeth. Cliff shuffled across the landing to the office; the officers were all talking, so he waited outside until he caught William's eye and made signs to ask if he could go in for the ashtrays. William nodded and indicated the door, which Cliff slouched through, returning moments later with the full ashtrays, which he emptied back in the bucket by Christian's cell.

"It says Mr C Dickens and Miss E Shaw." Christian gasped.

"It says what? It can't say that; they're lying, 'cos I said I wouldn't see her."

"It does say that. I can read, you know." He looked at Christian; distress etched the boy's face.

"Can you check again?"

Cliff sighed, nodded and wiped the ashtrays out before returning to the office. He made his way back towards Christian.

"I'm right. Mr C Dickens and Miss E Shaw, she must be your mother then?"

381

"No, she's not. They're just trying to trick me into seeing her by saying it was my mother coming, when it wasn't."

Disappointment overwhelmed Christian and he screwed his eyes tight shut to prevent himself from crying.

"What've I said then?" said Joe, puzzled by Christian's reaction.

But Christian shook his head fiercely and walked back to his cell, pushing the door closed behind him.

Just before twelve o'clock Charles Dickens and Miss Shaw arrived in the segregation unit, where they were ushered into the interview room. William came to the door.

"It's Thompson you want to see, sir?" he checked with Charles.

"If we can, please," said Charles.

Miss Shaw fidgeted restlessly, pushing her hair back behind her ears.

William walked across the landing, passing Cliff who was still mopping the floor, his unlit cigarette bobbing between his lips. He knocked three times, turned the key and opened the door. Christian was not on the bed, he pushed the door wider and looked into the room. From the bars of the high window, Christian hung limply, his body, lifeless, his face a dark blue. A red tie was knotted around the bar in the window, a reef knot tying that to a blue tie which suspended him. The chair on which he had stood lay in the middle of the floor next to a broken pair of glasses. There was a crash from the landing as Cliff stumbled to his knees, having followed William to the door and then silence, as William slowly pulled the cell door shut.

THE END

If you have enjoyed this book, please consider leaving a review on Amazon and/or Goodreads. Both will accept reviews even if you did not purchase this book from them. Reviews are there to inform other readers and they help a book gain visibility in a highly competitive market.

Thank you

Author's notes

While this work is fictional and none of the particular events portrayed happened, it is based on a certain reality. I have tried to bring to the surface what country life at the time was like and how insulated we were in those days from our urban counterparts, whose experiences were somewhat different. All the characters, with the exception of Peter, have been written in such a way as to have no resemblance to anyone living or dead.

If the book has a message it is to highlight the shocking number of young men who commit suicide while in prison. It would appear that the situation is worse now than it was then and if the public demand is to lock up more offenders, then they (the public) should have a duty of care to look after those people with humanity.

Acknowledgements

The production of this book, as with *Mary Knighton* and *Thisbe*, has been a team effort and the writing of the script was the easy part. Since 2015 when this happened Henri Merriam, in two weeks, transformed the 100,000 words of my handwritten, misspelt and grammatically disastrous scrawl into a readable typed copy.

This then sat on the shelf for a year or two until 2018 when once again Antonia Phinnemore took it in hand and edited it with meticulous accuracy. Since then my mainstay, Mary Matthews, took over and she has organised the production of the book. There would for certain be no novel if it were not for the work that Mary does. Thanks also to Julia Gibbs for the proof reading and Simon Emery for the layout of the cover. The cover design is by Brenda McKetty a nationally known book illustrator who lives locally.

Others have read the book and made comments which have been every helpful and I would like to thank the following; Mo Brown, Rosemary Hallworth, Roger Pierce, Janet Cunnington, Judy Rossiter and Margaret Bresse. I would also like to make a special mention of Mike Hirst who read the handwritten version but unfortunately died in late 2018. He was one of my very best friends from university days and I would like to dedicate the book to his memory.

Books by Thomas Richard Brown

Mary Knighton

Thisbe

A Knock on the Door

Coming Soon

Long Stop

Lightning Source UK Ltd.
Milton Keynes UK
UKHW011705120619
344291UK00001B/6/P